MIA EVERS

AND THE TWISTED SOULS

I0659570

ANGELA GUAJARDO

Gila Monster Press

Mia Evers and the Twisted Souls

Copyright © 2023 by Angela Guajardo

Cover by Bukovero

Published by Gila Monster Press.

ISBN: 978-1-961815-21-6

Join the Mailing List

Get informed on the next book release without worrying about any spam or filler. Keep an eye out for updates and chances to become a beta reader.

Sign up at AngelaGuajardo.com by scanning the QR code:

Chapter 1

I sat opposite Bylan in his office. He sat behind his sprawling desk, folded hands resting on the shiny surface, sleeves bunched at his elbows.

Mr. Redd was aligned with Dark.

My brain tried to process the revelation. Every last cell in my body screamed it couldn't be true as I scoured my memories for a moment where he might've brushed some dust off the sidewalk with the wave of a hand or nudged a door closed with Air magic. Something deep in the pit of my stomach told me there was nothing there, not even a spoken Fire rune to reheat a mug of coffee. "He's…" I couldn't finish the sentence. Every last part of me didn't want it to be true. It changed everything.

Bylan said, "Aligned with Dark. Lyra's certain of it." He removed a milky white bowl from a side drawer of his desk and set it in front of him. It had golden Light runes and a matching rod the length of his hand. He whispered something to the bowl and ran the rod along the rim. A sound like running a finger along the rim of a wine glass filled the room.

A wave of energy pressed against me, making me feel like I needed to pop my ears. Before I could force a yawn, the pressure lifted. Aha, a sound bowl. It would protect his office from eavesdroppers.

"And she's certain he doesn't have an attachment?" Vergo said. He sat in the chair beside me.

"Think about it. He's exhibited none of the behaviors Nurse Kor did during her attachment. He's been the same since day one. He shakes hands with parents and guides children around with gentle nudges. So no, something else is going on. As for what, there are quite a few possibilities, most of them not good. However, we can't presume his guilt. He's never done anything outright wrong. He may simply be an unpleasant fellow who's hard to like." Bylan gestured to me. "And for reasons you understand firsthand, he hides his alignment."

My chest rose and fell with a silent sigh. That's what I'd tried to do last year and at my previous schools.

"So then why tell us?" Vergo said. "You're not prejudiced."

Bylan glanced at the spirit cat. "So you and Mia can better protect yourselves and everyone we care about. Now that we know what he's capable of. Vergo, do you remember your interaction with Mr. Redd before Lyra and Mia showed up?"

"Now that you mention it, he somehow went under my radar. Either he's a very weak Dark who draws no interest from demons, or he's so powerful that he knows how to cloak himself."

"So a dead end for now." Bylan lapsed into thoughtful silence.

So Vergo had been hurting students for a long time. A sudden realization dawned on me. I dug my fingers into the armrests. "Were you the demon that killed Orton four years ago?"

"No," both Vergo and Bylan said. They looked at each other.

Vergo said, "How'd you know that?"

"Someone purposely summoned a demon to kill Orton," Bylan said. He opened a desk drawer and set a hardcover book before him. He flipped to a particular page and spun the book. He slid the book towards me and tapped a particular picture. "Here's Payton Arian Sorenson, the demon we crossed over yesterday."

"What?" I bolted to my feet and bent over the glossy pages. Rows of smiling faces stared up at me from inside rectangular boxes. Vergo hopped onto the desk. Payton was the only one not smiling. He looked bored and annoyed, yet somehow familiar.

"They expunged his student profile from records. This is the only place they must've overlooked. There are yearbooks in the high school library. Payton is in several years' worth. He was a transfer, like you. And he was a Dark. Based on what he did, it must've been tough for him, too. Only he went down a bad road." Bylan gave the bowl another ring.

"He's the Dark that killed Orton," I said in disbelief. Nausea rose in my throat. I leaned away from the yearbook. The killer had a human face. Here was the person who tried to kill my sister, too. "I hate him. He's a horrible person."

"He's the Light's problem now, thankfully," Vergo said.

"Don't be so quick to hate him," Bylan said. He stowed the yearbook, relieving me of its presence and its contents. "From what information Lyra and I gathered, Payton was a product of his environment. Society hated him for what he was, and he reciprocated that hate."

"Reciprocated?" I didn't know what the word meant.

"It means to do or give back the same," Vergo said.

"Yes. People treated him poorly, so he treated them poorly in return." Bylan frowned. "It's an understandable, easy route to take, but that doesn't make it right."

"He tried to kill my sister," I said. My hands balled into fists.

"I understand your anger and hate, and you're fully justified. But here's the thing—Lyra and I got a good look at the pieces of the box you destroyed. There were traces of Dark runes and residual demonic energy. It was a dabuk box."

My stomach flopped. "We covered those in history class. People make and use those for only a specific purpose." Anyone could create a dabuk box with the right tools and intentions. There were ten ancient, powerful ones tied to specific plagues, six of which were already found and destroyed. "Are you saying Payton was anchored to that box specifically for killing my sister?"

"Unfortunately, which means he may not've had a choice in the matter."

I dropped back into my seat. "Why?" I said in a whisper. I wasn't asking why the demon had no choice. That was obvious. Anchors like a dabuk box enslaved the soul it housed. Payton may or may not have been a willing participant. So why would any living soul want to kill my sister? She hadn't done anything to anyone, other than annoy me like all younger siblings did.

"This is where Lyra and I are left to speculation. Whatever the specific motives, it means that someone or something didn't want a Light around who could potentially ruin their plans."

Vergo said, "That doesn't make much sense. Wouldn't they go after you instead? You're the bigger threat. Bela's a youngling who doesn't understand what she's capable of."

"I don't think I'm out of the woods yet." Bylan leaned back in his chair and folded his arms. "She makes an easier target. If I have no Light student to mentor, then I no longer serve a purpose at this school. What better way to get rid of me than by getting rid of her?"

"Diabolical." Vergo flicked his tail in annoyance.

"I'm afraid she's still in danger. There's something going on at this school that I need to get to the bottom of. Without the Order of Leo backing me and with Lyra removed from her position, it'll be a challenge."

"How do I protect her?" I said. Bela was innocent and harmless. She'd done nothing to deserve this. Going to school shouldn't be a dangerous choice.

Bylan studied me a moment. "That's what we need to figure out. You're unusually powerful for someone your age. Lyra and I hope you can fill in where she no longer can."

"I'll do it." I had to.

The priest nodded. "Right now, we need information. The most critical pieces are finding out who made that dabuk box and who bound Payton to it. Orton was presented as the sole victim when Payton was alive, but he wasn't. And one thing the school probably doesn't know is that I do a lot of funeral services for this county. Payton took his own life shortly after expulsion and everything that followed."

"Such an act must've fast-tracked him to demonhood," Vergo said.

Bylan nodded. "I did Payton's funeral. A handful of people were there, including Mr. Redd. You see…he's Payton's uncle."

Vergo bared his fangs. "No wonder he came back to a location he loathed. How long has Redd been principal here?"

"He spent a few years at the high school and moved down to the middle school after the Payton incident four years ago. There are no records as to why, which is a clue in and of itself. As to who removed all this information, finding that out will expose how corrupted this district is."

Vergo said, "Word has it that the Volaires run everything this side of Marohu. Wouldn't it make sense that they're the ones behind all of this?"

Bylan shook his head. "No. I had a long conversation with their daughter, Gwen, after the incident with you. Gwen unwittingly made it clear that her family is prejudiced against Darks. She's been trained to feel the same. Besides, her family is too proud of the mining empire they've built. They care about money and mining, not demonic activity."

It would've been so easy to blame Gwen and her family for all this. She was easy to hate. If not the Volaires, then who? A demon's face with round red eyes flashed in my mind. I'd seen them through the principal's eyes. I sucked in a breath. "It has to be Mr. Redd."

"Lyra and I suspect something along those lines. He's been around for every incident. However, he's innocent until proven guilty."

I stood, my heart racing. "Bylan, I never got to tell you." Come to think of it, it had been strange for the middle school principal to show up at the high school when the four of us had snuck into the boys' locker room. I'd been so horrified over getting caught that I hadn't thought about how strange it was. That had to be Mr. Redd protecting his dabuk box. I told Bylan about the whole incident, including how my bracelet had stopped working after he'd taken it from me.

The Light priest studied me for a long moment. "That's some strong evidence, but there's too much room for doubt. He may be another Mr. Gauss. Regardless, we all have to be careful no matter what. For now, you need to go on as normal. Go to class, do your homework, practice your violin, and stay out of trouble. Do nothing that would clue him in on our suspicions. He may be another pawn in all this who needs saving, too. Until proven otherwise, treat him with respect. He's still the principal of this school."

"Do you think the school board knows he's a Dark?" Vergo said.

"That's another very good question that needs answering."

A polite knock on the door startled all three of us. I thought of Ms. Weever before remembering she'd been fired. On top of that, it wasn't her crisp three knocks. The mystery person had tapped on the door several times, barely loud enough to be heard.

Bylan drew his brows together.

Vergo said, "That's a sound bowl, right?"

"One that should discourage anyone from knocking on the door. Instead, they should feel compelled to move on."

Bylan tapped the edge of the bowl and shoved it in a desk drawer. His robes swished behind him as he rose and opened the door. His shoulders stiffened and then relaxed. "Damien," he said cheerfully. "Good morning."

"Morning, Sanctus," Mr. Redd said in his casual drawl. He peered around Bylan's arm.

Our gazes met. My stomach clenched. By the Light, could he hear through the sound bowl charm? Vergo hopped in my lap, making me flinch, and whispered, "Steady, Little One."

Mr. Redd forced a fake smile. "Ah, there she is. May I steal her a moment before she has to go to homeroom?"

Bylan nodded. "Certainly. I was doing a welfare check. Mia's such a brave soul. You'd think nothing happened yesterday besides winning the bandyll championship." He held out a hand to me. "We can talk later. Go with the Light, child."

Heart beating a million miles an hour, I hopped out of my chair. Vergo landed on the floor. Bylan gave my shoulder a reassuring squeeze as I followed Mr. Redd into the hallway. His touch was full of warmth, calm, and confidence. I clamped my mouth shut, resisting the urge to beg him to come with us. I didn't want to face the principal alone. If he's the one who made the dabuk box, then he was the one trying to kill my sister.

My legs trembled with every step into the office. I clutched the handle of my violin case, making my fingers hurt. Mr. Redd shut the door behind us. I flinched at the thud of wood hitting wood. He set a leather-bound notebook on his desk, turned to the back pages, and sat. "Please, sit. You're not in trouble for anything. And don't worry about the time. I'll write you a late pass."

Vergo curled up under my seat.

Every instinct told me to run. With forced calm, I sat on the edge of the chair with my violin case in my lap.

He tapped the notebook. "Do you recognize this?"

"My personal records." How could I forget? That thing had followed me from school to school my entire education.

"I think you've earned another update." He grabbed a fountain pen from a coffee mug that read "World's Most Awesome Principal. Just Add Coffee." He was so not the world's most awesome principal. Mr. Redd turned a couple more pages and pressed the notebook's spine so it sat flatter. A clock ticked somewhere behind him as his pen scratched away. He wrote several lines before sliding my records towards me. "There. Some much-deserved praise."

I pulled the notebook closer and read his large script.

Mia has shown great character and a strong sense of morality and integrity. She sent two demons to the Light with the help of a Light priest, saving multiple students' lives and probably many more. She is living proof that Darks are not all bad and deserve the same kindness as any other alignment. She is a diligent worker, talented musician, and an asset in goal to the bandyll team. She shows great promise to do great things.

-Damien Redd, Toolena Mesa Middle School Principal

I read the words a few times, my chest tightening with anger. Sure, it was great praise. It was a nice thing put down in my records. Did he mean a single one of these words? He had to be the one who made the dabuk box, had to be the one trying to kill my sister. This was a lie to try to get me to like him so I wouldn't suspect anything. I clenched my fists. After all I'd done for him to gain acceptance and trust, he'd been manipulating me the whole time. He was a liar, and he did it casually. And I had to play along with this stupid charade. "Why are you doing this, sir?"

"I beg your pardon?"

"Why did you accept me into Toolena Mesa when so many bad things had happened four years ago?"

He narrowed his eyes. "I did something very nice for you. The proper response would be to thank me."

The thought of it nauseated me. "Thank you, sir. It's very kind of you. I appreciate it."

"That's better."

"I'd still like to understand why."

The principal's jaw muscles flexed. "Miss Evers, I thought I made it perfectly clear during that school

10

board meeting last year. Not only are public schools legally obligated to accept any student that applies, I also hold progressive views on Darks, as do many of the staff here."

Because *you're* one, I thought, but I kept my mouth shut and concentrated on breathing. I hated this man worse than I hated Gwen. She was a bully. But him? He didn't care about anything but what he wanted. And he wanted my sister dead.

"While we've hit a few bumps, I stand by my decision." He started to say something else, but stopped. "Why are you looking at me like that?"

Vergo said, "Check your emotions, Little One. I know it's hard right now, but don't give away your secrets before you have the chance to get to homeroom."

I blinked several times and took in a deep breath. "Like what?" I said to the principal.

"Like you want to start yelling at me," he said.

"I'm sorry." Ugh, I'd apologized to him. I needed to keep my emotions under control. "I didn't mean it. I'm just—"

"Stressed out?"

That much was true. I nodded.

Vergo pawed my shoe. "Step away from this conversation. Let's get on with our morning."

Oh, if only I could run out of here without giving rise to any suspicion. "What happened to Mr. Gauss?"

"Mia," Vergo said.

Mr. Redd's muscles worked as he clenched and unclenched his jaw. "Don't you worry about him. He mixed with the wrong people. He can't harm anyone anymore."

"Please. I want to know, for my sister's sake. I want to know she's safe."

A red sheen passed over his eyes, and a shadow passed over him. He forced a smile. "She's very safe now. You destroyed his demon's anchor and, with Sanctus Bylan's help, crossed it over to the Light. That demon can't harm anyone anymore."

He'd used Bylan's Order title again. Either he didn't know about the Light priest's expulsion, or presumed that I didn't know and wanted to keep up the charade. Whatever the reason, I hated him for it. "Why did he try to hurt my sister?"

Mr. Redd spread his arms. "Couldn't tell you. I'd love to know myself. Your sister's a sweet little thing. We're lucky to have her at this school." Either it was my imagination, or he showed a little extra teeth when he spoke about Bela.

"You don't think it's because she's a Light, do you?"

Vergo swatted my shoe. "Mia, let it go before you make a verbal slip." I swung my foot at him.

Mr. Redd's face hardened. "Again, couldn't tell you, but she's safe. You have my word. Is there something worrying you that you're not telling me about?" He raised an eyebrow and fixed me with a studious gaze.

My throat closed up. Bylan had entrusted me with vital information for my safety, and I was already losing control. I lowered my gaze to the floor, hiding my face behind my hair.

Vergo rubbed up against my legs, sending calm through me. "I know you're understandably upset, but this will make things worse if you keep on this way."

A cold breeze tickled the back of my neck. Something about the sensation set me on edge. I raised my chin and avoided looking directly at the principal. "No, sir. It's just that she came real close to dying the other day. I guess I need time to let it all sink in."

"Definitely give it some time to sink in." The homeroom bell rang, and we both glanced at the clock above the door. "Now, let me write you a late pass." He scribbled something on a green slip of paper and handed it to me. "Put your former math teacher out of your mind. He can't hurt you, your sister, or anyone ever again, the box is destroyed, and the demon is gone. You and Sanctus Bylan saw to that."

One more demon was gone. I resisted the urge to correct him. If he didn't know I knew about the one with a female voice and a crown of branches, then it was probably better to hide that information, too. "Yes, sir." I took the paper and hurried out of the main office, the blinding sunlight a welcome companion compared to the principal.

Vergo bounded alongside me, his little black legs moving double-time to match my pace. "That was a close one. We'll have to practice how you behave around him if you want to keep anything secret from him."

"I didn't mean it," I said defensively, slowing long enough to yank open the 6-8 building's door. I was the only student walking down the hallway.

"I know, Little One. If I'd been in your place at your age, I probably would've acted the same or worse. I was quite the hotheaded youth. You're probably going to feel rage every time you see him. It'll be a matter of being prepared to deal with your emotions."

"Now you sound like Ms. Weever."

"Hopefully, that's a good thing."

We turned down one more hallway, and I broke into a run despite it being against the rules. I needed classes to distract me, to give me something else to think about. Or to be left alone to read my latest Yuna book.

The crystal serpents, who'd been under the control of a wizard, had crafted a cape out of their scales and imbued it with magic that'd allow her to glide with it. After Yuna broke the wizard's staff, the serpents were freed from the mind control spell. The cape was their way of saying thanks.

I'd freed Mr. Gauss and Nurse Kor from demonic attachments, and Mr. Redd had given me more good notes in my records as a modest reward, but the gesture felt empty, thankless. Mr. Gauss had been shocked to see the demon.

Yuna was hunting for the wizard in the next book, and now I was on the hunt for the person orchestrating all this demonic activity. I was ready to dump all the blame on Mr. Redd because I couldn't help but believe the truth was staring at us from the principal's office.

A few doors from homeroom, I slowed to a walk, and Vergo matched my pace. And then it felt like I walked through a curtain of ice. My movements further slowed and so did Vergo's, but he gave no indication that anything was wrong. His strides fell into slow motion. I reached for the doorknob. It seemed like it took ten seconds for my free hand to move from my side to stretched out in front of me. I willed my body to move faster, but it froze in place with my fingertips an inch from the scuffed metal.

I closed my eyes in response to an icy gust. My long hair lifted away from my shoulders and fell back into place. Blackness filled my vision. My racing heart pounded in my ears, which the cold nipped at. This couldn't be—

Whatever held me in place let go, and I stumbled forward. A pale light shone overhead, revealing a layer of fog hiding the flat ground. I had no violin, backpack, or spirit cat.

A pair of giant, round red eyes opened in the distance. They bobbed to one side, then the other, and loomed closer, like two eyes of a dragon. A shadowy limb touched the ground where homeroom should've been. Fog rose and curled around claws as long as my legs.

I took a step back. The claws were too close for comfort, but I had nowhere to run. I'd been transported to the demon realm. At least now I knew how to get myself out.

Greetings, child, said a female demonic voice.

The power of it cut right through me, making me want to cover my ears. I flicked a wrist, summoning my protection shield. It was no better than hiding in a paper bag. At least it took the edge off the tingle crawling up and down my spine. A bubble of golden light enveloped and shimmered around me before going invisible.

A pleasure to see you again.

"What do you want?" I said. "Why are you and the principal trying to kill my sister?"

The demon tsked. *So direct. Where are your manners?*

"Answer my question."

You know, maybe if you were more polite, I might

15

be more inclined to entertain your questions.

The claws flexed, reminding me who had the upper hand, but I didn't care. "You tried to kill my sister. Give me one good reason to show you any kindness."

I'll give you two. The demon's head lowered several feet, and the ground vibrated as an entire foreleg lowered onto it. Fog rose around a scaly limb. The head tilted, crowned in branches, and rested against a curled paw. *One, that wasn't me who tried to kill your sister. That was another demon.*

"Liar."

Oh? So it was your imagination that you sent a pathetic demon to the Light?

"The Demon King said he was a pawn. I bet you were the one who told Payton to kill my sister." This one was a far more powerful demon. I wasn't sure if greater demons bossed around the lesser ones. I didn't see why not.

Such an imagination you have. I promise you, I had nothing to do with that. I had no interest in that mortal. I'm only interested in you, and you're in a bit of a predicament at the moment.

"I know how to get out of here."

She waved a giant paw. It was like watching a tree bend and sway in a storm. *I don't mean this right here and now. I mean your principal.* She rested her head back on her fist.

"I saw you through his eyes. You're working with him."

The red eyes narrowed. *No.* Her voice was cold, menacing. Anger came off her in waves, physically pressing me into the ground and sending ripples through the fog.

At first, her anger became mine, but the sound of my heavy breathing cued me in to calm down and deflect it. I fed energy into my shield, buffering myself from her emotions. My breathing quieted and my heartbeat slowed.

The menace left her voice, but it was hard and cold. *This brings me to my second reason. We share the same dislike for your principal. We both wish to see him removed from his post. I want to help you.*

This didn't…what? Since when did demons want to do anything besides meddle and ruin lives? "Why?"

It's personal. Maybe I'll tell you one day if you cooperate. She placed both paws on the ground and her massive head rose higher. *You may call me Tradereth, by the way. So will you show me some manners in exchange for my aid? You do have a Light sister that needs protecting.*

I took a deep breath and words of agreement lodged in my throat. Manners in exchange for aid. Was that a bargain in disguise? If so, that was close. "Please tell me what you have in mind, Tradereth." There. Take that. And that was a demonic name, nothing I could use in an exorcism or power circle to trap her.

The head tilted and the demon let out a thoughtful laugh. *A little better. Anyway, I'll help you expose your principal's nastiest secrets if you do one little thing for me. Consider it a fair trade.*

My spine crawled anew. She wanted to strike a bargain. "No. Never. Don't ever ask me again. I'm leaving now." I closed my eyes and concentrated on my breathing.

Not so fast, child. There'll be consequences if you turn me down.

I opened my eyes. "There'll be consequences if I strike a bargain." Dread filled me. I'd turned down Allosyr's bargain and Carlo had died because of it. On the other hand, an incomplete bargain with him had almost resulted in my death, or I'd been dead for a little bit, or something. I dunno. No one had ever explained it to me, and I didn't have time to wonder.

Oh, but of course. Every action has a consequence. Even the path of inaction has consequences. Accepting my bargain will have consequences, but refusing it will be worse. She rose onto all-fours and prowled around me. The pale light bounced off patches of scales and branch-like spikes. The ground trembled with every step she took. *Either I help you remove your principal from his high horse and you save your sister, or you find yourself sucked into his plans and at the receiving end of my wrath.* She stilled, bringing her head, which had to be half as big as my house, within feet of me, dousing me in the smell of tree bark and sulfur. *Choose wisely, Mia Evers.*

I shook my head. "There'll be no bargain. I can protect my sister without your help. Goodbye."

The round eyes became slits. *I think you'll come around in time. Good lu-uck*, she said, not meaning the latter in the least.

Calming and slowing my breathing, I let go of all emotions and freed myself of the demon realm, sinking into the fog and the ground. The falling sensation stopped. The hall lights shone on my outstretched arm. It was covered in frost. So was the rest of my body and my violin case. I wiped off the frost as Vergo shook out his entire body, spraying the carpet with white flakes.

"What on Aardra?" His eyes widened. "Mia, what

happened? We look like we've been touched by the demon realm.

My hand shook as I reached for the doorknob. Hate, rage, terror, dread, and desperation flooded my consciousness. I really just… And she wanted—

I fled for the girls' bathroom.

Chapter 2

"Mia, slow down."

His voice chased me down the hall. I didn't slow until I had to push the bathroom door open, throwing my weight against it. It slowly closed with a drawn-out groan. I bolted for the farthest stall, dumped all my stuff against the wall, and slammed the door behind me. Burying my face in my hands, the high pitch of my hyperventilation echoed off every last tile and metal surface. The metal door stung with cold against my knuckles.

Vergo slipped under the gap in the door. "Mia, what happened? Talk to me."

I tried every last trick and technique to get my breathing under control. Ms. Weever had drilled me endlessly on how to control my emotions. The harder I tried, the worse my throat hurt. It was like trying to breathe around a knife.

Why couldn't I get myself under control? This so wasn't like me.

Either I help you remove your principal from his high horse and you save your sister, or you find yourself sucked into his plans and at the receiving end of my wrath.

The exchange played in my head over and over— the cold, the fog, the demon's rage, everything. It latched onto me like a vivid nightmare that wouldn't let go. A sob escaped my throat. I couldn't breathe through my nose. I reached for the toilet paper roll.

"Mia, I don't think I've ever seen you this frazzled." He stood on his hind legs, looking up at me with big blue eyes full of sympathy, and stretched his front paws to my hip. "Oh, Little One, please talk to me."

His presence tried to fill me with calm, but whatever lingering trace Tradereth had left behind urged me to give in to despair.

No. I couldn't. That's what the demon wanted. I had to fight this so I could protect Bela.

With the help of scratchy toilet paper to clear my nose and Vergo's soothing purr, I managed to get my breathing back under control. I rinsed my face with tap water and carefully paper toweled it dry. The brown stuff might as well have been absorbent sandpaper, but oh well. Now my entire face was red instead of having blotchy cheeks. The red from my eyes was gone, hiding the fact that I'd lost it for a moment there. Instead, I looked like I'd been running. I ran my fingers through my hair, straightening it out, and grabbed my things.

"May I ask what happened?" Vergo said, a paw lifted tentatively.

"I'll tell you later. I need to get to homeroom." I didn't want to tell him about it. Ever. Talking about it meant reliving it. The images and voices were only starting to fade into a black, white, and red blur, and muffled sounds wrapped in a lingering chill. I shivered and left the bathroom.

"I understand," he said, bobbing his head. "Sometimes it's real hard to be a Dark, and no one but you can understand what you go through. Take all the time you need."

Something fluttered in my chest, something that felt good, peaceful. I stopped and studied my spirit cat.

He twitched an ear back, the cat way of raising an eyebrow. "What?"

It was so easy to forget he'd been a Dark, too, before becoming a demon. He'd gone through hardship, seen terrible things, and done equally terrible things. It was so easy to see him as a soul seeking atonement and putting up with being stuck with me. But he understood me better than anyone, except Ms. Weever. My chest twisted at the thought of her. I tried to think of how to express how much Vergo's understanding meant to me, but the thought of being open and honest about such things made my chest twist a second time.

I arrived at the door to homeroom. "Thanks."

I barely glanced at Mr. Gauss's substitute teacher, more dropping my late pass in the chubby lady's hand than giving it to her on my way to my desk. I sat sideways, not bothering to take my backpack off. I rubbed my hands and blew warm air into them. I had no clue how long I'd spent in the bathroom, much less in the demon realm. I could barely feel my fingers. I had enough time to stick my hands under my upper arms before the bell for first period sounded. Huffing a sigh, I retrieved my violin case and joined the masses out in the hallway.

Someone taller bumped into me and an insistent hand grabbed my arm.

"Whoa, you're cold." Sussi shook out her hand. "What happened?"

"I'm fine," I said reflexively, and tried to head to history class. She grabbed my arm again.

"You don't look fine. You look like you saw a—"

Go ahead. Say it with a bunch of people within earshot that weren't on our team.

She glanced from side to side. "One of *those* things."

Tears stung my eyes. I yanked free and made it a few steps down the hall before bumping into Deren. Sussi stood beside both of us, hands on her narrow hips. She was half a head taller than both of us. In our defense, she was rather tall for all of us being twelve.

"What happened? I thought you and Sanctus Bylan got rid of it for good."

"Can I tell you later?" I said, wiping my face. Ugh, stupid tears. Go away.

"Tell us what?" Deren said. His usual happy-go-lucky expression creased into a frown. "Mia?"

"Aw, look, it's the Losers Club having a meeting in the hallway." Gwen fixed the three of us with her smug smile. Even while being a jerk, she was pretty with her tawny hair, pale eyes, and tanned skin complexion that came with a lifetime of living in the desert. Most girls had knobby knees at our age, but her legs were perfect. Boys were always looking at her.

Next to her stood her best friend Nonaya, a girl that

would've been as pretty if it weren't for her long, sharp nose. She even had knobby knees, like Sussi and me. They both wore expensive autumn dresses, and Nonaya wore lipstick and eye shadow.

Chibya, a heavy girl around the same height as me, gave Gwen a pained expression. She was another of Gwen's inner circle and had been the first to smile at me last year. I didn't understand how they were friends. She dressed well. Her family had money, too, but she was so unlike Gwen and Nonaya. Chibya never said anything mean to anyone.

"Freaks," Gwen said, pushing both Sussi and me into Deren. Nonaya giggled into her hand and gave Sussi a shove as well, who balled her hands into fists. She took a step towards the two. Chibya moved in front of them.

"Sorry, Sussi. Gwen's having a bad day."

"That does mean she can take it out on me."

Chibya lowered her gaze. "I know. She was mean to me before homeroom. She didn't realize it until I told her."

"What did she say?"

"She commented on how fat I am. I almost cried."

"Did she apologize?"

Her round face grew pained. She shook her head. "She looked upset with herself, though."

Sussi tsked. "Why are you friends with her?"

Chibya shrugged. "She's usually nice to me. We have fun together."

"Whatever. I've got to get to class." Sussi turned her back on Chibya, who waved at each of us before running off.

Deren watched her weave among the throng of

students. "She's weird."

"You're weird," Sussi said, rolling her eyes.

Rubbing my cold arms, I said, "Are you and Chibya still friends?" The chill of the demon realm was finally starting to melt.

"Sort of." Sussi followed Deren's gaze. "She's always nice to everyone. She's hard to hate. I wish she wouldn't hang out with Gwen anymore."

"Maybe she'll stop one day," Deren said. "Anyway, talk at lunch?"

"Maybe," I said to the floor. Gangly arms wrapped me in a hug. I flinched, having forgotten to expect it. Deren made a habit of giving me a hug every morning before first period. It was nice. With all the terrible things I'd been through, it was nice to have a daily reminder that life was different now. Sure, there were demons here, too, but I wasn't alone anymore. I gave him a quick hug back and he let go.

Sussi raised an eyebrow, looking from one of us to the other. "See? You two *are* boyfriend-girlfriend."

I tilted my head back and groaned. "No, we're not."

"I'm making up for all the people who've been mean to her. That's all," Deren said. "It's not what it looks like." He took a step back.

"Still sounds like something a boyfriend would do."

"Well, stop it with the boyfriend comments already."

Sussi gave a noncommittal shrug. "Fine, fine. See you at lunch."

***

I did my best to get lost in the day's lessons and

forget about demons and bargains. Our history teacher, Mrs. Livy, gave us a lesson on the history of wands and how people had figured out how to make them. It gave me a new level of appreciation for having the wand I'd used to destroy the dabuk box.

Bleh. More demon stuff.

Language Arts was mercifully bland as we progressed through learning the five-paragraph essay—so many words! I dutifully practiced introduction paragraphs, hook, thesis statement, and all. Mrs. Cerda read my intro paragraph to the class, having liked it so much. It provided a much-needed boost to my mood, until she assigned us way too much reading for homework. Science and especially math failed to improve my mood. All we did in math was worksheets on how to graph formulas since we had a sub in place of Mr. Gauss. I tried to convince myself he was out sick and that he'd be back in a day or two. I couldn't help but remember his terror when he'd laid eyes on the demon.

What on Aardra had happened to my math teacher?

Come lunchtime, I didn't feel like talking. Vergo had me remove his collar long enough to encourage Deren and Sussi to leave me alone. They frowned and ate their lunches in silence. Deren gave me another hug before I headed off to do more worksheets outside Mr. Redd's office in place of tutoring.

If only I could persuade him to let Ms. Weever come back. Except for the desk, chair, and piano, her former office sat empty. And if only I could persuade him to leave my sister alone.

No, better not think of such things around him. I'd come too close to slipping already.

At the end of the day, I searched for my bandyll bag before remembering I had to take the regular bus home. I followed the throng of students along the sidewalks, teachers placed at intervals to make sure no one ran or got hurt. We all filed onto our respective buses without incident. The buses were painted a yellow that'd stick out anywhere in the world, and had rounded glass windows that made it look like a spotted caterpillar. The buses hovered close to the ground with Air magic, but the main cabin was high enough to require a few steep stairs to ascend before taking a seat.

Even though I'd ridden the bus without my bandyll bag this morning, I felt incomplete after hauling it around for months. It was like I was missing a part of myself. Winter sports started soon. Maybe I'd try out for one. Bandyll had caused Mom and Dad to pay a bit more attention to me, and they'd both expressed how proud they were. If only bandyll was year-round.

I sank into the front seat next to Bela and propped my knees up against the chair back separating the bus driver's seat from the rest of the bus. I propped my latest Yuna book up on my thighs when Bela touched my arm.

"Grandma says hi."

"Hi, Grandma." I opened to my bookmarked page. Grandma spoke to Bela a lot ever since her alignment manifested. Every now and then, she asked Bela to say hi to me on her behalf.

Bela looked at the top of the bus stairs, her brows knit with concentration, the look she got every time a ghost talked to her. "She says you need to protect yourself, too, and not just me. Mia, what's she talking about?"

Heaving a sigh, I closed my book. I'd read later. Of course I'd protect myself, too. "I don't know. Why don't you ask her?" Please don't say anything about demons. Just for one day, I would like to forget I was a Dark.

Bela stared a moment. "She says to be careful who you ask for help, and whatever you do, don't fight them alone. Who are you fighting?"

So much for that. I stifled a scream. Couldn't Grandma have waited for this message for when we got home? I couldn't have even a moment's peace on the bus. "Don't worry about it, Bela. You're safe. I'm here to protect you."

Her serious gaze bounced several times between me and a ghost I couldn't see before she settled back down next to me. "Okay."

I opened my Yuna book a second time. It was later. Vergo gave me a meaningful look. I ignored it, scanning for the paragraph I'd left off at, only to slam the book closed a second time as Bela talked about her day. I let out a long sigh through my nose and stared at the bus's rounded roof as my sister went on about learning the alphabet and her numbers. I made myself do a breathing exercise to calm down. She was being a five-year-old who wanted to tell her big sister all about what she'd learned. At least the book had absolutely no ghosts or demons in it. I dutifully listened all the way home until she could redirect her endless chatter onto our parents.

I hid in my room and read until dinnertime, the lovely aroma of hominy, pork, and chili sauce coaxing me out of my room. A bubbling pot sat on the stove, pieces of hominy and diced pork floating in a soup that matched the desert reds at sunset. A bouquet of garlic, salt, pepper, and chili rode on the steam. I inhaled deeply and my stomach growled.

Mom smiled and gave the pot a stir. "Thought that'd get you out of your room. I made pozole. I know it's your favorite soup."

I returned her smile while doing cartwheels in my mind. Pozole was my absolute favorite. "Thank you."

"Between saving your sister again and winning that championship, you more than deserve it. I also have some brownies ready to bake later."

Oh, man. I could've eaten brownies for dinner and been quite happy, but I loved pozole just as much. I helped Mom chop up some oranges and grapes and added blueberries for a fruit bowl, set the table, and ladled everyone a steaming bowl of the best soup in the world.

Dad gave me a kiss on my head before setting Bela in her booster chair between our parents. He looked so happy and content. His big arms and broad chest flexed under a tight t-shirt as he strapped Bela in. "Smells great, babe," he said to Mom. She popped him a big smile as she brought over a big bowl of salad.

We sat down to a wonderful dinner. I enjoyed every bite and didn't mind Bela's ramblings. Mom was happy, Dad was happy, I was happy. All felt good and right for once. My actions had created this moment, this happiness. If only I could make them this happy every day.

"So, Mia," Mom said while inspecting a blueberry, "what's next now that bandyll season is over?"

"There's a party next week at Coach's house."

"Party," Bela yelled loud enough to make my

eardrums vibrate. "I wanna go."

I winced. It took a moment for my ears to stop hurting. "Bela, it's for the bandyll teams."

"But I wanna go."

I opened my mouth and Mom held up a hand. "It's alright, Bela. We'll all have fun next week."

My sister clapped excitedly.

I said, "I might do a winter sport."

Dad brightened up. "You should see about doing club bandyll. You'll get some really good goaltending experience that way."

Mom's brows drew together. "Isn't that really expensive?"

"Babe, we make plenty now. Besides, it'll be good for her." He turned to me. "Would you like that?"

Did he even have to ask? I nodded eagerly. "Very much."

"You know, I played bandyll when I was your age and almost all the way through college." He absently rubbed at a shoulder. "I was on track to go pro, but I suffered a career-ending shoulder injury. Before that, I was one of the fastest skaters on the court. Other teams had a tough time getting a shot off around me."

"You played defense?"

He nodded. "Sweeper. They called me The Vortex. Wherever the ball went on our side of the court, there I was. I was one of the best at stealing the ball away or forcing turnovers."

Dad had never talked this enthusiastically about anything with me. His whole face lit up and he smiled as he talked about his bandyll career, a couple of records he set, including most blocked shots in one season, and a bunch of great defensive plays he'd made over the years. During playoffs of his junior year of college, an offensive player from the opposing team rammed him into the side of the court while Dad was in the middle of throwing the ball. He hit the wall in a way that tore his shoulder up. To this day, he didn't have full range of motion, but he seemed unbothered enough to launch into another story about how that season ended in a championship for him and his team.

"Man, those were the days," he said.

I soaked it all in, from the stories, his expression, and the tone of his voice. It was all pure joy, pure happiness. I couldn't remember the last time I'd seen him this happy. I had to resist the urge to go over and hug him, and tell him how much I loved him. I didn't want to break the magic of the moment.

Instead, Bela broke it with a big gasp.

Her head tilted back and her hair splayed out behind her as if she were floating in water. Her little body gave off a blinding white light. I shielded my eyes. The light coalesced into the figure of an elderly woman wearing a white blouse and embroidered white skirt that fell to her ankles. She wore white shoes. She had the same eyes and forehead as Dad. Grandma.

Dad bolted to his feet, looking ready to run.

Mom sat, staring openmouthed. "Ava?"

Grandma nodded to Mom and took Dad's hands in hers. He was a mountain of a man next to her tiny frame, but somehow she held him in place. "Jay, it's so good to see you this happy. You haven't been this way in so long."

"Ma? What are you doing here?"

"Watching over you and your family. You've all been through so much."

31

Dad tried to pull his hands free. Whatever strength the Light gave Grandma held him in place. Her transparent torso didn't move. Dad pulled a second time to no avail. His shoulders drooped and he turned his head towards the living room.

"Head up, my son. You're stronger than this."

"Why are you here?" His voice was thick.

"To help my family."

Dad grimaced. "Help us by leaving us alone."

Grandma shook his hands. "Jay, I've been watching over you since that day. I tried multiple times to reach you through your eldest, but you wouldn't listen. In fact, you shunned your own daughter for trying to reach out to you."

For years, Grandma's ghost had come to me, most of the time, to talk and see how I was doing. She witnessed my string of expulsions, my loneliness, and sometimes asked me to pass an obscure message on to Dad. The last time she'd tried was shortly after my enrollment at Toolena Mesa, but by then, I'd given up on talking about Grandma with him. She'd stopped talking to me directly once Bela's alignment manifested. I missed it and wished she would talk to me more.

"I'm disappointed in you," Grandma said to Dad.

He let out a rough laugh. "What else is new?"

She sighed. "Jay, I love you. I always have and always will. I know I wasn't very good at showing it, but I hope you'll forgive me for it. Despite being your mother, I'm only human. Still, my flaws caused you pain, and I'm sorry." Her voice was tight, regretful. "I wish I could go back and fix it, give you better memories. I hope you'll forgive me one day, but what's more important right now is that things are going to get tough for you and your family, and you need to not run away again."

Dad's arm muscles bulged as he tried to pull free.

Grandma's glowing grip held firm. "Start that by forgiving yourself."

Dad's face and neck reddened. Eyes closed, he grit his teeth and his chin lowered.

"Please."

"What do you care?" he whispered.

"I need you to find peace, to let go. I refuse to move on until you do." She took a deep breath, as if building the courage to speak. "The last time you saw me alive was in a hospital, connected to so many contraptions and charms, forcing my heart to keep beating and lungs to keep breathing. I was a shriveled husk of my former self, wrapped in pain and suffering, ready to die but forced to keep on living." She took his face in his hands, forcing him to make eye contact with her. "You did the right thing that day. You ended my suffering. Free yourself from this guilt haunting you so you can make more room for love."

Dad wrenched free. He took one tearful look at Grandma before grabbing the car keys and storming out of the house. The door slammed shut behind him, making the house tremble.

Grandma stared at the door for a moment before closing her eyes and shaking her head. Her white glow faded and she disappeared.

Bela sat in her booster chair, eyes closed. Her hair fell back around her shoulders and she slumped against the chair back.

Mom stood with her hands clamped over her

mouth, tears in her eyes. The sound of a Fire engine roaring to life rumbled outside and fell silent. Mom moved to the dining room window and peered outside. I caught a glimpse of our car kicking up a thin layer of dust as it headed towards the main dirt road. Mom darted to their bedroom and slammed the door behind her, shaking the house a second time.

That was something she hadn't done in months, not before Dad started his job at the mine. I took in the bedroom door, not quite believing what happened. Muffled sobbing sounded from within. My chest tightened.

"That was a dramatic reaction," Vergo said.

His voice bumped me out of my shock. I checked outside to see if Dad had turned around, but he and the car were gone. I released a drawn-out sigh.

Bela was fast asleep, mouth ajar and her chest rising and falling with every breath. She looked so peaceful. I carefully set her on the couch.

No longer in the mood for brownies, I cleared the table, put away leftovers, and cleaned the kitchen. I'd learned long ago that Mom waking to a clean house after a rough night helped her find a better mood faster. Once the last piece of silverware had been dried and put away, I carried Bela to her bed and tucked her in.

Grandma's spirit must've completely drained her. I placed her favorite stuffed rabbit under her chin. Just in case, I stroked her song stone to life. A piano's gentle song trickled through the air in legato notes, making me picture a night sky full of twinkling stars.

Vergo sat silhouetted in the doorway, the tip of his tail casually tapping the floor. I got up and left the door open behind me, in case she needed anything in the night.

White spots in the booster seat snagged my attention. They looked feathery. I crossed the living room, and sure enough, a few pure white feathers lay on the edge of the booster seat. I picked them up. The down was soft and silky between my fingertips.

"Where'd those come from?" Vergo said.

"I don't know." I searched the house for a white bird. All the pillows and cushions on the furniture were intact and stuffed with cotton or whatever. I checked all the windows in the house to make sure they were closed, which they were. As far as I knew, there weren't any white birds living in the desert. Most were earthy colors, and some flaunted bold colors, like our neighbor's desert chickens. Even the mythical thunderbird was said to have plumage the color of stormy clouds.

Well, I had a lot of homework. I placed the feathers on my desk and got to work. Bad grades would only make my parents more upset.

Chapter 3

I was almost done with my reading assignment when I heard the front door thud closed. Vergo and I exchanged glances. I set my pencil on my notebook and snuck into the kitchen. A shadow of Dad's figure paused by his and Mom's bedroom door before slowly opening it. The door let out a small creak. He slipped inside, closing the door behind him. I tiptoed across the house and crouched beside the door, which had a big enough gap between it and the floor to stick my hand through, big enough to eavesdrop.

"You came back," Mom said, surprised.

"Yeah, sorry, babe. I didn't mean to upset you."

"Please don't ever leave like that again."

"I won't."

They both fell silent long enough for me to contemplate sneaking back to my room, but Mom's voice rooted me in place. "What was Ava talking about?

I thought she passed in her sleep."

"I don't wanna talk about it."

"Jay, I do. It's clearly upsetting you and I hate seeing you upset. Please tell me what happened."

Dad huffed a sigh. "I have to get up in a few hours for work. I need some sleep."

"No. You're not getting out of this that easy. Stop trying to handle everything by yourself. I'm your wife in all things, better or worse. Talk to me about this."

They both fell silent again. I crouched closer to the door, lowering my ear to within inches of the gap. I tucked my hair behind me to make sure it wouldn't be visible. Only a wedge of soft orange light seeped out into the living room. I placed my hands in the shadowed space.

"She wasn't the best mom in the world, but I couldn't handle seeing her like that."

"Your mom is your mom," Mom said. "There's a special bond between mother and child no amount of terrible parenting can destroy. I think we're all meant to love our parents even when we hate them. I'm not sure how to explain it."

"No, I get it. I think you're right. My mother was terrible. All she had was criticism for me. She didn't even know how to be proud of me when I played college ball. All she wanted to do was nitpick every little mistake I made. I avoided her for years, but I rushed right back to her when she got real sick. You'd figure I'd let her suffer alone after all that, but I couldn't."

"It means you're a good person, Jay. You're not heartless."

"*She* was," Dad said bitterly.

"Maybe not anymore," Mom said. "She apologized."

"But did she mean it? You heard her. She refuses to move on until she gets her way."

"But she's right that you need to forgive yourself."

"Oh, you're going to side with her in this?"

"No, you moron. You're my husband and I love you. I'll always take your side no matter what. If you'd stop jumping to conclusions so fast—"

"Sorry, Brecca. I didn't mean it. It's just…this is hard to talk about."

"It's okay. I forgive you." There was the sound of a gentle kiss. "I completely understand if you're not ready to forgive her. That was probably the first time in your life you heard her express remorse."

"It was. She was always frowning, always disappointed. No wonder Dad left her."

"But you still love her."

"In some effed-up way, yes."

"Welcome to being human." There was a kissing sound again.

"Thanks for putting up with me," Dad said.

"Hey, you put up with my craziness, so we're even."

There was another moment of silence before Dad spoke, his voice tentative. "Do you think…do you think I did the right thing that day?"

"With your mom?"

"Yeah."

"Do you think she would've suffered more if you'd done nothing?"

"Hours, days, weeks? Yeah. I don't know why the doctors insisted on keeping her on life support for so long. It was like she was already gone when I got there. It was like there was a body in the room, but there wasn't a person. Dunno if you get what I'm saying."

"I get it. And I do agree with Ava that you did the right thing. I hope you can forgive yourself for it one day."

"I'll try."

"That's all I can ask of you."

Mom and Dad made noises that cued me it was time to go back to my room. When I was little, I'd had no idea what those sounds were. I thought someone was hurting. Now I was old enough to know exactly what was going on.

Relief washed over me as I tiptoed across the house and into my room. Vergo followed me inside and hopped onto my bed. "Ah, family. Every last one of us is messed up in one way or another."

"There sure seem to be a lot of families happier than mine," I said, thinking of Deren's family. They were always happy and kind. Sure, their mom yelled at her sons a lot for goofing off and stuff, but the boys never got angry and they apologized before going right back to what got them in trouble in the first place. Deren loved his family and knew he was loved. There wasn't anything messed up about them. And they most certainly didn't have to deal with demons like I did. I was going to have to figure out how to deal with Tradereth sooner or later, like I had to with Allosyr.

Okay, time to distract myself with reading. I reached for the hardcover book on the floor next to my bed.

Vergo said, "That's what it looks like. I assure you there isn't a single family without its drama, black sheep, and tenuous relationships. Perfect doesn't exist, yet we all strive for it."

"I don't get what you mean."

Vergo lifted a paw to groom. "Honestly, it's an exhausting conversation. It's something you'll understand with time. Just know that you're not alone in your familial struggles."

***

The next few days passed in a blur. I was able to act more like myself. Deren and Sussi never bugged me for details about what had freaked me out the other day. Mom and Dad were cheerful again, but Dad seemed constantly distracted by something. Since he smiled and kissed me on the head every day, I didn't bug him about it. We both had things we didn't want to think about. Anything to avoid causing him to storm out of the house again.

Come Friday, there was no desk waiting for me outside Mr. Redd's office. I double-checked the hallway, but it was gone. I went to the front desk.

The front office had a vaulted ceiling and cabin-like walls. Decorations for The Seven's Seed hung all over the place, even though it was over a month away. The Seven's Seed was a holiday that celebrated a new year and the first seven humans blessed with alignments. Conspicuously absent among the elemental decorations were any that represented the first Dark, Tenebron. Ms. Weever had been the first to teach me about him. Multicolored streamers and paper cutouts blanketed the office, but no black to represent Darks.

Coach Desi Khamai and a second front office lady, whose name escaped me every time, sat behind a tall desk. The unnamed lady read a book while Coach chatted on the vine with, by the sound of their conversation, a parent. She turned at my arrival, her tight curls bouncing, and her face brightened with recognition. She gave me an enthusiastic wave made bigger by long pink nails that she must've resumed wearing now that bandyll season was over. Desi wrapped up her conversation and let the vine curl back towards the ceiling.

"Hi, Mia. How are you today?"

"I'm good, thank you. Do you know what happened to my desk?"

"It's not there?" She leaned past the adjacent wall to peer down the hallway. "So it isn't. That's strange."

Mr. Redd's office door swung open and he stepped out, turning his head the opposite way before spotting us. He smiled, but there was no warmth. He waved me over. "You're in luck. We have a new tutor for you."

My stomach flopped. All hopes of Ms. Weever coming back were snuffed out. I'd been hoping they'd be unable to find another person and be forced to bring her back.

Coach beamed. "Aha, that explains it. Enjoy your new tutor, Mia." She was cheerful, far too cheerful and indifferent to Ms. Weever's absence. Maybe she was trying to help me get over it, or maybe she didn't care who my tutor was. I'd never seen her and Ms. Weever hang out, so maybe they'd never formed a friendship. Still, her good humor stung. It felt like I was the only one sad to see Ms. Weever go.

No, Bylan and Nurse Kor had been upset, too. I wasn't alone.

I approached Mr. Redd with practiced calm. I hated him, wanted to express my rage, but I compartmentalized those emotions, stuffing them in the back of my mind while presenting an air of calm politeness. For all I knew, Tradereth was trying to coax rage to the forefront. I refused to give her the satisfaction of having her way.

I walked over, Vergo beside me, and out stepped a tall man with a lean build and a scrutinizing gaze. He rubbed his goatee and stopped, our eyes meeting. The slight bow in his back straightened and he fixed me with his intense gaze, as if looking for flaws in my appearance.

Mr. Redd held out a hand to me. "Mr. Muradon, this is your student, Mia Evers. Miss Evers, meet your new tutor."

The tall man held out a hand as big as my head. "Sig Muradon, at your service." His tone was formal, polite. My hand disappeared inside his, but his grip was gentle. We shook hands and I took a step back to avoid breaking my neck while trying to hold eye contact with him.

"Alright, have at it," Mr. Redd said.

Mr. Muradon's lip curled in a slight frown. "Thanks. I think I can handle it from here."

Fists on his hips, the principal sized up my new tutor before reluctantly returning to his office. The door thudded hard against the frame.

"Delightful introduction," Vergo said.

Mr. Muradon frowned at the closed door. "What have I gotten myself into?" he muttered to himself, then took a deep breath and shook his head. "Anyway, let's get started, shall we?" He waved for me to follow, leading me into Ms. Weever's office. Traces of incense and her perfume lingered in the air.

My heart ached. She really wasn't allowed to come back.

My new tutor sat on the edge of Ms. Weever's desk and adjusted his overcoat. He wore dress pants and shiny shoes, and his coat was big enough to pass for robes, making him look a tad wizardly. He needed a pointy hat to complete the outfit. He gestured for me to sit in the chair I'd used almost every time I came in here.

I set my backpack on the floor and sat on the edge of the chair, unable to bring myself to get comfortable. Vergo curled up under me. All of Ms. Weever's things had been replaced by Mr. Muradon's, including a violin, dozens of books, magical objects, and a few pictures lining the shelves behind the desk. A different desk calendar, pens, and notebooks sat atop the desk, complete with a bronze name plaque.

Mr. Muradon pursed his lips. "You look very unhappy."

"This isn't your office," I said.

He tilted his head in bemusement. "They warned me about your attachment to Ms. Weever. I'd like to point out that I'm not the one who fired her. She did that to herself."

"She was protecting me." I held my chin higher.

"From?"

Vergo stuck his head out from under the chair. "Careful. We don't know if he's friend or foe."

I looked away from my new tutor. "Demons."

"So I heard. I almost didn't take this job. This district seems to have some major issues, but I also heard that you and a Light priest took care of things. I can't say I've ever heard of a Light and Dark working together like that in my lifetime."

"That's the way it used to be," I said, clenching my fists. "I bet you didn't know that."

Mr. Muradon smiled. "Actually, I did. I'll have you know that Ms. Weever and I went to the same school for Darks. We had all the same teachers and everything."

"A boarding school?" Going to the same school as Ms. Weever sounded like a great idea.

"No, it was a private school in the city. It was only for Darks, giving us a break from prejudice and allowing us to focus on our studies and hone our skills."

"Maybe I should go there instead."

He wore a pained expression. "How old are you? Twelve? Sorry, that school was forced to close before you were born. You'll have to make do with Toolena Mesa, unless you've got somewhere better in mind."

I slouched. So much for that.

"I'm sorry. I know it's hard to be a Dark. We encounter hate wherever we go. Even though it would've put me out of a job, I would've wholeheartedly recommended that school to you."

"Why was it closed?"

Mr. Muradon let out a weary sigh. "Simply because it was a school for Darks. The school was accused of existing for the sole purpose of producing necromancers. A bit of publicity and the place was burned down in a riot a few weeks later.

"Sounds about right," Vergo said. "If you don't understand it, then it must be evil, therefore destroyed."

"Anyway, I'm not trying to impose on what Ms. Weever did with you. She's an incredible individual—intense and sometimes scary—but a brilliant, talented

Dark with a knack for scoffing at authority figures."

That described her perfectly. I forced myself not to smile. I was angry at him for taking over her office.

"By the sound of what happened, that hasn't changed."

"No. She's amazing. She didn't deserve to get fired."

Mr. Muradon looked askance at Mr. Redd's office. "Judging by your principle, I'm inclined to agree. Anyway, it's unprofessional to talk with you about such things. I wanted to let you know that I think highly of Ms. Weever and bear her no ill will. I hope you'll give me a chance."

I folded my arms. "We'll see."

His mouth crooked into a smile. "She definitely left her mark on you." He reached for a booklet I recognized, and I cringed.

It was the brainwashing garbage the school board wanted me to use to continue my studies.

He held it between two fingers like it was a dirty sock. "Your principal told me this has been the focus of your studies for a while now. I would like to know your opinion of its contents."

I gave the book the look of loathing it deserved and my new tutor busted out laughing.

"That answers that." He tossed it in his garbage pail by the door. "Go ahead and throw away your copy. We won't be needing it."

Okay, that made it a little harder to hate him. I fished my copy out of my backpack and added mine to the garbage. I was tempted to ask if we could go outside and light them on fire, but that probably wasn't a good idea, even though he felt the same way.

45

"The school board expects me to pick up where you left off in that nonsense. I'd prefer to pick up where Ms. Weever left off. Word has it you're way ahead in your alignment development that I'd dare call you a prodigy."

"Who says I'm ahead?"

"Your principal, for one. Despite his flaws, he speaks highly of you. You're the main reason why I said yes to this job. What has Weever taught you so far?"

"A lot." She was still teaching me, covertly sending notes via Bela's backpack. She'd been teaching me this way for weeks, fearing for all our safety and not wanting to make me easy prey for demons. Despite all she'd taught me, I had a ton to learn. My latest lessons focused on more powerful protection circles and a stronger energy bubble. The latter drained me quickly, so I hadn't practiced it much yet.

"Like?"

I shrugged.

"Do be more specific. I don't want to prepare a lesson just to be told she's already covered it."

"No point in being stubborn, Little One," Vergo said from under the chair.

I mentally filed through everything we'd covered from the start of sixth grade to about one quarter through seventh. I told him about learning the mbira and then switching to violin this year. I'd learned a variety of protection circles, started learning how to differentiate the energy signatures of various demons, locating cursed objects, and the Crossover Ritual. I withheld the exorcism lesson under the Order of Leo and the song I'd played to strengthen the power circle that wrapped around the cavern floor. I wasn't sure if

Bylan and Nurse Kor could get in trouble for that, much less if Mr. Muradon could be trusted with such information. Grandma had been right when she warned me about choosing who I asked for help. My new tutor would have to do way more than hate the same lesson book to earn my trust. I explained how I could play a circle's song on my violin and figure out a rune's notes by looking at them.

My new tutor perked up. "Can you really?"

"Yeah. Even Ms. Weever was surprised I could do that."

"You are a prodigy. Not many seasoned Darks can do that. Even I can't. I'm lost without a circle's sheet music, unless it's a simple one I've memorized. Would you mind showing me?"

I shifted in my chair. "Right now?"

"Please." He gestured to the open space between his desk and the upright piano.

I'd done a zillion charcoal drawings of power circles in the space. Ms. Weever had done many demonstrations, and I'd played several more on the violin. I flipped the latches on my violin case and retrieved my bow and a rosin block. I'd learned the hard way that a bow would do nothing but glide soundlessly along the strings if there wasn't enough rosin on it. I'd thought the brand new violin my parents bought me was defective until Mrs. Stirling, our orchestra teacher, taught me about its purpose. My rosin was plain old pine resin. Other rosins were imbued with power and enchantments to strengthen circles and spells.

Bow properly rubbed, I stood in the middle of the open space and shouldered my violin, picturing a basic protection circle's runes and their song in my head. My fingertips moved along the neck and I swayed a tempo. Confirming that my memory was correct, I raised my bow and played.

A light breeze rose from the floor. Runes winked to life with a purple glow in the four nautical corners of my forming circle. Curved lines wrapped around the runes, protecting and connecting all of them. As soon as I played the last note, the circle flared in brightness before settling into a subtle glow, humming with power.

Mr. Muradon took in my circle with wide eyes reflecting the purple glow. "Impressive."

I played the circle's song in reverse, canceling it out. I inhaled deeply as energy returned to me, feeling like someone pressed on my stomach. The process energized me.

My new tutor browsed his bookshelves, plucking free a book. He skimmed the pages, turning to a particular one, and held it up. "Do you know this circle?"

I drew my brows together. At first glance, it looked familiar, but upon closer inspection, it was a circle I'd never seen before. The four runes were *colli*, *sustri*, *gabo*, and *prasi*, a combination of protection and binding runes. The lines circling and connecting the runes created several rings of protection and binding. Two of the runes looked like the curvature of knuckles on a fist, *prasi* the curvature of a shield, and *sustri* looked like a rope or snake. The spidery runes laid out their notes before me, a song that moved with the cadence of heavy footfalls. "What kind of circle is this?"

"Can you play it?"

My fingertips played out the series of notes on the strings. It was a different song, but the sequence felt correct, right. "Yes. Hold the book still." I shouldered my violin again as Mr. Muradon held the book in two hands. Vergo came out from under the chair and sat up, tail curled around his paws. He watched with open curiosity. Studying the page, I played the song in my head again before raising my bow.

I played the circle's heavy song slowly, carefully, making sure every note came out in the correct order. Simpler circles would form if the song was played incorrectly. However, it'd be a weaker version of the perfect thing. It would also drain me of energy far faster than a properly conjured power circle. More complex ones would give me backlash if I messed up, dishing out anything from physical injuries to hospitalizing and even killing me. It all depended on the circle's purpose and potential power.

Judging by the runes and number of lines, this circle was simpler. The runes flared to life one by one with purple light, kicking up a fresh breeze. Lines formed between and around the runes as if someone were drawing them. The circle drew energy from me, feeling like gravity pulled harder, and the glow hummed with power.

Lowering the book, Mr. Muradon grinned broadly. "You really are a prodigy. You must teach me how you do that."

My mind blanked out at the request. Me teach my tutor something? Crazy. I was a student, not a teacher. I didn't know how I figured out a circle's song. I just did it. All the notes were right there, in the runes.

Vergo tentatively approached the circle, the glow

giving his eyes their night eye sheen. He flattened his ears. "Mia, this is a binding circle. I hope this was to satisfy his curiosity. You have no business learning this circle for a few more years."

My satisfaction deflated. That was the first time I'd sight-read a circle's song. I'd always practiced drawing it first, and then used a dampening rune on my violin so nothing would happen, even if I played a song correctly. I canceled the circle out. "Mr. Muradon, what was that circle for?"

"Protecting yourself while binding a demon to your will, something I don't anticipate you putting to practical use for at least a few more years."

Vergo said, "He has no business showing you that circle. Binding demons is something you don't want to attempt until you're a master at controlling your emotions and you've physically and mentally developed past the delightful phase of raging teenage hormones. As impulsive as I was, even I knew better than to touch such circles."

"Why did you have me play it?" I said to Mr. Muradon.

"Because the only backlash if you failed was that the circle wouldn't form, simple as that." He returned the book to its place among the shelves. "I want to pick up where Ms. Weever left off with your training. You clearly have incredible potential. She did you a huge favor by fostering your talent and encouraging you to grow as a Dark." He fixed me with his scrutinizing gaze. "I intend to build on that. I hope you're ready and eager to be my student."

"And I hope his intentions are good," Vergo said.

Chapter 4

Mom snuck me off to the bandyll party without Bela noticing, saving us all from a meltdown. Coach Viro lived partway down a straight dirt road that went on forever. It drew a line that got lost in the distant mountains. A long row of cars lined each side of the road. I hadn't wanted to arrive early or on time. Part of me didn't want to be here at all. Parties meant socializing. Socializing meant having something to say. Just about everything on my mind needed to be kept secret. Hopefully, I'd be able to hide in a corner and go unnoticed while everyone else had fun. I'd brought my Yuna book, just in case.

It was a cookie-cutter neighborhood, all the houses the same one-story rectangular shape, the front doors and windows in the same location, and everyone had the same large cinderblock fence lining their back yards. The only way to tell Coach's house apart was the abundance of party decorations, including floating bandyll balls with our Miners mascot on them, confetti hovering over the rooftop like a swarm of multicolored fireflies. Happy voices chatted and shouted in the back yard, and the latest pop music blared from song stones. I followed the arrows pointing to the backyard entrance, stopping at a wooden gate with a hand-drawn "Congrats Miners!" sign hanging on it. School color streamers framed the wide gate. I adjusted the beach towel draped over my shoulder and braced myself as I entered.

I must've been the last to arrive. The entire A and B teams sat, stood, ran around, or splashed in the pool. A colorful buffet sat on a long row of tables, complete with lemonade, iced tea, jalapeño poppers, chips and salsa, assorted meats, snack foods, salads, cookies, and cupcakes—everything a teenager would want to eat. Spiral sticks stood over the food at intervals, wards to keep bugs off the food. The music was even louder on this side of the gate.

I managed to take only a few steps when teammates turned.

"Mia!"

I took an involuntary step back as a small herd of bathing-suit-clad girls charged towards me, big smiles on their faces. Kelsi, our big eighth-grade forward and best shot on the team, grabbed one wrist, and Ansa, one of my defensemen, grabbed my other wrist. My teammates dragged me deeper into the yard, all of them talking over each other.

"Come play volleyball with us."

"You've got the try the food. It's amazing."

"What took you so long to get here?"

"Why did you bring a book? You totally don't need

that."

My mind blanked out as my feet carried me at a jog past the food and to the lounge chairs ringing the pool. Ansa draped my towel over one of the chairs, and Kentra, my sweeper, set my bag on top. A large chunk of the B team was splashing around in the pool kept warm by the glass roof standing high over the water. It was divided into rectangular panels that moved to catch the sun and heat up the water. While we were about a month off from winter, Toolena Mesa was relatively close to the equator, and thus experienced warm autumns and mild winters. Snow didn't happen every year at this elevation, and it was a coating that lasted a few hours at best if it did.

The air had a nip, but the sun was warm on my skin. My teammates dragged me away from the pool and to the square sand pit for some volleyball. Sussi stood on the other side of the high net, wearing a bikini. She gave me a wave and a smile. Half the girls wore bikinis, while the rest of us wore a one-piece. I kicked off my sandals, but left my t-shirt and shorts on. How any of them were brave enough to show so much skin was beyond me.

The sand was soft and warm between my toes. Vergo flopped down by one of the net poles and closed his eyes. He'd probably nap through the whole party. I stood in the back row, where Kelsi pointed.

"Mia, have you ever played volleyball before?"

Oh, man. Would they think I was uncool if I hadn't? I didn't want to get caught lying about what I did and didn't know. I had only seen snippets of volleyball in action, and we had yet to learn it in PE. "Er, no. I'm sorry."

Ansa said, "It's okay. Don't feel bad. We'll show you how."

With a bit of coaching, they taught me how to bump and hit the ball, and soon I was too engrossed in the game to worry about having to talk to anyone. We spent a good chunk of time retrieving the ball from various parts of the yard, and a few times had to bug the next-door neighbor to get the ball back. We all sucked, so I didn't feel bad anymore. We smiled, giggled, and thoroughly enjoyed volleying the ball around until hunger took over.

I helped myself to a heaping plate of what amounted to probably all the food I'd eat in a day. Everything looked and smelled so tasty that I didn't want to miss anything. I joined Sussi and a few other teammates at a round wood table with another spiral bug-repelling stick. The lemonade in our cups sloshed around until we all got settled down. Gwen and a few B team players sat at the table next to us, Gwen as far away from me and Sussi as she could manage. Dunno why she decided to eat at the same time as us, but whatever. She glared at me, but I rolled my eyes and turned to my heaping plate.

Kelsi, Ansa, and the others devoured their food and headed for the pool. I ate half of what I grabbed and nursed my lemonade, which was the right balance of sweet and lemony, and relaxed with Sussi, both of us listening to the upbeat music. I felt so fat and stuffed after so much tasty food.

She smiled for once, instead of projecting her usual grumpy indifference. She said, "So what are you going to do now that bandyll's over? I'm already bored."

I snuck a glance at Gwen seated with a couple of

other teammates. "I'm not sure. My dad suggested club bandyll, but I don't know if I'm good enough."

Someone at the other table snorted. Gwen's gaze darted away from me when I looked up. Her teammates were talking about something, but the timing of her snort was suspicious. Was she really eavesdropping? I wouldn't put it past her.

Sussi acted like she didn't hear the snort. "I think you are. You'd have to try out, but I bet you'd make our team. Every team always needs goalies. Most players want to be a star on offense and get all the attention for scoring goals. Dunno why."

"Me neither." While my skating skills had improved quickly, I couldn't see myself trying to navigate the entire court in hopes of getting a shot past another goalie and all the other players.

"Defense is where it's at."

"Agreed. Doesn't your club team already have a good goalie?"

"Yeah, but you're better."

"No, she's not," Gwen said, her tone dripping with snobbery.

I clenched my teeth, torn between snapping back at her or keeping quiet and taking it. I really didn't want to get in trouble at a party, especially with Coach right there by the food. Gwen stood near us, looking down her nose at me.

"Go away," Sussi said. "You're not even part of this conversation."

"We're part of the same club team, so I have every right to be part of this conversation." Gwen put her fists on her perfect hips. She was one of the braver ones who wore a bikini. While her chest was small, she clearly had one, unlike me. I was flat as two pancakes. I tugged at my championship t-shirt. She also had an hourglass figure while I was a mere rectangle.

Sussi said, "Well, we don't want to talk to you, so go away." She folded her arms over a chest as flat as mine.

"No. I don't want her on my team." Gwen folded her arms as well.

Sussi leaned forward. "It's not your team."

"Whose dad bought the whole team new uniforms last year?"

"That doesn't make it your team. No one told him to do that."

"And who's captain of the team?"

Sussi's eyes narrowed. "You're not the only captain. Get over yourself."

"Maybe it's not a good idea for me to try out for the team."

Gwen rounded on me, jutting her chin out. "No, it's not. Stay away."

"You're jealous because she made the A team and you didn't."

Gwen opened her mouth, but only managed to scoff.

Sussi leaned forward in her chair. "You also know she's a better goalie than Mattie. Mia's made stops we only wish Mattie had made in the past."

"There's nothing wrong with Mattie in goal. She does fine. Mia's not getting on the team and that's final."

"You're a real selfish jerk. I hope you know that."

I said, "Sussi, it's fine. I don't have to be on the club team. I don't see the point if she's going to be that nasty all the time."

Sussi rounded her glare on me. "No, you should be on the team. And you need to learn to stand up to her, or she's never going to stop being mean to you."

"Sound familiar?" Vergo said.

I leaned over. "Shut up," I said to the cat under my chair, anger rising to a simmer.

"Was that to me or to Vergo?" Sussi said, eyes narrowed.

"Vergo." I folded my arms and looked away from everyone.

"Who's Vergo?" Gwen said.

"None of your business," I said before I could stop myself. If we had bandyll gear on, I so would've tackled her. That was one of the fun things about this sport. You could beat each other up and not do any real damage. I'd shoved a bunch of players who'd skated into me. Right now, Gwen was pushing against my patience.

"Excuse me? Don't talk to me like that."

"Then leave me alone. We weren't even talking to you. You were the one who butted in on this conversation."

"You're the ones who started talking about *my* club team."

Sussi said, "Mia should play for the team. Didn't your dad agree with Coach that you need to practice teamwork?"

"Yeah, but he didn't say I had to with *her*." Gwen jutted her chin in my direction.

Sussi gave her a nasty smile. "Maybe if I whine and complain to the coaches and my parents enough, they'll kick you off the club team and we won't have to deal with you anymore."

"I'd like to see you try." Gwen rounded on me. "Stay off my club team. You suck at bandyll and you're nothing but an evil Dark who needs to learn her place in the world."

I was so sick and tired of being hated for being a Dark, so sick and tired of Gwen's crap and her hate. I'd done nothing to her and tried to ignore her, but she regularly went out of her way to make my school life unpleasant. Something in me snapped. I jumped to my feet and got in her face.

Her eyes widened, actually widened.

"You're a real jerk. You've been mean to me since the day I got here. You've been controlling and a bully, and when you no longer wanted me as one of your fake friends, you threatened everyone who would dare to try and make friends with me. Deren was the only one brave enough to stay my friend and he was the only one brave enough to help you to the nurse's office after you got sick." I trembled all over, but I didn't care. I couldn't take her abuse in silence anymore.

Gwen looked me up and down. "You made me sick."

"Shut up. You were bullying me again and I got fed up with it for once. I know what I did wasn't right, but I risked my life and fixed it as soon as I could. You should be thanking me for being halfway decent, despite how you treated me."

"Thank you? You're stupid if you think I will ever thank you."

I ignored her. I didn't care what she thought anymore. I had more venom and she was going to take it whether she liked it or not. "And then you get mad at me when I made the A team and you didn't. You did that to yourself because you're so stuck up and selfish, but you're too stupid and arrogant to see that. Coach saw right through you. I bet you whined and threw a tantrum like a child, until your parents got sick of hearing it and talked to the school."

"That's not true." Her face reddened. What a liar.

I took a step closer and Gwen took a step back. "No one likes you because you're so mean. Everyone pretends because they're afraid of you. You have no friends. You're nothing but a bully and a loser. The only person that likes you is my sister, and that's because she doesn't know any better yet."

One moment, there was rage all over Gwen's face. In the next instant, it was all shock. She tried to glare as her lips trembled. "I hate you," she said, her voice barely audible and a tear running down her cheek. She ran into the house.

The glass door slid closed. Not one player or adult followed Gwen. Conversations and play resumed, and a few parents helped themselves to the food.

"Dang, you got her good. I'm proud of you," Sussi gave me a victorious smile and patted me on the back.

"As am I," Vergo said. "She needed to hear every last word. Good job, Little One."

I breathed hard. That was a lot of words I'd spewed in a short amount of time. I should've been proud of myself for finally standing up to Gwen. I meant every word, even the no friends part. I dropped in my chair, trying to figure out what I'd done. Trembling struck me in waves. I clenched the armrests.

I'd stood up to a bully. It needed to get done, but not like that. I'd become as mean as her and I'd hurt her feelings. She actually had feelings to hurt. She was human, like me. How could I be proud of myself if I'd acted no better than my enemy?

Sussi said, "Mia, why do you look so upset? You should seriously be proud of yourself."

I shook my head.

"Dude, it took me way longer than you to finally stand up to her. No one stands up to her. You're, like, my hero right now."

"I'm not a hero." I grabbed my towel and backpack from the chair by the pool and went inside. I needed to go home.

Chapter 5

I'd hardly visited Nurse Kor's office for all of seventh grade so far. Between her strange behavior that motivated me to leave her alone and clued us in that she needed an exorcism, and then needing to leave her alone to help her stay under Mr. Redd's radar, I'd stopped seeing her after bandyll was over.

Today, however, I needed something to distract me from everything. I'd brooded over my confrontation with Gwen, tried to decide whether to go forward with club bandyll or take a stab at another sport, worried about Mr. Muradon and whether we could trust him, tried to think of ways to get Mr. Redd to expose his true colors, and stressed over the demon Tradereth and the bargain she wanted to force on me. On top of all that, Dad was pensive and acting distant towards both Bela and me. His behavior made Mom irritable, but she cooked, took care of the house, and tended to my sister.

I felt ready to explode if at least one thing didn't go right.

I rushed out of math class (we still had a sub) and, instead of heading to lunch, made a beeline for Nurse Kor's office and ignored the vines pawing at my ankles. They were harmless. They helped her feel out a student's energies and what ailed them. Many a student had tried to fake being sick. All had failed. She was a Florakin, a Kindred that had a special affinity with vining plants.

Nurse Kor sat reading a medical book, all three of her sick beds empty. A large peony sat in her hair above one of her ears. She had short hair, striking green eyes, and a studious gaze. When I first met her, I thought she was an elf from one of my books. Well, an elf in scrubs. Today's scrubs were patterned with palm trees and fae parrots, a tropical bird that looked more fairy than bird, except for its large beak and talons.

She looked up and blinked. "Mia, what a pleasant surprise. How are you doing?"

Sometimes I really hated that question. On top of everything else, I was wondering about Mr. Gauss, which had been no small source of worry. Some time had passed, giving me hope she had some information by now. I ignored the question. "Mind if I sneak having lunch in here today?"

She raised a brow, then gestured for me to sit on the bed farthest from the door. She made another hand gesture at the doorway and vines crept closer to the frame, lines of green coiling along the painted metal-like arms of an octopus crawling its way along the ocean floor. Dozens of triangular leaves curled up to resemble horns. Not only could she use plants for healing, she could also use them to enhance her senses. The coil of vines she always kept hidden up a sleeve crept up her neck and coiled around an ear, covering it in leaves. Creepy. Neat, but creepy. I shivered and rubbed my neck.

Nurse Kor yanked one of the blue and white curtains closed, blocking our view of the doorway. "So what's up?"

I took out my chicken, cheese, and veggie burrito from my backpack and held it in both hands. Thank the Light I'd been awake enough to make it before the bus came. "I've been wondering about Mr. Gauss lately. Have you been able to find out anything about what happened to him?" If we could find out what he was up to, then we'd figure out what Mr. Redd wanted, and I could figure out what Tradereth wanted. Almost everything demons said was a lie or misleading.

She grimaced. "Not exactly."

Okay, that wasn't an outright no. "What do you mean?"

She leaned closer, hair spilling over her shoulders. "The police took him away that day. There are records in the county police department of the school turning him in and the police picking him up. They booked him into the Eagle Tail County Jail, but that's where the trail stops cold. There's no record of a release, a transfer, or anything. Ms. Weever visited the jail. Boy, does she have questions for him. But anyway, she got there and they said he wasn't there. The front desk person showed Weever redacted records confirming that he wasn't being held there."

"What's redacted?"

"Oh, it's a document with certain blocks of text

covered up so you can't read them. It's a legal thing they have to do sometimes. Anyway, Ms. Weever double-checked the newspaper, which provides a daily jail log, and he was in there, picture and all, for the attempted murder of a minor, so we know for a fact that the police hauled him away."

My stomach roiled. That was the first time anyone had used the m-word to describe what nearly happened to my sister. It was an ugly yet truthful word. I pushed the thought aside. I needed answers. "So now what?"

"Weever's been checking the entire state plus neighboring states' jail records. So far, he's nowhere to be found, which is really, really odd and worrisome. Authorities should be out of their mind with concern over losing track of a person with such charges, but she said the people at Eagle Tail seem indifferent. The sheriff said the paper was wrong."

"Why would a newspaper lie about a jail log?"

"Exactly. When it comes to this stuff, all they do is print information from police reports. They have no motive to lie."

"So then the sheriff is lying. Why would he lie?"

"That's a very good question with a wide variety of very worrisome answers."

Vergo nudged my elbow. I took his collar off and he said, "Sounds like we're in greater danger than any of us realized."

Nurse Kor nodded, frowning. "That's what it sounds like. That has me wondering what kind of man Fabian really was."

I was no longer hungry. With no bandyll practice or games to motivate me to eat, I set my burrito on the sick bed. "Who do you think he was?" If Mr. Redd had made sure Mr. Gauss had gotten arrested, then either he'd done the right thing, or he was pretending along with the police.

Leaning back, she puffed out her cheeks and exhaled. "That's a very good question. There are things that suggest he was a bad person, and there are things that suggest he was an innocent bystander in all this. I don't know."

"Well, tell us," Vergo said. "Maybe we can offer an objective view."

She gave us a pained smile. "Part of me doesn't want to know. I'd almost rather never find out so there's always the possibility that he was all good."

Vergo stomped a paw on the bed. "This is no time for Heimerling 's cat. We need to be certain if it's alive or dead."

"Heimer-who?" I said. And what cat might be alive or dead?

He shook his furry head. "Never mind." He turned back to the nurse. "Knowing his motives will give us a very good idea of whether the events happening at this school are isolated or part of a much larger plot. Based on what you've told us about the police reports, I'm inclined to believe the latter. Start talking, madame."

Her shoulders slumped. "I honestly don't know what to think. We were both smitten with each other when we first met. I had butterflies, couldn't breathe and everything. He could barely speak. He was so nervous when he asked me out before the school year started." She softened into a reminiscing smile. "We went on several dinner dates and he didn't gift me the box until shortly after the school year started. I thought it was such a strange thing to give, but it was so pretty, and there was something about it that made me unable to refuse it."

"The demon's influence," Vergo said with a grimace.

The nurse winced. "You think so?"

"As a former Dark, I know so."

"Wait, you were—?"

"Yes. What can you recall of his behavior when he handled the box?"

She thought a moment, biting a lip. "He was real nervous, like he was afraid I wouldn't take it or something."

"Did he touch the box or did he gift it to you all wrapped up?"

Nurse Kor scrunched her brows.

"He touched it," I said, remembering the day he'd had a wooden box with doors on his desk. "He'd had it in his classroom. It was there on the first day of school. One of the little doors popped open when he accidentally elbowed it, and he closed it."

"I can't say I remember this," Vergo said.

"That's probably because you were too busy making fun of me."

"For what?" Nurse Kor said.

The cat's whiskers rose as he smiled. "Madame, you weren't the only one smitten with that man. He's a dashing fellow, I give him that. Even the students noticed."

The nurse gave us an amused smile. "He told me how various students left him love notes, even Gwen."

Vergo busted out laughing. I winced. Not only would I rather have no one ever know about my crush, but the mention of Gwen made me clench my teeth.

"Let's not talk about her right now."

Nurse Kor studied me. "I heard you gave her a much-deserved earful over the weekend. All the students are talking about it."

I felt the color drain from my face. "How'd they find out?"

Vergo said, "You weren't exactly soft-spoken during your tirade. There were teammates sitting a few feet away who heard the whole thing, and Sussi had a front-row seat."

I buried my face in my hands. "What if she went to her parents about it?"

"What, and show the whole school that she needs Mommy and Daddy to stand up for her? No. She's rotten, but she's not stupid."

I dug my fingertips into my forehead. "Can we go back to talking about the box now?"

They looked at each other, and Nurse Kor shrugged. "As you wish. So anyway, yes, I saw him touch the box, now that I think about it."

"Did he behave any differently while handling it? Were his emotions different from when he wasn't in contact with the box?"

"Honestly? Yes. He was more confident and forthright, if not a little pushy."

"Any anger or anything to make you feel uneasy?"

"You're asking a lot of my memory. Remember, I was getting sick a lot and was feeling irritable all the time."

"True."

"So what does it mean that he touched the box?" I said, picking up my burrito. I didn't feel like eating, but my stomach growled.

"Two things," Vergo said. "One, either a Dark placed some protections on him so he could somewhat safely handle the box. There's no such thing as being entirely safe when dealing with demons. Or two, the demon sent to meddle with you—" he nodded to Kor "—had little interest in him and had specific instructions to focus strictly on you."

"Because I'd been near the Crossing Ritual for you?"

"And the Demon King wanted something in exchange for losing me. Simple as that."

She crinkled her nose. "That's so cruel."

"That's the Demon King for you," Vergo said, flatting his ears in dismay. "How did your boyfriend behave after the exorcism?"

"I…actually broke up with him. I didn't know what to think or feel. I needed to be alone for a while."

Whoa, she'd broken up with him? I hadn't been able to tell. They'd both carried on as normal—well, Nurse Kor as normal as possible after being exorcised and learning that a demon had been controlling her for months.

"How did he take it?"

"He was understandably upset," she said with a nod, "but he got over it pretty fast and stopped talking to me altogether." One corner of her mouth curled into a frown.

"That may be a clue as to what his true intentions were."

The nurse grimaced.

Vergo scooted closer and curled his tail around his paws. "Or…that was the demon tugging his strings and redirecting him to Bela. He *was* present during both attacks."

I poked the cat with my wrapped burrito. "Do you remember Mr. Gauss's face after we severed the attachment?"

"I was a bit preoccupied with making sure the demon kept its distance from the three of you."

Vergo had transformed into a panther a second time during that encounter, buying Garrett and his coyotes time to add their power to my circle, giving us the boost we needed to overpower the demon. Mr. Gauss had thrown up before getting a look at our foe. "He was so surprised I thought he was going to pass out."

"Maybe he's a good actor."

I wanted to believe Mr. Gauss was the bad guy as much as Nurse Kor did. His kindness towards me had seemed genuine. I didn't want to believe it had all been an act to get at my sister. "Maybe he was a pawn. I mean, he had a demonic attachment. You know when that happens, you're not always in control. Maybe the good things were his real self and the bad things were the demon."

"Can someone willingly let in a demon?" Nurse Kor said.

"Of course," Vergo said. "That's something Wild Darks are notorious for."

"But Mr. Gauss was an Earth," I said.

"Alignments don't matter." He placed a sympathetic paw on my knee. "I know it's not the picture any of us want to paint. It would be nice to think the whole world is good and kind, but we can't afford to avoid staring the ugly truth in the face because it makes us unhappy."

I dumped my burrito back in my backpack. Food

was so out of the question, growling stomach or not. "I know."

Vergo sat up as tall as his little body could manage. "I don't think we're going to discover Gauss's true nature based on pure speculation. There are too many ways to interpret his actions."

"How do we find out the truth?" Nurse Kor said.

I sat up straighter myself. "We go to the source."

"We don't know where Gauss is," Vergo said.

In hopes of getting some answers when Allosyr had been haunting Miss Wren's homeroom, I'd reached out to Orton Totes' ghost. While he'd been unable to give me much to go on, he'd helped. "No, but we can get in contact with Payton."

Chapter 6

Mom, Bela, and I sat together at a table in Bylan's back yard, waiting for him to finish making preparations inside. He'd invited my dad, too, who'd declined, claiming he wanted to catch up on sleep over the weekend. It was a fair excuse, but he'd stiffened as soon as Bylan mentioned something about a ghost while on the vine with Dad. The excuse immediately followed. The Light priest didn't push him. Guess this meant that, Light or Dark, Dad wanted nothing to do with ghosts.

The table was made of blown glass of varying colors, giving the impression that our chilled water sat on a sunset. I was afraid of touching the table for fear of breaking it. Despite spending a lot of time at Sussi's house, I was intimidated by such open displays of wealth.

Bylan's back yard was a literal oasis in the desert.

It had a massive garden of raised beds lined up in tidy rows, a canopy of vines to shade it from harsh desert sunlight; an orchard bursting with lemons, oranges, grapefruits, and pecans ready for picking; and a stone water feature half as tall as the house. The sweet scent of fresh citrus rode on the late autumn air. Birds of paradise flitted among the trees, singing their sweet songs and flashing stunning colors that urged me to get up and pet them.

The patio itself was custom-laid stone chipped from a larger rock and linked together like a jigsaw. A matching stone path drew a straight line to the two-story house. A glass door slid open and an old lady stepped out, carrying a tray. What was it with rich people carrying stuff around on trays? I mean, it was neat and all, and made me feel special because someone had taken the time to present snacks in such a way, but I couldn't do the same at home, unless I wanted to use a cake pan.

The old lady was Mrs. Bylan, a sweet person with a slight limp, glasses, and curly hair. She looked every bit like a grandma from her flowery clothes, pleasant smile, and heavy build.

Mrs. Bylan set a plate of nuts, cheese, fruit, and dried meats on our table. She popped a wrinkly smile and headed back inside.

I reached for the grapes when the patio door slid open yet again. A tall lady with rich blonde hair and ice-blue eyes marched out. Her knee-high black boots thunked on the stone with every step, and her layered skirts swished with her hips. My breath hitched. Ms. Weever. I hadn't seen her since the day she'd covertly handed me the cloth without Mr. Redd finding out. I launched out of my chair.

While I wasn't the hugging type, I knew in my heart of hearts that I absolutely needed to hug her. She'd saved me from expulsion and empowered me to stop a second demon. She'd taught me so much and genuinely cared about me.

Ms. Weever's hard stare softened and she stopped. She spread her arms, and I slowed down to avoid toppling her over as I wrapped my arms around her corset. The material was frilly and itchy, but I didn't care. She was here. Arms wrapped around me, her chest rose and fell with a long sigh.

"You're taller than I last saw you," she said.

"I missed you," I said.

"And I you. Hopefully, today will set us all on the path to right some grievous wrongs." Ms. Weever squeezed me a second time and together we headed for the table.

Mom brightened. "Ms. Weever. So nice to see you, and under slightly better circumstances."

They shook hands. "Please call me Lyra."

"Dare I ask how you've been, Lyra? Mia told me what happened. There's something seriously wrong with this school."

Ms. Weever took a seat and poured herself some water. "Busy, to be honest. We all have far more questions than answers." She took a sip. "Now, I don't mean to be rude, but may I ask why your youngest is here?"

Bela stood on her chair, bracing her hands on the super expensive table. "I get to learn how to talk to ghosts."

Mom tried to hold on to her smile as her brows

drew together like she'd wished Bela hadn't said that.

Ms. Weever raised a penciled eyebrow. "I thought you already knew how."

"Bylan says I can learn how to do it when I want to."

Mom turned away from us all. "He wants her to learn how to do that kind of thing on command, so she can better control who talks to her and when."

Ms. Weever considered my mom over the rim of her glass. "Why does this sort of conversation make you so uncomfortable? You have two children with amazing gifts."

Mom searched for the right words. "I know. It's… This kind of thing has caused our family so much trouble. And I don't understand what's going on."

"How hard have you tried to understand?"

Mom's grimace was full of guilt. "Good point. I'm here, at least."

"And your husband?"

Mom shook her head. "He's worse than me and I only recently learned why."

"Do tell. I'd like to understand."

Mom shook her head again. "It's rather personal."

Ms. Weever raised her glass in a small salute, as if she understood.

One of the colorful birds flew over to Bela. It had velvety purples and blues in its plumage with a collapsible red mohawk of feathers on its head. While it was smaller than Vergo, its wings spanned the table's width, revealing deep greens and browns on the underside. The bird looked like a feathery dragon with a lizard-shaped mouth that ended in a beak, talons large enough to wrap around fingers, and a whiplike tail.

Bela let out a yelp and Mom shooed it away. The bird jumped back, opening its toothless maw, and squawked at her. She swiped at it a second time. It hopped and bit a knuckle, then spread its wings and hissed, its feathery body puffed up. It backed towards Bela, as if shielding her from Mom.

"Birdie, be nice." Bela stood on her chair and patted the bird's back. Its feathers calmed and it rubbed up against her hand. "Hi, birdie. I'm Bela." The bird trilled a few notes and hopped onto her arm. Bela dutifully stroked its velvety chest. It cooed and closed its eyes.

Mom gawked at the blood trickling down her hand, then glared at the dragon bird thing. She sucked on a knuckle.

"Sorry, Peeve hasn't quite mastered good manners."

We all turned at the sound of Bylan's calm, soothing voice. He and his wife approached us, he carrying a lumpy bag.

"Peeve?" Ms. Weever arched an eyebrow.

"Yes," Mrs. Bylan said. "He is our pet bird named Peeve. We literally have a pet peeve."

"Clever," my former tutor said.

Mrs. Bylan held out an arm. Peeve cheeped at Bela and flew over, the sunlight highlighting the various shades of blues and purples, and alighted on the outstretched forearm and nudged her shoulder. The old lady scratched under his chin. "He favors Lights and tolerates me, a Water. Isn't that right, Peeve?" She made kissing noises. Peeve mimicked the sound and tapped her lips with his beak. "Now, apologize to the lady." He huffed and ruffled his feathers. She booped him on the beak with a finger. "Be a gentleman and apologize."

The feathers flattened. Peeve turned on Mrs. Bylan's arm and bobbed his head, covering it with one wing. "Ra-ra." He plucked a green feather from his breast and placed it on Mom's knuckle. The feathery fibers became stuck to her skin like glue, stopping the bleeding. He squawked and flew off to the lemon trees.

"Sorry about that. Piasa wyverns are rather possessive."

"It *is* a wyvern," Vergo said from his spot in the seat next to me. "Where on Aardra did you get it?"

Bylan set a lumpy cloth bag on the table. "I must admit, he found me during my mission abroad decades ago. He came to me with an injured wing. I healed him and he never left. He didn't much like the long overseas trip I had to take to get back home, but here we are today. He's a faithful companion that enjoys keeping local birds away from the fruit trees." He touched the metal chair back, his gaze lowered to the bag. "Are you ready for a lesson today, Bela?"

"Yes, Sanctus Bylan." She hopped off her chair and stood next to the Light priest, her eyes a few inches above the tabletop. Little fingertips gripped the edge.

Bylan took objects out of the bag one by one, setting several candles, crystals, a necklace, and some chalk on the table. He pointed to the necklace, a little silver medallion engraved with a power circle, complete with runes, laid inside a ring of silver. "This is for concentration and protection." He put it on and, using some white chalk, drew four runes on the sidewalk, lining them up with the four nautical directions. "These are for more protection and to give the spirit something to anchor to." He dusted his hands off and set the candles and blue quartz crystals in a ring around the runes. "These are for helping channel the spirit. The flames and stones also provide a bit of energy, so we don't get so drained."

Bela's gaze grew serious and she nodded. I wasn't sure how much of this she took in. She acted like she absorbed everything.

Bylan stood inside the circle, facing east. Closing his eyes, he spoke the rune's words. Glowing white lines etched themselves into the stonework and the runes flared to life, humming with power. White sparks darted at the wicks, lighting the candles. The priest held his hands out, palms up, his eyes closed. "Now for the interesting part." He chanted something in another language with the cadence of a poem. The circle's energy tugged at me. Mom stood mesmerized by it all. Her feet carried her around the table, stopping only when Ms. Weever held out an arm. Mom shook her head and blinked several times.

My former tutor leaned closer. "He's connecting with the spirit world. Since our souls are connected to our bodies, we feel the pull, too."

Rubbing an arm, Mom took a step back.

"It's okay. There's nothing to be afraid of. It's a positive indicator that you're not some soulless doppelgänger."

Mom cringed, wide eyes fixed on the circle.

Bylan's voice rose as he repeated the chant. The candles flared higher. He took a deep breath. "Payton Arian Sorenson, I call thee forth. Come forward and speak to me. You will not be harmed."

A cry that was a mix of rage and pain emanated from the circle. At first, I thought it was Bylan, but his mouth was closed, his face etched with concentration. The flames danced as tendrils of smoke swirled around the priest, the cry getting louder as the smoke coalesced into a humanoid figure bound in chains.

"Who dares disturb my limbo?" Payton was a lean teenager, shirtless, and with hair that was short on the sides and a fallen-over mohawk ringing half of his face. Golden chains bound his hands behind him. While he was somewhat see-through, his dark eyes burned with hate strong enough to want to see the whole world destroyed—at least, that's what his presence felt like. There wasn't a single drop of empathy or compassion in his soul. While no longer a demon, he was still a monster.

"I am Alexander Bylan," the Light priest said in an authoritative voice. "I've called you here. We wish to speak with you."

Payton glared at each of us. Mom picked up Bela and cowered behind Ms. Weever. My former tutor's chest rose and fell with deliberate slowness. Bela watched with rapt attention, a finger in her mouth. She remained perfectly relaxed under Payton's glare.

The teenage ghost rounded on Bylan. "Release me. I have no business with you."

"You do now," Ms. Weever said under her breath.

"We have questions for you," Bylan said.

"I don't care." The chains went from gold to molten. Payton grunted, clenching his teeth. "Ask and I will answer."

"What was the nature of your attachment to Fabian Gauss?"

"Really? That's what you want to know?" Payton looked around the yard, his eyes narrowing when he spotted me. "You again? How could you send a demon to the Light like that? You're a Dark. You have no business trying to touch the Light."

"And you had no business trying to hurt my sister."

He studied Bela and me a moment before breaking into a wicked grin. He licked his lips. "I see the resemblance. I wonder why he didn't have me try to make a morsel out of you, too. You're clearly too soft to be a Dark."

Soft? Right. What an accurate description of me.

Not.

"Answer Bylan's question," I said.

Payton laughed. "What are you? His lapdog? Darks answer to no one."

Ms. Weever took a step closer. "You're a ghost, now, and not a Dark. You're dead. You have no alignment anymore."

He yanked against his chains, which flared up, making him wince. "I'll always be a Dark. Not even death can take that away from me."

"Then, by all means, demonstrate your ability to summon a demon."

He glared at her, his arm muscles straining against his chains.

"I'm waiting."

Payton opened his mouth and screamed. I covered my ears as it echoed out over the desert. The birds in Bylan's grove flew off, minus one that flew towards us. Peeve landed on the table near Mom and Bela, talons sliding across the glass, red mohawk feathers flared, body puffed up, and wings spread. He let out a shriek that made the ghost wince. Payton used profanity to tell the bird to get lost.

Bela gasped. "He said a bad word. Payton, apologize to Peeve."

Putting a hand over Bela's mouth, Mom said, "Bela, shush. Don't talk to him."

"Ah, the morsel has some courage. How cute. That courage is going to get you killed one day, little girl. I hope I'm there to see it."

Bylan made a fist and the chains seared into Payton's soul again. "I'm waiting for an answer."

"I'm getting there, old man. Be patient." Payton turned back to me. "See how superior these Light monsters think they are? I see that you're cooperating with him. Give it up. It'll backfire in the end. The world is a hateful, loveless place for Darks. You're only tolerated so long as you prove yourself useful. The moment you start thinking for yourself, acting for yourself, they cast you out and blame you for all that's wrong with the world. I tried to fit in and failed. You're clearly trying to do the same. Don't waste your energy. You'll never fit in."

"You're wrong," I said.

"You know I'm right."

Ms. Weever folded her arms. "Really? The victim's speech? Could you be any more cliché?"

Payton studied my former tutor. "Ah, the Dark that foiled my first attempt at devouring the Light morsel. Tell me, is the world any nicer a place for Darks today than it was four years ago?"

"Just because it's not balanced doesn't mean it's a lost battle. If you want to be a melodramatic defeatist, then by all means… The rest of us, however, live in reality. Every day is an opportunity to make the world a better place, no matter how small a part of it."

He rolled his eyes. "So you're one of those sappy types."

"Mia, do you see what he's trying to do?"

"Yeah. If he'd said all that before I met you, I would've believed every word of it." Payton thought he had all the answers, thought he knew how the world worked. He had no hope that things could change. While things were far from perfect at Toolena Mesa, a bunch of things had changed for the better. I had friends. I had a better understanding of how my alignment fit in with the others, that it was part of the whole. I didn't need to stick to the shadows for as long as I lived. My mom was getting braver, and Dad had shown that he still loved me.

"Enough stalling," Bylan said. "Tell me the truth about the nature of your attachment to Fabian Gauss."

Payton huffed a sigh and fiddled with his chains. "If you want to know so badly, he was a willing participant. I took great pleasure in watching him fool you all, especially that nurse lady. Even Fabian thought he was in love with her for a little while there, until I reminded him of what he needed to do. The weakling was starting to have second thoughts, but I snuffed them out."

"Who bound you to the dabuk box?"

Baring his teeth, Payton fidgeted with his chains more fervently. "Why do you want to know that? Does it matter?"

"Very much so. Tell me."

Grimacing, he took a deep breath. "A member… of…the Order of Tenebron."

Both Bylan and Ms. Weever inhaled sharply.

"It still exists," she whispered.

Bylan said, "Was it your uncle, Damien Redd?"

Payton smiled. "No. He's not stupid enough to leave such a trail of evidence."

"But is he the one who wanted the Light child dead?"

The ghost turned his head away and continued to strain against the chains. "Yes," he said through clenched teeth.

This time, my mom gasped. "Monster." She hugged Bela tighter and Peeve hissed.

"How big is the Order of Tenebron?" Ms. Weever said.

"Wouldn't you like to know?" Payton said.

"Answer her question," Bylan said.

The ghost tugged furiously at his chains. He tried to fight the compulsion to speak, but words forced themselves out. "The cosmic pendulum is always swinging. It's in the Light, but it's poised to swing back into the Dark. Change is coming. Darks are long overdue for some justice. You're all just pawns, even my uncle. Now, release me. I've had enough of this."

Bylan curled both hands into fists, his wrinkled face stern.

That was a face I dared not cross.

"No. We need to know more about this Order and its plans."

Payton strained against his chain. They glowed and made his wrists smoke. He acted like he couldn't feel it. He tilted his head back and screamed again, making my eyes water and eardrums vibrate. Something white shot out of his mouth and soared out of sight. Peeve took off after it in a flurry of flapping wings. Payton's body fractured. White light bled through the cracks.

Bylan sped through a flurry of martial arts-looking movements. The candles snuffed out and his circle flared with white light. "Payton Arian Sorenson, I release you back to your limbo. Goodbye."

Payton's body grew more and more transparent until he vanished altogether. "You're too late, old man. You can't stop what's coming. No one can."

Bylan dropped to his hands and knees, gasping for breath. The neck of his robes was soaked through with sweat. Ms. Weever knelt beside him while fumbling around inside a pouch tied to her waist. She produced a small vial holding a clear fluid and uncorked it. "Here, take this. It'll help you recover."

Bylan gratefully accepted the vial and downed the liquid in one gulp. "Thank you."

Peeve landed on Bylan's shoulder, its mohawk feathers collapsed and head drooping. "Gone. Gah-gone. Ra-ra."

Bylan petted Peeve's head and laboriously rose to his feet, causing the wyvern to flap his wings to maintain his perch. "It's okay, Peeve. Thank you for trying."

"What happened?" Ms. Weever said. "What was that thing that shot into the sky?"

"I have no idea."

Chapter 7

"Mia, let's go. We're leaving." Mom grabbed her purse and took off for the house.

I remained rooted in place. We'd gotten some critical answers, but now I had about a hundred more, the most pressing surrounding Mr. Redd and his role in all this, and what the heck was the Order of Tenebron? Judging by how Bylan and Ms. Weever reacted, it wasn't a good Order. Gauss was a part of it, Mr. Redd was probably a part of it, and how on Aardra could Bylan not know what Payton released from his mouth?

"Brecca, what's wrong? Don't leave yet."

Hugging Bela to her, Mom whirled around. "What's wrong? Are you kidding me? You have no business teaching my daughter such dangerous things. She barely turned five."

Bylan's mouth creased into a frown. "Regardless of her age, there are forces at work trying to kill her. This

84

means she needs to learn as much as she can as soon as she can, so she can protect herself as best she can. We're not always going to be around to protect her. Bela needs to learn how to protect herself, and quickly."

"It sounds more like her father and I need to get the principal fired as soon as possible."

"Were it that easy, Brecca," Ms. Weever said. "You heard Payton. The Order of Tenebron is alive and well. That means we have no idea exactly how large it is, who's a part of it, etcetera. Trying to run and hide won't make anyone any safer."

"Getting rid of Mr. Redd will make Toolena Mesa safer."

"You're presuming that every board member is an ally."

Bylan said, "We have to act as if every last one of them is an enemy."

Mom's eyes widened. "That's paranoia. That's no way to live."

"That's prudence," Ms. Weever said. "That's how we all stay alive."

"No. Mr. Redd needs to be gone. You're crazy if you think I'm going to send my youngest back to school with that monster there."

"That's exactly what you're going to do," Bylan said. "The last thing we need is to show our hand. Redd mustn't know what we know. I'll place a few extra wards and a tracer on her. I'll be forewarned the moment danger approaches."

"You yourself said none of us can always be there to protect her. What better way than to keep her as far away from that man as possible?"

"I understand where you're coming from," the

Light priest said. "I have children of my own, along with grandchildren. Nothing is more important than the safety of my family. I'm trying to help you do the same."

"Then why? How am I supposed to feel good about sending either of my children to school under such circumstances?"

"We need to know who our enemies are before we make any major decisions. The longer we keep the enemy complacent, the better."

"I don't see how anyone on the school board is an enemy. They were eager to expel Mia, until Bela's alignment manifested. It was only then that their tune changed, and with *your* help."

"Obviously, I had good intentions, but I don't know what the school board had in mind when they learned of Bela's alignment. It could very well be evidence of their benevolent intentions, or they could've seen it as an opportunity to prevent another Light from growing and maturing into a powerful force the Order of Tenebron loathes."

Much of the fire in Mom's eyes snuffed out as she frowned. "I've never heard of such an Order. Maybe Payton lied."

"Souls sent to the Light can't lie, even ones in limbo. You saw the chains."

"What did they mean?" I said, meaning the chains.

"They mean that Payton is on a path to atonement different from Vergo's. He can no longer revert back to demon or ghost, but he isn't wholly with the Light. Unlike demons, he's bound to tell the truth."

Ms. Weever took a step closer to my mom. "The Order of Tenebron is ancient, dating back to shortly after the Triallum, the period when Darks were hunted and killed, along with—"

"Along with those who weren't Darks, but were accused of being one. I remember that from History class," Mom said, frowning. "My family has a history of producing Darks. Jay and I see how much Mia struggles to have a normal childhood. We were worried Bela would be one, too. And now to have all these…d-demons on top of everything. Is there nowhere safe?"

"No." My former tutor shook her head once. "Which is why we need to face this problem head-on. The Order of Tenebron formed in response to the Triallum. They would love to do to the Lights what has been done to Darks. In their minds, Lights are the true enemy of society."

"Payton seemed awfully convinced of that," Mom said.

"Bad decisions create monsters. Not everyone learns how to rise above adversity. Some become consumed by it. It seems to be some people's nature to take such a path, like that Payton child. I don't see him ever rising out of limbo."

"The Light will wait for him," Bylan said, his gaze softening.

"How sentimental," Ms. Weever said.

"It may take years, centuries, or even millennia, but such emotions are exhausting to maintain. His rage will break and the opportunity for healing will set it. Shinjan will patiently wait. Every last soul is worth it."

"I hope you're right, Bylan. I don't see what the point is, but I hope you're right."

"Peace for the soul. Anyway, this could get very

deep and philosophical." He returned to his bag on the table and took out another silver necklace. Two overlapping directional arrowheads pointed north and south and had a pattern of knots woven in one continuous line over and around them. In the middle of the arrows sat three raised runes. "I had a feeling we'd learn some sensitive information." He held up the necklace. "This is a silence charm. Whoever takes on the vow of silence gains protection from accidentally speaking about such things outside of a protected conversation. It'll save us from mental slips and subtle meddling so the wrong people and…things can't learn of our conversation."

"There's only one drawback," Ms. Weever said. "Should anyone press you about a silenced conversation, you will find yourself unable to answer. Your forced silence will clue the questioner in that such things have been discussed."

"She's right," Bylan said. "The vow isn't perfect, but it's better than giving away clues without realizing it. Brecca, we need secrecy for the sake of your daughters' safety. Do you understand?"

Mom huffed a resigned sigh. "I still don't like it."

"None of us do," Ms. Weever said. "Unfortunately, we can't go to the police. There's clearly someone involved with the Order of Tenebron there, too. That's the only way I can explain Gauss's disappearance."

Mom reluctantly set Bela down and together they returned to the table.

Bylan took a head count, pointing to all six of us, including himself, and took out six silver chains from the bag. "Brecca, you understand that Bela must take the vow, too, yes? While she doesn't understand what's going on, she's the most vulnerable to giving up information."

"Whatever keeps her safe." She squeezed Bela's hand.

Bylan nodded and hooked six chains to the medallion at even intervals. He directed all of us to stand in a circle. We moved away from the table in order to stand close together. Bylan wrapped a chain around each of our wrists and had us hold it. We looked like one big, silvery spiderweb. Bylan wrapped the final chain around his wrist. "I'm going to speak an incantation. At the end, I'll ask, 'Do you accept this vow?' Each of you needs to respond with 'I do.' And then, from that moment on, today's information will be protected."

He placed a hand on the medallion and closed his eyes. He spoke the runes on the medallion. It flared to life with a blue glow. The glow flowed along the knots and outer edge of the medallion. Warmth seeped up the chain, caressing my wrist. I felt a connection to everyone present, like I held each of their hands. Bylan took a deep breath. "O Light, protect all present and empower this medallion with the vow of secrecy, for much has been spoken that needs protecting." He listed all the sensitive information, from communing with Payton, all the information he revealed, and what we needed to do next. "And these are all our secrets. We ask you, O Light, to silence our tongues, protect our secrets, and grant us grace should our secrets be probed." He turned to my former tutor, eyes closed. "Lyra Weever, do you accept this vow?"

"I do," she said with a nod.

Bylan repeated the process with each of us and we

spoke our agreement, even Bela. Mom paused before saying the two words, her tone full of resignation. The Light priest nodded. "O Light, I accept this vow. Let it be so."

The medallion jerked in his grip. Another wave of warmth seeped up the chain and the medallion snapped into six pieces with curvy edges.

Bylan hooked his free end to his medallion, forming a necklace. No wonder each chain was almost as long as my arm. "It's done. You can either wear the medallion fragment or leave it somewhere safe. The closer it is to you, the less likely anyone will try probing you for sensitive information."

"Pretty. Mommy, put it on, put it on." Bela held up her wavy triangle of silver.

Kneeling, Mom obliged and Bela hopped in place.

Ms. Weever stowed hers in a pouch. "Thank you, Bylan. I best get going. We clearly have a lot of digging to do and allies to find." Her icy gaze swept all of us. "Stay safe, everyone."

I wrapped her in a hug, which she returned.

"Stay brave if not for yourself, then for your sister."

"I will."

Mrs. Bylan held up a finger. "Give me a moment before you head out." She bagged the snack food for us to take home while the rest of us sat outside. Bela doted on Peeve with lots of pets and chin scratches. Ms. Weever scribbled away in a notebook, pausing now and then to think. Mrs. Bylan soon returned with two paper bags. She bent over to pick something up off the ground, where my mom had stood with Bela before being coaxed back over. Mrs. Bylan handed one bag to

Mom and one to my former tutor. "Stay safe, everyone." She held out her hand to her husband. "I found these over by the door. Can't say I recognize them."

She deposited two fluffy white feathers onto his outstretched hand. He passed them through his fingers and turned them over several times before glancing at Bela.

"What is it?" Ms. Weever said.

"It's nothing. Probably from one of my birds." He said the words quickly, too quickly. Ms. Weever raised a penciled eyebrow. We all had too much to think about already. Pocketing them, he escorted us out to our respective cars.

***

The rest of the day passed peacefully. Dad listened to a pro bandyll game on the living room song stone, the announcers' voices filling up the house. Mom acted like nothing had happened while Bela played with her toys, pausing now and then to cheer when Dad cheered and to yell at the song stone whenever he yelled. He accidentally swore once and was swiftly reprimanded by my sister.

I listened to some of the game. All it did was make me want to play. Something about listening to a bandyll game going on without my participation made me feel restless, so I retreated to my room to get to some homework done and practice a few power circles on my violin. With the aid of a dampening charm clamped by my tuning pegs, the instrument made sound only loud enough for me to hear. Mr. Muradon had given me a few different ones to learn, ones that didn't worry Vergo in the least. In fact, they were the same circles Ms.

Weever had suggested in her latest note secreted to me via Bela's backpack.

I let both arms drop by my sides. "By the Light, I forgot to tell Ms. Weever about Mr. Muradon."

Vergo looked up from the foot of the bed. "And tell her what, exactly? Hey, an old crush of yours is tutoring you now? He said so many nice things about you, Ms. Weever. Did you two date while at school together? Do you still like him?"

My cheeks burned. He had an annoying knack for knowing what I was thinking sometimes.

"Let it be, Little One. She's a very private person. She'd probably rather not be reminded that her own school was burned down out of hate."

"Fiiiiiine," I said and raised my violin. Adults could be so boring. With a huff, I focused on my sheet music. The notes were a tricky sequence and were taking me forever to memorize.

I did a double-take.

Did I…see a note move?

I peered closer. A note in the middle of the page twitched. Instead of flinching away, something forced my face closer, as if pulling me in. I tried to resist as cold seeped into my limbs.

No. Not again.

"Vergo." The foot of my bed lay outside my peripheral. I tried to free my head, my arms, my legs, anything, but the pull into the demon realm was too strong. The note that'd twitched engulfed the entire page, my music stand, and the whole bedroom. Darkness swept over me.

A cold, muted light shone down from above, illuminating what looked like my bedroom. My bed sat next to me, my music stand right next to it. On my other side sat my desk with all my books and my backpack on it. I had a window, a bedroom door and my closet door. Everything looked like it had been drawn with strokes of white paint and filled in with black and grays. I had no violin.

You and your allies are meddlesome creatures.

Tradereth's powerful voice sounded like it came from all around me, like I was surrounded by song stones projecting her voice. I turned in place, but saw no demon.

But I'll admit that contacting Payton was clever. He was such a good little pawn, inept as he was, but he will be missed.

I tried to concentrate on my breathing. A tightness gripped my chest, making my heart beat double time. I needed to get out of here. I had nothing to say to this demon. I closed my eyes only to have fear force a scream into my throat. I clenched my teeth, letting out only a stifled moan that left me gasping for breath. Why couldn't I focus on being calm in her presence? She was just another demon. All she wanted was to manipulate me.

And was doing a good job of it, too.

What's the matter? Afraid, dear child?

Something whipped past the window. I jumped, knocking over my music stand. I righted it and summoned my protection shield with a flick of my wrist.

Something rattled the bedroom door. The white outline of the knob turned. I threw myself at it and locked the door. Something banged on it. I backpedaled, tripped on my bed and fell. The door strained against the lock, the corners pushing past the trim. It rattled and vibrated, and then fell still. The knob jiggled, trying to turn one way and then the other, and fell still, too. I poured more energy into my shield, making it ripple with a flash of golden light, and tried to concentrate on my breathing.

What sounded like gigantic claws raked across the roof. I shrank into my bed. The roof would tear off any second. Claws would dive in and snatch me up.

The sound of heavy claws tearing into wood fell silent, making the thumping of my heart and heavy breathing seem unnaturally loud. I forced myself to take deeper, slower breaths.

I stopped breathing altogether as my closet door swung open. A shadowy figure stepped out, solidifying into an older woman with draconic horns. Sharp ridges followed her brow ridge, curled over human ears and curved up and beyond her head. Short bangs covered her forehead, and more hair fell to her shoulders behind the horns. She had round eyes similar to the demon's and matching red irises. The shadow of her form solidified into a black skirt, matching black blouse, and heeled dress shoes. Her heels clacked along the floor as she marched over to my desk. She moved gracefully, like a dancer, taking a seat in my chair with a flourish.

I slowly sat up.

"Let's have a chat, you and I." She fixed me with her red-eyed gaze, compelling me to look at her.

I couldn't stop studying the varying shades of red and flecks of black in her eyes. Her pupils were slitted like a cat's. While she'd taken on a more human form, she clearly didn't want me to forget she was a demon. "We have nothing to talk about."

"On the contrary." She pivoted sideways and draped an arm over the chair back. She examined long human nails. "I must admit I didn't give you much to go on last time we spoke. I shouldn't have been so surprised you turned down my offer."

"How many times do I have to tell you that I'll never bargain with you?"

She held up a finger. "You don't know that."

"Yes, I do."

A bright red sheen flashed in her irises. "No, you don't. Now, do be a good girl and show your elder some respect."

I thought about telling her I had no respect for demons, but what was the point? I sat up straight and my legs trembled, stopping me from standing. I wanted to meditate my way out of the demon realm. I seemed unable to concentrate on anything but her face and horns. I stayed quiet, earning myself a smile that surprisingly lacked fangs.

"As I was saying, I'm convinced that, with a bit of useful information, you'll see the advantage of striking a bargain with me."

I clenched my teeth, biting back a retort.

She paused to savor my anger spike, going so far as to lick her lips. "You see, I know all your despicable principal's deepest, darkest secrets, and I can show you how to use them to remove him from the picture and make all your lives safer."

"And how do you know these things?"

"I have my ways," she said.

"How do I know you're not lying?"

"A fair question. How about I show you a vision of what once was?"

I folded my arms. "And how do I know that won't be a lie, too?"

Tradereth tilted her head. "Simple. I have nothing to gain from lying about this. Even better, you can cross-reference the vision with physical records in the living world. It's far easier for demons to fabricate what can be than what was. Any idiot with a lick of sense can figure out when we try to lie about the past." She leaned forward. "So… Care to see one of his deep, dark secrets?"

She hadn't used any phrasing that could've been interpreted as a bargain. It was a pure, one-way offer. "Fine. Show me the vision."

"Deal." When she saw the look on my face, she smirked. "No, that wasn't a bargain, little girl. Relax." Standing, she interlaced her fingers and stretched her arms, cracking her knuckles. "Your despicable principal is responsible for fostering and feeding Payton's hate of the world. He shaped the boy into a monster." She scanned my room, settling on the music stand. She turned the head ninety degrees and pressed it down to waist height. "Since they were and are Darks, I was drawn to both of them. I watched the whole thing from the shadows. These are my memories." She touched a long nail to her forehead and it sank in, creating ripples in her pale skin and sinking up to her knuckle before pulling it back out. A green undulating cloud sat pinched between her fingers, silver swirling in its heart. She cupped it in both hands, concentrating, and deposited it on the music stand.

She said something in a harsh, guttural language that made a chill crawl up my spine. Demonic? Something about it made the inside of my ears burn.

"Come closer, child."

Eyeing the cloud, I slowly stood.

"They're just memories. They can't hurt you physically. As far as emotionally, that depends on your constitution. Anyway, do brace yourself. Your principal…well, you'll see." She spoke a few more demonic words. The green cloud shot out in all directions, engulfing my entire room and blinding me.

A woman's echoing voice filled the darkness. "You're a Dark, Damien. What do we do?"

"Why are you asking me?" Mr. Redd's voice echoed as well. "It's not like my life has been easy." The memory was shadowy, the lady and Mr. Redd mere fragments of their complete bodies. Their faces and torsos were clear, the rest of their bodies lost in shadow, as if that's all Tradereth remembered. Fragments of a kitchen surrounded them.

"But you've survived and overcome."

"Because I chose to become strong, instead of a victim."

"Please teach my son to be the same." She looked off into the shadows and Mr. Redd's gaze followed.

"I'll do my best."

A green cloud engulfed the scene like a tornado blowing in. The shadowy scene shifted to a school hallway, Mr. Redd standing before a boy of six or seven, his fists on his hips. The boy was crying.

"Stop crying, Payton. It won't make people any nicer."

"Why do they hate me so much?"

"Because you're a Dark."

"So?"

"It means you're different from them. You're the

only Dark in this school."

"I don't want to be different." He sniffed and wiped his face. His eyes were hard and full of hurt.

"You can't change being different, but you can change how you react to them."

"How?"

"Stop crying, for one. Don't let them see that they can make you cry. You're stronger than them. Be meaner too, if you have to."

"Meaner?"

"If they hurt you, you hurt them back."

"But my mom said—"

"Your mom told me to make you strong. Right now, you're a victim. This stops now."

Payton's shoulders shuddered and he sniffed again. "Yes, sir."

The green cloud swept through again. The scene shifted to a school playground. An older Payton squared off with a boy inside a ring of middle school students. The onlookers chanted "Fight, fight, fight!" and pumped fists in time with their echoing words. Teachers ran towards the circle. Payton and the other boy took swings at each other and collided. Payton shoved the other boy off, who then sucker-punched him. Payton folded. The other boy kicked him in the face before two teachers yanked him away, clamping onto his arms. The boy smiled with the same smugness I was used to seeing on Gwen's face.

I felt sorry for Payton, feeling even worse as the circle of students laughed. A third teacher stood over him. Hands reached, but stopped when Payton looked up. The teacher recoiled. "Payton Sorenson." He took a step back. "Go get yourself cleaned up."

Footsteps echoed closer. Mr. Redd shoved his way through what remained of the circle. He roughly yanked Payton to his feet and carried him off. Laughter and taunts followed them both.

Payton yanked his arm free and he wavered on his feet. His uncle grabbed his arm again and roughly guided him into the nurse's office. A lady looked up in surprise. It was Nurse Kor.

"Leave," Mr. Redd said.

Nurse Kor closed her textbook and scurried out.

Mr. Redd slammed the door, pushed Payton onto a chair, and grabbed a few items from a medicine cabinet. Payton slumped in the chair, jaw clenched, and eyes hard. There was no hurt left. It was all rage and hate.

"Stop sulking." Mr. Redd soaked some gauze with peroxide.

"I lost."

"Because you're weak."

"I'm sick of being weak. I want to make him pay for this." He gestured to his bloody face. "I want to make them all pay."

A wicked smile touched Mr. Redd's face. "Alright." He dabbed at his nephew's face. "What do you have in mind?"

"I want to make them too scared to pick on me anymore. I want them to be afraid of me. I want them to be afraid of Darks."

"Now you're talking."

Payton sat up straighter. "All my tutor teaches me is protection circles and stupid, useless songs. Tell him to teach me something more useful."

Mr. Redd turned Payton's head, examining his nose. A fresh trickle of blood dribbled out. He shoved some rolled gauze up the boy's nostril. Payton winced. "I doubt Mr. Syllis will risk his job for that."

"You know such things, don't you?"

"I do."

"Then you teach me. I want to learn. I want to be stronger than everyone."

Mr. Redd's grin broadened.

The green cloud swept through a third time, revealing the Toolena Mesa's high school football field. More of the scene was filled out with fewer shadows filling in the gaps. A fresher memory. Dozens of boys in pads and practice jerseys were lined up in the middle of the field. A handful more jogged laps around the track.

Among the joggers was Payton wearing a tank top, jogger shorts, and sunglasses. His crest of hair curved around one side of his face. He ignored the football team, while some of the female runners flirted with them.

The football coach blew a whistle. Most of the team jogged over to the water jugs by the bleachers. Three players jogged over to Payton, two of them blocking his path. They were big, broad linesmen. His face remained neutral behind his sunglasses as he tried to sidestep them. The two players moved back into his path.

"Get out of my way," Payton said.

"Get off our field," said a boy whose voice I recognized.

I squinted. He was half a head shorter than the other two boys, but was built like a sprinter. I'd seen that same build in a picture in Mr. Redd's office. I inhaled sharply. "Orton Totes." Unlike the memories, my voice didn't echo.

The memory froze as Orton took a step closer. We stood a few feet away on the track, a front-row seat to the scene.

"How are you surprised? You already know he's the boy Payton killed."

"I—" There'd been no word that Orton had been anything but a model student and star athlete. People loved him.

"Didn't know he wasn't the only victim in all this?" Tradereth said. "Yes, poor corrupted Payton was painted as the sole villain, which couldn't be any further from the truth."

Gwen had acted the same way when I gave her Allosyr's sickness. At least at the bandyll party I'd done nothing worse than make her cry. I didn't feel good about it. Honestly, I felt relieved over not having to hold all that in anymore.

Tradereth rolled her wrist and Payton squared up with Orton, who removed his helmet.

Orton said, "You don't belong here, freak."

"Go tell that to my coach. I'm running warmup laps, like the rest of my team."

One of the other two boys pushed him, making him stumble. Payton caught his balance and adjusted his sunglasses. "Do that again and I'll make you pay for it."

"We'll get you expelled," said the boy who'd pushed him.

"Don't care. I already know everything I need to know. Clearly, you three need to learn to be afraid of me."

"We're not afraid of freaks," Orton said.

Payton held a fist near his chin. His fist glowed purple and crackled with tiny sparks of lightning. The glow reflected in his sunglasses. "I'd be glad to test that."

All three football players lost their grins. The one that had pushed him said, "Orton, what's that?"

I had no idea either. Ms. Weever had never given me such a demonstration.

Orton flourished his hands, forming a triangle with his thumbs and index fingers. The motions were similar to Bylan's. A white rune appeared inside the triangle. "Hurt my friends and I hurt you."

"Then stay away from me and no one gets hurt."

"Do you know what Orton's alignment was?" Tradereth said as the two boys stared each other down.

"No. He never—" Based on the glow's color and the familiar movements. "He was a Light, wasn't he?"

"Correct. And as a Light, he thought it was his moral duty to seek out Payton and make his life miserable."

Sounded a bit like Gwen.

Payton glamced between the three boys, his gaze settling back on Orton. He grinned like he had a nasty idea. He straightened up and lowered his hand, the glow and sparks vanishing. "You really would love a fight, wouldn't you?"

"Can't wait for the day you finally grow a pair."

Payton's grin broadened. The only thing he was missing were fangs. "Oh, you'll have your fight, alright, one you can't win. If you think I'm going to fight fair, you're dead wrong. I've learned a few new tricks. You'll find out what they are soon enough."

"That sounds like a threat."

"It is."

"I should report you to the principal."

"But you won't because you know that'll make you look like a coward."

Orton crinkled his nose and said nothing, the gears turning behind his eyes.

"Orton, don't listen to him," the pushy linesman said. "He's trying to bait you."

"More coward talk. Do what you want. It doesn't matter to me." Payton walked around the two linesmen and resumed jogging.

The one that'd pushed him moved to grab him.

Orton said, "Let him go. This is a waste of time."

"What about what he said?"

"He was lying, just talking big to avoid a fight. He's the real coward."

The green cloud swept the scene away, replacing it with a darker one of Payton standing inside a glowing power circle. The runes were the same as the binding circle Mr. Muradon had shown me. Giant paws with claws half as long as my body thudded on the shadowy ground, one at a time. Payton fearlessly looked up at the triangular head looming over him. It had way too many eyes.

"The one named Orton Totes… Kill him. Kill him slowly."

The countless eyes squinted with glee. *Gladly*, it said in a deep, rumbly voice with an echo.

Darkness swept over the memory, which flaked apart, one piece at a time, and drifted away, revealing the demon realm version of my bedroom.

"You know the rest," Tradereth said, taking a seat. She crossed one slender ankle over the other.

I remained standing. "Why exactly did you show me all this?" None of it helped me expose the truth about Mr. Redd. It further confirmed what I already knew.

Her expression remained aloof. "First, to show you that I can show you anything from the past you need to know. With such information, you can set up your despicable principal to catch him in a lie. Wouldn't you consider that an advantage?"

I wished Vergo was here with me. I really could've used his guidance at the moment. He'd know what to say. All I could think of how sensible the demon sounded. "I guess."

"See? You've made the first step towards coming around to my way of looking at things." She flicked her hair with a hand. "Second, these memories serve as evidence that support a truth you can only take as an accusation. Redd was quite eager to see Orton dead because the boy was a Light, but he wouldn't dare risk his position to remove the boy himself. That's one reason why he cultivated Payton into the monster he became."

"I heard he was moved to the middle school principal position after Payton's death." Crap. I probably shouldn't have said that. It was a piece of information the demon didn't need to know I knew.

"You are correct. While the school board doesn't know about his alignment, they were concerned about the familial connection. Instead of removing him from a post that's hard to fill so far outside the city, they shuffled staff around and stuck him in his current position, somewhere he most certainly doesn't belong."

Yeah, he didn't belong. Ugh, this was so creepy agreeing with a demon. "What did Mr. Redd do to you to make you hate him so much?"

Tradereth gave me a measuring gaze.

My words must've caught her off guard. No one hated someone for the sake of it. There was always a reason. Gwen had made up a reason to hate Deren and eventually found a reason to hate me. This demon had to have a reason to hate my principal.

The demon broke into a sly grin. "Strike a bargain with me and I'd happily tell you, as part of the bargain."

"I don't want to know that badly." Part of me did, though. I had a feeling that was a very important piece of information, but it wasn't worth a demon's bargain to learn it.

She pouted. "Pity. Anyway, despite you sending his nephew to the Light, he hasn't lost sight of this goal. He's quietly scheming at the moment. He knows it's dangerous to make another attempt on your sister's life anytime soon, but he won't stop trying. Still, she's a painful reminder of the pawn he lost not once but twice. There's no telling for how long he'll remain patient."

I shook my head. I didn't know what to say. I needed to get back and tell Vergo this. I needed to tell everyone. Maybe it'd be worth the risk going straight to the school board with this information. Maybe even Mrs. Volaire would listen. Maybe Gwen could get her mom to listen. She loved Bela for some strange reason. I'd do anything, include swallow my pride and suck up to Gwen, if it meant keeping my sister safe.

"This is why I'd like to offer protection for your sister in exchange for one little thing: you become my new anchor."

Okay, not anything. Besides, could she even protect Bela? What was the catch? Allosyr giving me the power to cure the sickness had had a terrible catch.

"Ooh, hesitation. How delightful. You're finally starting to come around." She cradled her chin in one hand.

"No. You'd twist it. Demons always twist bargains to get the better end of the deal."

"Of course we always get the better end of the deal. That's why we call it a bargain and not a fair trade. So, are you willing to risk your sister's safety and turn me down again, or will you consider my offer?"

"The answer's still no." It was tempting, I gave her that. Maybe this was how Ms. Weever felt before striking a bargain with Allosyr after losing her son. I didn't know how we were all going to keep Bela safe. We'd already had two close calls. But to become a demon's anchor? Definitely a no.

"Are you sure? He became my anchor after you all uprooted me out of your beloved nurse."

By the Light, he was her anchor. I understood this was bad. How bad I wasn't sure. I hadn't had a lesson on demonic anchors yet.

"Think about it." Resting her elbows on her knees, she leaned forward. "So long as he's my anchor, I'm bound to carry out his will. Who do you think attracted Payton to take care of your sister?" She paused. "All me. If you become my new anchor, he can no longer give me commands. I can't harm your sister, unless you tell me to. Everyone you care about becomes safe from me."

I shook my head. "There has to be another way. A bargain can't be the only way."

She tilted her head. "Oh, you can turn me down and see what you can do on your own. However, if you refuse me, there'll be consequences."

I shook my head again. Every instinct said a bargain was a bad idea. There had to be another way to keep Bela safe and take Mr. Redd down. Tradereth was trying to get what she wanted, nothing more. My sister's safety meant nothing to her. "Why do you want me to be your anchor so badly?"

"Like I said, strike a bargain with me and I will tell you everything."

"I'm sorry. No. I can't do it." Why did I apologize to a demon? Ugh. Habit, maybe.

Her body swelled as she stood. Her horns scratched the dark ceiling as she towered over me. She had to be ten feet tall. "Are you sure that's the answer you wish to give me?"

"It is," I said with a nod while a tiny part of me screamed at me to strike the bargain. My heart raced anew. I needed to get out of here.

Her eyes glowed red. "Then, Mia Evers, prepare to suffer. Considerably."

Chapter 8

Under the protection of some white sage burning in one corner of my room, I told Vergo everything, including my first exchange with Tradereth that had left me hysterical. The spirit cat listened intently to it all from the foot of my bed, letting me speak without interrupting. He hissed when I described the bargain the demon offered and then apologized for the sudden outburst. The hiss had come before he realized what he'd done.

Repeating the events filled me with dread. Part of me wondered if I'd made the right choice. Of course, it felt like having to choose between asking Gwen to be my friend or asking Mr. Redd to babysit Bela.

"Please tell me I did the right thing."

Vergo nodded. "Oh, most certainly. No advantage a demon can give you is worth the sacrifice."

"But what about the suffering she promised?"

"We'll handle it as it comes."

I grimaced at my desk chair. Something told me that wasn't going to be good enough.

"At the very least, you're not alone in this, Little One. Until we discover how she plans to make you suffer, there's little we can do to prepare other than be ready to react."

I hugged one of my stuffed animals, a large lizard with multicolored eyes I'd named Giggo while learning to speak. I'd had it for as long as I could remember. It was permanently stained with dirt along the stitching lines, despite how many times Mom washed it. At least it always smelled clean, like a flower garden in full bloom. "Do you remember Tradereth from when you were a demon?"

"I'm afraid not. Demons don't exactly socialize with each other. They're far more interested in the mortal realm and what chaos they can cause. She and I could've crossed paths multiple times without so much as glancing at each other. Demons consider each other about as much as humans consider ants. There's only interaction when one becomes a nuisance to the other, like that time I pulled you into the demon realm and unwanted visitors manifested in the distance."

I shivered at the memory. "We need to send her to the Light."

"You need to detach her from her anchor first. A Crossing Ritual will fail if an anchor is in place."

"I don't think Mr. Redd'll let us exorcise him."

"We don't need his cooperation, but that's not the real problem. Judging by how her presence affects you, which tier of demon do you think she is?"

I'd been trying to avoid this, to not think about it

this whole time. I clenched Giggo's tail. It'd been painfully obvious what she was since my flight to the bathroom. Ms. Weever had forced me to face such energies enough times to be unable to deny the truth. "Arch," I whispered.

"And she's already demonstrated her ability to escape, even if we exorcise her."

"We can prepare for it this time. We can place wards around that cavern so she can't escape."

"That'll result in a fight. You'll need far more than you, Bylan and Weever, if any of you want to walk out of there alive."

"Bylan and Ms. Weever have to know people who'd help."

"Possibly, but you're presuming they'd willingly put their lives on the line for one demon that will eventually be replaced. No, we have to approach this another way."

"No. We have to get rid of her. We have to send her to the Light. Like Payton, she'll no longer be a threat."

Vergo slowly inhaled and exhaled, thinking. "I understand where you're coming from. While no longer having to deal with this particular demon would be nice, the Demon King has too many minions at his disposal for that to make a difference. We have to find a way to expose and destroy the Order of Tenebron. Attack the root, not the stem."

"What does that mean?"

"It's a figure of speech. To kill a weed, you need to remove it from the root. If you tear it at the stem, it'll grow back. Tradereth is the stem and the Order of Tenebron is the root. If it turns out that we need to cut a few stems before we can remove the root, then we'll do that, but only if we have to."

I wanted this demon out of my life. How could he not see that? She needed to go, needed to be uprooted. Wrapping my arms around my shins, I clamped my stuffed lizard between my chest and legs.

Sheets shifted under my feet as little paws walked closer. Vergo rubbed up against my shins and hands. "Stay strong, Little One. She hasn't lifted a claw yet and you're already suffering. Don't let her mere threat cause you suffering." He purred, but it failed to pierce my anxiety.

"I can't stop this feeling of dread that it'll be worse to not give her what she wants than to accept the bargain and all the consequences that come with it."

"That's what she wants you to think."

Then she's very persuasive, I thought. Regardless, I believed Vergo. My battle with Tradereth hadn't begun and I was already losing. "She's so subtle. How do I protect myself from this?"

He flopped onto my feet. I rubbed his chin, making him purr louder. "There's no fast, easy fix. The best thing you can do is learn to catch yourself when you have these thoughts and redirect them to somewhere else, to something that leaves you feeling empowered."

"Stop thinking about her and her bargain every time I catch myself doing that?"

"Yes. Specifically, think of something you know beyond a doubt you have control over. Like you know you can hug your lizard, you can slow down your breathing, or you can play your violin, even if it's a simple scale. If you can do that one little thing, you empower yourself to push her out of her thoughts because you have better things to do than sit there and feel afraid. The goal is to regain your sense of control. Does that make sense, Little One?"

"Focus on what I can control, instead of on what I can't?"

"Precisely." He affectionately licked my hand.

***

Dread returned on Monday morning, when Deren wasn't present to give me my morning hug. I stayed in the hallway until the first of five tolls sounded and slipped into Mrs. Livy's class before I could be marked late. The last time he'd been absent, it was from the sickness Allosyr had given him. I couldn't help but think it was happening all over again. It took all my willpower to resist dashing to Nurse Kor's office and calling him.

I was certain I'd failed my history quiz, even though I read each question multiple times. My mind wouldn't stop circling back to Deren and the reason for his absence. I ended up circling random answers and submitting it at the end of class. Vergo tried to tell me that focusing on my quiz was something I could control. His sage advice was so much easier said than done. The day passed in a haze of anxiety, colors, and sounds. I pretended to take notes and follow directions until lunch. I followed the crowd from the 6-8 building to the cafeteria, automatically stood in line and collected a colorful meal from the cheerful lunch ladies, and sat across from Sussi at our usual spot among the rows of long, noisy tables. Deren's seat was conspicuously empty.

Sussi fluffed her mashed potatoes with a spork. "What's wrong? It's not Gwen, is it?"

"No. I'm worried about Deren."

"Why? He's probably out sick. Everyone gets a cold this time of year."

"Trust me, it's not that."

Vergo hopped onto Deren's chair. "Want me to explain it to her?"

I looked away and nodded. "Please."

The spirit cat hopped onto the table and placed a paw on Sussi's shoulder. Since he touched her, she could see him. She flinched, flicking a spoonful of potato onto the table. She scooped it back up and ate it. Vergo touched her shoulder and brought his mouth close to her ear. He told her about Tradereth, the bargain she offered and the suffering she promised.

Sussi's eyes widened. "You think she made him sick, like he did?" She nodded in Vergo's direction.

"That's what I'm afraid of."

"That's messed up. Still, you need to call him first to make sure you're right. He could totally just be sick."

And she totally didn't understand what it was like dealing with demons. I shoved some mashed potato in my mouth before I could snap at her.

A tray plunked down where Deren normally sat. Garrett plopped onto the seat and shrugged off his backpack, pausing when he noticed the two of us. Avoiding eye contact, he said, "You two don't mind, do you?"

We shook our heads. I didn't mind. He wasn't the bad kid I thought he was. He was strange alright, but he certainly wasn't mean.

Sussi said, "Not at all. You came in clutch for us during that incident with the—" She glanced at the table adjacent to ours. She had maybe three feet between her and the next four-person section of table.

She leaned closer. "You know…that thing."

"Anytime," Garrett said and helped himself to some mashed potatoes and breaded chicken.

At least we could count on him as an ally. He honestly had turned the battle with the demonic version of Payton. I'd been on the verge of failing before he and his coyotes came in and added their power to ours. "Why did you help us that day?"

"Because the three of you don't treat me like I'm some freak," he said and ate another bite. "Where's Deren?"

Guilt roiled in my gut as a tray of food squeezed past Sussi's head. Chibya sat next to Sussi, settling down with a rosy-cheeked smile.

"Hey, Chibya," Sussi said. "I feel popular today. What brings you here?"

"I finally reached my limit with Gwen this morning. She made another mean comment about my weight before homeroom. I told her to stop. She got mad and called me a few names. I called her a few names back and we took off in opposite directions."

"Nice. Welcome to the group."

"Thanks. So what were you all talking about before I butted in?" She pushed her tray in and propped an elbow on the table.

Sussi glanced at me. "Can I tell her? We need all the help we can get."

"Tell me what?"

"Not here," I said. "It's too dangerous." To drive my point home, Mr. Redd drifted by our table, hands clasped behind his back. He nodded to the four of us. "Good afternoon, kids," he said politely—too politely —and moved on.

I shuddered. As much as I wanted to warn them about Mr. Redd, it was probably a good thing that I couldn't. They were safer not knowing how dangerous he was. They could act normal around him.

"My house?" Sussi said.

"Oh, I'd love to," Chibya said. "We haven't hung out in so long."

"And whose fault was that?"

"Sussi, you know I didn't avoid you by choice."

"I'm not blaming you, dummy."

Chibya blinked. "Oh. That's good to hear. I was so afraid you were mad at me for it."

"Real friends don't tell friends who they can and can't hang out with. I mean, I hope you never hang out with Gwen again, but…"

"I get it. Thanks."

Garrett and I ate in silence while Sussi and Chibya caught up a bit. They chatted about their families, and Chibya shared some gossip about Gwen. She'd sulked all weekend and hadn't stopped calling me nasty names, until she and Chibya clashed. She beamed at me. "I so wish I'd been there to hear everything you said. You're the reason I finally built the courage to stand up to her, too."

I stopped with my spork halfway to my mouth.

"Honest. Thank you."

I fumbled for words before a coherent thought surfaced. "I'm not proud of what I said."

"Don't say that. You said nothing but the truth. If she doesn't like the truth, then she should do something about it. She's so stuck on being a bully. She likes it when people are afraid of her."

Wow. Just wow. Maybe she had deserved it after

all. Still… "I made her cry. How does that make me a better person than her?"

Chibya's eyes widened. "You made her cry?" She said it loud enough for the students next to us to turn their heads. "She so left that part out."

"You should've seen the look on her face as she ran into our coach's house." Sussi regaled Chibya with all the details and paraphrased my tirade as best as she could remember. Nearby students listened, mouths agape. Towards the end of the story, Sussi pointed to Chibya's untouched food. "You should hurry up and eat, by the way. The bell's about to ring."

A pained expression crossed her face, and she blushed. "I don't know why I grabbed food. I'm not feeling hungry."

"I'll take it, if you want," Garrett said.

Chibya slid her tray over.

***

I called Deren's ley line coordinates as soon as I got home. While lunch had helped me regain my focus, it hadn't stopped me from thinking about him and what might've happened. The sound of crystals clinking against each other played in my ear, until Mrs. Sevine said, "Hello?" She sounded exhausted.

"Hi, Mrs. Sevine. It's Mia. Is Deren around?"

"Certainly. Let me go get him."

Leaves rustled as their end of the vine changed ears. Deren said, "Hi, Mia. What's up?"

He sounded healthy and his usual upbeat self. "Hey, Deren. Are you okay? I noticed you were out today."

"Er, yeah."

That was an unusual response. "Are you sick?"

"No. I'm fine."

I inwardly sighed with relief. "Where were you then?"

"Home. We…we needed a family day."

Worry crept over relief. "Oh." He wasn't sick, but he wasn't happy either. "Did something happen? Is everyone okay?" My heart pounded so loud I wouldn't have been surprised if Deren heard it over the vine.

Deren fumbled for words. "Mia, if I tell you something, promise not to tell anyone else?"

Oh, no. I turned my back to the rest of the house. Our vine was on the far side of the kitchen, opposite the dining space and living room, where the rest of my family hung out. Since I called Deren now and then, they paid me no mind. I lowered my voice. "Of course."

He was silent a moment. "My dad was fired from his job at the mine."

Deren was one of four boys. That was a big, expensive family to feed and take care of. "Oh, no. I'm so sorry."

"Thanks. We spent all day selling our livestock."

"May I ask why they fired him?"

"That's the thing. We don't understand. They fired him for stealing. They didn't even say what he stole. He's been there for twenty years. He hasn't so much as been written up for anything. We all know Dad's not a thief. It doesn't make any sense."

"No. You're all good people."

"Thanks.

"What happened?" Vergo said.

I covered the vine leaves over my ear and told him. His eyes widened. "Oh, no. You don't think…

117

Tradereth?"

It took a moment for my brain to put two and two together. My hand fell away from my ear, dread and guilt filling me. "Oh, no."

"What?" Deren said.

"I—" What was I supposed to say? *Hey, Deren, a demon tried to force me to strike a bargain with it. I told it no, so it's on a mission to make me suffer and decided to start with you and your family. What do you think of that? You still wanna be my friend?*

Something sank in a zigzagging path past my face and landed on the ground. A burnt piece of parchment lay by my toes. It had a tiny script on it. I crouched, the vine stretching to stay with me.

It was a tight, spidery script that read, "The suffering has begun. Enjoy."

I recoiled, stretching the vine to its limit. It tugged on my ear.

The note turned to dust and dissolved.

No, I couldn't risk losing him as a friend. "Deren, remember that demon that appeared after we placed a protection circle around the main office?"

"Barely. I only got a quick look before hitting the ground." He let out a nervous laugh.

Deren had curled up on the ground, hiding his head in his arms. I'd tried to rally him with a few nudges and words, but he'd been paralyzed with terror in Tradereth's presence. He didn't need to feel embarrassed, though. Handling a demon's presence was tough, even with practice. "She's still around."

"Wait, really?"

"Yeah. We're going to all hang out at Sussi's in a few days. Can you make it? I'm going to explain to everyone what's going on." I'd explain everything that wasn't connected to the vow of silence, of course. I fidgeted with my silence charm hanging around my neck. Fearing Mr. Redd might probe me, I'd chosen to wear it at all times.

"I think so. Dad spent part of the day job hunting. He warned us we might have to move when he finds something, like as far as into the city."

"No." My throat tightened. Please no.

"I don't wanna move. None of us do. We like it here, and the rest of our family is out here, too. This is our home."

"I don't want you to move either. You're my friend." Unfortunately, moving might make him and his family safer, at least from the demon. As far as from the Order of Tenebron? Who knew?

Vergo bared his fangs. "Divide and conquer."

"Yeah, and you're mine," Deren said. "Dad doesn't want to move, so he's going to try his best to find something close, but he warned us about the possibility of moving. Here's to hoping everything will turn out okay."

"Yeah." I wanted to warn him that it wasn't, but a part of me wanted to cling onto hope. There had to be a way to stop Tradereth without accepting her bargain.

***

Deren showed up at school the next day. He smiled when he saw me heading for history class and gave me his daily hug. I gratefully returned it, inhaling the scent of cotton and dirt. It was a calm, earthy aroma I'd come to appreciate.

"Hey, not boyfriend-girlfriend." Sussi gently nudged us and wore a smirk, which vanished as she gazed past me. She frowned and folded her arms. "What do you want?" she said to the person behind me.

I spun around. Gwen and Nonaya both looked down their noses at us and wore smiles that made me ball a fist. I had no intention of swinging at either of them, but I would've welcomed the fight.

Gwen said, "So Deren, how's your family doing now that your dad's out of a job?"

He furrowed his brows. "How'd you know?"

She twirled her tawny hair around a finger. "Oh, you know, my father and I talk business now and then. I *am* expected to take over the mines after he retires."

Rage flared inside me. I took an aggressive step closer. "You didn't."

"I did," she said mildly and turned to Deren. "Your dad is welcome to beg for his job back. My dad might change his mind and take pity on you and your family."

Deren furrowed his brows. "What are you talking about?"

Gwen's wicked grin broadened and she gestured to me. "Ask her." She leaned closer. "Talk to me like that again and Sussi's dad is next."

I gaped. Sussi, however, swore at Gwen and punched her square in the nose, knocking her to the ground. Nonaya yelled at Sussi and charged. Sussi swung again. They pounded on each other with their fists. Blood appeared on their faces and knuckles.

A teacher yelled. Sussi and Nonaya kept swinging until Mr. Enti, our science teacher, yanked the girls apart. He was a retired military man with a muscular build and intimidating scarred face. He was a good head and a half taller than most students. Mrs. Livy hurried over and restrained Nonaya's arms while Mr. Enti struggled to restrain Sussi.

"Knock it off," he snarled in her ear. She flinched and then did a double-take. She looked at her fists and paled when she met Mr. Enti's glare. "What's gotten into you two?"

"She's lost her mind," Nonaya said.

"Gwen threatened to get my dad fired," Sussi said.

"I did not," Gwen said from the floor. She had both hands over her nose and tears streaming down her face. Her voice sounded stuffy. Blood dripped from her chin.

Mrs. Cerda, our language arts teacher, helped Gwen to her feet.

"That's enough," Mr. Enti said. "The three of you, come with me. And if anyone starts fighting again, I'll finish it. Now start walking." He let Sussi go.

The hallway was packed with students, a gap ringing us. Everyone stared.

Sussi massaged an arm as she led the way, snatching up her backpack mid-stride. Students parted for her. Gwen and Nonaya followed, with Mr. Enti bringing up the rear. Whispers filled the hallway. Students talked behind hands as they watched the small procession. I wished I could make out what they were saying.

"All of you get to class," Mr. Enti said, the veins in his neck popping out like tree roots sticking out of the ground. Students scrambled into motion, as did I.

I kept my gaze on the floor as hurried footsteps surrounded me. I slid into my seat, took out my notebook, and kept my head down as the bell tolled. On the fifth and final toll, an icy coldness gathered by a shoulder. My spine tingled. I stiffened as Tradereth's voice whispered in my ear.

Would you like to see Gwen Volaire suffer?

"Of course I would," I said under my breath.

Strike a bargain with me and I will make it so.

I didn't bother answering. My answer was no, a very reluctant no.

Chapter 9

The whole school knew about the fight before lunchtime. Garrett and Chibya joined Deren and me at lunch, Garrett taking Sussi's spot. He told us that Sussi had been suspended for a week, and Gwen and Nonaya had been given a week's worth of detention.

"How'd you find out?" Chibya said. A full lunch tray of rice and beans with sautéed veggies and a fruit bowl sat in front of her. She pecked at the grapes and cantaloup, chewing slowly and thoroughly.

"I have counseling every day in the main office. We couldn't do anything for fifteen minutes because Mr. Redd was that loud. He was so mad at both of them. Gwen tried to pin it all on Sussi, but that made him yell louder. And then he said something about telling Gwen's father about her threat." Garrett shoveled some rice and beans in his mouth.

"What did she say to that?" Chibya said.

Garett shrugged. "All I heard was Mr. Redd after that. I couldn't make anything out. By then, my counselor made us both focus on our session."

Mr. Redd hadn't yelled at Sussi and me much after we'd fought. Still, we hadn't drawn blood and Coach had been present to put a swift stop to it. And when I'd gotten in trouble last year, my earful hadn't been that loud. And that was Gwen Volaire he was yelling at, too. I dared not chalk it up to a bad day he was taking out on three students. I couldn't help but worry he knew more about what was going on than any of us realized.

No one saw Gwen, Nonaya or Sussi for the rest of the day or the rest of the week. I only heard from Sussi once when she called my house to unhappily inform me that she wasn't allowed to have anyone over anymore until she learned to stop picking fights. I tried to apologize, but she spoke over me, asking me to tell everyone else that the hangout was off. She hung up.

I wrote to Ms. Weever about Tradereth, her bargain attempt, and her promise to make us all suffer until she got her way. The letter grew in length as I told her about Gwen, the fight, and what had happened to Deren's family. I knew he didn't want me to tell anyone, but she and Bylan deserved a heads up. Anyone could be next, all of them a potential guilt trip to pressure me into giving Tradereth what she wanted. My wrist hurt towards the end. I rolled it a few times before stuffing the letter in a plain envelope.

More Seven's Seed decorations clogged up the main office the next day, including what looked like a swarm of multicolored fireflies dancing around the ceiling. Only six colors. No seventh for Darks. The aroma of ginger and mint filled the air, holiday scents, the smell of some semblance of winter. Nights were cold, while the days warmed to the point of not needing a jacket by lunchtime.

It being first thing in the morning, I wore my jacket over a winter dress. I also wore matching boots and black leggings. I unbuttoned my jacket and knocked on Bylan's office door. A few snowflakes and a couple of drawings decorated his door. Judging by the sloppy quality, Bela might've done them. A muffled voice invited me inside. A strong wave of mint greeted me as I opened the door.

"Why good morning, Mia." Bylan smiled, something about his aged face making it contagious and extra warm. He closed a notebook and set a fountain pen beside it. "To what do I owe the pleasure of your visit?"

Stepping inside, I held the door open. "I'm stopping by real quick. There's a letter in Bela's backpack for Ms. Weever. You should read it, too. A lot has happened this week."

All the warmth left his face. He nodded. "Thank you."

I waved and stepped back out into the hallway, closing the door behind me. I turned around and almost bumped into Mr. Redd as he whisked by.

He raised an eyebrow. "Good morning, Miss Evers." While his tone was cordial, he might as well have asked me why I was leaving Bylan's office.

"Good morning, Mr. Redd," I said, and hurried over to Mr. Muradon's office, my heart pounding faster than my footsteps. I'd come to terms with the fact that it was his office now. I didn't like it, but he had yet to give me a reason to hate him. I slipped inside and pressed my back against the door while I caught my breath.

Mr. Muradon's brows furrowed. An open book rested in his hands, and he gently set it on his desk. "Something wrong?"

Vergo passed through the door as if it weren't there. "You forgot me, Little One. I know that was close, but Redd wasn't close enough to overhear that exchange." He curled up under one of the two wood chairs.

Mr. Muradon studied me. I relaxed my shoulders and let out a slow breath. "Too many decorations," I said. I set my violin case on one side of the chair and my super heavy backpack on the other side. His studious gaze followed me. "I'm feeling stressed out." At least that much was true.

He nodded knowingly. "I get that. Seven's Seed isn't exactly an enjoyable holiday for Darks. Everywhere we look, we're reminded that we've been left out. Can't say I like this holiday much better than All Souls Day."

Ms. Weever had taught me the truth about All Souls Day. It used to be about bringing all the elements together, not glorifying Lights and drilling into everyone's head what made them superior to every other alignment, especially Dark. Seven's Seed celebrated six out of the seven alignments. All the decorations made it hard to ignore that fact. "I'm ready for it to be over," I said.

We had another month of this stuff.

Mr. Muradon smirked. "Same. But unfortunately, we can't control that, so let's focus on something more useful." He removed a beige soapstone bowl from one of the bookshelves and placed it on his desk. It was flecked with gold and black, marbled with white veins, polished to a shine, and carved with runes, power circles, and artistic patterns. He filled it with water. "By the way, when do you plan on introducing me to Vergo? I'd very much like to meet him."

I stiffened. I hadn't said anything about Vergo to him yet. "How'd you find out about him?"

"Mia, if I hadn't been told before I was hired, I would've found out thanks to students gossiping about him. However, I'm confused as to the size of this spirit cat. I've heard conflicting stories." He lit a white sage bundle and wafted the smoke towards the rest of the office with an owl feather.

With a huff, I removed Vergo's collar and introduced them to each other. My tutor was openly fascinated. Vergo sat on the chair with his eyes narrowed.

"I've heard it's incredibly rare for a soul to find atonement via this path."

"I haven't the faintest idea," Vergo said. "I wasn't exactly schooled in the history of spiritual atonement before being sent back."

"Your way of speaking is a bit different. When were you alive?" Mr. Muradon said.

"During the events leading up to the Necromancers War, and long enough after that to see our downfall. I was hanged for my crimes."

Mr. Muradon's eyes widened with excitement. "You're an uncorrupted relic from history. Do you have any idea how useful it'd be to know the real past, instead of the version we're all force fed?"

Vergo glanced at the soapstone bowl. "Are you

saying you want to scry into my past?"

"Yes. Those who fail to learn from history are doomed to repeat it. And we as a society are repeating it over and over. Centuries later, Darks are still hated and feared. If we can understand what went wrong and see how things were perceived from both sides, then we can figure out how to end this cycle of hate. Wouldn't that be a great legacy to leave behind once you've finally atoned?"

Vergo's ears flattened. "I'd rather not relive my past for the sake of your amusement. What's done is done. If you want to stop the cycle of hate, then both sides have to stop feeding into it."

"You're right in that regard, but people need to learn how. We need to learn what didn't work so we can try something new."

The cat growled. "Don't make me relive those memories."

"It's just one time."

"I don't care."

"Do it for Mia and her future."

Vergo shook his head. "You don't want to see what kind of person I was. I was no better than my demon self."

Honestly, I was overcome with curiosity. I'd heard an ugly, hate-filled version of the events from the Light side, the victorious side. Teachers from my previous school told me over and over that it was my duty to repent and ask forgiveness on a daily basis. I didn't understand why I was supposed to do such things when I hadn't played a part in that war. It was easier to give them what they wanted, instead of asking questions they didn't like.

To see history through Vergo as it really happened? How could I say no to that? "I don't care what you did. I want to know the truth."

"You may come to regret that," Vergo said with a grimace. "I did unforgivable things. You won't ever look at me the same."

Mr. Muradon said, "You're not who you were then. Your reluctance and shame are evidence enough."

"Please don't make me relive these memories," Vergo said to me.

Under different circumstances, I would've listened. My more curious side made me nod to my tutor, cuing him to begin the lesson. His shame meant little in the face of learning how to try and end the cycle of hate.

Vergo's blue eyes widened. He hopped off the chair and scurried to the door as runes flared to life all around him. He rammed head-first into the door with a teeth-clenching thud and toppled over. He shook out his head. "What on Aardra?" He spun around, fur bristling. He hissed at Mr. Muradon. "You never had any intention of giving me a choice. What kind of tutor are you?"

Mr. Muradon calmly added a black liquid the consistency of paint to the bowl. "A pragmatic one. I'm sure the Light will see this as an adequate part of your atonement process."

"That's not your call to make. Release me."

He sprinkled Vergo with some of the black liquid. "Mia, today's lesson is on scrying. There are multiple ways to do it. Every alignment has its ways. Normally, Darks scry demons and ghosts, but a spirit in limbo, like him, is available to us as well."

Vergo cried out in pain. His fur bubbled where the liquid had touched him. He reared up. His body bubbled and writhed all over. His limbs stretched and grew. I backed up next to my tutor as Vergo doubled over and continued to swell. Paws stretched into fingers. His face rearranged itself to human proportions. The ears dropped and rounded into human ones. His fur sank back into his body and reformed as a white tunic and black pants. Golden hair that matched Ms. Weever's grew to shoulder length and filled out into the shape of a lion's mane. His tunic-clad torso rose and fell with heavy breaths.

Mr. Muradon gawked. "That was unexpected."

Vergo examined his hands, flexing his fingers and turning them this way and that. He sat up on human knees and patted down his chest. Mouth ajar, he looked up. "What did you do?" He had a handsome face. His blue eyes were wide and had a wild sheen that made me take another step back.

My tutor held up the glass vial. "It's a typical scrying oil. I'm guessing it's what caused you to revert back to your human form. You weren't a spirit cat back then. So maybe—"

"Shut up and get this over with." Vergo stood on unsteady legs, rising to a few inches shorter than Mr. Muradon, who had to be the tallest teacher in the entire district. Vergo had a narrow build with corded muscles in his forearms and neck. A sharp collarbone crossed the "v" under his tunic, revealing a hint of a strong chest. "What are you staring at?" he said, glaring.

I shook my head, bringing myself back to the task at hand.

Mr. Muradon said, "Scrying is an incredibly useful tool, especially when it comes to gathering factual information. The only danger is that you're vulnerable while scrying. It puts you in a trance that makes you oblivious to the present world around you. Scry only in a safe location. Thankfully, we don't have to worry about that today." He set the vial aside and set a song bowl next to the scrying bowl. "Depending on how good at focusing you are, sounds make great focus tools. Regardless of your aptitude, I highly recommend using a song bowl to help you focus and sync up with the past. It grants you a better vision." He ran the rod along the rim of the bowl. A round, pure note filled the room, sending a wave of calm through me. He opened a second vial and used a thumb to spread a line of golden oil across his forehead. "Hold still. This is a blend of mugwort, wormwood, and eyebright."

A pressure slid across my forehead, dousing me with a garlicky scent mixed with sage. I resisted the urge to touch my forehead.

Mr. Muradon approached Vergo and hesitated.

Vergo nodded reluctantly. My tutor reached for his forehead and a hand snatched his forearm. Vergo glared at the tall man. "I don't approve of some of your teaching methods. You have yet to convince me that you're a benevolent man. Consider this your only warning that if you ever do anything to harm her or set her on the wrong path, I'll exact vengeance." He roughly let go, leaving behind white indents in my tutor's skin.

Mr. Muradon frowned. "Consider your warning heeded." He rubbed a line of oil across Vergo's brow and set the scrying bowl at his feet.

The three of us stood around the bowl. One of my hands disappeared inside Mr. Muradon's and Vergo firmly gripped my other hand, his touch cold like any other ghost's.

Mr. Muradon said, "Focus on the water and the sound of the song bowl. Let them guide you to the past. Let your body grow heavy and relaxed, open to the messages that await us."

The darkened water drew me in like a steaming bowl of soup set on a dinner table. The lingering note eased tension out of my limbs. The longer I concentrated, the more the water filled my vision, until my eyes closed of their own accord.

"Vergo, take us back to the events leading up to the Necromancers War. Tell us your story. Teach the lessons that must be learned. Let all be laid bare."

Vergo's grip tightened, a wave of anxiety coming off him. I squeezed back.

"O Light, grant us a vision of what was so it will not be again."

A force pulled me downward and a wind rushed through me. I opened my eyes. Instead of the office, I stood alone at the edge of a city made of stone. Square buildings were built into the side of a snowcapped mountain. A group of robed men stood next to a dirt road, facing me. The front of each of their robes was marked with the Dark symbol, a northeast facing crescent moon with three pointed lines hanging from the southern end. The two outer lines had one barb each.

A voice that wasn't my own said, "We strike tonight. This arrogance and repression ends now." It was Vergo. I was him. I tried to move his legs, but the memory held me in place as the other people nodded. They threw hoods over their heads and dispersed.

The memory shifted as if someone had placed a

different picture in front of me. Stars filled the sky above the same stone city. Lights shined from countless windows and little tendrils of chimney smoke disappeared into the twilight. I stood with a ring of robed figures lining the edge of a gigantic power circle. As one, we dropped to our knees and pressed our hands to the ground. The power circle lit up, shining on each hooded face with purple light. The circle hummed with power, making my arms vibrate.

"Bakakodozu, heed my call. We ask for your aid to right wrongs, to be an instrument of our rage and bring justice to those that hate us." A tornado wind buffeted me. Golden hair flicked in and out of my vision and Vergo's hood rhythmically bumped against the back of my head.

Giant claws surged out of the ground, reaching skyward. They gripped the ground as a second set of claws shot out. A massive head rose like a black moon peering out over the horizon. It surged upwards as the rest of the demon's emaciated body followed. It crouched on long, clawed black feet and its back emanated smoke. Its hip bones and ribs stuck out against tight, leathery black skin.

Feed me your hate. Your rage. Feed me your wrath.

My whole body vibrated with the demon's heavy voice.

Vergo chanted a spell. The other hooded people did the same. Lines of red and black pulsed towards the demon. Its body grew with every beat, stretching beyond the circle. Its body jerked and an arm shot out. Spikes and boils erupted. Muscles and tendons thickened. Its other arm rose with a jerk and it grew to match the other arm's size. A massive, leathery wing emerged from its back, and then another.

The demon reared up, towering taller than any building in Marohu. It grew and grew, until each claw was twice as big as man. Three whiplike tails sprouted from the base of its spine. They cut through the air, cracking with the intensity of a lightning strike. The demon roared, making the ground shake. Wings blotted out the sky.

A massive roar answered Bakakodozu's from miles away, as did another from miles in the opposite direction. Black shapes outlined in a purple glow loomed over the landscape.

"I am wrath incarnate," the demon said and turned for the city. His voice boomed like thunder. Three tails whipped by like a fast-moving low cloud. The ground shook with every step it took. "I am justice."

The other distant shapes descended on the city.

The memory shifted to a molten, smoking ruin under a bleeding sunrise. The entire city was nothing more than a stony landslide resting against the mountain. The demons were gone.

The memory shifted again. I looked down at miles and miles of sprawling countryside from high up a mountain, Vergo's hands braced on a stone wall, a finger tapping. Below me lay a mix of ruins and new buildings, a city partially rebuilt. Hundreds of tiny figures moved along the roads.

"There's been a message from the Light Order," a voice said from behind me.

I turned. A robed man with the Dark symbol on it handed over a tied scroll. I tore it open. Fragments of the letter were visible. Most of it was blurred, having been lost to time. The letter told Darks to stand down or die. I crumpled the scroll. Vergo said, "See that they get the message that we won't ever stand down."

The man with graying hair nodded, a wicked smile touching his thin lips. He turned and the vision flickered as he walked off.

I stood in the middle of an open, rugged desert among the front lines of a massive army. Opposite us stood another massive army clad in white, gold and silver. The Army of Light, like the history books described. Tens of thousands of them spanned the desert from horizon to horizon. With a command from someone farther down the lines, Vergo and his allies conjured summoning circles. On the other side of the battlefield, white-clad soldiers raised their arms skyward and engulfed their army in light. It grew blinding, washing out the memory.

I knelt before a tribunal of people clad in white and frowning down at me from row upon row of stone benches. A Light priest wearing a golden and silver suit of armor paced between me and the tribunal. More half-naked people knelt on either side of me, mouths gagged, hands bound behind them and chains attached to metal collars around their necks. My mouth filled with the taste of linen and a bitter litmus, keeping my tongue as far away from the gag as possible. Saliva drooled down my chin as my mouth fought to retain moisture.

The pacing man clasped his hands behind his back, taking one slow step after another, studying each bound person as he passed. He spoke with a cultured, arrogant voice. "I thank you all for your cooperation. Your sacrifice for the sake of your followers will not go to waste." He looked askance at Vergo. "You'll be used as an example before we methodically eradicate your loyal followers."

My lunge was cut short by the chain connected to my collar. Metal dug into my throat, making me choke. I leaned against the chain, wrestling with the bonds immobilizing my fingers and tying my wrists together. I couldn't draw a rune if I wanted to. My chest tightened as I struggled to breathe around the gag.

The man gave me an all-too-familiar smug smile. "We've all learned from this war that Lights are the ones who must establish balance." He resumed pacing. "Darks clearly have no place in all this. You lot exist to create chaos. This is unacceptable. Any members of the other alignments who disagree with our assessment will be cast in with your fate, we'll make sure of it. This world needs balance. Anyone who seeks to unbalance it does not belong. We'll have absolute order." The man reached the end of the line and paced back towards the center of the room. "As for all of you, you'll helm the efforts to clean up your mess. You'll literally be worked to death. Your alignments will be suppressed. Executioners will monitor your every move. They'll kill you at the slightest hint of rebellion. Should you miraculously survive the cleanup efforts, you'll be hanged. So count every breath you draw from here on out a blessing until the Light casts you into damnation. This war will be nothing more than a bad memory and a strong lesson."

My vision blurred into a patchwork of ruddy colors And then all went black.

My head snapped back and I gasped for breath. The white office ceiling stood over me and I held two different hands, one warm and one cold. Mr. Muradon breathed hard as well. Vergo stood with his head bowed, golden hair shielding his face. The swirling water in the bowl stilled. We released hands.

Mr. Muradon said, "The winners sure painted a more noble picture of how they handled their victory." He smothered the white sage.

Vergo's hair turned black and shortened. His clothes stuck to his shrinking body, transforming back into fur. He dropped to his hands and knees, fingers shortening into paws and nails curling into claws. A tail sprouted. He crouched with his belly pressed the floor, down to cat size, his head hanging low. He took in his black paws with white toes before retreating to inside my backpack and out of sight.

Mr. Muradon lit some incense and set it on the chair. "Should help him shake off the bad memories." He gestured for me to take a seat and leaned against the corner of his desk. "So what did you think of what we saw?"

I gave my backpack a little extra space, sitting in the far chair. I wanted to pick him up and hug him. I wanted him to be back in human form so I could hug him better. Their failure to beat the Lights in the war had been a prolonged death sentence full of more suffering. Sure, they didn't go about standing up to oppression in a noble way, but instead of people questioning Lights, it'd only made things worse. "Neither side did the right thing and the war changed nothing; if anything, it made things worse for Darks."

"It did make things worse, unfortunately. Have you learned about the Dark Huntsmen in history class yet?"

Sounded ominous. I shook my head.

"During the Revival Age, the period following the Necromancers War, the Grand Light Order formed a special group called the Dark Huntsmen. It consisted of people from the other six alignments tasked with hunting down Darks and their sympathizers who went into hiding. Legend has it that they succeeded in eliminating every last known Dark. The interesting thing is that this might be true."

"How? I thought alignments were genetic." That theory held with my mom's side all the way to me. But then Bela's alignment threw that off. Mom and Dad had no recollection of a Light ever being in the family.

The corners of his mouth curled with skepticism. "It seems like it, but society has been tracking alignments since that particular war. There's data suggesting that's true, and there's also contradictory data. Instead, there's a pattern suggesting that a geographic region impacts alignment distribution. Data patterns follow this more closely, but when you cross reference it with the passage of time, it doesn't hold up either."

"Is it random?"

"The Grand Light Order is pushing the explanation that it's mostly random, with Light and Dark having lower odds of manifesting than the other five." He spoke animatedly, his face bright with excitement and enthusiasm. "There's a desperate push to make society believe that." He shook his head. "It seems true until you run the numbers and cross reference with major events throughout history. Then the true pattern emerges."

I had no idea what he was hinting at. Shrugging, I held up my hands.

"Here, I'll give you a hint. There was a huge surge in Darks being born after the war and during the time of the Dark Huntsmen. Light numbers have been in steady decline ever since. Ask Sanctus Bylan. It's not common knowledge, but I'm sure he knows. The Light Order eventually disbanded the Huntsmen."

The Necromancers War and the events surrounding the Dark Huntsmen's efforts spawned a spike in Dark numbers? Why? And one of the old ladies at the Order of Leo had said something about there being fewer Lights born lately, when we brought in Bela after her alignment manifested. "Our actions affect which alignment manifests in a person?"

"Exactly." He stood and emphasized his words with hand gestures. "As for on what scale, we don't know. There's a theory gaining momentum that there are forces at work making sure Darks are a part of society all around the world. All efforts to eradicate Darks throughout history have failed. The Grand Light Order is worried that their time in power is coming to an end. The forces that be want balance. Lights cannot eradicate Darks any more than Darks can eradicate Lights. We're all part of some cosmic whole. We're all equally important in achieving balance."

This was a crazy theory. I didn't know how to wrap my mind around it. I'd been told all my life that I had no place in the grand balance of things. There was one question I'd never had the chance to ask anyone, though. "What is so important about balance? Ms. Weever mentioned it a bunch, but I don't get it."

He popped a sympathetic smile. "Okay, so maybe we both got ahead of ourselves. She was reassuring you that you do have a place in this world. I'm sure all the city schools tried brainwashing you with negative comments."

I nodded, my heart sinking. He'd nailed the truth.

He waved dismissively. "Throw all that away. Darks are part of the balance whether Lights want to admit it or not."

"What balance?" Ugh, would any adult please start making sense about this stuff?

"Oh, sorry." He leaned back against his desk. "It's probably something you won't entire understand until you're older."

I stifled a groan. "Adults keep telling me that."

"Okay, okay, you're wise beyond your years—"

I heard that a lot, too.

"—so maybe you'll understand. The balance all us boring adults are talking about is a key component of peace and happiness in our lives. Nature lives in fragile balance that's constantly fluctuating to compensate for imbalances that threaten the survival of one species or another. Human society fluctuates, too, hence the strange pattern in elemental alignments. Lights are overpowering the balance, which, as you and I know all too well, isn't bringing the peace and happiness we should all be enjoying. I think our numbers are rising and theirs are falling for the sake of a happy balance. And if we're going to achieve that, we need to figure out how to do this the right way. Does that make any sense?"

No, but I wasn't going to admit it. Pretending to be wiser beyond my years, I nodded.

Chapter 10

I spent the weeks preceding Seven's Seed holiday vacation trying to wrap my brain around this whole balance thing. I understood it was something important that involved every last human being and that it was important to happiness. Mr. Muradon built lessons off of Mrs. Livy's history curriculum, using events coinciding with the fluctuating alignment numbers. I saw the correlation, but I couldn't understand why or how human actions influenced alignment numbers. I also didn't understand what exactly he wanted me to do with all this information. And since I was already having a hard enough time understanding all the other stuff, I didn't want to feel stupider for telling him I didn't understand the point of these lessons.

Since we were going to start the next unit at the start of the next calendar year, I was so relieved when the last day of the quarter, the last day before vacation finally arrived. It felt like it took a whole year to get here.

Mom seemed to be going through the motions as of late. Dad was working hard, but he hadn't been the same since Grandma channeled herself through Bela. This carried over to Mom in a form of a distant, pensive gaze, simpler meals, and me picking up the slack on dishes and keeping the house clean. I missed bandyll, but the lack of games and practices afforded me the time needed for housekeeping and homework.

Dad had bought Bela and me new Seven's Seed dresses to wear. Mine was white with a silver lace half-jacket and matching shoes and flower hair clip. I wore black leggings to show silent support for my alignment. I should've worn all black, but I lacked the courage. At least Ms. Weever wouldn't be there to shame me with a disapproving frown. Mr. Muradon was more understanding.

Bela wore an adorable white winter dress with gold embroidery, white lace, and a matching gold half-jacket and flower hair clip. She chatted away about how she was looking forward to showing all her friends her new dress, all the food and treats we were going to get to eat, and the games her teachers had prepared. Mom usually reacted with short responses sprinkled throughout Bela's inexhaustible chatter. She quietly braided a lock of hair on either side of my sister's head and secured them together with a white hair tie.

Bela said, "Do you think Sanctus Bylan will like my dress?"

Mom continued to fuss over my sister's hair as if she hadn't heard.

Bela's little brows drew together. "Mommy, are

you listening?"

Mom blinked a few times. "Hm? Yes, Bela. Keep telling me your story."

She stomped a foot. "No. I asked you a question."

Mom's fingers paused in their raking and her eyes widened. She had dark lines under them. Was she not sleeping well, either? "Oh, I'm sorry, sweetie. What was your question?"

Bela pouted and folded her arms. "Why aren't you listening anymore? You're always sad."

Lines creased around Mom's mismatched eyes as she forced herself to finish tending to my sister's hair. "I'm sorry. I'm not trying to ignore you. I have a lot on my mind."

"Then have less on your mind. I don't like it when you're sad."

Light bless her blunt, honest heart. I said, "Bela, that wasn't a nice thing to say to Mom."

Distant gaze devoid of any happiness, Mom forced an empty smile. "It's okay, Mia. She wasn't trying to be hurtful, were you, sweetie?" She turned Bela around and kissed her nose. My sister giggled.

"No. I love you, Mommy."

A scrap of happiness deepened her smile. She kissed Bela again. "Alright, you two enjoy the festivities. I'll be here when you get home." Mom kissed the top of my head and ushered us out the door.

The school bus was decorated for Seven's Seed with paintings in every bulbous window and a hand-painted sign that read "Happy Seven's Seed!" The bus driver gave each of us a leaf-wrapped piece of chocolate. Bela ate hers. I stowed mine in my backpack, catching a glimpse of a sulking spirit cat taking up the same space as a couple of textbooks and notebooks.

I zipped my backpack closed and braced for a day I was going to try to enjoy. At the very least, I had no tests to worry about and teachers weren't allowed to give us homework over the break. Today was for pure enjoyment and community.

The elementary campus looked like an enchanted patch of desert with all the little orbs of light dancing in the air and charmed fairy dolls flitting among them, little arms sprinkling more orbs over our heads.

Teachers wore their holiday best and handed out little candies that were greedily snatched up. I accepted one from Miss Wren, my sixth-grade homeroom teacher. She graced me with a hug, wishing me a happy Seven's Seed, and I stopped by Bylan's office. I had another letter for Ms. Weever. In it, I'd finally geared up the courage to ask her about Mr. Muradon and if they'd dated when they went to school together. There were a bunch of other things, including a couple of quizzes she'd sent me to complete. My new tutor was the part I was most eager to hear a response to.

The office door was propped open with a block of rose quartz. Bylan stood before his rows of books, chin in one hand, searching for a particular volume. "Good morning, Mia," he said, eyes on the books.

"Morning Bylan. I have another letter for Ms. Weever." I held up an overstuffed envelope and set it on his desk. "Bela didn't bring her backpack today."

"I'm surprised you have yours."

"I feel weird without it." I'd managed to leave my violin at home. I couldn't bring myself to do the same with my backpack. "And Vergo likes to curl up in it."

"Is he still brooding?" Bylan freed a choice

volume, studied the cover, and set it back on the shelf.

"Yeah. I wish I knew how to help him feel better." Vergo was still upset. He hardly spoke anymore. I wanted to blame his moods on Tradereth, but not only did I doubt a demon could affect him this way, he'd been upset ever since my scrying lesson. Yes, I'd seen a glimpse of the terrible things he'd done, but it hadn't changed my opinion of him. If anything, I missed his sarcastic remarks and running commentary on my life. Sure, I often found them annoying, but their sudden absence was painfully obvious. I tried a few times to coax him out of his mood. Each time, he acted as if he hadn't heard me.

"Give him time. This may be part of the Light's lesson for him."

Well, it was a stupid lesson, but I kept the thought to myself.

"Anyway, I'll make sure the letter gets to Lyra. I'll see you at the lunch feast." He grabbed another book, looked at it, and put it back.

I waved even though he wasn't looking and headed out of his office. The metal door leading outside swung closed behind Mr. Redd, who wore a white suit and gold tie. His dress shoes were black. He nodded to me as he passed. Pushing the metal door back open, I looked over a shoulder. The principal entered Bylan's office. He seemed to do that every time I stopped by. Nothing ever came of it. I headed to homeroom.

Like All Souls Day, our shortened school day was crammed with fun and games, and lessons hidden inside them. Mrs. Livy had us play memory games that tested our knowledge of Aardra's creation story.

Legend had it that two divine forces battled over

dominion of Aardra, breathing life into our world at the same time. Both shed blood and tears on our world, infusing it with magic and the essence of their souls. This led to the birth of the first Light and Dark humans, Lux and Tarn. Lux breathed a consciousness into the Air, giving birth to Ard, the first Air, and infused a campfire with another consciousness, giving birth to Vur, the first Fire. Tarn molded clay and stone into the first Earth, named Er, and bathed in a mystical hot spring, giving birth to Woad, the first Water.

Lux and Tarn fell in love with each other's work and together created Gen, the first Kindred. And from that day forward, all of humanity became shepherds of the elements.

Despite Tarn's role in all this, he wasn't represented anywhere on campus. He was hardly mentioned after Gen was born.

I successfully matched up my characters and events with the corresponding facts, coming in second for the fastest completion time. Garrett beat me by four seconds, winning himself an orange chocolate Shinjan idol. He kindly shared a piece with me even though Mrs. Livy awarded me a wooden teardrop necklace carved with the Light symbol, a south facing crescent moon with five narrow diamonds crowning the north side. It was pretty. I'd give it to Mom or Bela later. We listened to a story on the song stone in language arts, played with elemental charms in science with the goal of knocking over wooden cup towers, plotted out ornaments in math class under the guidance of a substitute teacher (we still didn't have a new math teacher), and watched a staff-versus-students basketball game during PE and elemental tutoring blocks. Coach

Viro, Mrs. Sterling and Mr. Muradon dominated the boys- and girls-basketball teams while I snuck in some reading on my latest Yuna book.

After receiving the cape from the crystal dragons, they told her about a wizard tower that touched the clouds. That was probably where the wizard had retreated to. And if she was going to climb that tower, she was going to need help. Yuna made a reluctant trip back to her home kingdom to recruit allies. The satyrs and serpents lacked the power to face so much concentrated magic. The basketball game concluded as Yuna faced her father, the very person who had banished her from the kingdom. Her mother was in the throne room, too, and was the only reason Yuna hadn't been automatically thrown into the dungeons.

I reluctantly returned my book to my backpack, but brightened up at the thought of the feast and getting a chance to hang out with Deren and everyone else. Sure, Gwen would be there, too, but she pretended we all didn't exist after getting detention. She didn't even look at me during homeroom.

Since three grades couldn't fit into the cafeteria all at once, tables were lined up to snake around the edge of part of the playground and ringed the cafeteria inside and out. There were no tables to sit at. Teachers split us among three long lines of students to load up plates. A bouquet of delightful aromas filled the air, causing my stomach to growl. Honeyed biscuits, tamales, stuffed jalapeños, assorted grilled meats, snack foods, pastries, cookies, cupcakes, fruits, raw and cooked vegetables, salt, pepper, butter, casseroles, and more. For once, I was grateful for the Volaires. No city school had the funds to serve a feast half this size. Sure, the Volaires might do this every year to flaunt their wealth and earn brownie points, but I wasn't going to complain. And there were brownies, too.

Vergo poked his head through the side of my backpack and sniffed the air. He gave the endless line of tables of food a longing look before disappearing back inside.

I joined Sussi and Chibya in line. Sussi gave me the same casual wave she greeted everyone else with, and Chibya's eyes squinted with joy as she waved. Deren came up behind me and greeted us all. "Where's Garrett?" he said.

Sussi pointed over to the chain link fence.

Garrett sat propped up against the fence with a loaded plate, feeding his two coyotes, Snooter and Longears. The coyotes wagged their scruffy tails and took turns licking Garrett's fingers. His aide stood with her back to the scene, tending to her plate of food. She'd gotten used to Garrett's coyotes at some point. She stood alert and relaxed.

"That works."

With exception of Chibya, we all loaded plates to the brink of collapse. Chibya grabbed a few pieces of fruits and vegetables after Sussi nagged her to eat something. She'd been doing this a lot lately, but in her defense, her face didn't look as round.

We joined Garrett and his coyotes to enjoy our Seven's Seed lunch. I stuffed myself silly on tamales and jalapeño poppers, and filled up my dessert stomach with cookies, a brownie, and some cupcakes. Oof. I felt ready for a nap by the time I threw away my plate. At least we'd be boarding the buses soon.

Sussi set her backpack on the ground and took out

four round objects wrapped in swirling colors of a concealment charm. "Hey, I got you all presents."

Beaming, Chibya inhaled. "Aww, Sussi, you didn't have to, but thank you." She accepted a glistening ball half the size of her head.

I automatically held my hands out for the ball she offered. Exchanging gifts was part of the Seven's Seed tradition. No one in my circle of friends had mentioned exchanging gifts.

"Relax," Sussi said. "I wanted to do this. It's just a little something." She gave the last two shimmering orbs to Deren and Garrett.

Feeling selfish, I reluctantly stroked the orb, dispelling the concealment charm. The shimmering sank to my palm and vanished, revealing a small wicker basket stuffed with candy and a small stuffed cat that looked like Vergo, including the white patches on his chest and toes. My heart melted. It was so cute. I hugged it to my chest. "Thank you, Sussi. I love it."

She popped one of her rare genuine smiles.

She gifted each of us a candy basket complete with a small stuffed animal. Garrett had a coyote, Deren a white dog like the two giant beasts that roamed his property, and Chibya had an owl. We all thanked her and Chibya squeezed her in a group hug.

"I actually got you something, Sussi," Chibya said. She gave the rest of us a pained smile. "I'm sorry I didn't think about the rest of you. I'll come back from vacation with more presents."

Deren and I both waved dismissively, both of us taking turns saying it was okay, telling her to not worry about it. I said, "I didn't bring anyone anything, so really, don't worry about it."

"I got you something, Mia," Deren said. He blushed.

I froze. He got me a gift? "Really?"

He snatched a swirling orb out of his backpack and held it out to me. "Yeah."

I looked at it and then at him and his hopeful gaze. "Are you sure?"

"Definitely. I wanted to. You're like the best friend I've ever had."

"You mean girlfriend," Sussi said loud enough for us to hear.

I tilted my head back and Deren sighed in frustration at the exact same time as me.

Chibya leaned closer to Sussi. "Are they going out together?"

"They don't think so," Sussi said, "but don't tell them that or they get real mad."

"I can see that," Chibya said.

Deren shook his head.

"Do we bother correcting them?" I said.

"No point. Here." He deposited the orb in my hands.

I glanced at him one more time before building the courage to stroke the concealment charm. I understood he wanted to give me a present. I felt like such a terrible friend for not thinking of this. He was my best friend. The charm fell away, revealing a cord necklace strung with several polished, multicolored stones marbled with white. Oh, my goodness. It was gorgeous.

"I made it myself. It's a protection charm." He pointed to each stone as he named them. "It's made with rose quartz, fire agate, labradorite and one piece of emerald." One small green stone sat nestled in the middle, faceted like a diamond. There were seven stones in all, three on each side of the emerald.

"I love it. How did you find all these?"

"I'm an Earth, duh." He gently draped the cord around my neck and tugged the ends so the stone sat over my heart. "The emerald was the hardest to find. My dad helped. Most of the good stuff is in and around the mines, but the whole desert has neat stuff lying around. This region used to be a chain of volcanos millions of years ago."

Sussi said, "We're not, like, gonna blow again any year soon, are we?"

Tilting his head, Deren's gaze grew distant. Hundreds of voices filled the air with happy chatter and play. We were our island of five people among everything going on. Deren shook his head. "Naw. The land has settled. We're good."

Sussi visibly relaxed.

I touched the stones. There was a positive energy to them, one in an elemental language I didn't understand, but instinctively knew was good. This was the sweetest thing ever. I knew they were all looking, but I didn't care. I threw my arms around Deren and hugged him tight. After a moment's hesitation, he hugged back.

Chibya said, "Wait, so they really don't think they're going out?"

Sussi snorted.

Deren's chest rose and fell with a huff. He let go and faced them. "No, we're not. I'm not ready for girl stuff."

"And I'm not ready for boy stuff," I said. Why couldn't anyone else believe that he was being kind to be kind, and not because he was my boyfriend?

"Why can't you all believe we're just friends? I don't know how to be a good boyfriend, and I don't wanna do that gross face and hand stuff I see Nonaya and Bo doing."

I grimaced. Not at what Deren said, but the unpleasant image of Gwen's friend Nonaya and her boyfriend Bo with their mouths all over each other, and Bo's hands on a very personal space of Nonaya's body. The teachers got super mad when they caught them, giving them both a week's worth of detention. They made out every day, anyway. Ugh. "I don't know how they like it."

"I don't either, but I've caught my parents doing the same thing," Dere said.

"Mine, too!" Oh, thank goodness. I wasn't the only one.

"I like being friends with you, Mia," Deren said with a nod. "You're fun, and things are definitely anything but boring."

"Thanks. I like being friends with you, too."

Sussi made kissing noises.

We both glared at her and told her to shut up at the same exact time.

Chibya laughed. "You two are funny."

Deren shouldered his backpack. "Wanna go for a walk?" he said to me.

I wordlessly shouldered mine. I waved to the others and we walked side-by-side, making a lap around the square sidewalk that ringed a large playground full of students have fun and eating.

Deren lowered his gaze and lines creased his forehead. "My dad found a job a few miles down at the restaurant, so it looks like we don't have to move."

"That's good."

"Yeah. Silden and Alden are working the fields, helping harvest cabbage, parsnip, and stuff. The farm owner lets them take a little home every day as part of their payment, and he even gives us honey. And our neighbors are giving us some eggs and food, too."

"So are you all doing okay?"

"Yeah. Everyone's been real nice and supportive. I told Dad I'd work, too, but he said no. Mom suggested I offer our neighbors help with their livestock as a way of showing thanks for their support. Dad thought that was a good idea." He smiled. "So did our neighbors. So now I'm scooping a lot of chicken, cow and horse poop every day after school."

"Eww." It was gross, but it needed to be done. Dad had said something about wanting some chickens. Mom flat out forbade it, saying she didn't want so much stink so close to our house. When Mom wasn't struggling with feeling real sad, she kept the house immaculate, despite Bela's efforts to leave her toys everywhere.

Deren shrugged. "It feels good to help. And Mrs. B even gives me a fresh, hot churro now and then as soon as I finish. I'm having fun."

"That's good. Are your brothers having fun, too?"

"Alden is, but Silden is upset because he's missing his senior year of team roping. He's trying to hide it because he understands the money stuff. It's not making it any easier knowing he's missing his last year of school sports."

"Yeah, I'd be upset, too."

"Dad says he's still looking for something better so we can all go back to being just kids again. He doesn't like any of us working. He wants us to save it for when we're all adults, saying something about how childhood is so short. He must've forgotten how long it takes to grow up. I'd love to be an adult. I wouldn't have to get up for school all week long and there'd be no one telling me what to do anymore."

"Seriously." Adults liked to complain to us "children" about how we were all in such a rush to grow up and that we should enjoy it more. Growing up was rough. Even I would rather be an adult already. I could do more to help my parents. "Does this mean you still might move one day?"

"Yeah," Deren said.

"Do you think he could get his job back at the mine?"

He shrugged. "He hasn't said anything about that."

Someone called my name. We both stopped. Bela ran towards us, her face red and tears streaking down her face.

"Mia." She bowled into me and hugged my legs. "I wanna go home."

Deren and I looked at each other. I held my sister's shaking shoulders. "What's wrong? What happened?" She cried harder. I hefted her into my arms. Boy she was getting heavy. She was too big for this. I sucked it up for her sake. Bela clamped her arms around my neck and shoulders. Both our weights pressed my feet into the ground.

Deren helped me remove my backpack one arm at a time and Vergo hopped out. His tail remained low to the ground, his ears pricked towards Bela.

I headed for the main office. Bylan would help me calm her down. Deren held the decorated door open for me and jogged down the short hallway and tried

Bylan's doorknob. It was locked. He tried a second time and knocked on the door.

No one answered. A broken cookie lay in front of the door. I thought of picking it up by I didn't want to touch it.

"Maybe he went home already," Deren said. "He never hangs around for anything."

A trickle of dread crawled up the back of my neck. Something wasn't right. Deren raised his hand to knock again. "Stop," I said and jutted my chin towards the empty name plate. Each office door had the words "Office of" painted on them in all capitals and a brass nameplate of the corresponding staff member beneath it. Bylan's was missing. And so were Bela's handmade decorations. Little rectangles of sticky residue were the only hint anything had been there.

Deren did a double-take. "Weird."

Hiking a snuffling Bela up in my arms, I walked over to the front desk. Festive music filled the air. The top of Coach Khamai's curly black hair stuck out over the high countertop. I walked around to the side, where she and the other front office lady were able to enter and exit with ease. Coach sat alone, tapping a foot in time with the music and double-checking report cards. She tracked her progress with a fingertip while bouncing her gaze between a card and a thick packet of spreadsheets. "Coach?"

"Give me one second," Coach said without looking up. She checked the last few grades, stuffed the report card in a labeled envelope, and tucked it behind the last envelope in a shallow box. She flipped over the packet and covered the next report card, and put on a big smile that vanished as soon as she noticed Bela. She stroked her song stone, lowering the volume. "What happened? Did she get hurt?"

"I don't think so." She'd run up to me without any trouble. "Do you know where Sanctus Bylan went?"

Bela cried louder.

Coach frowned. My stomach flopped. She waved me closer and whispered, "I don't think he's coming back. Mr. Redd was in the office with him for a good while, and then Sanctus Bylan loaded up his car with all his belongings and left. He did not look happy. Mr. Redd removed his nameplate and threw it away." Vergo padded off towards Bylan's office.

"Did Mr. Redd look happy?" I said before I could stop myself.

"That's a strange question." She raised an eyebrow.

"I'm sorry. That was really rude of me."

Coach popped me a sympathetic smile. "I'll pretend you didn't ask."

"Thanks. Sorry."

Coach thought a moment. "Your sister stopped by here not too long ago. She tried to get into Sanctus Bylan's office and then talked to, I'm guessing, a ghost before running off. Next thing I knew, you and Deren showed up with her. Anyway, don't worry about it. Go enjoy the last bit of fun and games before it's time to load up onto the buses."

No. She wasn't telling me everything. "Coach, please tell me what happened. You have to know."

"Even if I do, it's not appropriate to talk about such things with students."

Vergo returned. "Everything's gone. I don't think he's coming back. Something's not right with this. He acted perfectly normal this morning."

I gently set Bela on her feet. She clamped to my waist, hiding her face. I stroked her hair. She was so small and had been through so much already. "Coach, you've heard about the stuff I deal with, right?"

"Yeah. You're one brave kid. I don't think I could do what you do, even if I was your alignment. I don't know how you do it."

"I have to. And I need you to tell me what you can."

"I really shouldn't. Please go back to the feast."

Okay, time to take a risk. She didn't give me the impression that she was under Tradereth's influence, but it was a possibility. "Coach, there are things going on that I need to get to the bottom of. I need to know why Sanctus Bylan left so suddenly."

Coach turned to the pile of report cards and bowed her head. "I don't know what Sanctus Bylan did, but it was severe enough for Mr. Redd to dismiss him from campus. The school board will decide whether he stays or goes. I'm sorry, Mia."

Bela cried harder.

Chapter 11

I tried to put it all out of my mind on Seven's Seed break. I desperately needed one day to forget about everything and enjoy life. Dad was home and happy, and had an extra day off. Mom was a little more cheerful, and Bela was her normal bubbly self after waking up to a bunch of presents in the living room.

Vergo quietly watched us all from beside Bela. Mom and Dad had given me permission to remove his charm collar for Bela's enjoyment. They sat on the couch, watching Bela and me open a handful of presents, Dad with an arm wrapped around Mom. She leaned against him, an arm around his waist, head resting against his broad chest. Bela stroked the concealment charm around her last present, revealing an interlocking block set to build stuff out of. She squealed with delight and locked Vergo in a hug. His blue eyes widened.

"Do be a little more gentle, Tiny One. While it doesn't hurt, it most certainly is startling."

Bela laughed and hugged him again without making his eyes pop out.

"Better. What have you got there?"

She lifted the drawstring bag. Little wooden blocks clacked together. "I'm gonna build you a house."

"But I already have a house." His tail lazily flicked behind him.

"This one's going to be for you."

I opened my final present, two more Yuna books. I hugged them to my chest, inhaling the scent of fresh cut paper. "Thank you, Mom and Dad." This had been the most thoughtful Seven's Seed I could remember ever since my alignment manifested. We were a real family again despite the issues haunting us, Dad was home and Mom was smiling. I resisted the urge to enjoy it too much for fear that Grandma might try to channel herself through Bela at any moment.

"Yes, thank you, Mommy and Daddy." Bela upturned the bag, dumping multicolor blocks all over the wood floor. I clenched my teeth at the wave of thuds. Hopefully she hadn't scuffed the floor.

Dad chuckled. "You're welcome, girls. I've been wanting a Seven's Seed like this for a long time."

"Me, too," Mom said and snuggled deeper.

Dad reached under a couch pillow and held up a rectangular box. "Babe, I've got something for you, too."

Mom inhaled with delight. "Aw, Jay, you really shouldn't have. I meant it when I said to make the girls happy."

"You're one of my girls, too." He kissed her.

Mom delicately took the box, her mouth ajar, and removed the lid. Her mismatched eyes lit up. "Jay. By the Light." She held up a silver necklace with a glittering diamond the size of a marble. "It's magnificent. Where on Aardra did you get a diamond like this? Please tell me you didn't—"

"I found it in the mine. The diggers must've overlooked it so I took it. The Volaires are rich enough as it is."

"This thing is worth a small fortune."

"You're worth more to me than any fortune." He took the necklace and put it on her. Mom tossed her hair back and admired the necklace. "Do you like it?"

Mom lunged, pressing her lips to his. Dad went wide-eyed before wrapping his arms around her. They both inhaled deeply through their noses. Mom slid onto his lap.

"Eww, Mommy and Daddy. No kissing." Bela made a disgusted face.

Mom and Dad broke apart, smiling and breathless, and then went back for more. In one swift motion, Dad picked Mom up and carried her off into their bedroom, the door closing behind them.

"I think she liked it," Vero said.

I gathered most of my presents and retreated to my room. I needed more than one wall to separate me from what was about to happen. I deposited my books and new clothes on my bed and came back for my sage bundles, violin maintenance supplies, and a collection of holiday treats.

Two more white feathers lay among the blocks. I picked them up. They were equally soft and downy, like the others. I held them out for Vergo to see. "Did you see where these came from?"

He did a double-take. "I would very much like to. This is the third time I'm aware of this happening. Bylan seemed bothered by them, which means he must know."

I wasn't sure when we were going to get the chance to ask him, considering he was no longer accessible at school anymore. I didn't want to think about that, though. Not today. I added them to the other two feathers on my desk and put away my new clothes.

Vergo curled up in his usual spot at the foot of my bed and closed his eyes.

I added new socks to my sock drawer and studied him a moment. "Are you feeling any better? I'm really worried about everything going on."

"Give me one more day. I understand terrible things are going on. I just…need time."

I folded a shirt. "I don't know why you think some of those memories were so bad. I saw what happened, but they did nothing to change my opinion of you."

His furry chest rose and fell with a sigh. "That's because you didn't see the true aftermath. That was one of several heavily populated cities we destroyed. I and my brethren committed genocide. And then I had the audacity to feel outraged when Lights killed my wife, daughter, and one of my sons. The Weever name was nearly wiped from the face of this world while my actions led to many generations of families coming to an abrupt end. You didn't see the carnage from the Necromancers War. The land is scarred to this day. And you didn't see the beatings, whippings, and torment I underwent as I was forced to rebuild one of the cities. And you didn't see the joy masses of people felt when they finally watched me hang." He curled up with his back to me. "No, Little One. One does not remember these nightmares as one remembers washing the dishes."

No wonder he'd been so adamant about not reliving them. My chest tightened. And here I thought my life was bad. It was hard, sure, and I had my inconsolable moments. Knowing so little about Vergo's past, I hadn't entirely understood, but now I did. I knew enough to acknowledge his pain and loss.

I silently closed my dresser drawer, took Vergo into my arms, and sat propped up against my pillows. Vergo struggled. I held him pinned to my chest. He pushed a bit more before finally collapsing against me, his body taut. He trembled all over. A sob escaped him. I held him tighter, resting my chin against him. He broke down into sobs and dug his claws into my shirt.

I cried with him. His pain became mine for a while before a calm overtook me. He continued to cry for what felt like hours, but I didn't care. Something told me he needed this. I ended up falling asleep with him on my chest, getting woken by Bela. Eyes itchy from crying, I rubbed them.

Bela stood in the doorway with a hand on the knob. "Mommy says come eat."

"Okay, be right there." At some point I'd slid down onto my side with Vergo lying against me. I slowly sat up. Vergo yawned, his ears stretching behind him, making his eyes look like little slits as he stretched his front legs.

"I'm going to stay here, if you don't mind," Vergo said.

I affectionately scratched his head and joined the

rest of my family for a holiday lunch. He felt better. I felt better. He needed a bit more time to recover from letting go of all that negative energy.

***

Vergo made good on his promise to talk about my worries the next day. He was back to his attentive, observant self. The dark cloud was gone. Pain loomed around him, but no longer controlled his moods.

I sat at my desk with Vergo in front of me, sitting between a stack of books and a messy pile of sheet music. I'd practiced every day but Seven's Seed. "I think we need to do that stem thing you mentioned."

"I think you're right, unfortunately. Losing Bylan's protection at the school is a major blow. She'll grow bolder. We need to do something about your principal, and quickly."

"Should Bela stay home? Is it safe for her to go to school anymore?"

"That's a good question." He thought for a moment. "This has become a fine balance between hiding what we know and keeping ourselves safe. Go get your mother. I'd like to speak to her without causing your father distress."

I did as told, pulling her away from reading while Dad napped beside her on the couch. Mom raised an eyebrow, then set her book down and followed me back to my room.

Vergo moved to the edge of my desk and curled his tail around his paws. "Greetings, madame. There are important matters I would like to discuss with you."

"Oh, um, okay." Mom folded her arms and leaned against the doorframe.

"Mia and I are concerned about Bela's safety at the

163

school. Bylan has been removed from his post for mysterious reasons. We believe that this may make Bela more vulnerable to the foe at hand."

Mom's eyes widened. "He was fired?"

"We're not sure. He was either fired or left for hasty reasons. He could've been threatened for all we know. The reality is he's no longer there to protect your youngest. This concerns me deeply."

"I can't send either of my children back to that school then. This is terrible. Mia, we're going to have to find another school for you and your sister."

"One that'll happily enroll a Dark?" I said.

Mom opened her mouth to retort, but stopped. "Crap. You're right."

Vergo said, "Let Mia and me scope things out, get a feel for what the enemy is up to."

"No. It's too dangerous."

"We can protect ourselves. It'll be alright."

"Absolutely not."

"Mom, it'll be okay. I'm not afraid." As thankful as I was for knowing she worried about my safety, I needed to figure out what Mr. Redd was up to.

Mom gave me a pained smile. "That's very brave of you, sweetie, but I don't want to risk it. We're already bound by a vow of silence."

"Then you know we can't hide forever. We have to do something about it."

She let out a resigned sigh. "Let me go call Sanctus Bylan. We'll see what he says." She walked off, the tail of her blouse billowing behind her.

Vergo stared into the kitchen. "That went about as well as expected."

"Maybe we shouldn't have said anything to her."

"No, we need to keep Bela safe. We'll figure something out." He studied my sheet music pile. "I have an idea. May I teach you something?"

"Teach me what?" I said. Vergo hadn't taught me anything beyond the protection circle I kept fully charged around the house. He also coached me through power circles and corrected my violin posture. He had to be part of the reason I was able to learn everything so fast.

"I think it would benefit us all greatly if you learned how to do remote scrying. The only challenge is we'll need something from the person we intend to scry."

"Mr. Redd?"

"Exactly. We need to go to school next week."

Mom returned and waved me over, eyes livid. "Sanctus Bylan wants to talk to you," she said with forced calm.

Vergo and I exchanged confused looks. I headed into the kitchen, put the vine to my ear and it coiled around, leaving a leaf in front of my mouth. "Hi, Bylan," I said, unsure if he was angry, too.

His resonant voice filled my ear. "Hi, Mia. I thought of calling you sooner, but I didn't want to interrupt your holiday vacation."

I didn't care about that. Normally, I would've observed formalities and asked him how his holiday was, but I didn't have the patience for it today. "What happened? Bela came running to me, all upset. The front desk lady said she spoke with a ghost outside your office."

A leaf tickled my ear with a sigh. "Damien has been keeping a close eye on me all year, even before the Payton incident. It got worse after that. I'm sorry. I was so deep in thought that I forgot about the letter you left on my desk."

My stomach flopped and I felt all the color drain from my face. Oh, no.

"He got to it before I did. He read the whole thing and confiscated it."

Oh, no. Oh, no. Oh, no. He knew I was receiving lessons from Ms. Weever. He had to be anything but thrilled to find out I was keeping contact with her. And that Bylan was helping.

"Mia, what was in that letter?"

"Nothing about the demon stuff. I returned my completed quizzes and asked her about Mr. Muradon."

"Nothing that compromised the secrecy of our intention to expose him as the enemy?"

"No. It was a short letter. I asked her how she was doing." Vergo stood at my feet, looking up at me. My face heated. "And I asked her if she liked Mr. Muradon and stuff when they went to school together."

The vine fell silent for a moment. "Simple gossip. So then he's having me fired for helping you stay in touch with a former staff member."

"Why? That's not fair."

"It's a code violation. It's unprofessional to do what I did."

"Couldn't they have told you to stop or something?"

"Not when there's a demon about. No. While the letter appears innocent, it implies that Lyra's aiding you. The fact that she helped you locate the dabuk box means she's a threat to whatever scheme he's part of, which means she's grooming you to be a threat as well.

And by me helping the two of you, I've marked myself as a threat as well."

"But you're a Light. Can't you talk to the school board? There has to be someone there that'd believe you if you told them the truth about Mr. Redd."

"I thought about it. Damien must've known I'd consider that course of action. He somehow found out about my expulsion from the Order of Leo. He told me that if I went to the school board to make any complaints or wild accusations, as he put it, he'd inform the board about my anathema status, which would make them side with your principal. So no, we're on our own in this. We have to find another way to expose him without making it look like we're crying wolf."

"What do we do now?" My heart sank to my feet.

"We regroup. All is not lost. We'll stop him and his demon one way or another, and then we will focus on the Order of Tenebron. We can do this."

Chapter 12

Bylan was so confident. I was not, especially after I asked Vergo to explain what he meant by divide and conquer. He said it was a war reference. One way to defeat an enemy was to divide an army into smaller, more manageable chunks and destroy them piece by piece. First, Mr. Redd had removed Ms. Weever, and then Bylan. Deren had almost been removed and we weren't allowed over Sussi's house, further dividing my army of allies. Vergo tried to comfort me. I felt ready to fold under Tradereth's pressure to strike a bargain with her. I couldn't face an archdemon alone. And the longer this went on, the more she would make me and everyone I cared about suffer.

"You're ruminating again," Vergo pointed out from his side of the car. We were on our way to the club bandyll facilities for tryouts. I'd almost decided against trying out. Sussi told Kelsi about my uncertainty. Kelsi intercepted me between classes before Seven's Seed break and urged me to try out, promising to buffer me from Gwen should her ugly side show its face.

That was the last bit of the motivation I needed to ask Dad about club bandyll. He was ready to head out before my alarm went off to get up and shower. I barely ate enough breakfast by the time he had my bag in the trunk. If it weren't for Mom, we both would've forgotten my water jug.

I sat in the back with my jug secured between my feet, the ice cubes rattling every time the car turned. The Fire engine hummed away under the hood and Dad had the song stone on. A bunch of men and women talked about the holiday break and how pro bandyll teams were getting ready for the second half of the season.

Ruminating was a fancy word for thinking a lot about something. It's what Vergo said every time he caught me thinking about Tradereth and her bargain. It was how he got me back to thinking about what I could control, instead of feeling overwhelmed by what I couldn't.

I took a deep breath and pet him to let him know that I'd heard his words. I could try out for club bandyll. I could ignore Gwen if she decided to be a jerk. I could focus on what I wanted the coach to see. I could control how I performed during try outs.

Yes, bandyll was a great distraction from all my problems. I sat up straighter.

A giant oblong cylinder of a building rose up before us. Big red letters that probably lit up during sporting events read "Charming Wash Arena." Sections of glass rose from ground to roof along the front, framed by massive roots that rose up and ringed the edge of the roof. Several blocks of restaurants sat opposite the entrance and a massive parking lot lay next to everything, with a pair of hotels at the end.

Dad turned down a road that led to the massive facility and parked among the car cluster in the last bit of morning shade created by the arena. Several more cars pulled into the spaces next to us as other girls retrieved bulky sports bags from trunks. In his excitement, Dad carried my bag for me. I and several other girls I didn't recognize converged on a wide sidewalk leading to the arena. I did a double-take at one particular girl.

Ugh, Gwen. She narrowed her eyes at me. She walked slightly bent under the weight of her bandyll bag, a sharply dressed man walking beside her. Mr. Volaire. He looked ready for an expensive dinner party. He had the same tawny hair and striking blue eyes as his daughter, but his face was stuck in a slight frown and as if he were deep in thought.

The frown turned in Gwen's direction. "What are you scowling at? Such an expression does not become a Volaire, especially not in public."

"I apologize, Father. *She* is here."

I stiffened and drifted to the other side of my dad, shielding myself from view.

Mr. Volaire squinted at me in my peripheral. "Oh, the goalie from the A team."

"And the one we talked about a while back."

His face hardened. "Ah. That one."

So they had talked about me prior to firing Deren's father. I clenched my fists. I couldn't believe she'd stooped so low to get back at me. I walked close to Dad all the way into the arena. A bored usher sitting on a round stool manned the entrance. He wore a white dress shirt, black vest, and black pants. He directed parents in one direction and players in the opposite. Paper signs hung from ropes blocking off sections of the facility, including concession stands with their giant windows covered by ribbed sheets of metal. Despite the lack of cooking, a hint of popcorn and hotdogs lingered in the air.

Dad and I lined up behind a few other families separating us from the Volaires, whom the usher greeted by name.

Mr. Volaire said, "Good morning, Bill. Did you have a good Seven's Seed?"

"I did, sir," Bill said with a deep nod, almost a bow. "Very relaxing. You, sir?"

"Busy, but good. Business stops for no holiday."

"So long as business is good."

"That it is, that it is. Catch you later, Bill. And Gwen, do be a good girl and play flawlessly."

"Yes, Father. I will." Gwen headed for the locker rooms and Mr. Volaire hung back, inspecting a handheld device I didn't recognize.

Once we reached the front of the line, Dad handed me my bag and kissed my forehead. "Good luck, Mia. Play your heart out and I know you'll make the team."

"Thanks, Dad." I shouldered my bag.

Dad and Mr. Volaire politely greeted each other. Mr. Volaire said, "How's your youngest doing? My daughter is absolutely smitten with her. She doesn't go a week without mentioning how adorable Bela is."

"She's doing well and is having lots of fun with her Seven's Seed presents. I wouldn't be surprised if she worked for you one day as well. She has a knack for building things."

"Charming. I'll let her enjoy her childhood a little longer before exposing her to the rigors of hard work." Mr. Volaire winked and Dad laughed.

I followed the signs directing me to the locker room. Energetic voices drifted down the concourse. Bands of white reflecting from the overhead lights moved with me along the tile floor. There was an excited energy to this place, as if all the years of bandyll played in this facility had left a piece of themselves behind with every game.

A hand touched my shoulder as I turned for the locker room.

A sharply dressed man stood behind my shoulder. "Mr. Volaire. Good morning, sir."

"Good morning, Miss Evers. May I have a moment before you head in?"

I wanted nothing more than to run into the locker room. I sidestepped out of the way of two girls entering. Mr. Volaire moved with me. Vergo stood close to my feet, eyes locked on Gwen's father.

"Thank you. I promise I won't take up much of your time. You do have somewhere to be. I wanted to compliment you on your excellent performance this year with the Miners. Was that really your first time playing bandyll?"

"Yes, sir."

"Impressive. With raw, coachable talent like that, I'm sure you'd make an excellent addition to the Hornets."

"Thank you. I'm going to do everything I can to earn a spot on the team."

"Glad to hear it." Instead of happy, his tone was pure business. Did this guy know how to be happy? He waved me closer. Too scared to refuse, I shuffled my feet and he leaned in. He smelled of metal and expensive cologne. "As fine an athlete as you are, I heard about your heated conversation with my daughter. I understand she isn't always agreeable, but I expect you to never, ever talk to her like that again. If you ever have an issue with her again, you'll take it up with me and I'll handle it. Do you understand?"

I took a step back and my legs shook.

"Is this man serious?" Vergo said. "Mia, are you going to stand up for yourself?"

"I—"

"That's it. I've had it. Mia, I demand you take my collar off right now. It's time I put an end to this idiocy."

"Mr. Volaire, Vergo wants to talk to you."

His face morphed into blank confusion. "Who?"

I bent over and removed the collar. Vergo shook out his head. Mr. Volaire let out a small cry of dismay and took a step back. "What on Aardra?"

Vergo flattened his years. "Now you listen to me, good sir. Your beast of a daughter fully deserved every last drop of venom spat at her that day." He reared up on his hind legs with a front paw pointed at Gwen's father. "Your daughter is not some innocent little angel Mia suddenly felt like bullying one day." Vergo grew to his full human height in two seconds flat, his fur transforming back into his tunic, pants, and leather boots. He stood half a head taller than Mr. Volaire and held a pointed finger under his chin. Vergo looked at his finger, and then at himself. "Oh. This is convenient."

Mr. Volaire's eyes bulged out of his exceptionally pale face.

Vergo fixed Mr. Volaire with a stern look and gestured to me. "This child has been at the receiving end of your daughter's cruel amusement from the day she set foot in Toolena Mesa. Your daughter is a bully and a tyrant, two things I highly doubt you want used to describe your progeny. Why do you think a talented athlete like your daughter nearly missed playing school bandyll? She needs a serious attitude adjustment if she's ever going to take over your business one day. As of right now, she's breeding hate and resentment, not loyalty and pride. She's not a leader. She's an arrogant dictator. Since you're her father, I leave it up to you to decide whether this is acceptable."

Mr. Volaire stared, his hands held protectively over his chest.

Vergo narrowed his eyes. "Did you not hear a single word I said?"

Mr. Volaire blinked several times before straightening his posture, his eyes wild. "May I ask what are you…Vergo?"

"I'm a soul sent by the Light to serve this child here." Vergo protectively wrapped an arm around my shoulders. His whole body was cold, yet felt solid as a flesh-and-blood human. "I'm bound to her, having to go wherever she goes, so I have a front-row seat to all that happens to her. I can provide every last detail of the exchanges between her and Gwen if need be."

"The Light sent you? To assist a Dark?"

"Yes. Ask Sanctus Bylan if you don't believe me."

Mr. Volaire raised an eyebrow. "The school board is to review Mr. Redd's case for firing him."

"On what grounds?"

"That I cannot say. My wife hasn't informed me as it's none of my business, but she's upset with the development. She's rather fond of the old man."

"I can assure you Mr. Redd is not fond of him. He seems to have an unusual dislike for Lights."

"Damien has been with the district for well over a decade. Toolena Mesa has had the privilege of graduating a handful of Lights during that time. If you have any issues you'd like to bring up, please talk to my wife instead. I'm not involved in such affairs."

Vergo nodded. "Certainly. So back to the main topic then. I'll make sure Mia upholds her end of observing civility so long as your daughter does the same. Do we have an understanding, good sir?"

Mr. Volaire studied Vergo. "Light spirits cannot lie, correct?"

"Correct."

"I'll talk to her. She knows the consequences of lying to her father."

"Thank you. And now I have one question for you. Why did you deem it acceptable to have Deren Sevine's father fired for Mia's outburst?"

"I beg your pardon?" Mr. Volaire looked genuinely confused. "He was fired for stealing. It had nothing to do with the events at the bandyll party."

Vergo furrowed his brows at me. "Did we perhaps misinterpret? No, she—"

I stepped forward. "Mr. Volaire, Gwen bragged about getting Deren's dad fired and threatened Sussi's would be next if I ever talked to her like that again."

"Did she, now?" Mr. Volaire's gaze hardened with inward rage as his face grew pensive.

"I'm sorry, yes."

"So that's why they fought," he said to himself. "It all makes sense."

"So she didn't tell you to fire Deren's dad?"

His hard gaze focused on me. "Goodness no. She plays no role in such decisions. I talk to her about goings on and let her test decision-making ideas on me, but she's decades away from deciding who is fired or hired. Mr. Sevine's grievous lack of judgement earned him his dismissal. I don't understand what motivated him to do such a thing after twenty years of loyal service."

"This is most certainly a peculiar turn of events. I hope you get all sorted out, Mr. Volaire."

"Thank you. Anyway, we best let Mia get ready for tryouts. The Hornets have been hurting for an exceptional goaltender. Thank you both for your time." He gave us both a slight bow and headed off, his stride purposeful and confident.

Vergo watched him leave. "Decent fellow. I think he had no idea about his daughter's true nature. She's in for a nasty shock when she gets home."

I nodded. "If he didn't fire Deren's dad because Gwen told him to, then—" I was about to ask how it happened. Memory of the note from Tradereth resurfaced. Of course. She was the real force behind all this.

Vergo said, "Gwen must've found out about it through her father, and then lied to get under your skin."

"I hate her," I blurted. Despite all I'd been through, I didn't hate people. I wished they'd not hate me. But Gwen? Ugh.

"I think she's about to get her comeuppance for all her bad behavior."

"What's comeuppance?"

"Means she'll finally be punished. Now off with you before you're late." He pushed me towards the doorway.

I hurried down a hallway lined with pictures of bandyll athletes and tried to turn into the locker room, but an unseen force held me back. Did they magically bar the way for lateness?

"Ah, Little One?" Vergo stood in the doorway, arms outstretched and a foot in front of him braced as if to stop him from sliding. His face was contorted in a grimace. "You're about to enter a locker room full of minors. I'm not a cat at the moment and I appear to have a significantly shorter tether while in this form."

"Change back?"

"I'm trying. I don't know how."

I held his collar. I ran over and slipped it on his wrist. Since the spirit concealment charm didn't work on me, I had no clue if he was invisible to anyone else.

Vergo looked at the simple band around his wrist. "I hope it works or this is going to be rather awkward."

The hallway leading into the locker room was L-shaped. An empty first row of lockers greeted me, followed by louder voices chatting away. I poked my head in the locker room. Dozens upon dozens of girls donned bulky bandyll gear. A few looked up, including Sussi. She brightened and waved.

I waved her over. Drawing her brows together, she waved for me to come to her. I shook my head and waved urgently. She shook her head. I nodded and waved again. Rolling her eyes, Sussi slid over on her inline skates, towering over me.

"What's your problem? Get over her and get geared up."

"It's Vergo. I need to see if you can see him."

The annoyance in her expression softened into confusion. "Okay?"

I called to Vergo and he stepped past the bend in the hallway. Grimacing, he held his arms awkwardly at his sides, looking anywhere but at us.

Sussi's expression remained confused. I said, "You don't see him?"

"Should I?"

I let out a sigh of relief. "Thank the Light. It still works."

"What are—?"

"I'll tell you later." I grabbed her wrist and jogged deeper into the locker room. The leathery smell of bandyll gear filled me with excitement. I didn't realize how much I missed it.

Vergo slipped into the locker room, shielding his face with his tunic and giving me a flash of a muscular stomach before disappearing behind the first row of lockers. I snorted.

"What are you so cheerful about?" Gwen said.

For once, I felt like she couldn't hurt me. I felt emboldened as I removed my sneakers. "Had a nice chat with your dad. I like him. He's scary, but I like him, like Mr. Enti." Mr. Enti was the teacher who restrained Sussi during her fight with Nonaya. He was big and scary, but we all knew he cared about us. He simply lacked patience for drama. Mr. Volaire was scary, but he showed respect for others.

Gwen crinkled her nose. "You're lying."

"You wish. He's looking forward to having me on the club team. Said something about being an excellent addition to the Hornets."

She looked as if she didn't believe me. "What about the other stuff?"

Ah, so she did know her dad was going to confront me about what I'd said at the party. "We talked about that, too. He's going to talk to you again later. He was pretty shocked by what I had to say." Sure, Vergo had done most of the talking. I didn't feel like explaining my spirit cat to her.

Gwen shook her head. "I don't believe you."

It didn't matter what she believed. It didn't change the truth. I barely finished putting on all my gear when a whistle blew deeper inside the facility.

A man yelled, "Alright, ladies. Ten laps, ten laps. Go, go, go."

I somehow managed to stick behind Sussi as we spilled out into the rink. We organized into single file as we swerved up and down the curved edge of the court. The court looked bigger than the one at school, but that might've been due to the endless rows of cushioned folding chairs stacked high over the court. Parents sat sprinkled among the chairs, everyone's gazes fixed on us.

Students, staff, and parents had crammed onto the bleachers and all around the court during playoffs. Their presence motivated me to play harder, try harder for saves, and embrace a must-win-at-all-costs attitude. Imagining this arena packed with cheering fans gave me pleasant chills. I had to make the club team.

I'd done some running over break. I quickly learned that skating used leg muscles a bit differently than jogging. I blocked out the burning in my quads as much as I could, focusing on the back of Sussi's practice jersey to help myself keep up.

At some point during the laps, Vergo had reverted back to his cat form. He camped atop one of the goalie nets. Thank the Light. Literally.

A tall bear of a man wearing skates stood on center court. He watched us all and blew his whistle after the last girl completed her tenth lap. We grouped up in front of him, our breathing a chorus of huffing and puffing.

"Sounds like y'all got a bit too relaxed over break. We'll fix that." His gaze swept over us. "Welcome to tryouts for the U-13 Hornets. My name is Andre Tokket. You can call me Coach Tokket or Coach. I've led the Hornets for nearly a decade now. Over the course of eighteen years, I played in the NBL for various teams, including the Thunderbirds. I made it into the playoffs ten of those years and helped my teams win a Wayne Champion Cup twice. I've coached and assistant coached several professional teams, earning three more Cups. And now I'm here, away from all the hassle and politicking to help kids like you make something of yourselves. I don't tolerate laziness or poor effort. I build championship teams around players hungry for glory. If that doesn't describe you, then please see yourself out."

No one moved. Our breath was quiet. The whole arena was quiet enough to hear the central air humming away up in the rafters.

"Excellent," Coach Tokket said with a straight face. "Let's begin."

Like Coach Viro, Coach Tokket worked us through conditioning drills followed by drills that tested our passing, skating, aptitude in all positions, minus goalie.

I'd gotten better at passing. As a goalie, I had to in order to help my team put a stray ball back in play. I was a little better on defense, but I kept trying to snatch the ball as if I had a goalie glove on, giving the offensive group a rebound to send to the net.

The whistle blew on my latest accidental goaltending attempt. Everyone held their position as Coach Tokket skated over. It was like standing next to a bear reared up on its hind legs. Despite his gray hair, huge, muscular arms strained against the confines of his long-sleeved shirt. "What's your name, kiddo?"

"Mia Evers, sir—Coach Tokket."

"Mia, are you a goalie?"

"Yes, Coach."

"Great. Go suit up."

Best words I'd heard in my life. A hint of a smile touched Coach's face and he nodded towards to the locker room. I eagerly skated off, fumbling with the straps of one scoop, then the other and carried them under an arm as I skated up the curved edge of the court and entered the locker room. I barely registered what my hands did as I strapped on my leg pads, swapped out a smaller chest guard for bulky goalie's padding, and switched to a goalie helmet, scoop and glove.

Next thing I knew, I was standing in goal. A whistle blew. A shooting drill ensued. I stopped shot after shot, each thud of a ball in my glove or off one of my pads filling me with a spike of joy. I got down and ready, blocked a ball, dropped it off to the side, and got ready for the next shot. Block, drop, move. Block, drop, move. My reflexes came automatically, like I'd done this my entire life. It felt like ages ago since the championship game. Blocking shots made me feel alive and unstoppable.

"That's my girl." Dad stood on the other side of the flexible glass lining the court, a huge grin on his face.

I smiled to myself. Yes, this was the main reason I loved playing bandyll. It made my dad happy and proud.

Shooting drills soon turned into a scrimmage. Another girl suited up for goaltending. She must've been Mattie, the goalie Sussi had mentioned during our argument with Gwen.

Apparently I was put on the side with the less skilled players. Kelsi, Gwen, and several other girls peppered me with shots as my defense struggled to keep them at bay. Kelsi and Gwen snuck a few goals in only because I had moved to block another shot that swiftly turned into a second opportunity. I couldn't get to my feet fast enough to stop them. It was my job as goalie to minimize rebounds, and the defense's job to back me up when catching the ball wasn't an option. I was annoyed that those shots got past me. I made note of the sequence of events that led up to each goal in hopes of avoiding a repeat.

Coach swapped me and Mattie after Kelsi buried her third goal in the net. I spent the next fifteen minutes watching from the other side of the court as Mattie faced shot after shot, reacting a hair too late, missing cutting the angle, and getting caught out of position time and time again. Coach mercifully blew his whistle after the tenth goal snuck between her leg pads.

We took a water break and sat in the middle of the court. Like Coach Viro, Coach Tokket thanked us all for trying out and let us know that the final roster would be mailed out tomorrow. He politely bade us enjoy the rest of vacation and told us to stay on top of our grades. We carefully stood on our skates and Coach pulled me aside as everyone but Sussi, Kelsi, and Gwen rumbled off to the locker room.

He placed a giant hand on my shoulder. It was big enough to crush my skull. Thankfully, the man belonging to that hand smiled. "That was an excellent performance today, Mia."

"I let four goals in."

His smile broadened. "While goalies are the last line of defense, it takes a whole team to let one in. I can teach you some techniques that'll further your goaltending skills."

"I'd love that, Coach."

"Excellent. Welcome to the team."

Gwen rumbled closer. "No, Coach. Don't do it."

His smile vanished and he straightened to his full, intimidating height. "Don't do what?"

Gwen puffed up. "Put her on the team. We already have Mattie. We don't need her."

"Based on Mia's performance, I'd say she has earned herself a spot in net."

"She's a Dark. She doesn't belong on my team."

"Your team?" Coach drew his brows together. "Since when has this been your team?"

Gwen fumbled for words.

"That's right. This is not your team. You're not the one running it. And as far as anyone's alignment, I don't care. Bandyll is a physical team sport, no magic involved. It is about bringing people together with a common goal, not dividing ourselves over differences. Gwen, I value having you on my offensive line, so you better decide what's more important—working together or getting distracted by differences. And you better figure it out fast." He swept an arm out. "There are a lot of girls who'd love your spot. Now go hit the showers. I don't want to see you again until you've made a decision."

Shoulders hunched, Gwen skated off.

Coach placed a hand back on my shoulder. "You ignore that outburst, you hear? She's not in charge. I am."

"Yes, Coach."

"Now, you hit the showers too and enjoy the rest of your vacation."

I joined Sussi and Kelsi, who slapped me on the back and congratulated me on making the team. Kelsi said, "This year is going to be epic. I can't wait."

"Seriously," Sussi said. "I can already smell the brass from our next trophy."

Mr. Volaire and Dad stood in the front row, both of them looking unhappy. Great. They'd heard the whole thing. This was a part of my life I could've done without either of them witnessing. I avoided their gazes all the way into the locker room.

Gwen sulked in silence as we all showered and dressed in fresh clothes. I tried to hurry through everything. Gwen beat me out of the locker room, where both our fathers waited.

Mr. Volaire's eyes looked ready to catch fire the moment he spotted his daughter. He snapped his fingers and pointed towards the glass doors. Gwen started to say something. He shushed her. "Not a word. Get to the car. Now."

Gwen bowed her head and walked, her father

keeping stride beside her.

Dad wrapped an arm around my shoulders, his gaze full of concern. "Has she treated you like that all this time?"

I hesitated. Did I admit it or not? I didn't want him to get mad, not even at Gwen and her dad. "She used to be worse. Vergo talked to Mr. Volaire before tryouts, though." Dad gave me a skeptical look. Skipping the part about Vergo transforming into a human, I told him the whole thing on the way to the car.

Dad popped the trunk open. "I wish you'd said something sooner. I don't like hearing people treat my daughters like that. And tell Vergo thanks for me."

Vergo held his chin high. "My pleasure," he said, even though we both knew Dad couldn't hear him with the collar on.

Chapter 13

Mom drove us in on our first day back to school. Despite what Bylan told her over multiple ley line calls, she couldn't stop stressing over our safety. It was annoying, but Vergo pointed out that it was a way a parent showed love for their children.

Oh, fun. Something else an adult told me I wouldn't understand until I was older.

While I believed him, it didn't make dealing with Mom's anxiety any easier. She made us stick with her all the way into the main office. Coach Khamai greeted her warmly, but Mom held her in a stern gaze as she set her hands on the countertop. "Bela told me about Sanctus Bylan's sudden departure. I hope you can understand this worries me. I'd like to know who the school intends to tutor her from here on out."

Coach's smile strained to stay on her face. "I'm afraid I don't know. I'm not involved in the staffing process."

"Then can you tell me if the school is taking steps to ensure all our children are safe? Without Sanctus Bylan around, I fear for their wellbeing. There have been several major incidents at this school since we've been here, and all of them were handled with his help. And now he's gone. Why?"

Coach searched for words. She frowned. "I'd suggest you talk with Mr. Redd. I honestly don't know, and if I did, I wouldn't be allowed to discuss it with you. He might be able to say more."

Mom yanked her hands off the counter. Talking to Mr. Redd was probably the last thing she wanted to do, especially after the vow of silence. I'd gotten a few months of practice pretending I didn't know some of his secrets. I was able to bury the thoughts every time I saw him. But Mom? She'd probably struggle against the vow of silence and put herself in a compromising position.

Coach said, "If it makes you feel any better, the school was heavily warded over break. There are protection circles around every building. Wards and other protections saturate the fences, and the school board is in the process of hiring a new Light priest to tutor Bela and keep an eye on things. The school property also has wards lining all four sides. I think this is the safest the campus has been since it was built."

"That's good to hear," Mom said.

A door down the hall opened and Mr. Redd appeared. He brightened at the sight of us. "Mrs. Evers. What a pleasant surprise. No wonder you didn't answer your line. I've been trying to call you. Please come into my office. I need to speak with you."

Mom paled. Using the counter so the principal couldn't see, I squeezed Mom's hand, willing calming energy into her. I wasn't a Light, but she straightened up.

"Oh, good," she said, sounding anything but thrilled. "I need to talk to you, too." The words came out reluctantly. She hugged and kissed Bela, and then hugged me, putting her mouth by my ear. "Wish me luck."

"Good luck, Mom," I whispered back.

"Thanks. Stay safe."

I caught a glimpse of the terror on her face before she disappeared inside Mr. Redd's office.

Vergo padded off after her and bumped his head into the wood door. He shook his head out. "That eel bat. He warded it."

With no way to eavesdrop on the conversation, Vergo and I headed to homeroom. Hopefully, Mom would stay somewhat calm and get us at least one clue to go off of. Garrett and I waved to each other as we passed, and I caught a glimpse of Gwen and Nonaya sitting in the back of the room before sitting down. Gwen looked away, and Nonaya gave me a nasty look. I ignored them both and instead focused on morning announcements, bouncing a knee until the first bell finally rang.

I tried to hurry off to history class, but had to slow down to share our customary morning hug with Deren. We waved good day to each other and he jogged past me. Before I could take three steps, someone elbowed me in the ribs. I hunched over and reached back.

Nonaya looked down her nose at me. "Stay away from Gwen. Don't look at her. Don't talk to her. Don't even talk about her."

"Can I bite this one?" Vergo licked a cheek.

"I'll handle it," I said to him and took a step closer to Nonaya, resisting the urge to punch her. She so deserved it. "Don't tell me what to do. I don't care—"

"Or what?" she said with a smug smile.

I stood so we were mere inches apart. We were even in height, but she was bony while I had muscle from months of bandyll. She'd whined for weeks over the bruises Sussi left on her, who acted like her split lip and pair of bruises didn't exist. Bandyll was good at making girls tough. "I'm not afraid to get suspended for putting you in your place. Touch me again if you wanna find out if I'm serious." *C'mon. Do it, please. Give me an excuse to hit you.*

All the fight left Nonaya. She gave me a wide berth and mumbled something about me leaving Gwen alone. She disappeared into the mass of students, robbing me of a chance to vent my frustration. Oh, well. It was better I didn't do anything to get in trouble. I turned towards history class and stopped.

Sussi stood in the middle of the hallway, arms folded and a big smile on her face. Students veered to either side of her, paying neither of us any mind. "So glad I got to witness that." We fist-bumped and headed to our respective classes.

***

A large pillow with four tassels, some incense, and sage sat in the middle of Mr. Muradon's office. I hadn't seen the pillow before. It was big enough to sit on.

"Good morning, Mia, and welcome back from break," Mr. Muradon said. "Go ahead and set your stuff by the chairs. You won't be needing them today."

"What are we doing?" I sat cross-legged with my feet on the floor. The pillow was comfortable, leaving my hips a little higher than my ankles, and making it easy to sit up straight. All meditation techniques required good posture. I so needed one of these at home.

"Our first unit of the quarter will be on protecting your thoughts from demons. We Darks are under constant bombardment. To protect ourselves from their influence, it's good to establish some crucial boundaries. I probably should've taught you this sooner, but I got caught up in the whole balance unit. So on to the next. You know how to meditate, right?"

I nodded. "Ms. Weever made me learn it." I absolutely hated meditation at first. My attention wandered all over the place. It took me weeks to be able to focus on nothing but my breathing and heartbeat for five minutes. I'd cried a few times out of frustration. Ms. Weever made me get right back at it day after day, until one day I realized I was holding my mind in one place for fifteen minutes at a time. Now I could slip into a meditative state in seconds if I wasn't too stressed out over one thing or another.

"Alright, let's get started." He rubbed his hands together. "I have a feeling this'll be a short unit."

I wiggled around a little to settle into the perfect spot and set my hands on my knees, touching the tips of my thumbs and forefingers together. My tutor lit a smudge stick and wafted the smoke around the office with an owl feather. I straightened my back. It was very good at sneaking in a hunch.

Mr. Muradon moved a chair to sit in front of me. He rested his elbows on his knees and interlaced his fingers. "Demons can linger around humans without attaching and listen in on an unprotected mind. They unearth our deepest fears and turn them into reality. They discover our greatest hopes and sabotage them. They take our goals and tear them up. They find repressed memories and emotions and bring them to the forefront, torturing us and turning us into people we aren't.

"Thankfully, everyone has the innate ability to repel demonic probing, but demons can weaken our mental defenses and take root. By the sound of the stories floating around, you've already had your share of dealing with demons. This has made you vulnerable. Demons have learned that you're powerful and adept at your abilities. You're a tasty beacon shining into their realm."

I tensed. "They can see me without crossing into the realm of the living?"

"They can see your energy as they can see mine and your friends and family. We look like little blots of light to them until they take a portal into our realm. That's why demons and ghosts often look like shadows or blots of darkness to us. Darks are bigger, shinier blots. And with all your interactions with demons at such a young age, you've turned yourself into a tantalizing soul."

Vergo lay curled up under the other chair. "He's right, unfortunately. This may be why Tradereth has taken great interest in you."

"Why does it make me tantalizing?"

Mr. Muradon sat up straight. "Because you've proven yourself to be an excellent instrument of chaos, should a demon take over you. If they can control every last one of your thoughts and emotions, they can persuade you to carry out every last whim and will of theirs. For the demon, it's like being alive again."

I tried to say something about Payton, but my mouth wouldn't open. It was like my jaw muscles became stuck closed and my lips went limp. All I could do was breathe through my nose. The little triangle of silver hanging from my necklace warmed against my skin.

Oops. Thank goodness for the charm.

Maybe something like that had happened to Payton. Mr. Redd could've directed demons to him, helping shape him into the monster he became. And since that was all he knew, it's who he was in limbo.

Okay, time to change my focus to the lesson at hand.

Either Mr. Muradon didn't notice my sudden inability to speak or he chose to ignore it. His face grew serious as he lit an incense stick. "Becoming more adept at our alignment is a double-edged sword. While we can better protect ourselves and others, and better channel our abilities, we also increase our risk of demonic influence."

"No wonder Ms. Weever was so mad the other schools didn't teach me much."

He winced. "Yep, not the smartest decision those schools made. Anyway, this meditation technique is called patreycit, the ancient term for 'protect the mind.' It places an energy barrier around your mind that demons can't easily penetrate. If you practice this once a week, they'll never get in. So let's get started. Sit comfortably with your back straight. Slowly close your eyes as you count backwards from five in your head."

I did as told, everything going calm and dark at the end of the count. I inhaled the scent of sage and incense. My limbs grew heavy and my head felt like it floated, detached from the rest of my body, light and free.

Knock, knock, knock.

The rap of knuckles on wood, sounding like three loud bangs, startled me out of my meditative state.

The office door opened and Coach Khamai stuck her head in. "I'm sorry to interrupt, but we got a call from Mia's mom. Mia, grab your things and go sit by the front desk."

"What's going on?" Mr. Muradon said.

"Something happened at the mine. She's on her way to the school to collect both Mia and Bela."

I felt all the color drain from my face. "What happened?"

Coach shook her head, making her tight curls bounce. "I don't know. That's all I could gather before she ran off."

I grabbed my backpack and violin, and waited in one of several chairs by the front entrance. Seven's Seed decorations were plastered to the walls. All the charms that'd hovered near the ceiling were gone. My imagination ran wild with possible scenarios. Maybe there'd been an explosion or a collapse and my dad was either seriously injured or dead. I pictured the three of us standing over him lying on a gurney at the hospital, barely clinging to life.

"Calm down, Little One," Vergo said, touching my arm with a paw. His voice was full of concern. "We don't know what happened. For all we know, there could've been an accident and they sent workers home to make room for cleanup. He could be perfectly fine."

I wanted to believe him, but my imagination was too persuasive. I hugged him to my chest.

The echo of two pairs of footsteps carried into the front office, followed by the people making them. Bela and Gwen. I sat up. What was *she* doing with my sister?

Gwen dropped to one knee and gave Bela a hug. "See you later, Bela. Hope everything's okay."

Bela hugged her back. "Bye, Gwen."

My chest tightened with rage. How could she hug someone like Gwen? Why did she even like her? Why did they like each other?

Standing, Gwen spotted me and froze a moment before leaving the way they came, her footsteps stomping down the tiled floor. Bela came over and sat next to me, her feet dangling a good foot off the floor. Vergo hopped onto her lap and rubbed against her.

"Greetings, Tiny One."

"Kitty." Bela wrapped him in a tight hug, making his eyes widen.

"Why do I subject myself to such torment?"

Time passed with agonizing slowness as we waited for Mom to arrive. Vergo purred away as my sister petted him, giving her a few licks now and then. It felt like the entire school day had passed before the glass doors swung open. Mom scooped Bela into her arms and told me to hurry. Vergo and I followed her to the car. I stuffed my backpack between me and Bela, and rested my violin case on my lap. The car launched into motion. I clung to the door and my backpack as we turned onto the main road. A car honked behind us. Our car's Fire engine roared and Mom sped down the dirt road. I dared not speak until we got home, which didn't take long.

I stepped out, inhaling fresh air tinted with the smell of cow. Mom's crazy driving left me feeling like I had a ball of worms for a stomach. I followed her and Bela inside, and checked for Dad in his customary spot on the couch.

He wasn't there.

The question sat on the tip of my tongue, but the wild look on Mom's face warned me to say nothing. My voice would only set her off. I cautiously took a seat on the couch. Bela ran for her blocks and busied herself with them. Vergo joined me on the couch, watching Mom's every move with open concern.

Mom paced up and down the length of the kitchen, running her hands through her hair. Her face was red and eyes watery. Normally, she hid in her bedroom when she got worked up. I braced for her to storm by me every time she reached the living room side of the kitchen, but each time she turned back towards the laundry room.

I fought the urge to get up and clamp my arms around her. If she could hold still a moment, then maybe she could calm down enough to tell me what'd happened. As a Dark, I didn't have any abilities to calm other people.

But Bela did.

Bela seemed oblivious to Mom's distress. She was completely engrossed dismantling a house she'd made for Vergo. I understood she was young, but it annoyed me that she didn't show more empathy for Mom's distress. "Bela, I don't think you shouldn't be playing with your toys right now. Mom's real upset. Did Bylan teach you how to help people calm down?"

Bela stopped with a block in her hand and looked at Mom. She dropped the block and ran over. "Mommy, what's wrong? Why are you sad?"

Mom gave Bela a gentle nudge. "Go back to your blocks sweetie," she said in a thick voice. "I'm fine."

"No, you're not. Your aura's all prickly." Holding out her hands over Mom's stomach, Bela stuck out her tongue. Her brows drew together and she grunted. "Mommy, I can't make the prickly go away." She breathed harder. "I can't make it go away," she said in a tight voice, and buried her face against Mom's thigh.

"It's okay, sweetie. Thank you for trying."

"She's probably taking on your mother's distress," Vergo said. "She's not yet powerful enough to override another person's emotions.

Mom disappeared with Bela into my sister's room. Crying sounded from within. I stood in the doorway. Mom lay Bela down on the bed and stroked on her lullaby song stone. Gentle, calming music mingled with Bela's crying. Sitting on the edge of the bed, Mom ran her fingers through my sister's hair. The cries slowly softened into tired moans, and then silence. I returned to the couch.

Mom reentered the living room with her head bowed, arms folded, and tear streaks on her face. She tentatively approached me, her gaze averted.

"I don't know how to tell this to you, Mia," she said in a thick voice. "Bela's too young to understand. I never thought we'd have this conversation. He's always been so careful about not getting caught. And then I thought he'd put all that behind him."

Dread crept into the back of my mind. "What happened?"

"I should've known," she said to herself, clutching her Seven's Seed necklace. "That's the only way he could've gotten a diamond like this. He must've gotten greedy and gone back for more."

"Mom, what happened?"

Fresh tears welled in her eyes. She turned her back to me. "You know how your dad was gone a lot for the last several years?"

"Yeah. You always said he was working."

"That's true to a point. He was working to find us food, new clothes as you and Bela outgrew yours, stuff we needed around the house, and so on. The whole truth is that he stole everything. Companies would fire him when they found out about your alignment. Coworkers' children would tell their parents about you, and that would be the end of one job or another."

"So then it really was my fault all this time."

Mom spun around. "No, Mia. Don't believe that for one second. Your father and I love you very much. It was other people's fear and stupidity that cost him his jobs and not you. Never you. You've done nothing wrong. Your alignment is part of who you are. That's it. You've done nothing to make people fear and hate you. The Grand Light Order and all those idiots are the ones teaching society to hate and fear Darks. Why do you think we turned down enrolling Bela in the Little Leo's Academy?"

"I thought—" I filed through memories from the day we brought Bela over to the Order of Leo. The Light priests had been so eager to snatch Bela up and stuff her into their academy while ignoring my presence. "Oh. You don't want her turning into one of *them*."

"Right. And Lyra was right about me not trying hard enough to understand your alignment and being as terrible as the rest of society. I'm sorry. It must be very confusing and difficult for you to grow up."

I looked at my shoes. "It is."

"I'm sorry. Your father and I want nothing but happiness for the both of you."

"What happened to Dad? Is he okay?"

Mom buried her face in her hands. "He was arrested at the mine. He was caught stealing precious gems. He set off a security ward and that was it. He was caught in the act. I received a call from the county jail. They'll call me again when they set the court date. Oh, Mia, I thought he'd put an end to this behavior. It isn't at all fair to put you and your sister through this."

"What'll happen to him?" All I knew about jail was that that was where bad people went for doing bad things. I believed Mom's explanation for Dad's years of thieving. It made sense—the being gone at odd hours, stuff showing up in our house in the middle of the night, Mom's constant anxiety every time he left, her offhand explanations for Dad's absences, everything.

"I don't know."

"What if it's a demon that made him do it? Made him go back to stealing stuff again?"

"I don't know, Mia. He's stolen so much in the past. I don't think a judge will care."

Such a tormented, malleable soul. He should've listened to his mother.

Tradereth's voice came from behind my neck, sending chills down my spine. Picturing fangs dripping with saliva, I hopped off the couch and backed away, but there was nothing there.

I conjured my protection energy shield and focused on calm. Mom's distress had to be more than enough to draw a few negative souls. I'd have to refresh my wards later.

"What if I can prove it? There's still at least one demon around. The timing is real suspicious."

No judge worth their salt would believe a child, especially not a Dark child. Give it up, Mia Evers. Your father is lost to the justice system.

Mom shook her head. "I don't know. I don't have a good feeling about this."

Your father is mine, child. He let me in well before I revealed myself to you. Give it up. I've already won, unless you'd like to strike a bargain, of course.

Chapter 14

Mom kept us home for the rest of the week. On the upside, it saved me from having to face everyone at school while my dad was in jail. On the downside, I had to take care of Bela and the house. Mom barely left her room, emerging now and then to eat a few bites of food I'd prepared. She spent time in the living room now and then, when Bela got worked up. Mom might as well have been a stuffed animal propped up on the couch. It stopped Bela's tears, but she was unusually quiet for a bubbly, social child.

Between Dad's absence and uncertain future, and Mom's and Bela's anxiety, I couldn't concentrate on anything, not even reading. Tradereth savored all of our misery, popping in now and then to thank us for the emotional feasts. My only escape was the conditioning runs for club bandyll. The rocky, uneven terrain forced me to concentrate on my footing and little else, allowing me to empty my mind of everything until I returned to the house. Running probably saved me from getting sucked into the whirlwind of emotions devouring our home.

Come Saturday, someone knocked at the front door. Since Bela was taught not to answer the door without any of us present, she hopped in place. "Hurry up. Someone's here."

I crossed the kitchen and Bela used both hands to yank the door open. Bylan and Ms. Weever stood on the front porch. Eyes stinging, I took turns hugging both of them.

"You two are a welcome sight for sore souls," Vergo said from his perch on a dining chair. "We should've thought of calling you sooner."

We entered the house. Ms. Weever closed the door and Bylan returned Bela's hug. He said, "You've been through a lot over the last few days. Has there been any word about your father yet?"

"I don't know," I said. "Someone called, but they wouldn't talk to me. Mom only took the line when I told her it was the courthouse. All she did was listen and then go back to her room."

"She didn't think it prudent to inform you of what the call was about?" Ms. Weever narrowed her eyes.

"I leave her alone when she gets like this. Talking to her only makes it worse."

"When she gets like this?" Ms. Weever's voice rose half an octave. "Is this behavior a regular occurrence?"

Face heating, I fumbled for words.

Bylan said, "It's okay. You don't need to explain. We'll see if we can put an end to it today. Where is she?"

I pointed to the bedroom door. "I'd wait for her to come out."

"Not happening." Ms. Weever threw the door open and stormed inside.

I stood behind Bylan, and Ms. Weever put her fists on her hips, taking in the lump that was my mom. Sheets and blankets formed a sloppy nest. Bare feet shifted and Mom sat up.

"Lyra," Mom said, sounding surprised. "What are you doing here?"

"Get up. Your family needs you."

"And I need my husband. Leave me alone."

"Your daughter called Bylan. She's worried about you. Get up and get yourself to the dining table."

Mom's tearful gaze found me cowering behind Bylan's voluminous white robes. Lines creased her face. She swung her legs over the side of the bed and sat there, head bowed, face hidden by long, dark hair like mine.

Ms. Weever shifted her weight to one leg. "What are you waiting for? Let's go."

Mom's body rose and fell with a sigh. "I'm trying."

"No, you're not. You're just sitting there."

Mom turned her head. "Go away."

Ms. Weever tilted her head back. "Light, give me patience in this moment." Lowering her arms to her sides, she stood before Mom and put a hand on her shoulder. Mom flinched. Closing her eyes, Ms. Weever concentrated for a moment. Her brows furrowed. "Hm." She retrieved a glass vial of a clear liquid from a hip pouch.

"What's she doing?" Bela said to Bylan. She stuck a finger in her mouth.

"Hunting," Ms. Weever said. She held the vial over Mom's head and whispered something to it. It momentarily pulsed with a silver light before reverting back to looking like plain water. Ms. Weever held the vial there for a long moment before passing it over the rest of Mom's body. Mom sat there, looking away from everyone, her shoulders hunched. Ms. Weever scanned every limb, every extremity, every last square inch of Mom's body for…something. She came back to Mom's head a second time, touching it in a few places before pocketing the vial. "Bylan, this is all you. There's something about her that's out of balance. I don't know what it is. She doesn't have an attachment, active or residual."

Bylan entered the bedroom, robes swishing along the wood floor, and placed a hand on Mom's head. He sucked in a breath through his teeth. "Brecca, how long have you been like this?"

"Like what?"

"This emotional turmoil." He draped a purple sash over Mom's shoulders. "Extreme bouts of despair, high anxiety, hopelessness, lethargy, and everything else you're feeling."

Mom thought a moment and shook her head. She shrugged. "I don't know," she said in a tight voice.

Bylan turned to Ms. Weever. "Be patient with her. This is a severe case." He took Mom's hands in his and rubbed her knuckles with his thumbs.

"A case of what?"

"We're not sure what to call it. I've seen her disposition in many people in my years at the hospital. It's like their souls are half-dead, their minds a torturous prison. In the meantime, we've dubbed it melancholia.

It could very well be demonic in origin, like the sickness Allosyr caused. Demons plant such seeds and watch the chaos unfold."

"Then what do we do? I came here fully expecting to exorcise her, but that's not the case."

"We'll do a blessing ceremony. It can help, but it won't solve the problem."

Ms. Weever, Bela and I helped Bylan set up an energetically neutral space in the back yard. Our yard was little more than a patch of dirt that lay open to the rest of the desert. Some plants were green in the middle of a mild winter. Most of the landscape was varying shades of brown and would stay that way for at least another month, until the seasonal rains arrived.

We set a lawn chair in the middle of a power circle. Bela helped Bylan draw in the dusty ground, lined the circle with crystals under his guidance, and he sprinkled various herbs over the space. Ms. Weever and I took turns using my violin to ward off the ghosts wandering the desert, along with any other negative energies that might try to attach to Mom.

Ms. Weever handed my instrument back. "You've come a long way since you started on the mbira. Your sound is much cleaner and your transitions between strings are far smoother. I think once you're fully grown, your fingertips will hit the notes with more ease. You're close as it is already."

"Thank you." Hopefully, I'd be nice and tall one day, a desirable trait in bandyll goalies. I was a few inches shorter than Ms. Weever, who was tall.

Bylan explained to Bela everything he did. She asked questions now and then, and he explained the purpose of the circle, the herbs, and everything else.

She took it all in with open curiosity. Once preparations were complete, they went back inside to retrieve Mom. They each held a hand and guided her onto the lawn chair. Mom's hair was a mess, her gaze distant and face puffy from days of crying on and off. I clenched my teeth. I wish Bylan and Ms. Weever hadn't seen my mom like this.

"Brecca, where's my sash?" Bylan said.

Mom blinked and looked down. "Hm? Oh. I don't know."

"I'll get it," Bela said and ran inside.

"Why did you remove it?" Bylan said to Mom.

"I don't know. I don't even remember taking it off."

"What's the last thing you remember before we came and got you?"

Mom thought a long moment, biting her lip. "You rubbing my hands."

Ms. Weever said, "What would make her forget a chunk of time?"

"A lot of things, honestly. Emotional trauma, ruminating, stuff like that. She could've been so busy with what's weighing on her that she could've absently removed the sash. Why? Are you worried it's something more sinister?"

Ms. Weever lifted an arm in a half-shrug. "It's what I'm used to dealing with."

"This isn't the first time a melancholia has reported life going by without noticing."

Bela hurried over to us, dragging one end of the sash along the ground and the rest bunched in her arms. I ran over to help. She said, "I've got it."

Not wanting to trigger a tantrum or tears, I let her

pass without my help, wincing as one end drew a line in the loose, topmost layer of dirt.

Bylan thanked Bela and draped the sash back over Mom's shoulders. He dusted off the dirty end before fussing with the sash so it lay flat. With Bela's help, they performed the blessing ceremony. Bela kneeled with her hands on Mom's bare feet. Bylan stood behind Mom with his hands on her head. He chanted words in another language, causing the circle to flare to life with white light. All the herbs he sprinkled inside the circle rose into the air and swirled. The aroma of lavender, lemon balm, passionflower, chamomile, and more filled my lungs, spreading a sense of calm and peace. I breathed deeply.

Bylan stuck a hand in the swirling herbs, and then moved like a martial artist, ending with an arm out, palm up. The herbs gathered on his outstretched hand. He tossed them outside the circle and withdrew a vial from a sleeve. He sprinkled Mom with the liquid and spoke a few more words in her ear. Her eyes blinked several times. She stretched her limbs as if she'd woken from a full night's rest.

"When are we starting the thing?" Mom said.

"We already did it," Bylan said. "How do you feel?"

"Oh. Like I finally got a great night's sleep for the first time in a month. And I feel calm."

"Good, good." He returned his sash to his shoulders. "I have a few charms I want to give you."

We regrouped inside the house, and Mom was gifted with a necklace and four bracelets to wear during waking hours, and several crystals to keep under her pillow. Bylan explained their purpose was to help her energies regain balance and repel negative outside energies. Grimacing, Mom eye's glistened at all the stones and jewelry. She put everything on and stuck the stones under her pillow before rejoining us at the dinner table.

"Gosh, I feel like a black cloud has been lifted," Mom said as she took a seat. "I feel more like myself." We all had a glass of chilled water. A bowl of nuts and dried fruit sat in the middle.

"I'm relieved to hear it," Bylan said as Ms. Weever lit a smudge stick. "Make sure you wear all that every day. You have a very severe case of what we call melancholia. You'll revert right back to your former state without them."

"Will do." Mom took one look at me and Bela, and buried her face in her hands. "I'm such a bad parent. I can't believe I neglected the both of you like that."

Jaw muscles flexing, Ms. Weever stared pointedly at the table.

"It's okay, Mom," I said. The words were automatic. Her shutting down like that wasn't okay. I hated it. I didn't know how to make it stop, especially when neither I nor my alignment had triggered it. "I love you." At least that much was true.

"Thank you, sweetie. I love you, too. Thank you so much for taking such good care of Bela and the house. I don't know what I'd do without you."

Ugh, more stuff I wished no one was around to witness. I felt a need to come to my mom's defense and reassure Bylan and Ms. Weever that my mom was a good mom. She had bad days and needed help getting through them.

"Relax," Bylan said, placing a hand on my mom's.

"Not only have you been through a lot, it's highly likely that a demon has amplified your reaction to everything. You weren't yourself because outside forces blocked you from reacting better. Don't be so hard on yourself."

Mom's gaze lowered to the table. "I'll try." Mercifully, her eyes remained dry.

We were only a week into a new year and I think I'd had all the crying I could handle from Mom.

"That's all we can ask of you." Bylan reached for the food bowl. "And this brings me to our other area of major concern. First, Deren's family, then me, then Jay, and now Brecca. I was hoping to avoid this, but I think we need to take care of Tradereth. We need to do another exorcism. Tradereth will only keep looking for more ways to pressure Mia into accepting her bargain."

"That'll be fun," Ms. Weever said. "Damien will be an even more unwilling participant who *wants* his attachment. We need allies. There's no way we can do this with just the two of us."

"I'll help," Mom said before I could.

Two? Why on Aardra would Ms. Weever not want my help? I'd proven myself an adept Dark, hadn't I?

"With exorcising a very powerful demon?"

"Yes. You yourself pointed out that I need to learn to face this stuff head-on, instead of hide from it. I can help, can't I? I'm an Air."

"Yes, every alignment is involved in an exorcism," Bylan said.

Ms. Weever said, "I certainly appreciate the offer, Brecca, and I'm glad you want to help. I'd like to warn you that you'd be putting your life on the line. We exorcised a demon from Amity last year, and it nearly overpowered us before escaping back to the demon realm." Her icy gaze turned to me. "A certain Mia Evers foolishly decided to give us a hand without realizing the risk."

"And what would've happened if she hadn't helped?" Vergo said from the chair next to me.

"Not another word out of you," Ms. Weever said. "I haven't forgiven you for your transgressions."

"Nor do I ever expect you to. That doesn't change the fact that Mia helped the both of you when you desperately need it."

"I want to help, too." As scared of standing up to Ms. Weever as I was, I held her glare of death. "You're not the one she's constantly pushing to strike a bargain to make her stop messing with my family and friends. I want to help with the exorcism so I can stop worrying about everyone I care about, including you."

"I think she makes a fair point," Vergo said.

"Shut up," Ms. Weever said, earning a heavy sigh out of the cat. Vergo ducked his head, curling up on the chair and out of my tutor's sight. Ms. Weever's glare softened a fraction. "I understand you want to put Tradereth in her place so she can't meddle with any of us ever again, but you don't understand how dangerous exorcising an archdemon is. I dare say we got lucky the first time around. I don't think she was ready for a fight, so she fled."

Bylan said, "I have mixed feelings about letting you help, Mia. It's as dangerous as Lyra says."

"Can I help?" Bela said.

Everyone told her no.

"Absolutely not," Mom said. Bela's lip quivered with impending tears. Mom tapped my sister's quivering lip. "You'll be in charge of protecting the house instead. It's going to be a very important job. None of us will be able to do that, but you will. That's how you're going to help, okay?"

Bela pouted as she considers Mom's words. "Okay."

I inwardly let out a breath of relief. Tantrum averted. Still, that left one burning question unanswered. I turned to Mom. "So what about me?"

Bylan said, "If we do this right, I think we can include you, but only if you promise to protect yourself should things go wrong."

"And that means no playing your violin without permission," Ms. Weever said.

"I promise," I said with a nod. "Anything to be a part of the exorcism."

Bylan turned to Mom. "Are you okay with this?"

She gave the Light priest a wan smile. "No, but I don't think it's fair to leave her out."

"And are you willing to help?"

"Yes. I have to protect my family. I have to do something right."

Bylan nodded and stroked his chin. "So then this means we need to find a Fire, Water and Earth willing to help us. Amity will say yes, providing us a Kindred. Kindreds technically aren't part of the exorcism ritual, but that Garrett Antcil lad certainly helped in the battle with Payton. I'll ask around for the last three."

"I will, too," Ms. Weever said. "So how are we going to drag Damien into that cavern under the Order of Leo?"

"Looks like there's another kidnapping in our future," Bylan said with a wan smile. "We have carefully orchestrate this one. Tradereth is probably anticipating this move."

Chapter 15

I was forced to babysit Bela on the day of Dad's trial. I'd begged and pleaded. I wanted to be there to support him, to have a chance to speak in his defense. I didn't care that I was a Dark and that people didn't want to hear about demons being involved. Like Mom, they needed to learn to face this ugly truth. Demons were out there, up to no good, and people like my dad suffered because of it. I pointed this out to Mom. She shook her head.

"Absolutely not. You're both staying home. I don't want you to see your dad like this. It's already hard enough on him."

"But—"

"No. My answer is final. I never want you to see your dad as a criminal. I don't want to hurt you with such memories. And I don't want your dad to see you from the other side of the courtroom. Think of how much that'd crush him."

Vergo had his collar on today. He sat by my feet, watching events unfold. "I know you don't want to hear it, Little One, but it's best that you stay home. I urge you to respect your mother's wishes."

I sighed through my nose. Neither of them understood. I wanted the chance to defend my father, and not leave it up to a bunch of strangers to decide Dad's fate based on the evidence they had.

Mom grabbed her purse and the car keys. Bela and I stood by the door as Mom opened it. She gave us quick kisses goodbye.

"Bela, please behave for Mia. Play with your toys, practice the stuff Sanctus Bylan taught you, and listen to your sister."

"Yes, Mommy," Bela said.

Mom closed the door behind her.

Despite repeatedly being told no, I wanted to throw the door open and bolt into the car. The Fire engine roared to life. Just no. She couldn't leave me behind like this. Any moment and the door would swing open, Mom would wave me over and together we'd head to the courthouse.

The engine's hum drifted farther and farther away, until I could no longer hear it.

I ran to my room and closed my door. I threw myself onto my bed, flopping face down. I didn't know whether to cry or scream. Instead, I settled for staring at the sunbeam shining on my bedroom floor, warm and indifferent to what went on in my life.

Cat paws walked up my back, stopping at my shoulder. "Go away." I rolled onto my side and curled up into a ball.

"Would that I could, Little One," Vergo said, "but we are bound together by forces beyond our control."

"Why didn't you convince my mom to take me with her?"

Vergo tried to sit on the edge of my bed. I pushed him off. He settled for sitting in the sunbeam, his blue-eyed gaze annoyingly patient. "Because if I were your father, I wouldn't want you to see me like that, either. My one son that survived got to watch me get whipped and beaten, worked like a beast, and slowly starved to the brink of death. I'll never forget the rage and pain in his eyes." He hung his head. "If I could go back and shield him from all that, I would. If I were your father, I wouldn't want you to see me treated as a criminal. I'd want you to always remember me as a loving parent and provider."

"But the judge and everyone else don't know about the demon. Tradereth had to have made him go back to stealing. It changes everything. He shouldn't be punished for something he wouldn't have chosen to do on his own."

Vergo fixed me with a flat gaze. "Think how that sounds in a world that hates Darks and doesn't want to be reminded that such things exist."

He was right, but I looked away. I wasn't in the mood to admit I was wrong.

Bela stood in my doorway, frowning. When had she gotten there? "Daddy won't be coming home," she said.

I sat on the edge of the bed, my hair spilling over my shoulders. "You don't know that."

"Grandma told me."

"Well, tell Grandma she's wrong."

Bela's eyes welled with tears. Leaving my door open, her little feet thumped across the house and out of hearing range.

Burying my face in my hands, I heaved a sigh. "I shouldn't have said that." I needed to go for a run to clear my head and take a break from thinking about anything, but I couldn't until Mom and Dad got back home.

"Dare I remind you to breathe?" Vergo said. "I wish I could make this all stop. I hate seeing you upset like this."

I flopped onto my back and stared up at the ceiling. I didn't like being like this either. I said a lot of dumb and mean things when upset, but didn't know how to stop myself. Fur brushed the fingertip of the hand I hung over the edge of the bed. I scratched Vergo's head. At least he didn't hate me for being a jerk. He hopped onto the bed and curled up against my waist, making my side vibrate with his purring.

Like always, a purring spirit cat was calming. My breathing slowed and my anger melted away into blank calm. I could think again. I needed to apologize to Bela. She'd done nothing to get snapped at.

I scratched Vergo between the ears and crossed the house on silent feet, ears straining for sniffling. The house was quiet. Not even any wandering ghosts meandered around the yard. Bela lay in her bed, hugging a stuffed animal.

Instead of walking in there and apologizing, I retrieved my violin. I had some sheet music from orchestra class. I quietly set up my music stand, adjusting the neck so it held the sheet music at eye level. I shouldered my violin, gave my brain a moment to adjust to reading music, and played.

The song was steady and gentle, the notes rising and falling like deep breaths, telling the story of a lone wanderer heading towards a sunrise. The tempo gradually picked up as the song progressed, the notes rising with the sun I saw in my mind. The wanderer's steps plodded onward, steady and determined. It was a song of hope and strength, one meant to inspire people to keep going.

I snuck a glance at Bela. She sat up, clutching her stuffed rabbit. The orange glow of her night light shone on her serious face. I played through the rest of the song, my fingers methodically working their way up and down the violin's neck, my arm guiding the bow along the strings.

The notes rose and quickened. The imagined wanderer crested a hill and was presented with a majestic destination nestled in a green valley, complete with a river. Whatever happened to Dad, we'd find a way to get through this. We'd reach the destination we desired.

Rabbit in one arm, Bela came out into the living room.

"I'm sorry for snapping at you," I said.

"Grandma says that was nice of you to play that song for me. It's pretty."

"Thanks. You hungry?" What better way to make up with my sister than with food?

Her little eyes lit up and she nodded.

I cut up some strawberries and kiwi for Bela to munch on while I made us breakfast burritos. The house filled with the tasty aroma of eggs, bacon, potato, and salsa. Bela and I ate together at the table with Vergo watching on from the chair between us. Both our moods brightened on full stomachs. She helped me clean up by wiping random spots on the bottom cabinets and pushing in chairs at the dining table.

To further make myself be a good big sister, I let her read several of her schoolbooks to me. Each book was about twenty illustrated pages, each page with a three- to five-word sentence. Bela haltingly read the words aloud and pronounced each one correctly. I half-listened while progressing through more of my Yuna book.

Yuna's father, the king, had denied her help. Her mother tried to persuade him, but he gave his final word and dismissed Yuna. Her mother, unfortunately, couldn't defy the king's wishes. Instead, she pointed Yuna in a new direction, telling her to seek aid from dryads in a neighboring kingdom. They were powerful magical people who might be able to help. Yuna set off alone on her horse, only to be attacked by the trees themselves as soon as she ventured inside the dryad forest. The leaves had a poison, causing her to pass out. When she woke, she was imprisoned in a dungeon made of stone and roots. She had no weapons, no armor, and her mouth was covered by a cloth that made her unable to speak.

Some robed person with green and brown skin stood outside Yuna's cell when the front door of my house opened. I stuffed a piece of paper between the pages and closed the book.

Mom shut the door behind her, her movements slow. Her gaze swept the living room, passing right over us.

"Hi, Mom." I tried to sound light and pleasant, but

I knew something was very wrong.

"Mommy!" Bela hopped off the couch and wrapped Mom's legs in a hug.

Mom stared off at nothing as she absently placed a hand on Bela's shoulder.

"Where's Daddy?"

"He won't be coming home for a long time."

"Like not until tomorrow?"

Oh, Bela. Bless your innocent soul.

"No, longer. Much longer. They connected your father to a string of thefts over the past few years around Marohu. He tried to steal from the mine in the same exact way as these other unsolved crimes. Your father admitted to all of it. He pleaded no contest."

"What does that mean?" I said.

"It means years of jail time. Investigators linked dozens and dozens of thefts to him. He's broken into various jewelry stores and such, and then pawned the items for money to buy food and clothes, and pay rent and other bills. He explained all this to the judge, who seemed sympathetic. Since Jay destroyed a lot of property, he has to serve jail time."

"For how long?"

"For too long," she whispered. "Ten years or more." She removed Bylan's necklace and bracelets, and disappeared into her bedroom.

Like Mom, I retreated to my room and sat on my bed, at a loss for words. Ten years? I'd be well out of high school before I saw him again. Bela would be in high school. We'd grow up without him there for us. He wouldn't get to watch me play bandyll. And what were we supposed to do about Mom?

I felt like I should be crying, but no tears came.

Maybe I was supposed to be angry and throw things, but my room was a blur of colors.

Well, Mom was home. I needed to go for a run.

***

Mom recovered somewhat the next day, determined to not hole up on us. She moved slowly, wore a pensive frown, and got upset over strange things, like dropping something on the floor. Bela kept asking me about Mom's behavior. I kept telling Bela to make sure to stay on her best behavior and do things that made Mom happy. Bela did her best to behave, but she was five years old and acted like it. Her neediness triggered Mom's short temper. Mom caught herself time and time again, apologizing to Bela after each outburst.

At least Mom was cooking, cleaning, helping look after Bela and even drove me to my first official club bandyll practice. Like tryouts, a line of cars trickled into the lot. "This is a really nice facility. When's your first game?" Mom said as she pulled into a parking spot. While her words showed interest, her tone lacked energy.

"Not for another month or so." I wrung a strap of my bandyll bag. I couldn't wait to feel the thump of a ball in my glove as I made a save.

"I'm looking forward to it. Your father would've loved to have been there." Her voice grew tight as she clutched the steering wheel. "You'll have to write him all about it."

"We can write to him?"

"Yes. And visit now and then, and talk to him on the vine. He isn't completely out of our lives."

"Can he come to my games?"

The wheel creaked in her hands. "No. Head on in,

sweetie. I'll catch up in a minute."

Vergo and I looked at each other. This past week had been a crash course in learning what topics would make mom cry. Anything that required mentioning Dad was a bad idea. However, since Mom mentioned him first, I thought it was safe this time. I hiked up my bandyll bag on my shoulders and followed a line of players into the arena.

Club bandyll practice was similar to middle school bandyll. We had the same warmup routine, similar drills to hone skills, stretching routines and overall practice flow. During the fall season, opposing teams had the same exact pre-game warmup as us. Apparently, someone had decided this was the perfect routine, so everyone did it. There were only two major differences between club and middle school practice. Middle school focused on a lot of fundamental skills and basic strategies. Coach Tokket taught us plays and honed our positioning strategies, making us do certain actions over and over until the whistle blew and my body moved without thinking.

No wonder Sussi, Kelsi, and Gwen were so good. They had so many strategies and tricks at their disposal. They all knew several ways to counter opposing moves and tactics.

I even learned how to anticipate shots. There was a fundamental flow to bandyll that involved using the curved walls and player positioning to create openings to take shots. And then opponents would stand in certain places to block my line of sight to a shooter in one spot so they could take a shot while I couldn't see. I even made Kelsi work harder to score on me.

Towards the end of practice, we scrimmaged one

half of the team against the other. Another stark difference between my two bandyll teams was the roster size. Middle school had only fourteen players per team, two for each position. Club bandyll had a twenty-six-person roster, two goalies and twelve each on offense and defense, making it possible to play against ourselves.

Coach teamed me up with Sussi and a bunch of girls whose names I struggled to learn. We spent most of the time with helmets on to protect us from flying bandyll balls and getting smacked by scoops. I spent most of the time seeing the backs of purple and gold practice jerseys. I learned everyone's number quickly. I probably wouldn't learn names until we all wore game jerseys, which conveniently had everyone's surnames on the back.

Gwen and Kelsi were teamed up on the opposing side, meaning Coach Tokket wanted me to work. Mattie, the other goalie, was on the team and in the other net. It was a field of purple on gold versus gold on purple. Coach blew his whistle and tossed the ball skyward. Scoops reached for it.

As anticipated, Kelsi came away with the ball. She spun past Twenty-Nine, who had a long ponytail that often blocked one digit or the other. Kelsi rolled to my left. Sussi and Eighteen trapped her in a vice, forcing her to pass. The ball sailed across the court and into the scoop of Forty as she caught air above the ramp. A shot came at my head. I deflected it with my scoop, redirecting it to Sussi, who squeezed past Kelsi and handed it off to Seventy-Seven. Everyone sprinted for the far side of the court, leaving me alone in net. Well, almost alone. Vergo camped atop the net, using it like a hammock.

My offensive line wove back and forth, moving the ball from player to player with swift, accurate passes. Three players wove through what was called the triangle formation, a strategy designed to slowly pull the defense out of position and open up a shooting opportunity. Seventy-Seven received the ball next to the net and shot. Mattie stuck out her glove, deflecting the ball back into play. Twelve players moved towards me like a flock of purple and gold birds on wheels.

Eight used the curve edge to skate up and around Nineteen, forcing her to give chase. Sussi somehow closed the gap as Eight came right at me. Sussi smacked Eight's scoop, sending the ball rolling. I gloved it and Coach set up a face-off to my right. Kelsi took the face-off against Seventeen and won. Sussi blocked access to the middle of our half of the court, forcing Kelsi to pass once again. Kelsi, Gwen, and Thirteen worked through the triangle formation, each of them taking a turn skating to the center point of my side of the court before passing the ball as one of my defenders moved in for the block. The goal was to draw the defense away from the middle, making it a one-on-one shot between me and the shooter. Their defensive line rotated in a wedge formation that always left two players in the middle of the action while allowing a third defender to help on offense. The offense shouted to each other, calling for the ball or where a teammate should move. My defense shouted to each other, calling out who to cover, slowly packing tighter around me.

Gwen rolled to the center spot with the ball as Twenty-Nine got sucked into covering someone else, leaving an open lane on me and my net. I squared off with her. She threw the ball. I lunged for the top corner, but the shot flew way wide and clunked into a scoop outside my peripheral. I turned. Kelsi lobbed the ball across the court to in front of the goal box. I swung at it, but it sailed past unhindered and straight into Eight's scoop. She buried the ball in the open half of the net.

The whistle blew, and the three of them skated into a group hug.

"Nice pass," number eight said to Gwen, who smiled.

"Thanks. Nice goal."

We reset with fresh legs on the court and began with another tossup. My center, number ninety, tipped it to my sweeper and the six of them charged onto the opposite court.

It was neat how each group played a little differently. Our starting line played fast and loved to attack the net. The secondary offensive relied more on passing back to defense for long shots using screens on the goalie. Most goals were scored off of redirections, meaning the offense bunched up outside the goal box and gave the ball a tap with a scoop, bumping it on a new trajectory and often past the goalie, who was in position to intercept the ball's original path. The more Coach Tokket mentored me, the more this became the only way anyone could score on me, besides pulling both me and defense out of position like the first line did.

Forty-four skated to the front of the center line, forcing a defender to draw closer to cut the angle on net. Forty-four fired the ball over the defender's shoulder. One of our teammates stuck out a scoop as Mattie reached for the high save. The ball deflected off the scoop and bounced between Mattie's leg pads for the goal. This time, my offensive line gathered in a group hug as Coach's whistle blew. We swapped out the entire lineup again and reset at center court.

Despite Gwen's flaws, she and Kelsi worked well together on offense. They always seemed to know where the other was without having to look. Their passes found each other more often than not, and they almost always got a shot in before losing possession as a team.

Kelsi skated the ball in close to the net, nearly squeezing past Sussi, who swatted at the scoop holding the ball. I pressed the side of my body against the vertical post, blocking off a sharp-angle shot. This left a good chunk of the net open on my other side. Great shooters would take advantage of a close slice of open net if I didn't cut it off. I angled a skate against the post so I could push off it if Kelsi crossed the ball.

Kelsi crossed the ball, sneaking it between scoops of two different defenders. The pass found Gwen deep into the wing. I pushed to the other post to cut off a sharp-angle shot from the other side. She rolled backwards and fired. I stuck out my scoop, but the ball skimmed the tip and into the back of the net.

Dang.

Gwen and the others did the group hug before she skated over to me. Her expression was calm, neutral, not one hint of a smug smile.

She said, "You would've deflected my shot if you were a little farther ahead of the net." Her tone was equally calm, not one drop of negative criticism. She sounded like Coach. "You were too far in. If you come out a little more when you swing around like that, you'll cut off both the sharp and far angles."

My brain blanked out. Where was the "you suck" comment? The smug smile? The usual Gwen?

"Does that make sense?" Gwen said.

Pushing confusion aside, I repositioned myself for a sharp angle shot, but with the heel of my skate against the post, instead of my toe. "Like this?"

Gwen skated backwards to her shooting spot and squinted. "Yeah. There's hardly any open net." She skated over to the bench before I could figure out whether or not to thank her.

"I wonder what her dad said to her," Sussi said, holding onto the net.

I flicked the ball towards center court. "No idea. She didn't even give us any mean looks in the locker room."

"I know. It's weirding me out. I almost miss it."

I playfully shoved Sussi, making her roll away. "Don't say that." We both giggled.

"I said almost."

Chapter 16

Nurse Kor sneaking me off to the hospital to save Deren had been crazy. Kidnapping her to exorcise her had been crazier. But sneaking over to Mr. Redd's house under the cover of night to incapacitate and kidnap him? I was so expelled if this plan failed.

Mr. Redd lived on the opposite side of town, surrounded almost entirely by open desert cast in silvery moonlight. There were a whopping three other houses in sight with lots of cows and horses in between, metal fences marking off where one expansive property ended and the next began. The farm animals paid the eight of us no mind as we moved from bush to bush, sneaking closer to a ranch house with light shining from several windows. Bylan and Ms. Weever had parked their cars on the other side of several hills. Nurse Kor coaxed the mesquite trees and tumbleweed bushes to stretch their branches and provide us some cover, making our movements easier. And Zekary, a lady's man of a Water that Ms. Weever had recruited, had provided us with water-filled goggles charmed to give us night vision. I lifted the goggles to prove to myself that it was nighttime and not dusk, that we weren't as easy to spot as the goggles made us look like we were.

Mom had almost backed out of helping. After Dad's sentencing, she'd called Bylan to tell him to find another Air. He somehow talked her off the ledge and convinced her to help out. And now she brought up the rear of the group with me, her hair pulled back in a braid to keep it out of her face, should there be an elemental battle with Tradereth. She and I both wore black yoga pants and black shirts.

Bylan and Ms. Weever led the way while holding various objects probing for wards and scanning for ghosts and demons that might alert Mr. Redd of our presence. Bylan had thrown my brain for a loop when I'd first seen him in black pants and a black long-sleeved shirt. I'd only ever seen him in his white robes, until tonight. I'd thought he was someone else when he came by to pick us up and drop his wife off to babysit Bela.

We crept within a hundred yards, and so far, nothing.

"You sure we're not acting too paranoid?" Zekary said.

"We're dealing with an archdemon," Ms. Weever said, her gaze fixed on two rods pointing ahead of her. "What do you think?"

"I'm more worried about the exorcism part than this." Zekary wore all black and had a nose ring, hair dyed blue, and nails painted black.

"Well, worry about this part, too. The demon may already know we're here and is letting us get close enough to trap us."

Bylan relit a sage bundle, and Mom made some hand gestures, spreading the smoke so it enveloped us. White sage was a natural shield against getting detected by demons. I'd frequently used smudge sticks so Allosyr hadn't been able to overhear conversations or see what I was doing. If Tradereth wanted to find us, if she hadn't already, she'd have to cross into the realm of the living.

Zekary whispered, "Oh, yeah. I'd totally forgotten about the time we—"

Ms. Weever shushed him. "Reminisce later. Anyone sense anything yet?"

"Just one person inside," said Ergon, the Fire Ms. Weever had recruited to help us. Ergon was a short, stocky man with gelled, spiky hair dyed red and orange to look like flames. Like the rest of the group, he wore all black, his jeans super baggy. He also had a steel chain looped from a belt link to a lower pocket at his knee. Ms. Weever had argued with him about not wearing it. He reasoned he could use it as a weapon should the need arise.

"Just one? What about his wife?"

"I'm sensing the same thing," Zekary said. "No pets to speak of, either."

"I never did a funeral for her," Bylan said. "Maybe they divorced. I don't recall her being at Payton's funeral."

Ms. Weever said, "I've heard him talk about her with Desi, though, as if she's alive and with him." Her rod crossed. She turned and led us around the problem spot.

"Maybe she's visiting family or something," Ergon said.

"All the better for us," Zekary said. "Means we don't have to deal with her or explain to her what we're doing to her husband."

"Then let's make sure we get this done right tonight," Bylan said. He and Ms. Weever guided us into the back yard, avoiding the blocks of light that spilled out onto the rocky ground. Gerund, an Earth Bylan had recruited, used hand motions to move the dirt so we could sneak silently. He was a bulky man, big and strong enough to carry a person on each shoulder and jog a mile without stopping. Mom helped Bylan cover us with a fresh round of sage. We crouched by one corner of the house, away from a neighbor's livestock and out of line of sight from the nearest house.

Bylan faced us all, his wrinkly face serious. "Lyra, Amity, and I will sneak in and incapacitate him. If anything happens, get back to the cars and get out of here."

"What about all of you?" I said.

"Don't worry about us," Ms. Weever said. "You'll all go to the school board, the Volaires, the police, and expose the truth about Damien Redd. Depending on what happens, he'll most likely be unable to conceal his secrets."

"What about the vow of silence?"

Bylan lifted a chain from around his neck, revealing the silver wedge of a silence charm. He held it in front of his mouth. "By the Light, the truth will out, thus I speak with Shinjan as my witness." The charm pulsed blue and shattered.

The charm around my neck shattered, too, the pulse of magic jabbing my chest. Mom reached for her chest, as did Ms. Weever.

"Problem solved," Bylan said. "If you tell enough people, the truth will reach the right ears. Even the Order of Leo might step in, but let's hope we don't have to resort to that. Exposing this mess won't help Darks."

"How will we know if something went wrong for the three of you?" Mom said.

"You'll know," Ms. Weever said. She, Bylan, and Nurse Kor snuck off to the front of the house, Ms. Weever with her lock charm in hand. Ergon held out his hands, softening the ground ahead of the trio. They moved in perfect silence and disappeared around the corner.

I tensed. I didn't like that we were separated. I understood the need to leave us behind. It didn't make things any easier to accept. I wanted to be in there with my former tutor, wanted to be at her side while we took steps to right so many wrongs.

I turned to lean against the house when a strong hand gripped my upper arm, yanking me away.

Ergon patted my shoulder. "Might not want to do that," he said. "Don't want to find out the hard way what kind of wards have been placed on the house."

Holding my arm, I backed up next to Mom and Vergo, and she wrapped an arm around me. That was close.

Everyone stood with an ear turned to the house. I strained for the sound of struggle from within, shouting, anything. With the exception of the occasional call of night hawks and winter desert bugs making occasional buzzes and clicks, it was silent.

We all flinched when a horse snorted. Zekary chuckled softly. "No, not at all nerve-wracking to wait like this," he said. Ergon and Gerund smiled.

Mom folded her arms. "How long should we wait?"

"Not much longer," Ergon said. "I sense them in the same room. I think they already knocked him out."

Zekary's attention shifted to inside the house. His brows rose. "Hey, I think you're right. Damien's heart rate is slowing."

"How do you know?" I said.

The blue-haired man smiled. "Human blood is mostly water. Waters can feel blood flow like we can feel out where water is hiding underground. We can also feel how fast it flows. Makes it easier to detect lies when interrogating people."

"They're heading out," Ergon said.

A moment later, Bylan rounded the corner with a vine-covered man draped over his shoulder. He moved laboriously, his breath heavy. Gerund hurried over and transferred Mr. Redd's inert body to his shoulder. The principal looked like a child compared to the giant man. He led the way back to the cars at a fast walk that forced my much shorter legs into a jog. Nurse Kor hurried beside him, staying close to her vines.

Gerund stopped. "Hey, hey, hey." Mr. Redd's body writhed.

Nurse Kor held both hands near him, her face tight with concentration. An arm lifted away from Mr. Redd's side, making a vine snap. "Bylan, help."

The Light priest huffed over and touched Mr. Redd's forehead. "Hold your breath, Gerund." Gerund inhaled deeply, and Bylan sprinkled something over the principal's nose. "Rest, child of the Light. I'll let you know when it's time to wake." The arm slowly sank back against the rest of the body. The hand hung limp. Nurse Kor's face relaxed. "Alright, let's hurry."

Gerund stretched into a jog, with Nurse Kor beside him. The rest of us did our best to keep up, but he stretched his lead to the cars. We caught up and everyone but Gerund and I took a moment to catch their breath. I breathed quickly, but the short jog was nothing compared to the rigors of bandyll practice, especially with goalie gear on.

Gerund stuffed Mr. Redd in the back of Bylan's car. Ms. Weever, Bylan, and Nurse Kor hopped inside.

Ms. Weever tossed her keys to Zekary, who caught them. "Crash it and I'll kill you."

Zekary smirked. "Relax. She's in good hands. Besides, that was ten years ago."

"And I haven't forgotten or forgiven."

"How nice," Vergo said. "I'm not the only one she holds a grudge against." Since he wore his collar for safety's sake, I was the only one who heard him.

Ms. Weever said, "Ergon, please go make sure Zek behaves. Brecca, go with them. Mia, get in here. You're going to help me."

I climbed in the back next to Nurse Kor and removed my goggles. Bylan and Ms. Weever sat on either side of Mr. Redd. Gerund's bulky frame settled down in the driver's seat. Vergo curled up under my feet. Bylan's car was a white limousine with room for six in the back seat, and held a small apothecary cabinet in front of the trunk. The seats were made of soft black leather, the seats themselves running parallel to the windows instead of two rows facing the front. Gerund slid a section of glass open and turned his head. "Where to?"

"The Order of Leo," Bylan said.

Gerund turned all the way around, his face incredulous.

"I'll give you more directions when we get there. We're not going to the basilica."

Gerund visibly relaxed and fired up the engine. It purred with the intensity of a growling lion. "Was gonna say. Does Zek know where we're going?"

"He'll figure it out," Ms. Weever said.

Gerund steered us onto the road, and a pair of headlights peeked over the top of the apothecary cabinet. Mr. Redd fidgeted again. Bylan placed a hand on the principal's forehead. The principal flashed a grimace before falling still.

"Mia, you're going to help me keep the demon suppressed. She clearly wants out this time."

"She?" Nurse Kor said.

"Yes. Demons take on aspects of who they were when alive, including their voice." Ms. Weever donned one necklace and wrapped the other around her wrist and Mr. Redd's in a figure eight. She handed me two necklaces. "Mia, do the same with yours."

They were identical silver bead necklaces with tiny runes engraved into each bead. I wore one around my neck and looped the other around my wrist. I hesitated. I really didn't want to hold my principal's wrist. This was the man who wanted my sister dead for being a Light, the man who had less than honorable ambitions for me and my future, the man who'd corrupted his nephew on purpose.

"I know it's not pleasant. Suck it up."

Wincing, I looped the second necklace around his wrist and held on.

Mr. Redd's body twitched. He groaned and convulsed.

Nurse Kor held out her hands in the principal's direction, guiding her vines to coil tighter. Mr. Redd flexed both arms and held his fingers like claws. The vines strained. Some snapped, allowing his arm to stretch farther. Ms. Weever held his wrist in both hands, and her face reddened as she tried to pull his arm down. A hand reached for me and his wrist twisted in my grip, turning his fingers towards me.

"Look out," Vergo said.

I let go, falling back in my seat. A length of black tar stretched between my palm and Mr. Redd's wrist. I cried out in dismay. "What is that?" I reached to tear it off. Ms. Weever seized my wrist.

"Hold still." She drew a small knife and stabbed at my palm.

I screamed, expecting pain to explode in my hand. I tried to pull away. Ms. Weever held fast as she pressed the dagger tip into my palm. There was no pain. I didn't even feel metal against my skin. Instead, there was a coldness and a frantic energy trying to soak through my skin. The tar writhed. Ms. Weever slashed at it, cutting most of it away. The end attached to Mr. Redd's wrist flopped onto his lap. Bylan dashed salt on the mass. The mass recoiled from the salt, creating holes around each granule before retreating inside Mr. Redd's arm. Ms. Weever stabbed at what remained attached to my palm. It froze, looking like a bunch of twigs. The coldness faded and what remained of the black mass flaked away, drifting upwards and dissolving.

"Okay," Ms. Weever said. "We'll do something else." She and Bylan slumped back in their seats to catch their breath.

"What was that?" I said.

"That was the demon trying to latch onto you in an attempt to free itself. Don't touch him again. She wants to use your inexperience to her advantage."

"Please don't tell my mom this happened." The last thing I needed was for my mom to freak out over an archdemon trying to anchor to me.

"Tell her what happened?" Ms. Weever said with a crooked smile. When she noticed my confusion, she winked.

"That was a joke, Little One. She's pretending to have no idea what happened."

"I don't get how he keeps pulling out of his sleep," Nurse Kor said.

"He's drawing on the demon's power to fight it," Ms. Weever said. "They both know what's coming. This is going to be an intense exorcism."

"You mean mine wasn't?"

Ms. Weever thought a moment, her gaze growing distant before nodding. "Yours was up there, to be honest. But this is going to be the second time, a rematch, so to speak."

As if Mr. Redd and Tradereth heard, he fought against the vines.

Nurse Kor twitched her hands and the vines coiled around the principal. "My poor babies are so mad at me right now. I owe them big time after this."

"Your vines?" I said. The nurse nodded. "They have feelings?"

Nurse Kor tilted her head and made a face. "Kind

of. They don't feel like we do. Plants know good and not good, and that's it. Like rain is good. It helps them grow. Too much rain is bad. It suffocates them. They don't feel love, fear, hate, sadness, and such. It's just black and white, good and bad. That's it. Their current task is causing pain."

However fast Gerund drove, the trip to the Order of Leo felt way too long. Mr. Redd constantly struggled against everything thrown at him. Bylan wiped sweat from his brow repeatedly, and Nurse Kor had fewer and fewer vines to restrain him. The Order of Leo shone bright in the night, lights positioned all over the castle-like basilica, illuminating its many turrets. We drove along the edge of the expansive facility, past several parking lots, and onto a road concealed by mesquite trees. Rocks bigger than the car rose up on both sides, and we plunged into total darkness around the next turn. The car veered down. This time, I remained calm.

Lights, spread out like spots on a caterpillar, illuminated the tunnel. The car's headlights shone on a spiraling path that led us deeper underground. I breathed slowly, urging my stomach to accept the endless turning with grace. A hand touched my stomach, and a cooling calm spread. Nurse Kor removed her hand and gave me a small smile.

"Saw you struggling."

I nodded gratefully.

The endless spiral straightened out. Two giant stone doors loomed in the headlights, the cave ceiling lost in darkness. The dotted pathway of lights arced to the ground, casting long shadows lost in the cavern ceiling. The headlights veered away from the doors as Gerund parked the car. Zekary pulled in next to us and the three of them stepped out.

Mr. Redd struggled again for a moment. Bylan retrieved the wheelchair from his trunk, and he and Ms. Weever strapped him in, going straight for the silver cuffs on top of the leather straps. Nurse Kor adjusted her vines so they wouldn't get pinched under the straps.

Bylan draped his purple sash over his shoulders as he led the way to the giant doors. The sun and a handful of Light priests were carved into one side, robed arms raised heavenward. The moon and more priests were carved into the other side, arms also raised. Between them and split evenly between the doors sprawled a contorted demon. Hopefully, this was how the impending exorcism played out.

"In the name of the Light, open this door." Runes lit up all along the doorframe and floor. The sun and moon blazed as well. The doors swung inward. Stone rumbled and then the doors stopped, thudding against something. Bylan and Ms. Weever exchanged looks, their brows drawn together.

"I take it that wasn't supposed to happen," Zekary said.

The doors had swung far enough for us to pass through single file. Bylan peered inside, hands braced against the carved stone. His hands fell away and his shoulders dropped. "No," he said in a hoarse whisper.

"Gerund, get these doors open now," Ms. Weever said.

"Don't bother." Bylan backed up, his face drawn and pale. "The room has been destroyed. There's nothing left."

"Maybe I can fix it," Gerund said. Bylan limply waved at the exorcism room. Gerund jogged past him and stepped halfway inside. His head turned one way, then the other, and his shoulders slumped. He turned back to us, a frown on his face. "That's not something I can do alone."

"How bad is it?" Ms. Weaver said.

"The whole cavern's collapsed. I can tell you it looks like a massive hole from above. We need about a dozen Earths to move that much rock."

"We don't have that kind of time to gather that much help."

"Even if we did," Bylan said, "the circle's destroyed."

"Can't you remake it out here?" Nurse Kor said.

"Not from memory. And I didn't bring any books with me. There's no way any of us could've anticipated this move."

"Again, something we don't have time for," Ms. Weaver said. Her unhappy gaze snapped to me. "You don't happen to remember it, do you?"

Cringing, I shook my head. "I'm sorry, no." I remembered reading the runes and playing their song, but the circle itself? No. I didn't have that kind of memory, especially when it hadn't crossed my mind that I'd need to do another exorcism so soon.

"So now what?" Zekary said.

Mr. Redd jerked in the chair. His head tilted back. A back liquid seeped through his skin, turning him into a black, humanoid figure.

Ms. Weaver went wide-eyed, her blue eyes full of terror. "Oh, no. Everyone help. Now." She jammed both necklaces on Mr. Redd's neck, pulling tight as if trying to choke him and the demon.

I took a step back as the adults swooped in. I had

my violin, but no knowledge of what to do as a Dark. The only lesson on exorcisms had been with Nurse Kor. And considering the demon's reaction when I touched Mr. Redd's wrist, it was probably best that I stayed back.

Gerund made some sharp hand gestures. Rock thrust upwards, enveloping the wheelchair and arching over Mr. Redd's lap. Zechary yanked water out of a canteen, threw it around the principal's torso like a lasso, and froze it, pinning the principal's arms to his sides. Mom formed a ball of air between her hands and shoved it in Mr. Redd's mouth, blocking him from speaking. Ergon rubbed his hands together. They glowed red and caught fire. He thrust his hands outwards, surrounding all of us in a ring of fire.

Bylan moved behind the wheelchair. The moment his sash touched the black forehead, an unseen force knocked us all onto our backs. The fire died, ice shattered, and a roar escaped Mr. Redd's throat. A thick tendril of blackness shot out of his mouth, the end reshaping into claws. Those claws dug into the ground. A second tendril shot out and formed a second set of claws. The tendrils morphed into two giant spider legs standing over us. A third tendril shot out, morphing into a head crowned with tree branches.

Finally. Such a weak vessel.

Ms. Weever stood and brandished a wand. Tradereth swatted it away. Wood clattered onto stone. The demon crouched over Mr. Redd and her round red eyes, turning towards me, curved with glee.

You'll do nicely.

Before anyone could react, before I knew what was going on, blackness enveloped me. My back hit the rocky ground and I bounced off it. Gravity pushed on me, pinning my arms and back to the ground. An icy energy surrounded and filled me, wrapping me in its chaotic joy, filling me with destructive power. I felt energized, a hundred feet tall.

And then I felt nothing.

Chapter 17

I felt a pressure over my mouth when I came to. Something scratchy pressed against the back of my head. I tried to move my arms. Something held them pinned to my chest. I popped my eyes open.

"She's awake," said a faraway, muffled voice.

My head spun. The interior roof of Bylan's car loomed over me in a blurry haze. When did I get in here?

"Mia," a closer, hysterical voice said. Hair brushed my cheek. A pretty face with mismatched eyes blocked out the roof. Mom's face. "Mia, are you okay? Please tell me you're okay."

I tried to sit up. Hands pushed on my shoulders.

"Hold still, Mia," Mom said, her voice sounding like I had cotton stuffed in my ears.

I squeezed my eyes shut, willing the dizziness to go away. I breathed through my nose. There was something over my mouth, blocking me from opening it. I tried to sit up only to have hands stop me again. I tried to speak. A muffled moan came out.

Bylan leaned over my other side, his aged face lined with worry. "We've magically bound your mouth for safety's sake."

What an Aardra for?

Mom said, "Bylan, please tell me she's going to be okay."

I pushed against the hands on my shoulders and made a series of sounds in a terrible imitation of speech. I willed them to understand that I wanted to be allowed to sit up. My chest rose and fell, my breath a high-pitched wheeze through my nose. What on Aardra was going on? Why was I bound all over and why wouldn't they let me speak? My head felt like it floated off the floor and the world spun anew.

A cool hand touched my forehead and leaves crept into my peripheral. "Relax," Nurse Kor said. Calming energy trickled into me, slowing my breath and dispelling the dizziness. My heart thudded against my chest and I desperately wanted to rip off whatever covered my mouth. The lack of mobility made me want to panic and struggle. I wanted to feel my arms move.

"Brecca, she'll be okay if we take the right steps," Bylan said.

The right steps? What had—? The sight of Tradereth coming out of Mr. Redd's mouth flashed in my mind. After that, there'd been darkness, a pressure, a sense of great power, and then me waking up in here.

Ms. Weever leaned in next to Bylan, blonde curls spilling over her shoulders. "Tradereth has anchored herself to you."

A voice whispered behind my ear, making my skin prickle. *Yes, child. You're going to be an excellent anchor. You're my instrument of chaos now.* Tradereth chuckled.

Oh, no.

"We didn't want to take any drastic measures without giving you a say in what we did."

Without giving—? I gave her an indignant groan that sounded like a child whining. I had an archdemon attached to me. We needed to fix this fast.

"Let her sit up," Ms. Weever said to Nurse Kor.

I sat up and hands dragged me backwards, leaning me against the leather divider that separated the driver's seat from the rest of the car.

Bylan and Nurse Kor kneeled on either side of me, Mom beside the nurse and Ms. Weever opposite her. Ergon and Zekary sat by the apothecary cabinet and Gerund watched on from outside, his bulky frame filling up the doorway. Vergo sat curled up under a seat by Mom. Every last one of them had lines of worry all over their faces.

Their distress is so delightful, don't you think? Tradereth's voice shifted to behind my other ear. *If only you could've seen the panic as I attached myself to you. They thought I was going to turn around and attack them right then and there. So silly, these mortals. No, I have what I want now. We're going to savor every delicious moment together.*

I let out a distressed groan. By the Light, please take this thing off my mouth. I strained against the white cloth wrapped around my torso from shoulder to hips. It held me in place, making me look like a partially wrapped mummy. I huffed through my nose.

Ms. Weever said, "If we're to release you, we need to suppress your alignment."

I sat still, a fresh chill going down my spine. Suppress? Mr. Redd had been an anchor for who knew how long without suppressing his alignment.

How cute, Tradereth said. *A temporary solution. Do they really expect you to go the rest of your life without being able to use your alignment? Would you want to live that way, child?*

No, I wouldn't. No alignment meant no way to protect myself or others, no more power circles, no magical protections. Despite the troubles my alignment caused, it wouldn't stop me from being a Dark and facing all the social challenges that came with it. Suppression meant Tradereth couldn't use me. Maybe? I wasn't sure.

"Would you agree to that?" Ms. Weever said.

What choice did I have? Stay trapped like this or at least be able to talk while trapped another way? I nodded. Mom squeezed my knee, her eyes watery.

"Oh, sweetie, I wish I'd never let you come."

She's the reason you were allowed to come. The Light priest and your former tutor would have never agreed to it without her consent. If your mother was in her right mind, she never would've agreed either. She's so easy to manipulate. A little nudge here, a planted thought there, and now I have a new anchor. Suppressed or not, it doesn't matter. I'll accomplish my goals. Let your friends and family think they're safe.

So this was how Yuna felt when she woke in the dryad king's dungeon, trapped and powerless, in no control whatsoever. How were we going to fix this?

Ms. Weever placed one hand on my forehead and

the other on my sneakers. She breathed a heavy sigh through her nose and closed her eyes. She took one deep, noisy breath after another, and soon an invisible force tugged at my feet and pushed on my head. Something inside me—my energy?—sank towards my feet, shrinking away until it vanished. Ms. Weever spoke the names of several binding runes. Heat flared on my forehead and feet. My skin stung. The car tilted one way and everyone tilted the other as I slumped sideways. Mom and Bylan guided me upright.

An emptiness sat in the pit of my stomach. Where my bones were, there was nothing, as if they'd become hollow. The rest of my body held their shape around where the bones used to be. I tried to conjure my protection circle. My awareness hit a mental wall. I pictured the golden energy shield, but it was no more real than a daydream.

Bylan touched the cloth covering my mouth and spoke a rune's name. A face mask like one surgeons wore fell on my lap. It was pure white and embroidered with a coin-sized power circle. I gulped in a breath through my mouth, the skin on my face feeling cold after being covered for I didn't know how long.

"This is awful," I said. My former tutor turned her head away.

"Awful, but necessary," Bylan said.

"I know." I never should've come.

Mom wrapped me in her arms and cried into my hair. "Oh, Mia, I'm so sorry."

"Hold yourself together, girl," Ms. Weever said, fists balled on her thighs. "We're going to find a way to fix this."

Such sweet despair. Such thirst-quenching tears.

I scanned the interior of the car. "Where's the smudge stick? I can hear her talking."

Zekary produced one from the apothecary cabinet with Bylan's help, and soon the car was filled with bitter smoke. *We'll chat later, Mia Evers*, Tradereth said as the first tendrils enveloped me. *We still have a bargain to strike.*

I breathed the smoke. It didn't need to be in my lungs to work, but it helped. With my alignment suppressed, I couldn't sense her presence. Her voice was just another voice. It could no longer make my spine tingle. At least there was that perk.

"Is she gone?" Bylan said.

I nodded. "She still wants to strike a bargain with me."

"What does that mean?" Mom said.

Ms. Weever slid onto one of the seats. "It means we can't send Tradereth back to the demon realm. We have to send her to the Light, or she's going to keep coming back for your daughter."

"What does she want with my daughter?"

Ms. Weever's icy gaze circled back to me.

I looked at my sneakers. "She called me her instrument of chaos. She didn't say anything more specific."

"It means she intends to use you to cause pain and suffering," Ms. Weever said. "Demons like to use us all to set things in motion that will cause tragedy and chaos, generally on a large scale. And since we know the Order of Tenebron is alive and well, we begin to understand why Tradereth has singled Mia out."

"Because she's a Dark?" Mom's face lined with fear. No, not that look again.

"Not exactly. It's her potential as a Dark. You do realize she's a prodigy, right?"

"Honestly, I had no idea."

Ms. Weever narrowed her eyes. "I thought you said your family has a history of producing Darks. How do you not know?"

Mom grimaced. "No one really talked about it. I don't know their developmental stages."

Ms. Weever motioned towards me. "She's well ahead of the curve to the point where she's figured out how to do things even I don't know how to do. She can look at runes and figure out their song. I haven't met another Dark who can do that. Your daughter's special. She's capable of great things. On the downside, this means demons know she's capable of great horrors, should they be able to twist her to their will."

"I can't live the rest of my life with my alignment suppressed," I said. Arms bound, I swung out a leg to catch my balance as I tipped sideways. Mom helped right me.

"Let me get you out of this," Bylan said, slipping a finger under the white cloth by my shoulder.

"You're right, you can't," Ms. Weever said. "And we have no intention of forcing you to do so. Bylan and I will do some research so we can safely exorcise you and destroy the demon in one go."

Mom gestured to the destroyed cavern. "Can't we make that circle again?"

Ms. Weever grimaced. "Tradereth most likely will try to kill your daughter out of spite in addition to putting up a major fight, putting all of our lives on the line as well."

"Out of spite? What spite?"

"For taking away her anchor. If she can't have Mia, then no one can. Thus is the way of demons."

"Of course it's this complicated," Zekary said as he relit the smudge stick. Fresh tendrils of smoke wafted across the car.

Vergo placed a paw on Mom's hip. "Lyra's right, unfortunately."

Mom jumped. Realizing it was Vergo, she placed a hand over her heart. "I forgot you were here."

He asked Mom to remove his collar. She did without hesitation. Gerund, Zekary and Ergon all went wide-eyed.

"Whoa, what's that?" Zekary said.

"A spirit cat," Bylan said as he peeled a layer of cloth off, revealing a second complete layer. He swung his arms around me, removing the next layer and freeing one of my hands. I gratefully flexed my fingers and rolled my wrist. The Light priest gently held my hand as he retrieved some sort of crayon from his less voluminous black sleeve. What was it with him and hiding stuff in his sleeves? He said, "Vergo used to be a demon. He's an excellent source of information."

"Used to?" Gerund said from outside the car.

Bylan explained the whole episode about Vergo's former demonhood, how Bylan and I had crossed him to the Light, and how Shinjan had sent him back as a spirit animal to help me and to repent. During his explanation, Bylan drew a protection and binding power circle on the back of my hand and activated it with a few words. He unwrapped my other hand and did the same. An ache like having the flu traveled up my arms and into my stomach before vanishing.

Ugh, more suppression. Hopefully, he and Ms.

Weever would figure out how to safely rid me of Tradereth sooner rather than later.

"Dude, I want one," Zekary said.

Vergo flattened his ears. "I'll have you know I'm not a pet."

"Alright, mister not-a-pet, how do we get rid of an archdemon without it killing Mia?"

"Simple," Vergo said, "you outwit a demon at its own game." He hopped onto my lap and faced everyone. "It's like a chess game. With the limitless lifespan of being a demon, they spend ample time scheming and plotting. They have a hundred different ways to accomplish their goals. We need to do the same and think like a demon. We need to anticipate Tradereth's moves and outmaneuver her; essentially lure her into a trap that looks like she's going to get what she wants and—"

"No. Too complicated," Ms. Weever said. "She's had too much time to think things through. I have a feeling we played right into her hands with our exorcism attempt."

Tradereth's revelation that my mom was the reason I was allowed to come replayed in my mind. I shivered. "We did."

"What makes you say that?" Zekary said. He studied me with open curiosity and a hint of concern in his scrunched brows. Mom watched with watery eyes and a tight grip on my knee.

No. I couldn't say it in front of her. She didn't need the guilt, didn't need to know a demon was meddling with her, too. She was already having a hard enough time staying motivated with Dad gone.

Ms. Weever's icy gaze bounced between me and

my mom. "Demons are subtle meddlers. With all the time she spent with Damien, she's had plenty of opportunities to influence me, Bylan, Amity, Mia and who knows who else? We're never going to outmaneuver Tradereth. We're going to have to do this a different way. We need a Light Order's help."

"You're kidding, right?" Zekary said. He wore a pained expression.

I sure hoped she was. They were the last people we needed to go to for help. If I went there and explained to them that I had an archdemon anchored to me, what would they do? Lock me away like some criminal? Kill me and force Tradereth to find another anchor? Find a way to permanently suppress my alignment?

"I wish I was," Ms. Weever said. "I don't see any other way to gather a powerful enough group to take on an archdemon. Honestly, we're probably fortunate we didn't get to attempt it ourselves."

"What will they do to me?" I said. Part of me wanted to hug Vergo to my chest. My arms remained glued to my lap.

"I'm not sure I like this idea," Bylan said. "The organization has gotten worse over the years. There's a good chance they'll slam the door in our faces. They certainly won't listen to me."

"What do you mean?" Mom said. "You're a Light priest. You're one of them."

He frowned. "Not anymore. They marked me as anathema as soon as they found out I'd helped Mia, a Dark, deal with a demon. I've been stripped of my rank and cast out. It's how I was able to become Bela's Light tutor. The Order of Leo denounced your entire family the moment you turned down the Little Leos Academy.

"That's absurd." Mom balled her hands into fists. "I mean, they seemed a little off that day, but not so outright biased. What's wrong with them?"

"That's how bad it's become. In the past, I would've been told to never speak of it again after telling them about working with a Dark. The whole thing would've been swept under the proverbial rug, and that's it. Nowadays, the Grand Light Order wants total control." His gaze grew distant. "Honestly, they need to fall."

"Like that's ever going to happen," Zekary said.

Bylan's face hardened. "No mountain is too big to crumble. Anyway, enough of this. Lyra, I advise against approaching any Light Order. They're not allies by any stretch of the imagination."

"I have to try."

"You're a Dark. They won't listen to you."

"They might when I tell them about the Order of Tenebron."

"They won't believe you. Drop the idea, Lyra."

"No. You can channel Payton. He's a soul in limbo, bound to tell the truth. We can make him tell a council everything he knows."

"And how are a Dark and an anathema going to gain an audience?"

Ms. Weever opened her mouth.

Bylan said, "And don't even think of forcing your way in. You'll be tackled and arrested before you can figure out which way to the council chamber."

Ms. Weever scowled at the car floor. "I'll figure something out."

"What if one of us went?" Zekary said.

"And did what?" Ms. Weever said.

"Told them about the Order of Tenebron, and that we have a friend in need of help."

"You'll be tossed out," Bylan said. "Without any evidence, you'll be marked a lunatic and escorted off the premises."

"Well then, let's get some evidence."

Chapter 18

Despite having an archdemon trapped in my body, the ride home was mercifully uneventful. The desert passed us by on either side of the highway in moonlit darkness. Mr. Redd lay on the car floor, out cold, one of Nurse Kor's vines wrapped around his arm to make sure he stayed asleep. Bylan had refreshed his sleep spell, too, also just in case.

No one said anything, everyone's eyelids looking heavy. It was well past midnight, well past everyone's bedtime, especially mine. Prioritizing my sleep, especially during bandyll season, I religiously stuck to a nine o'clock bedtime. I leaned against Mom while Vergo dozed in my lap.

Instead of parking behind the hills, we pulled into Mr. Redd's driveway after Zekary and Ergon both confirmed that Mrs. Redd wasn't home.

"Thank the Light," Zekary said as Gerund put the

car in park with a metallic click. The car gently sank to the ground as the Air charm that caused cars to float was switched back to dormant. "We could definitely use a break after tonight's setback."

"We need a lot to go right," Ms. Weever said, stepping out of the car.

I stepped out as well, and no one said anything. Good. I needed to stretch my limbs after being bound and cooped up in the car.

Gerund carried Mr. Redd inside and set him in a living room chair with an open book in his lap. He set the principal's arms in a way to make it look like he'd fallen asleep reading. "Hope he reads a lot," Gerund said, inspecting the principal's slumped form.

"Doesn't matter," Bylan said, pushing up his sleeves. "He won't remember a thing."

Ergon shuddered. "I'm out. Memory revisions freak me out. There's something not right about it." He disappeared down a narrow hallway.

Bylan placed his fingertips on Mr. Redd's temples. "There is an ongoing debate about the ethics of memory revisions, but I think we get a pass in this scenario. The last thing we need is for him to contact the Order of Tenebron before we can save Mia." Bylan closed his eyes and tilted his head back.

"Speaking of them," Zekary said, inspecting a lamp with crystal tassels, "there's gotta be evidence somewhere in this house."

Ms. Weever crinkled her nose as she took in the heavily decorated living room. It looked more like a space to look at than to live in. There were so many breakable items on the coffee table nestled between the couch and comfy chair, a wooden case full of more breakable decorations packed behind glass and oil paintings in gaudy frames covering an insufficient amount of the flowery wallpaper.

Zekary laughed behind a fist. "What's the matter? Not a fan of the decor?"

"Hardly. There's definitely evidence of the wife everywhere. Everyone pick a room and start looking."

"For what?" Zekary said.

Ms. Weever gave him an incredulous look. "I don't know. Pamphlets, books, trinkets, cursed objects, anything that seems unusual or sinister. Feel out the rooms. See if you encounter anything negative. Bylan and I will take a closer look if you think you've found something." She crossed to the coffee table and held her hand over the porcelain figures. Each figure was a hand-painted animal, lizard, sprite, or bird.

Mom led me into the kitchen and we started in one corner, me with a smoking smudge stick in one hand. Vergo sniffed around the cupboards and under a round table with a square tablecloth. The kitchen was as heavily decorated as the living room, minus the porcelain figures and oil paintings. Instead, the table had a ceramic fruit basket with matching salt and pepper shakers and napkin holder. The table was set for two, complete with silverware wrapped in cloth napkins. Jars, jugs and cooking paraphernalia lined the counters, everything having a specific place.

Mom checked inside the fridge. I checked cupboard after cupboard. It was all pots, pans, food containers, cleaning supplies and such. Everything was perfectly ordinary. I even checked under a stack of dish towels tucked in a drawer. No books or pamphlets.

The eight of us plus Vergo regrouped in the living

room, everyone empty-handed. Ms. Weever pointed. "Everyone check a different room, just in case." We all took off in new directions, Mom and I ending up in a small guest bedroom that looked like it hadn't been used in years.

The bed was perfectly made, the blankets flat and with no depression in the middle to hint at years of use. The dresser had all but one empty drawer, the last one holding extra sheets and pillow cases. The closet was full of extra comforters and pillows, along with some camping gear. An old cast iron sewing table sat in a corner next to an old fashion wash basin complete with an oval mirror. Not one object gave off a bad energy or seemed like a tool for the Order of Tenebron. I kept trying to spread my awareness in search of negative energy, only to be reminded each time that I was suppressed. Had I always used my alignment this much? I felt so blind without it. I might as well be blindfolded. Doing my best to search the room with what tools I had, I carefully checked between and under the folded sheets, and felt around the drawers for hidden compartments.

We regrouped a second time, empty-handed like before. Nurse Kor rubbed sleepy eyes while Bylan stood by Mr. Redd, who snored softly.

"Are we perhaps overlooking something?" Zekary said, running a hand through his blue hair. "Like something really obvious and we don't know it?"

"Maybe," Bylan said, "but I suspect this house is perfectly ordinary. Whatever he's up to, he's made a point to not leave any evidence in his own home."

"Seems like he's thinking ahead like a demon," Ms. Weever said, frowning.

"Maybe that's why his wife isn't here," Ergon said, fiddling with the steel chain attached to his baggy jeans. "She must be a part of the Order, too. She's probably at one of their meetings or something."

"Maybe we're looking in the wrong spot," Zekary said, turning to Gerund. "Anything underground?"

"Hey, good thinking." Gerund held his hands out and stomped the ground. He tilted his head one way, then the other. "Nope. Just some irregular patterns, probably from when this house was built. Sorry, no secret basement or underground chamber. It's solid bedrock all the way to the water table."

"There has to be something we're missing," Zekary said. "This guy has to be part of that Order."

"Most likely yes," Ms. Weever said, rubbing an eye. "He's clearly taking great pains to not get caught. Let's go. This is a waste of time."

We scanned the house to make sure we left behind no evidence of our snooping. We tweaked the lay of pillows, checked drawers to make sure all folded items were the way we found them, and made sure the floor was free of shoe prints. Gerund smoothed out the ground, erasing all our trampling before we climbed back into the cars.

The ride home was mercifully quick. Mom and I quietly entered the house to find Mrs. Bylan sleeping on the couch. Mom woke her with a gentle touch to a shoulder.

The old lady's eyes popped open. She took in the both of us and her face brightened. "Welcome home. How'd it go?"

"I don't wanna talk about it," Mom said in a low voice. Bela was fast asleep in her room, the glow of her nightlight spilling into the living room. "How was Bela?"

"An absolute sweetheart." Mrs. Bylan stood and stretched out her back. "She even connected me to my late mother, letting me know that she loves me and is watching over me. Bela has such a strong connection to the Light for someone her age. She's a blessed child. The Light has big plans for her."

Mom winced. "Thank you. We'll have to talk about this some other time. Mia and I are exhausted. Let me see you to your car."

I retreated to my room, dragging my feet, and set the smudge stick in a bowl on my desk. Its protection would fade at some point in the night. At least my alignment would be suppressed, blocking Tradereth from making a pawn out of me. Hopefully, it also meant she couldn't enter my dreams. Vergo waited outside my room, until I let him know I was in pajamas. I curled up with a book in hand and blankets over my legs. Vergo curled up in his customary spot at the foot of the bed.

I couldn't bring myself to open the Yuna book, couldn't bring myself to lie down and close my eyes. I had an archdemon anchored to me. And she still wanted to strike a bargain. What did she want from me? Why me? Why not another Dark—an adult Dark even? Even after what Ms. Weever said, I didn't feel special or powerful. Everything I'd done since arriving at Toolena Mesa had been accomplished with great struggle and a lot of help. She'd even had to rescue me from the demon realm. Wouldn't a real prodigy have figured it out herself? Or maybe not have gotten herself stuck there in the first place?

Vergo lifted his head, blue eyes watching me. He

twitched an ear. "Something on your mind?"

And once again, he was surprisingly perceptive. I set my book on the floor and wrapped my arms around my shins, resting my chin on my knees. "I'm scared."

He sat up. "I was wondering when you were going to say something. You've been awfully quiet since that whole fiasco."

"What happens if they can't exorcise me in time?"

"We'll find a way, Little One. It's possible. The problem is that everything hinges on how Tradereth will react."

"How many people does it take to beat an archdemon?"

Vergo's gaze grew distant as sage smoke tendrils drifted through the air. "That's a tough question to answer. In my memories, you saw how many it took to summon one. And that was on purpose. There was no anchor, so it's easier to command a demon to return to its realm under such conditions. But with an anchor?" He looked at me. "It gives a demon leverage, an ability to resist command. Think of it like an untrained dog. A dog owner can easily call a trained dog to their side and tell them to do tricks. A summoning circle gives you that kind of power and command over a demon."

"We can't do that to Tradereth?"

"Unfortunately not. She's anchored to you. She's like an untrained dog. We can force our will on her, but she'll ignore it and do what she wants. In order to capture and contain her, we have to chase her down first. As soon as she feels that leash around her neck, she's going to lash out. And since you two are bound together, we have to make sure we protect you in the process."

Tradereth most likely will try to kill your daughter out of spite. Ms. Weever's words echoed in my mind.

I didn't know how to feel in response to that. I dealt with dead things all the time. Taking a last breath in the realm of the living wasn't the end. At the same time, I didn't want to take my last breath. I wanted to stay alive. "Do you think she'll try to kill me when we exorcise her?"

Vergo showed a flash of fang in a grimace. "Unfortunately. A less powerful demon would most likely flee and avoid a fight. But one as powerful as her? She's going to flaunt her power and make sure we know there are dire consequences for denying her what she wants. Whatever happens, we'll do whatever it takes to keep you alive and safe."

"Including suppressing my alignment for the rest of my life?"

Vergo's eyes narrowed as he studied me. "Is that you or the demon talking?"

I lifted my chin off my knees. "I don't know. I'm scared I might have to live with my alignment suppressed for the rest of my life."

"No one said you will. Lyra already stated that that's not an option. Fight this fear Tradereth is trying to impose on you."

"How?" I curled my hands into fists. I wanted to scream, to throw a pillow. Was this mounting anger not mine either?

"What's one thing in your control right now? It doesn't matter how small, so long as you know you can do it."

Nothing. Absolutely nothing.

I gasped. There it was, her influence, sitting deep in

the back of my mind, trying to twist anything and everything away from joy, comfort, happiness, hope, and all that was good. "Vergo, she's influencing me. How is she getting through the sage cloud?"

His ears lowered. "I was afraid of this. Smudging is more for clearing out the energies around and inside you. Demons are entities, not energies. Smudging also isn't the best tool for battling demons."

"What is?"

He gave me a pained smile. "Willpower. Your will to embrace the Light, hope, love and all that is good needs to be stronger than your willingness to give into darkness, despair, rage and the like. So what's one thing you can do right now that's in your complete control?"

I let out a slow sigh through my nose and looked around my room. Sure, breathing was in my complete control, but I wanted to latch onto something more than that. I needed sleep, needed rest to get my energy back and face whatever came at me next. As tired as I was, I felt restless. My Yuna book lay on the floor. I reached for it. "I can read." Maybe taking a break from reality would help me forget my problems for at least a little while.

"An excellent choice." Vergo curled up at my feet and kneaded the comforter, his purrs mingling with the sage-scented smoke tendrils.

I settled against my pillows and opened to the part where the dryad king interrogated Yuna, demanding to know why she had trespassed on his lands and why he shouldn't kill fairy scum like her. Her plight wrapped my thoughts up in the unfolding scenes. Mentioning her mother completely changed the king's attitude towards her. He freed her and returned her things. They had a long conversation over a tasty dinner and Yuna felt hope for the first time after her disastrous audience with her father.

***

The weekend passed in a blur of reading, practicing my violin, looking after Bela, and helping Mom around the house. Once again, Mom's gaze grew distant and her actions mechanical. Bela noticed, too, and her one tantrum made things worse. Mom didn't bother getting up Monday morning before school.

"Why is she still sleeping?" Bela said as I helped her get dressed as much as she'd let me. She wouldn't let me help her get her dress or socks on. At least she let me make sure everything matched.

"She's probably real tired," I said. It was a lie, but Bela was too young to understand this whole melancholia thing. She kept expecting to see Dad every day and got teary until I was able to distract her. At least she was accustomed to Dad already being off to work while we got ready for school. "Let her rest. You know you don't like it when we wake you up too early sometimes. Mom feels the same way, okay?"

Her little brows drew together in concentration. "She'll get cranky?"

"Right. Show Mommy you love her by letting her rest and not making her upset."

"Okay."

Mercifully, we made it to school without any more fussing. I kept my head down as I followed the throng of students off the buses. Footsteps pattered along the sidewalk, and the smell of dirt and flowers enveloped us.

"Keep your hands to yourself, Todd," Mr. Redd's

angry voice said over the din of dozens of students pointing and gossiping. His voice scared the nearby students to silence.

Like a school of fish avoiding a predator, the students gave our principal a wide berth. His face reddened with rage and he grabbed Todd, some gangly boy a few years older than my sister, by the loop atop his backpack. Thin arms flung out as Todd fought to stay on his feet. Another boy with ear-length hair that bounced with every step ran off, clutching his face.

"Walk, young man, or you will serve detention with me for the next week."

The second boy slowed to a fast walk and squeezed between two girls. The girls shied to either side and gaped at the boy.

Mr. Redd's rage turned back to Todd. "You have detention for the next three days."

"He started it," Todd said.

"And I caught you, not him, doing the punching."

"But—"

"Get to class," Mr. Redd said through his teeth and yanked Todd by his backpack loop back into the throng of nervous students.

"Someone's in a good mood," Vergo said from over my shoulder. Even though my backpack was closed, he had his head poked out, collar and all. I didn't understand how something from the physical plane could pass through solid objects by being in contact with him, but who was I to question how the Light made things work for a spirit cat? "I'm guessing he found out he no longer has a certain evil entity anchored to him anymore."

Yes, he did, said Tradereth with far too much

delight.

I flinched. She hadn't said anything since Zekary had lit the sage in the back of the car. Mr. Redd glared at every last student. I ducked behind some eighth graders and snuck off to Nurse Kor's office. Homeroom could wait.

The vines shivered as I walked by. The scent of lavender and a sterile environment filled my nose. Nurse Kor sat at her desk, as usual, measuring out various herbs and oils. "Nurse Kor, do you have any sage?"

She looked up, surprised. "Oh, hi, Mia. I'm afraid not. That was a Bylan thing."

Tradereth tutted. *How convenient for me that he's no longer here to be a nuisance. I'm looking forward to our first day of school together.*

"I'll be back," I said and headed for Mr. Muradon's office.

He paused in the middle of removing his long coat. "Why good morning. What brings you in so early?" He finished removing his coat and hung it on a hook behind his desk.

"Please tell me you have some sage."

"I do, but—"

"Please light it." I wrung my dress in both fists.

He raised an eyebrow. "What's wrong?"

I fumbled for words. While he'd given me no reason to suspect he might be part of the Order of Tenebron, Vergo was unwilling to fully trust Mr. Muradon. "Can I tell him?"

Vergo narrowed his eyes at my tutor. "I wouldn't risk it."

"Tell me what?"

264

Yes, go ahead. Tell him. What do you think he can do for you that no one else can? Walk away, child. No one can help you.

"I'll tell you later," I said to the floor and returned to Nurse Kor. I plunked on one of the blue cots and buried my face in my hands. A weight settled next to me and a hand rubbed my back. Such kind, loving energy. Energy that couldn't save me from an archdemon.

"What's wrong, Mia? Anything I can do to help?"

"I don't know."

Of course there isn't. Tell her. Knowing and accepting the truth will only make this easier to bear.

Ugh. Go away, you stupid demon. She wasn't even trying to hide her efforts to manipulate me. "Are you afraid of me now?"

Her hand squeezed my shoulder. "Of course not. I'm afraid *for* you, though. I want you to be okay, but I don't know how to help."

My backpack jostled and a small weight landed on my other side. Vergo walked across my lap and place a paw on the nurse's thigh. "Continue to be here for her. The demon's working to make her feel isolated and alone."

Oh, but you are alone, Mia Evers. They are all powerless to help you. Only I can. And you know how.

I clamped my hands over my ears. "Go away!"

The hand yanked away from my back and Vergo jumped to the floor.

Silence followed, pressing down on me with its loneliness. I didn't need my alignment to sense their shock and confusion.

Tradereth chuckled. *Oh, but we are bound together*

for the rest of your mortal life. Strike a bargain and we'll discuss when I can and can't talk to you. Until then, I will wear you down until you give in.

Nurse Kor said, "Do you mean us or her?"

"Her," I said. "I'm sorry. I didn't mean to scare you."

"Maybe you should go home until we figure this out. How is she able to talk to you while you're suppressed?"

"I don't know."

I'm an archdemon. My will is stronger than some silly spells and charms.

The thought of home meant being around Mom and her melancholia. I needed a break from that. "I don't want to go home. It won't make a difference." Home or school, Tradereth would torment me. I didn't have enough sage to block her out for days on end. The stick in the bowl on my desk was almost spent.

"Okay." Nurse Kor rubbed my back. "Come to my office any time throughout the day. I can make a sleeping draught if you think that'll help. Breathe, honey."

I forced myself to sit up. I took several deep, controlled breaths. "This is so hard. It's so easy to feel what she wants me to feel."

Bargain with me and I'll let your emotions be your own again.

Tempting. So tempting.

Exactly what she wanted me to think. I stood. "I'll stop by if I absolutely need it. Maybe lessons will help distract me."

"I hope so. I'm here for you in any way I can, Mia." Nurse Kor stood.

"And so am I," Vergo said. "Stay strong, Little One. Don't give her the satisfaction of seeing you despair."

Too late. He has no idea how easy you are to manipulate. Your prodigal skills as a Dark mean nothing against the will of an archdemon. Willpower is separate from alignment power. You are young, emotionally weak, and volatile. I can sense your growing desire to bargain with me. It's only a matter of time. Days, weeks, years? It makes no difference. I have all the time you do not.

Head down, I gave Nurse Kor a hug. Her nurse scrubs were soft against my cheek. "Thanks. I'll see you later."

Arms wrapped around me, backpack and all. "Take care, Mia. I'm rooting for you."

I headed back outside. The chill air was refreshing, invigorating. I breathed deeply as I headed for the back of the throng dispersing among the various buildings. Mr. Redd headed towards me, face red and mouth set in a scowl, his glare fixed on the door behind me. Guilt bubbled in my chest. He didn't look in my direction as the gap between us shrank.

Stay away from him.

An unseen force yanked me sideways. I threw my arms out and a hand caught me by the upper arm.

"Miss Evers—" Mr. Redd's eyes widened. He let go as if he'd been burned.

Idiot child.

He seized my arm again, his glare looking right through me. "Traitor!"

I cringed, pushing at his hand. "Mr. Redd?"

He let go and his face paled. "Miss Evers, I

apologize. I—" He fumbled for words. "Get to class. Right now." He stormed into the main office and the door slowly swung itself shut.

Vergo casually flicked his tail. "He slipped. He actually slipped." He turned away from the office. "Let's head to class. We'll talk when it's safer."

***

The day passed in agonizing slowness. Tradereth provided a running commentary on all my lessons, poking fun at all my teachers and classmates. Come lunchtime, I wanted to sit alone. I should've thought of packing my lunch. I would've headed straight to Nurse Kor's office. Instead, I stood in line for chicken tacos with a side of cheesy beans and rice, and joined everyone at our designated lunch table.

Sussi frowned. "What's wrong with you?"

Ah, yes. Friends. I'm going to take such pleasure in making them all turn on you, one by one, unless you bargain with me, of course. Do you want friends? Do you want to keep them? I mean, how hard would it be to convince them to stay away from you forever, little Dark?

My forehead tightened and my heart quickened. Please no. After years of no friends whatsoever, I had four.

Think about it. Can you bear to watch them turn their backs on you? Can you bear to be alone again?

Chibya and Deren mirrored Sussi's concern. Garrett kept his gaze on his food, listening. He didn't use his eyes to pay attention, but he noticed everything. I said, "Something really bad happened over the weekend. I can't say a whole lot here."

Once again, Mr. Redd's impeccable timing caused

him to wander past our table, hands clasped behind his back, gaze roving the noisy cafeteria. His face reddened and eyes narrowed at the sight of me. He walked on, gait slow and stiff.

"We're here for you," Deren said, placing a hand on my shoulder. His brows drew together. He squeezed. "Your energy feels weird."

I brushed him off. "It's probably not safe to touch me."

"It's not scary. It's… I'm not sure how to describe it."

Chibya, her lunch untouched, reached across the table and touched my hand. She recoiled. "Your energy feels real low or tiny or something."

I lowered my gaze to my tacos. They looked so tasty. They were made with love and joy. I didn't feel hungry, but I'd eat. I had to. Not only did I have club bandyll, I needed all my strength to contend with an archdemon. "They had to suppress my alignment for mine and everyone's safety. That's all I can safely say."

Deren gasped and leaned closer. "Suppress? That's, like, real extreme. They only do that to criminals. You've gotta tell us, Mia."

I shook my head.

"What if you wrote it down?" Chibya said. She produced a pencil and small notepad.

Yes. Tell them. Maybe it'll strengthen their resolve to stand by you. Or it'll work in my favor and push them away. Your choice.

I clenched my tray in both hands. And breathed. Tradereth was an archdemon, a master of subtlety and persuasion. And manipulation. She was trying to push me into uncertainty. It definitely seemed like a gamble

269

to tell my friends anything, but if it were one of them with a problem, would I want them to tell me?

Of course. I'd want to know everything in hopes of being able to help. I wrote one word on Chibya's yellow notepad with blue lines. "Archdemon." They all leaned over to read it.

"I don't know what exactly that is, but it sounds serious," Sussi said.

"It is." I tore off the sheet and balled it up. I'd stuff it in my milk carton later, just in case. "It might be safer if you all stayed away from me, until I'm not dealing with this anymore."

Staying away from them won't protect them. I don't need to be around you to influence them. Remember how I visited you when anchored to that evil small man. Every move you think of making, I've already got a counter-plan. I have plans within plans, moves and counter-moves. You have no idea what you've been swept into, Mia Evers.

"No way," Sussi said. "Friends stick together. I wanna help."

"Me, too," Deren said. Chibya and Garrett voiced their agreement, too.

I gave them a wan smile. "Thanks guys. It means a lot to hear that."

"Besides," Sussi said, "it's not like your parents would've let you come to school if you were really all that dangerous."

"Right," Deren said, smiling.

I forced myself to smile. None of them knew about my dad.

"And we've got our first game in a couple of weeks. There's no way you're missing that."

I sat up straighter and held up a taco, like I was toasting to something special. "Definitely." If there was anything I refused to let an archdemon ruin, it was bandyll. I could make Dad proud, imprisoned or not. The joy I felt while on the court was stronger than anything I'd ever experienced. That joy was mine to keep, and that was final.

At the conclusion of lunch, I headed to Mr. Muradon's office in a somewhat better mood. I had to stop believing every last lie Tradereth fed me. My friends showed no signs of wanting to abandon me even after my revelation. Sure, none of them fully understood what it meant to deal with an archdemon, but I didn't care. This part of my life was normal.

"Still want the sage?" Mr. Muradon said from behind his desk.

"Please."

He set a stone bowl on his desk, filled it partway with sand and lit a sage bundle. The bitter smoke filled the air. "Alright, you've gotta tell me what's going on."

Vergo flicked his tail in annoyance. "No way around it now. He knows something's up. Giving him the silent treatment will only raise suspicion."

I searched for words. What did I say? What did I not say? Was he an ally, or was his niceness an act? Honestly, it was one very long, deliberate act. Just in case, I'd reveal as little as possible. "An archdemon anchored itself to me without my consent over the weekend."

Mr. Muradon gasped. "How did this happen?"

Oh, we kidnapped Mr. Redd, attempted to exorcise him, and it backfired. Badly. "I'm not sure. It happened so fast. It showed up, I passed out, and then woke up with a demon talking to me in my mind."

My tutor studied me, his eyes narrowing. "It just showed up?"

Technically it had. One moment it was hidden inside Mr. Redd. The next moment, it burst out of him and transferred to me. "Yeah."

"This is very strange." He scanned his books, tapping each of them before moving onto the next.

"Indeed," Vergo said. "We should've rehearsed an answer, sage cloud or not. Demons, especially archdemons, don't anchor like that without motivation. Ask him if he knows how this might've happened."

I did as told.

Mr. Muradon said, "That's a very good question." He paused at a beige tome and took it out, studying its cover. The leather looked eerily like human skin. I shuddered. He said, "Did the demon happen to reveal why it has taken such great interest in you?" He flipped through the pages, pausing at a choice one.

"It said I was going to be its instrument of chaos, but it didn't say how." And there was one other thing. Maybe he could help me find ways to resist. "It also wants to strike a bargain with me."

Mr. Muradon's hands twitched. The book slipped and he caught it midair, bending a few pages. He smoothed them out. "What on Aardra for? You're so young."

I shrugged. "It didn't get more specific. The demon said it wouldn't give me any details until I struck a bargain with it."

"Troubling. Very troubling. We need to take steps to ensure your safety before we can figure out how to exorcise such a powerful demon. Archdemons are no joke." He rounded his desk and put his palm to my forehead. He recoiled. "You're already suppressed. Who did this?"

"Sanctus Bylan." I used his title, not sure if Mr. Muradon knew about the priest's anathema status. "I was scared. So was Mom. I'm still scared. I hate it, but we didn't know what else to do. Can you fix this?"

"Not alone, unfortunately. Let me try something." He flipped a few pages before finding the one he wanted. He pressed down the spine and smoothed the page.

Since he was so tall, I couldn't see the page. The creepy cover smelled of leather, making me shiver again. There were stories of Wild Darks that used human body parts to make stuff. Human-made objects held a power nothing else did. No matter what Tradereth tried to make me do, binding a book in human skin would never be one of them.

Mr. Muradon poured a circle of salt around my feet, checked his book, and whispered an incantation. Maybe if I wasn't suppressed, I'd have sensed something. He might as well have been talking to himself.

"What are you doing?" I said.

"You'll see in a sec." He flipped to the next page and placed a fingertip near the top. He chanted words that sent a tingle down my spine. The words were harsh and guttural, sounding nothing like human speech. I'd heard words like this only once before. Demonic? There were Darks that could read and speak the demonic tongue?

"Mr. Muradon, what are—?"

A swirling wind kicked up, sending loose papers

flying and knocking several objects off the bookshelves. His violin fell off the piano in a discord of hollow thunks. A darkness filled the room. My head tilted, mouth open. A tendril of black surged out. I tried to scream, but I had no control over my lungs, much less my trapped breath.

You will leave me with this one. Begone. The blackness morphed into the jagged shape of Tradereth's head, tree branches and all, before swirling with the wind and retreating back inside me. The sudden wind died as fast as it came. A few books fell off the shelves and loose papers zigzagged their way to the floor.

I doubled over. My stomach churned. Lunch wanted to reappear. I willed it all to stay down as I took one deep breath after another. The salt circle had spread out like a paint splatter.

The office door swung up. Coach Khamai's terrified face framed by tight, bouncy curls poked in. "What was that?

Mr. Muradon popped a guilty grin and snapped his book closed. "We're fine. Just had a little surprise. Sorry for the scare."

Coach backed out into the hall and closed the door with a soft click.

"That was fun," Mr. Muradon said sarcastically. "Let's not do that again."

"What were you trying to do?" I plopped onto the nearest chair, my legs shaking.

"Commune with it. Find out what it wants. It's unusual for an archdemon to take such interest in a child. Yes, you're a Dark, but why go so far as to anchor to you?"

I shook my head, at a loss for an answer.

"Sorry, that was a rhetorical question."

"So what do we do now?"

"I need to do some research. Dealing with archdemons is as serious as it gets." He put his fists on his hips. "In the meantime, let me teach you how to shut out a demon's thoughts. I'm not sure if it'll work on an archdemon, but it's worth a shot. It's better than carrying sage everywhere."

"Ah, he's not going be able to do that with your alignment suppressed," Vergo said.

"Mr. Muradon, my alignment."

He swore, and then covered his mouth. "Oops, sorry. Bad habit. But yes, you're right. Here, I need your hands." He held out hands twice as big as mine.

I clamped my hands to my sides. "What are you going to do?"

"Undo as much of the suppression as I can."

"Are you sure that's a good idea?"

"Do you want the demon to keep needling you for a bargain, or do you want to be able to shut her out?"

"I want to be able to shut her out, but not at the cost of her being able to do stuff through me."

"I'm not a Light. I can't undo everything Bylan did. Only another Light can, so you'll be safe."

"But not as safe." I remained put.

"How safe will we all be if you finally cave and give her that bargain she wants? You need to be able to protect yourself."

Vergo said, "Unfortunately, he makes a good point. With a partial suppression, Tradereth's ability to influence you will be limited, and if she can't keep pushing a bargain on you, then all the better."

I reluctantly stood. As much as I hated being

suppressed, this wasn't the solution I'd hoped for. "What can it do if I'm only partially suppressed?"

"I'm not sure. I never learned about this in school. My every instinct says you need to be able to protect yourself more than she needs to not be able to tap into your alignment. Please let me do this." He held his hands closer.

Vergo bobbed his head. "Go ahead, Little One. You need your shield if you're going to defend yourself from a monster."

A seed of doubt sat in the back of my mind. This couldn't be safe, couldn't be a good idea. Or was that Tradereth wanting me to stay suppressed, wanting me to remain unable to block her out whenever I was unable to hide inside a sage cloud?

Yes, it had to be her. That had to be why my suppression hadn't bothered her. I placed my hands in Mr. Muradon's. Large fingers closed around my hands. My face heated. This was how lovers stood together. While, mercifully, I didn't have a crush on my tutor, the nature of this contact wasn't lost on me. Hopefully, no one barged into the office. This would be beyond awkward to explain.

Thumbs brushed the back of my hands. Bylan's suppression runes flared to life with white light a moment before fading. "Okay, I can't undo this part, but…" He dropped to his knees and touched my shoes. "Okay, yes, this part I can do. Go ahead and sit. I don't want you to fall over."

I sat back down and Mr. Muradon, one hand on my shoes, and two fingers pressed to my forehead, whispered runic words. A warmth grew in my feet and spread up, like a revitalizing inhale. My alignment senses came back all at once, making my head spin as the energy around me became known. I could sense Vergo's location without looking at him, sense Tradereth's presence in the form of a creeping terror tickling the back of my mind and making my skin crawl. The myriad protection circles and wards vibrated against my awareness as I felt out the campus. A few ghosts wandered on the other side of the road.

I exhaled with relief. I could see again.

"You won't be able to do any power circles or place wards. At least now you can defend yourself. Now, let me teach you how to block a demon's whispers."

Chapter 19

Mr. Muradon showed me some mercy and sent me home with several smudge sticks. Tradereth hadn't said anything yet since I tried the medication technique, but it didn't mean that she wasn't trying to lure me into complacency. At least I emotionally felt better without being completely suppressed. I could keep the doubt, the despair and hopelessness at bay. I felt more like myself.

Mom was her unhappy self. She made dinner and spent time in the living room with Bela, giving me a chance to focus on anything but my sister. Sadness came off Mom's neutral face in suffocating waves. Being in the same room as her was painful.. Bela tried to get Mom to play blocks with her on the floor. Mom patted Bela on the head and told her to have fun. "I'm watching sweetie. Make me something, will you?" She redirected her attention to her latest book with a shirtless man and pretty lady on the cover.

"Okay, Mommy." Bela returned to her blocks with a hop before settling on the floor.

I retreated to my room. I had homework. I had the desire to get it done. Sure, I wished I never had homework again, but that was a part of school. On top of that, it'd only make Mom feel worse if my grades dropped. I set my backpack on my desk and undid the zipper.

"Go ahead and light a smudge stick," Vergo said. "Just in case. I want to discuss something."

I lit one of the four smudge sticks Mr. Muradon had given me and waved it around my room, spreading the smoke.

"You look like you're feeling better, by the way," he said.

I nodded, taking a seat on my desk chair. I faced Vergo on my bed. "I don't think entirely suppressing me was a good idea. Tradereth was able to make me feel whatever she wanted. Now I can keep her influence at bay."

He nodded thoughtfully. "Good. I'm relieved to hear it. I didn't like suppressing you, but I didn't know what else to do. This is such an unusual situation. Demons attach themselves to living souls all the time, but to turn a person into their anchor like that? Unheard of. I'm sure it happens now and then, but not enough for there to be writings on such things."

"Do you have any idea why she was so eager to transfer herself to me?"

"That's why I want to talk to you. You remember the traitor comment Redd let slip, yes?"

How could I forget? "Yes. I figured he meant

Tradereth."

"Right, but think of the implications."

"Implications?" More big words from a little cat.

"I mean why do you think he called her a traitor? What conclusions can you guess at by learning this tiny bit of information? That's what I mean by implications."

"He didn't want her to leave him?"

"Exactly." He scooted closer, his furry face bright with excitement. "Think about it. If he didn't want to be an anchor, he'd be relieved to have her gone. However, he's clearly upset to have lost her. He wants her for something. As for why he considers her a traitor, that makes things very interesting. With all the demons available to serve a Dark, he's taken a special interest in Tradereth. What drew those two together? Why was he so furious when he found out that she's attached to you now? If he cared about your wellbeing, then he would've shown concern. Instead, there was only rage."

"I see what you're saying, but I don't know what it all means." We already knew Mr. Redd was a bad man. We knew he was up to no good. He had to be a member of the Order of Tenebron. We just lacked—

"It means we need to delve into his past again. I'm going to give you a scrying lesson."

"With Payton?"

"No." He casually flicked his tail. "With Mr. Redd himself."

Terror gripped my chest. I clutched my chair. "He's not going to let me scry him."

"We don't need him. We only need something *of* his. If we do this right, we may be able to figure out where to find all the evidence we need to expose the existence of the Order of Tenebron to the Grand Light Order. I think that's worth the risk of sneaking into his office."

***

It was like Mr. Redd knew we were trying to sneak into his office. All week long, he was either in his office or near the main office. I tried every morning after hopping off the bus, before and after lunch, before and after tutoring, and at the end of the day before having to bolt for the bus. I even tried having Nurse Kor use her vines to check if the coast was clear during lunch one day. He was too close for comfort. Come Friday morning, I was ready to scream.

"This isn't working," I said to Vergo as I stormed out of the main office and on the way to homeroom.

"Then let's try something different," he said while riding in my backpack, his head sticking out. "I have an idea."

"It better be a good idea." I folded my arms.

"It's a fun idea. I'm sure Deren, Garrett, Sussi and Chibya will like it, too. We need them to create a distraction for us. Don't tell them why. Just tell them when."

I unfolded my arms. "Okay, now I'm interested."

"I'll tell you all about it in homeroom."

***

On the way to first period, I told Deren and Sussi I needed their help with something, and I'd give them the rundown at lunch. Deren promised to pass the word onto Chibya in science class, and I told Garrett after history class. He perked up, giving me one of his rare smiles while avoiding eye contact.

"Will you need Snooter and Longears, too?"

I pictured two coyotes running around the campus while several teachers and Mr. Redd tried to catch them. A funny image, but Garrett would get in major trouble. Everyone knew about him and his coyotes. "Nah. Leave them out of this. I don't want to get you stuck in detention for the rest of the school year. Mr. Redd's in a really bad mood."

"I've noticed. See you at lunch."

The day didn't pass any faster or slower than normal. I both dreaded and eagerly anticipated lunch. The plan might work or it might fail horribly. Mighty Shinjan, please let this work. Everyone but Chibya devoured our enchilada lunch. She took a couple of bites and settled for watching us all eat while she frowned. She'd gotten skinnier over the past few months, but she was still noticeably overweight. A few bites shy of skipping lunch entirely was helping.

I mopped up the last of the enchilada sauce with a piece of corn tortilla and wiped my mouth with a napkin. We all leaned in, our chins hovering near the table. I drew dampening and blocking runes on a piece of paper and activated them with a touch. While the meditation technique Mr. Muradon had taught me appeared to work, he taught me a few other things as well in case one technique alone wasn't enough. A wave of energy enveloped us and the din of hundreds of voices grew quieter. It was off-putting for the cafeteria to seem so quiet, but it also meant not even the students at the table next to us could hear. "Okay, here's the plan: I need you all to create a big distraction that draws Mr. Redd's attention away from me."

"Why? What are you going to do?" Sussi said.

I shook my head. "It's not safe to tell you. If any of

you get caught and he interrogates you, then we're all in a lot of trouble." I hadn't even told Nurse Kor.

Deren said, "Okay, what do you want us to do?"

"Set off the all the fire alarms at the same time in every building."

"Including the main office?" Chibya said.

"Yep. Every building but the cafeteria. Can anyone make some sort of communication charm so we can coordinate the alarms?"

"I can," Deren said. "When are we going to set off the alarms?"

"As soon as lunch is over. We'll use the time between classes as some cover. Everyone picks a building and as soon as everyone signals they're in position, we set them off."

"Easy enough," Sussi said. "I call the six-eight building."

Everyone else called a building, leaving me with the main office, and Deren took several rocks out of his backpack.

Sussi crinkled her nose. "Do you always carry rocks everywhere you go?"

"Yeah. I'm an Earth. I practice on them all the time, so please give them back when we're done." He whispered some runic words to the rocks and gave each of us one. "Give it two squeezes to let us know you're in position. Mia, give yours three squeezes to signal for us to set off the alarms."

Once the bell signaling the end of lunch sounded, we all hurried off in separate directions. I hurried off to a back corner of the main office while Vergo kept a lookout. Mr. Redd monitored my lunch wave, but he always marched right back to the main office, using the front door while I used the far door by Nurse Kor's office. My rock vibrated twice two separate times, signaling that two of us were in position. There was a red fire alarm switch right by her door. I squeezed my stone twice. Footsteps echoed down the hallways in the distance, probably by the front desk. Vergo ran to the end of the hallway that connected to the side hall. The main office had a c-shaped hallway that wrapped around the heart of the building, Mr. Redd's office nestled in the middle. My stone vibrated a third set of two, and then a fourth. Everyone was in place.

Vergo said, "He's by the front desk. Go for it."

I squeezed my stone three times, and then counted to three. I yanked the bar-shaped switch pained red and white, and ran out of the office, crouching behind a blue myrtle cactus bush as students filed out of every building. Shrill bells made my eardrums vibrate, drowning out students' voices. We were supposed to be quiet while walking to our safe zones. I'd never witnessed perfect quiet in all my years of fire drills. Mouths moved, arms raised, telltale signs that students were happy to have fire alarms interrupt learning.

Vergo popped his head through the wall. "The coast is clear. Hurry."

Oh, boy. This was it. Holding a strap of my backpack, I dashed inside all the way into Mr. Redd's office. The space was immaculate, the furniture and decorations sparse. My heart pounded away, punching my chest with urgency like a fist banging on a door. "What do I take?"

"Something he won't notice is gone for a few days."

I scanned the room, my whole body taut with

anticipation that Mr. Redd would barge in any second. His coffee mug? No. His pens? No. Notebooks? Definitely not. I couldn't sneak out his chair. What about the photos? No, he probably didn't handle those enough to make a strong enough connection for scrying a living person. I checked drawers in the cabinet the photo collection sat on. Nothing useful in there. I checked several desk drawers, pausing at the bottommost one. A leather-bound notebook rested atop a pile of folders and some notebooks. It looked exactly like my student records notebook. I opened it to the first page. My full name was handwritten in large, tidy script on a long black line.

"What is it?" Vergo said.

"My student records." Why on Aardra were my records in his desk and not with all the other student records?

"That'll work. He's written in it. Take it and get out of here."

I buried the notebook in the bottom of my backpack and ran out of the building. I rounded a corner. Mr. Muradon's towering frame stood out among the front office staff in the front office parking lot. I hurried over to him. His face lit up and Coach Khami merrily waved to me.

"There you are," Mr. Muradon said.

"Yeah. Sorry I took so long."

"You get lost or something?"

I gave them a wan smile that hopefully looked embarrassed instead of guilty. "I was on my way over from lunch. I hesitated between the cafeteria group and coming here. I figured it'd be quieter here."

"Until the fire trucks get here," Coach said.

***

The unscheduled fire drill ate up a good chunk of tutoring time. Mr. Muradon didn't seem in the least bit suspicious, not even when word got around that there was no fire anywhere.

"Kids pull pranks now and then," he said with a shrug. "I did stupid stuff when I was your age, too, so I'll take that over a Water flooding a bathroom or an Air sending mini tornadoes down hallways while everyone's transitioning between classes."

"Students did that back then?" Only once someone flooded the middle school bathroom. There's also a story about some Fire kid who melted a hole in one of the classrooms in the 3-5 building, but I'd never seen it. Elemental accidents and antics happened. The school had wards to protect the property.

Mr. Muradon popped a mischievous smile. "Of course. That's normal school stuff. All sorts of stuff happened before I went to the Dark academy. One time, there was this kid who puked, and then had a demon fling it all over the teacher everyone hated."

"Oh, gross."

He sat backwards on a chair, propping his forearms on the back. "Oh yeah. And it stank, too."

Instead of lessons, he ended up telling me story after story. I laughed and smiled until my face hurt. It was fun learning about my tutor as a kid. When the bell rang, his eyes widened. He glanced at his watch. "Okay, that one was on me, but I'm blaming the fire drill. Have a good weekend, Mia."

My final class passed in agonizing slowness. At least Mr. Redd hadn't shown up to summon me to his office. Part of me feared he'd notice my school records missing from his desk. At the same time, he could've simply forgotten to return them after making notes in it. Whatever the reason, I'd add my school records to the rest once I was done with the notebook and let him wonder whether or not he'd been the one to put them where they belonged.

Bela led me inside the house and the aroma of steak and beans greeted us. Mom stood in the kitchen, cooking up dinner. Thank goodness. A better day. Her hair was messy and her gaze distant, but she wore fresh clothes and the house was clean. Keeping a house organized by myself when a five-year-old lived in it was no easy task. On the weekends that I cleaned, it was like Bela ran around undoing everything as I moved from room to room.

Bela joined Mom in the kitchen. I gave Mom a quick hug and retreated to my bed. I felt tired enough to fall asleep after spending all week trying to steal something out of Mr. Redd's office. The sudden ability to relax hit me full force. I made myself to stay awake with my Yuna book until Mom called me to dinner. Bela talked enough for the three of us, asking about Dad only once. Mom's eyes watered at the mention of Dad and Bela fell silent, her brows drawing together. She nodded to someone across the table who wasn't there, or, rather, someone I couldn't sense. Probably Grandma again. Bela switched to talking about stuff she learned in school, helping ease Mom's tears away.

After dinner, my sister and I cleaned up the kitchen while Mom read in the living room. Once the last of the silverware was put away, I retreated to my room and took the notebook out of my backpack. I tossed it on my bed.

"Finally, the moment has arrived," Vergo said.

What do you have there, Miss Evers?

I stiffened. I'd almost forgotten about Tradereth after not having heard from her for over a week.

I set a sage bundle in a stone bowl.

Tradereth sighed. *This again? You can't keep this up forever. One day you'll slip and forget. One day, you'll give me a bit of delicious information I can twist to work against you. I'll know your plans and ruin every last one of them.*

"Whatever. Shut up." I lit the sage bundle.

Manners, Miss Evers. Keep that in mind if you want a fair bargain the day you finally bend.

Using an owl feather, I spread the smoke around my room, then settled down long enough to meditate for safety's sake and activated the same runes I'd used during lunch. Vergo guided me through drawing a power circle used for scrying and had me pour water on a black dinner plate set in the middle of the circle. The water turned the plate into a mirror that reflected my window and the white wall framing the curtains.

Under the gentle orange glow of a salt lamp on my desk, I sat with my shins brushing the plate and my school records on my lap, opened up to the back, where Mr. Redd had made notes. I took hold of Vergo's paws. He sat on his haunches, his balance relying on my grip.

"This would be so much easier if I were in my human form. Granted, I'm not sure how helpful I'd be. This is a Dark's method of scrying. At least it'd be easier to—" His blue eyes widened and turned blue. His paws shifted in my grip, sliding and expanding. I let go. In seconds, he transformed into his human self, complete with a white tunic, black pants and the same golden hair as Ms. Weever, swept back like a lion mane. He sat a head taller than me. While I'd seen him in human form before, it was jarring. I expected vertical irises and cat fangs or something. Every last bit of him was all human.

"Thank the Light for the small mercy." He took my hands in his cold grip.

I reflexively recoiled. "Sorry, you're cold to the touch."

"Ah, sorry. Don't think I can do anything about that." We held hands again and he took a deep breath. "Let's get started. And to give you fair warning, scrying takes a lot of practice. You can cheat and make it easier with the right tool, but obviously you don't have a scrying stone handy. Anyway, it will most likely take you a few tries to zero in on the part of the past we're aiming for. Let whatever memories you land on unfold. You'll tire yourself out faster if you fight it."

Vergo guided me through a meditation technique, his voice soft and gentle. My body relaxed. I felt alert and aware of the immediate world around me, my gaze locked on the water's surface. The coldness of his touch was no longer relevant. It was there, same as the air around us.

"That's it. Ease your awareness towards the water. Let it be all you see. Let it show you all. Now repeat after me. Mighty Shinjan, shine your light down on this circle."

I echoed his words, my voice low and strong.

"And protect all within… We ask you to show us truths… Please show us who Damien Redd is… Please reveal all we need to know… so we may better serve the Light."

I repeated the last part and my body grew heavy, like the air pressed down on me. The water rippled, sending rings bouncing into each other and obscuring the reflection. The ripples shifted, falling into a swirl. Either I bent closer or the swirling rose and spread. Something pulled me forward.

"Breathe. Embrace the pull."

I slowly inhaled. My body resisted the pull. I gently released my breath. The pull guided me forward, downward, into blackness.

A scene appeared as if someone had activated a light switch. A sandy playground with children running around. A redheaded boy stood by a rope climbing net. Two bigger boys, maybe seven or eight, stood over him, hate twisting their faces. "Get out of here, Damien. No one wants you. You're short and stupid, and you're a stupid Dark."

Damien charged the two boys, bowling one over. He punched the boy several times before getting clocked in the head. Damien thrashed around. The two bigger boys overpowered him, one wrapping him in a bear bug. Damien kicked wildly, clipping the second boy, who socked him in the gut. Damien doubled over, gasping for breath. The second boy punched him again, splitting his brow. Damien let out a cry of pain and dropped to all-fours. The boys laughed, kicked sand on him, and walked off.

Footsteps hurried closer. A lady in old-fashioned nurse clothes crouched beside Damien. "Damien," she said in a pained voice. She brushed sand off his shoes and examined his brow.

Damien pushed her away. The nurse stepped back, her arms clamped to her chest.

"I'm sorry, honey. I want to make it better."

"You can make it better by leaving me alone."

"Oh, honey, I wish I knew how to help you. I hate seeing you hurting like this."

"I'm not hurting." Damien rubbed his eyes with the back of his fist.

"I wish your father was with us. He'd know what to do. He'd teach you how to get the respect you deserve."

"Well, he's not coming back," Damien said, wiping his eyes again and spreading blood on a sleeve. He lurched to his feet.

"Please, let me clean your cut."

"No." He scowled at the playscape. "I'm fine."

"Honey, you're not fine. You need to learn to make friends or people will never stop picking on you."

"They need to learn to be afraid of me."

The nurse, who must've been Mr. Redd's mom, shook her head slowly. "That's not how the world works."

"I'll make it work."

I cringed. Mr. Redd was so cruel as a child. He was picked on as ruthlessly I was, but he reacted so differently. It was terrifying. Where had he learned to be hateful so fast, and what'd happened to his father?

As if they stood on a rotating surface, Mr. Redd and his mother swapped positions as the scene around them spun in a swirl of colors. He grew into a short teenager, and his mother paled and sickened. Red curls stuck to a sweaty forehead. A hospital manifested around them, his mom lying on a gurney floating over a small pool of water.

Mr. Redd stepped up to the gurney. "No, Mom. Not

you, too." Damien's eyes welled with tears. He held his mother's limp hand, pressing it to his face.

"I'm sorry, honey. I never meant to disappoint you. I'll hold on. I'll try to pull through for you. I love you so much. I'm tired, so tired. I need to rest."

"No, don't rest. You need to get up. Please."

His mother's eyes closed and her head sank deeper into the pillow. "Remember what I said about how the world works?"

"Of course. I'll never forget."

"And is your way of making the world fear you working?"

He grimaced and tears ran down his cheeks. His voice came out in a whisper. "No."

"Then try something else. Please try making friends. I won't be here for you much longer."

"Don't talk like that."

"Make friends, Damien. I know you can do it. You've always been able to accomplish anything you put your mind to. Now, let me rest. I'm tired."

"No. I forbid it. Open your eyes." He shook his mother's hand. The song stone beeping out his mother's heart rate slowed, dwindling to a full stop. It emitted a shrill tone like a wolf's howl. Mr. Redd screamed at his mother to wake up. Her body sank into the gurney. The small pool of swirling water stilled. Mr. Redd seized the song stone and dashed it to the floor. Shards flew in all directions. He breathed heavily, face red as his hair, and tears streaming down his face.

All his rage left him. He dropped to his knees and cried into his hands.

The scene was too much. I pulled back from it. Blackness flashed across my vision before Vergo and my bedroom reappeared.

Vergo blinked several times. "That was disconcerting. I almost feel sorry for the man."

"I do feel sorry." To be there when his mother died? Horrible. No one deserved to go through that, no matter how bad a person they were.

"I wouldn't waste any empathy on a human like him, but anyway, we're getting closer to the present. Let's go again."

I took a deep, calming breath and slipped backed into a meditative state. I focused on the present version of Mr. Redd, willing the Light to show me what I needed to know in order to stop him from whatever he was trying to accomplish with the Order of Tenebron. As if in answer, the scrying water pulled me into its depths.

An adult Mr. Redd with the first hint of graying sideburns sat across from a woman at the table in his kitchen. She looked similar to his mother, but had straight red hair that ended at her shoulders, glasses, and a blockier figure. They both looked concerned. The lady said, "I know things aren't progressing like you hoped with the Order. What if—" She wrung her hands, her left hand bearing a wedding ring. "What if we moved on, left it all behind?"

Was this his wife?

Mr. Redd's faced turned crimson. "And abandon all my hard work? No. We need to keep trying."

"Damien, this is exhausting. It's time to move on."

He studied the lady. Whether he was sad, angry, scared, or concerned, I couldn't tell. He straightened up. "No, there's other work to do."

Her expression transformed from defeated to

scared. She sat back in her chair, hiding her hands in her lap. "Do you mean—?"

"Yes. I think it's time."

"Are you sure? That's a lot to ask of me."

"You promised. It was why I finally agreed to marry you."

The lady, his wife, lowered her gaze to her lap. "Is there no other way to achieve your goals?"

"Lily, the Order's hard work is a slow process. One mistake could ruin everything. Molech knows how hard I've worked to build the Order up. You've seen what I've been through. I think it's time you took on a new role."

Her narrow shoulders rose and fell with a sigh. "Okay."

Mr. Redd and his wife stood. The chairs, the table, and the entire kitchen got sucked into a swirl of color that dissolved to black. Lily dropped to her knees. Chains appeared, connected to the ground and bound around her wrists. Her bangs obscured half of her face. Her one visible eye reflected terror in the surrounding firelight. Lily sat inside a giant power circle decorated with runes and a line formation I didn't recognize. Something about them made me cringe. This was a circle with bad intentions.

Six black-robed figures stood evenly spaced around the circle's perimeter. Black robes appeared around Mr. Redd, the hood down. The firelight made his hair look redder, as if it were on fire. In one hand he held a book and in the other a dagger. The other robed figures chanted something. The circle's lines and runes flared to life with purple light. Mr. Redd stepped inside, holding the book open. The purple glow cast thin shadows all around him.

The chains jingled as Lily shook. Two lines of tears on her cheeks reflected the purple and orange light. With great effort, she met her husband's gaze. "Do you love me?"

He paused. "I thank you from the bottom of my heart for your undying loyalty. I couldn't've asked for a better wife. You've served me well and you'll continue to serve me from the Demon King's realm. Do you accept the power he's about to bestow on you?"

Head bowed, Lily's body shook with a sob. "I accept."

Mr. Redd raised his dagger. "Hear me, Molech. I offer up Lily Sarka Redd as a blood sacrifice. Let her be reborn as your instrument of chaos. Grant her your power." He shifted, blocking Lily from view. The dagger glinted in the firelight and came down. Lily fell over, dead, the chains falling with her.

The six robed men chanted something in deep, harsh voices. It sounded like a rhythm more than a song. The words came out monotone, a syllable accented here and there. The circle's light flickered, a swirl of white mixing in. The glow brightened, then flashed with a crack of thunder.

Black claws surged out of the circle, followed by a slender black shadow arm. A head covered in black tree stumps rose into the air. The rest of the demon's body rose out of the ground and crouched before Mr. Redd, smoky tendrils of blackness dripping off of her as if she'd climbed out of swampy water. He looked the size of a puppy next to her. Tendrils dripped off her, hissing upon contact with the circle. Two round red eyes opened.

I am...reborn. The demon spoke in a booming woman's voice breathy from exertion. She examined her black body, turning her arms this way and that, and experimentally flexing claws long enough to wrap around a body.

Mr. Redd tossed aside his dagger, dropped the book, and held his arms up, the sleeves bunching at his elbows. "Welcome, great demon. What name has Molech bestowed upon you?"

You may call me Tradereth.

Tradereth! The female voice had sounded familiar, but I'd dared not jump to conclusions. He—that had been his wife. He'd killed his wife to turn her into a demon.

I pulled away from the vision. Blackness enveloped me a moment before Vergo's wide eyes locked on me, his mouth ajar.

Chapter 20

Ms. Weever was as shocked as me and Vergo when I told her about the scrying session. Lily Sarka Redd. Tradereth's mortal name was Lily Sarka Redd. She'd been Mr. Redd's wife. She wasn't alive and well. She wasn't a part of the Order of Tenebron.

Mr. Redd had killed her, had killed his wife for whatever goals he had. He was as bad as a demon.

"Mia, take a few deep breaths. I can hear you over the vine."

I touched the leaves wrapped around my ear. "Sorry. I'm still in shock." Vergo stood beside me in human form.

"I understand. I am, too. Even with what Payton told us, I would've never guessed this in a thousand years."

"Why did he do such a thing?"

"Selfishness," Ms. Weever said. "Pure selfishness.

He has goals. Everyone is a tool to him, nothing more. He's incapable of love or compassion."

"But he cried when his mother died."

"I guarantee you those weren't tears of mourning. They were tears of rage. He had no control over the situation and he knew it." The sound of rustling filled my ear. "People like him don't have empathy. He wasn't sad his mother died. He was furious he could no longer use her for personal gain. Does that make sense?"

"He doesn't care about anyone but himself?"

"Correct. People like him don't care what anyone else is thinking or feeling. To him, he's the only important person in the world. Only what he wants matters."

"How do people get like that?" Even with having a past like mine, he responded to the hate so differently. He was hateful and selfish from the beginning. But me?

"A rare few are born that way, but most are shaped by childhood trauma. Based on what you told me, he's the latter."

"Then how does he act so normal most of the time?"

"He can blend in with society because he's observed social norms and acts them out to get what he wants. He smiles because that's what people do in certain scenarios, like seeing a friend walking up to them. He expresses regret, remorse, and other appropriate emotions because he knows that's expected when someone dies. And he doesn't mean one damn word of it."

Vergo said, "He's a monster in every sense of the word but in appearance."

"So what do we do now?" I said to Ms. Weever. I agreed with Vergo wholeheartedly.

"You go on as normal while I reassemble the group. Having Lily's mortal name changes everything. I have connections that can do an investigation into her murder. There's a trail of evidence somewhere. Once we have enough to get a warrant for his arrest, we can expose him and the Order of Tenebron all at once. Mia, you did an amazing job with your scrying. You gave us all a real fighting chance."

"Do I really need to go back to school on Monday?"

"I'm sorry, yes. Go to school, do your homework, keep practicing your violin, go to club bandyll practice. I promise this investigation won't take too long. Hang in there for us."

"I will," I said.

"I know it's a lot to ask. Just think, every time you see him brings you a moment closer to the end of his reign of terror. His days are numbered."

We bid each other good night and I removed the vine from my ear. It coiled back towards the ceiling.

The patter of little feet on a wood floor drew closer. Bela, who was in bed before I called, crossed the kitchen, eyes half open. Sleep walking? She reached for both me and Vergo, one hand latched onto Vergo's and her other hand gripping my arm. Her head tilted back and an otherworldly breeze whipped up around us, making the vine leaves shiver.

"You must fight, Mia," Bela said in an echoey voice that sounded much like Mom's. Her hand squeezed my arm.

Vergo and I gasped. A powerful energy filled me,

coursing through my body like blood. The runes on the back of my hands flared to life with white light. Bela squeezed harder. I reached for her hand. An unseen forced blocked me from pushing her away. The runes dissolved in a puff of smoke.

"Danger is near. You must fight."

The wind died. Bela's grip slackened. She slumped forward and Vergo caught her in his arms. Small white feathers fluttered to the ground between us.

I braced myself, expecting Tradereth to manifest, but the house was still and peaceful, as if nothing crazy weird had happened. If the demon was around, watching and waiting, I sensed nothing through the sage cloud.

Vergo's gaze darted around before the tension eased out of his shoulders. He adjusted his grip on Bela and stood. "I guess whatever spoke through her didn't mean right this instant."

"How did she do that?"

"I haven't the faintest idea. This is Light stuff, something I know hardly anything about. In fact, I'd love to know where on Aardra these feathers are coming from." He indicated to the floor with his chin.

I picked them up. They were as soft as the ones I'd found on her booster chair months ago.

"That's the third time this has happened, right?"

"I think so." I followed him to Bela's room.

He lay her in bed and pulled the sheets up to her shoulders. "I saw Bylan's face that day. He knows something. I wonder why he wouldn't say what these feathers mean. It's not like Lights can raise demons."

"Let's ask next time we see him. You don't think it's a bad omen or something, do you?"

Vergo shook his head. "I don't know. I don't see a pattern in all this."

***

The following week of school was mercifully boring. Tradereth left me alone. Mr. Redd left me alone. Mom was deep in melancholia, but she dutifully got Bela ready for school, made dinner, got me to bandyll practice and back, and did all that other mom stuff. She slowly came out of it as the weekend arrived, eager to see my first club bandyll game. Coach Tokket put us through drill after drill, making sure we always knew what the plan was, no matter the situation.

"If you always have a plan, then you always see a way to win," Coach told us at the end of our final practice before game day. We all sat around the locker room, sipping water while he delivered his customary wrap-up talk. He wore his skates, making him even taller. "Our opponents will make adjustments and force us to figure out which plan to use against them. We have a bunch of plans and a bunch of plays. We'll keep them on their toes while they try to figure us out. In the meantime, we'll win."

Instead of being afraid of my first club game, like I had for middle school bandyll, I eagerly anticipated it. Coach had told me to expect a different level of play. I wouldn't entirely understand what he meant until I experienced it, but he encouraged me to stick to the plan and I'd do fine in goal.

Come late Saturday morning, Mom pulled into the arena parking lot packed with cars. Ours was one of several games scheduled throughout the day. Two teams, one white and green and the other blue and white, trickled out of the arena and into the lot.

Families, including me, Mom and Bela, sported purple and gold of the Hornets, and another group of new arrivals sported red and black. We followed the flow into the arena and Mom gave me a tight good luck hug inside the doors.

"You'll do great, sweetie. Do your best and I'll be proud of you no matter the final score. Dad will, too."

Knowing it was better to not add to any mention of Dad, I nodded. "Thanks, Mom."

"Good luck, Mia," Bela said.

I mussed her hair and joined my team in the locker room with a handwritten sheet of paper taped next to it that read "U-13 Hornets." The smell of sweat, leather and metal, along with the din of excited voices, surrounded me. I joined Sussi, Kelsi, and the rest of the team in gearing up.

Despite having plans and plays galore, my eager anticipation dissolved. I flinched at sudden noises and stared at nothing while I geared up. This was the real deal. I didn't want to disappoint my team or my family. I didn't want to prove Gwen right that I sucked. Yes, she'd been nice enough ever since Vergo set the facts straight with Mr. Volaire, but we weren't friends. We were teammates. That's it. When it was time for practice, we got along for the sake of the team. As soon as practice was over and our gear was packed, we didn't look at or talk to each other. Even Nonaya didn't bully me on her behalf at school anymore.

I double checked my laces for the umpteenth time to make sure they were nice and tight. My ankle hardly rolled, but I could shift my weight around. Good.

A horn blew from deeper within the arena, making me and a few other girls jump.

"Alright, girls. That's us," said coach from somewhere in the adjacent hallway. "Go get warmed up."

Sussi laughed and put a hand on my shoulder. "Relax. You'll do great. Just stick to the plan."

I nodded, not trusting myself to speak. My stomach felt like a brick. She helped me get my glove and goalie scoop on, and I followed her down the hallway. Vergo hopped on my shoulder and I brought up the rear of the procession.

A coldness gripped me. My movements slowed. The gap between me and Sussi widened, and it felt like I was trying to move through quicksand. Sussi froze mid fist-bump with Coach, scoop and fist inches apart. I gasped. It echoed in the sudden silence. I willed my glove hand to move so I could summon a protection bubble. Everything went black.

I stumbled forward as Tradereth's will released me. I wore my bandyll gear. My skates sank into what felt like deep mud. I couldn't see the ground through the layer of fog floating halfway up my shins, and as far as I could see into the gloom in every direction.

Welcome back, Mia Evers. Tradereth's voice echoed all around me.

"Hello, Lily Sarka Redd." I tried to free a skate. Whatever I stood in held me suctioned in place.

A giant shadow shifted in the distance, turning. Two round red eyes appeared high overhead, looking down. They tilted. Tendrils of fog passed in front of her face. *So that's what you were up to.*

"Lily, I command you to leave me alone."

The eyes squinted. Tradereth chuckled. *Nice try. That's not how this works. Knowing my name certainly helps you, but you need to know what power that gives you. Clearly you don't, little girl.*

"So then how does it help?" A long shot, but I had to ask.

A mist in the gloom parted as the red eyes drew nearer, revealing a shadow of a head with a crown of branches. Clawed paws big enough to crush a car stepped into view, pausing feet away. The head lowered to mere feet above me. *You insult my intelligence if you think I'd answer such a question.*

I shrugged. I wasn't sure what else to do.

Anyway, I didn't bring you here to banter. I have a question. Did you see how I became a demon? Did you see what that evil little man did to me? I saw your notebook. Clearly you scried into his past.

"I did."

Then you know he deserves justice. He's my enemy, too. Help me destroy him and his goals, and I'll reward you greatly.

"We don't need your help. We're already working on it." The eyes drew level with the top of my head, dousing me with cold and her terrifying aura. My legs shook, but my stuck skates saved me from dropping to my knees.

You dare deny me the justice I deserve? You're worse than him.

"Why haven't you done anything to him yet? You're clearly a powerful archdemon."

Because he knows the true power of names, Mia Evers. He's made sure that I cannot rise against him. You have no idea how hard it was to break his anchor. I'm just a tool to him. He never loved me. Her voice grew tight and full of rage. *He couldn't even bring himself to lie and say he did. I was too stupid to see it while in my mortal shell. All I wanted to do was please him. Nothing I did was good enough, not even my death.* The eyes rose into the gloom, looking down on me. *So I ask you again, Mia Evers, do you dare deny me the justice I deserve?*

Her rage seeped into me, filling me with the desire to scream until my throat was raw. My eyes stung. I needed claws to shred every last person who had wronged me, including Mr. Redd. Her rage became mine, but thanks to my lessons, and to my alignment no longer being suppressed, I noticed the emotional manipulation. I summoned my protection bubble with a flick of a wrist. I took a deep breath and exhaled the rage, the hurt, the betrayal. Calm filled its place, along with a trickle of fear in the back of my mind, tickling my spine. Tradereth must be suppressing her fear-inducing aura in hopes of making it easier to persuade me to help her achieve what she wanted.

I did feel sorry for her despite all she'd done. Was it enough to persuade me to strike a bargain with her? Definitely not. "He does need to be punished for his actions."

Then you see that you must help me. I cannot seek vengeance alone.

"If we work together, it'll be without a bargain."

No. You don't trust me and I don't trust you. A bargain is the only way we know both of us will make good on our parts. The ends justify the means.

"No bargain," I said.

Traereth's eyes narrowed. *I've already removed your father. Do you want your mother to be next? She's gripped in an awful internal struggle at the moment.* A giant claw swirled the fog. *Your father's absence has dealt her a terrible emotional blow. She's an easy target. Dare you risk her wellbeing? All she needs is a little nudge.*

My heart rate quickened. Dad's arrest and ensuing imprisonment had broken her heart.

Or maybe I should go for Deren Sevine first. She drew something in the ground. The fog rose up, morphing into a gray image of Deren. He smiled at me. *I can finish the job Allosyr did not. He clearly wasn't cut out for demonhood. I couldn't believe a mere child foiled him. He got what he deserved. But your beloved friend? An opportunity wasted. He and his family struggle to make ends meet. Surely, I'd be doing them a favor by giving them one less mouth to feed.* Deren's image collapsed back into the fog blanket.

"You're trying to scare me."

Am I now? She sounded amused. *Maybe I should go after your sister.* An image of my sister rose out of the fog, complete with a flower hair clip over one ear. *She's such a sweet, innocent little thing who doesn't understand how cruel life is. Why let her live long enough to experience such a harsh reality?* She swiped at the image, destroying it.

Rage surged to the forefront, filling me with a strong desire to punch the demon. No one was allowed to hurt my sister. "Enough," I said. "Mr. Redd is going to pay for his actions. My friends and I are making sure of it. You can either help us without a bargain, or you can leave us all alone. Ms. Weever knows your mortal name. She'll teach me what to do with it, so either leave us all alone or prepare to get sent to the Light one day."

Then maybe that's where I'll start. You feel awfully

safe while having her around.

"She knows how to fight you."

Who says it'll be a fair fight? The red eyes squinted with an unseen smile.

This was a waste of time. Why did I allow myself to talk with her for so long in the first place? "I've got a bandyll game to play. Good bye."

As you wish. We can continue this later, after I've taken some steps to demonstrate the consequences of your choices. One day, you'll see that a bargain is your best option. She casually flicked a black wrist, plunging me into darkness. The locker room hallway reappeared, unbearably bright. Sussi and Coach Tokket fist-bumped.

I rolled back into motion, closing the gap. The chill lingered. I didn't care. Tradereth was full of threats. Learning her mortal name must've made her desperate. She had to be trying to rush me into making a decision. Obviously, she'd make good on her threats to hurt people I cared about, if given enough time. I'd worry about that later. I had a game to play.

Coach Tokket placed a hand on my cat-free shoulder, stopping me. "You've got this, Mia. Forget about the whole game. Focus on constantly being ready to make a save. Play the game one save at a time and be our eyes in the back of the court. Okay?"

I nodded. This I could do.

His brows drew together. "How do you feel so cold?"

I shrugged and skated off.

Vergo dug his claws into my jersey to stop him from falling off. "What did she want this time?"

"Same as always. We'll talk about it later. I need to

focus."

The hallway spit me out into the team bench area. I crossed the gap and dropped down onto the court. The rumble of wood in my ears and the feel of wind on my face dispelled the chill. I followed the rest of my team in several half-laps while the red and black Scorpions team did the same. I skated over to the net and bowed my head. It probably looked like I was praying, but that explanation worked in my favor. Instead, I performed a blocking meditation so Tradereth couldn't bother me for the next twenty-four hours. I must've forgotten this morning.

Warmups helped me block out the demonic interruption. Each shot on goal honed my focus until I became aware of only the players on the court and our surroundings. During practice, we were surrounded by a ring of darkness. Today, ample light showed the hundreds of people filling up the lower half of the arena. Several sections had entire teams sitting together, color coding the seating arrangement. Purple and gold sat in clusters on our half of the arena.

A horn blared, indicating the end of warmups. We filed onto our bench and drank some water. An announcer sitting in a booth stationed between the benches stood and held a sound stone wrapped in vines close to his mouth. He took a deep breath.

"Welcome, everyone, to opening day of U-13 girls bandyll," he said in a sonorous voice. The sound stone carried his voice to magically connected sound charms, filling up the arena. I couldn't help but smile. We'd never had an announcer during school bandyll.

I elbowed Sussi. "Why didn't you tell me about the announcer? This is awesome."

She popped a mischievous grin from behind her face mask. "And ruin the surprise?"

The announcer introduced the Scorpions and their coach and read off the starting lineup. The players rolled out onto center court as their names were called and raised their scoops to cheers and applause.

The Scorpions looked like a decent team. Their uniforms were cool, but I liked ours more. Some of the girls were pretty tall. Kelsi was taller than all of them at six feet.

"And now to introduce the Hornets coached by NBL veteran Andre Tokket," the announcer said. Cheers and applause erupted all around our half of the court. We drummed our scoops on the waist-high wall separating us from the court. Feet stamped all around us, making it sound like rain pounding on a roof. The announcer worked his way through the lineup, saving goalie for last. "And today's starting goaltender is number ninety-nine, Mia Evers."

The sound of hearing my name spoken so loudly and with such excitement gave me goosebumps. I could barely breathe as I left the bench and rolled towards center court. People cheered. No one knew of or cared about my alignment. It was bandyll time. I smiled as I rolled by and bumped scoops with my other six starters, including Gwen. We were officially in truce mode.

Referees rolled onto the court. A whistle blew. Both our teams skated into position. I found my spot in front of the net and took a swig from my squeezable water bottle resting next to Vergo.

"Good luck, Little One. This should be fun."

Facing center court, I got down and ready. The rest of my team bent their knees and held their scoops ready at their sides. Kelsi rolled closer to the center line, squaring off with another tall girl. A female referee standing between them, ball in hand, pointed to Kelsi, who nodded. The ref pointed to the other center, who nodded as well. The whistle blew and a red ball the size of a softball launched skyward.

Kelsi won the tossup and nearly fell over as the other center rammed into her. Kelsi underhanded the ball to our sweeper. My teammates moved into the offensive zone and maneuvered around, looking for a decent shooting opportunity.

The Scorpions were a more physical team than anyone I'd faced. Kelsi led the attack during her shift with Gwen and Lonnie as her wings. They rotated through the triangle formation as they passed the ball around. We tried to pull them out of formation, but they were surprisingly fast. A scoop deflected Gwen's pass back to Kelsi, and it became a scramble for the loose ball. Skates and scoops knocked the ball around as everyone worked to stop the other team from possessing the ball. It bounced and rolled past center court. Sussi swooped in to help Gwen, only to get knocked over. Nika, my sweeper, barely beat a Scorpion to the loose ball and fired it up court before getting knocked over. The players shifted direction, rumbling back down into the offensive zone. Gwen and a Scorpion pushed and shoved as the ball rolled up the far end of the court, Gwen checking the player into the ramp before regaining possession. Two defenders swarmed her. She snuck an underhand pass to our right wing, Lonnie. My teammates reorganized into triangle formation again. Kelsi and Gwen squeezed in a shot apiece. Kelsi's rebounded off a goalie pad and Gwen's found a defender's knee, dropping her. A bandyll ball was heavy, hollow rubber with little flex in the material. It left a mark if it hit a spot with less padding. Once the Scorpions chipped the ball back to our half of the court, said defender rolled off to their bench on one skate.

We controlled the ball for most of the first quarter, taking a few shots and exchanging full-body blows all over the court. The Scorpions were fast and physical. We answered them hit for hit. Coach yelled directions from the bench, coordinating our efforts and adjusting positioning as we were able to hear him over the shouting, cheering, and rumble of skates. Much to our frustration, the score was zero-zero at halftime.

We retreated to the locker room for halftime, helmets and scoops off, everyone sipping at water and munching on orange slices. We were all sweaty, me more from wearing so much gear than anything. I had seen only ten shots in the first thirty minutes of play while we had dished out twenty shots that made it all the way to their goalie.

Coach Tokket stood before us with a clipboard under one arm, his gaze serious. "Keep it up, girls. You're wearing them down. They're fast and trying to force their way to our half of the court. We're playing smarter. I guarantee they're real frustrated right now. I bet you they're not used to being shut down like this. Teams like that try to hide a weak defense. This is how we're going to take advantage of that…"

Coach tweaked our positioning and assigned certain players to theirs, pointed out some patterns he noticed, and gave us words of encouragement that gave us energy without inflating our egos. The horn blared from within the arena. Standing, we grouped up, one scoop each piled in the middle. Coach put his hand on top of our scoops.

"They are fast, if not a little faster. I wouldn't be surprised if they have the stamina to keep this pace up. Keep playing smart, girls. I smell a goal for us. Stick to the plan. We'll get it. Hornets on three." He counted and we cheered before returning to the arena, the starting line returning to our positions. Vergo hopped back onto the top of the net and curled up.

I got down and ready as the ref rolled to center court for the tossup. The whistle blew and the ball shot skyward again. Kelsi mistimed her snatch, jumping too soon. The Scorpion girl arced around Kelsi with the ball and fired at me.

Both Coach Viro and Coach Tokket had taught me the importance of being ready for a shot every time the other team got the ball. Every. Time. I was physically in position to react, but my brain was in toss-up mode. My scoop hand moved automatically as my brain registered a need to make a save. I moved my whole body. The ball deflected off my scoop, then off the top of my helmet. Sussi and Jolen, my right fullback, rolled to either side of me as a Scorpion chased after the rebound.

Vergo laughed. "Nice save. I know I shouldn't laugh, but that's one way to use your head."

Easy for you to find it funny when you're not in goal, I thought sourly. One time, during a practice scrimmage, Kelsi scored a goal by shooting at Mattie's head from behind the net. The ball rebounded off Mattie's helmet and into the net. Kelsi laughed. Mattie didn't. Kelsi tried to sound sincere while smiling through her apology.

The rumble of skates brought me back to the players currently crowding me. A Scorpion tried to take a sharp-angle shot. I blocked it with a shoulder. Jolen snatched up the rebound and tossed it up to Lonnie right before getting checked into the side ramp. Two Scorpion players swooped in to intercept the pass, succeeding in tipping it, but not in stealing it. The loose ball bounced to center court and beyond.

Gwen swept past Lonnie with a defender right behind her. She scooped the ball up, rode the ramp, and spun to shake the defender. She rode the ramp down. Another defender swooped in to intercept. Instead of taking the quick shot on net, Gwen swerved past for a breakaway. The defender fell in her attempt to skid to a stop. The goalie crept out of the goal box and lifted her scoop and glove. The stands erupted in cheers and shouts. Gwen skated within arm's reach of the goaltender and took aim. The goaltender reacted, moving for the low block. Gwen swung her arm around like a softball pitcher and released the ball above the goalie's arm.

The goal horn blared. The announcer yelled, "And after nearly three quarters of play, the Hornets draw first blood." Our half of the arena erupted in cheers.

My team piled on Gwen for a group hug. My heart leaped in their direction. If I weren't in goal, I would've joined them. I raised my arms and whooped. What a goal. I was definitely glad to have Gwen on our team.

Both teams reset and we had another toss-up at center court. The quarter lasted only long enough for the announcer to identify Gwen as the goal scorer, when the goal was scored, and give Jolen credit for the assist.

Come fourth quarter, the Scorpions played like they were pissed off. They hit harder, fought more desperately for control of the ball, and forced us on defense. We snuck in line swaps as we could, but we hardly got in any shots, often having to resort to dumping the ball in their end to avoid running out of steam. Shots came at me from all over our half of the court. I made save after save, grabbing water between face-offs. I directed my defense around the net, helping them cover open players and block shots I knew were coming. My rigorous defensive efforts steadily wore me down, until coach called time out to give me a much-needed breather.

"We've gotta get back on offense," I said to Sussi, who was red-faced and covered in sweat.

"Believe me, we're trying," she said.

"Hang in there, girls," Coach Tokket said. "You're doing fine."

"But we've gotten three shots on net all quarter," Gwen said, frustrated.

"That's fine," Coach said. "There's five minutes of gameplay left. They're in desperation mode. They're thinking even less. On top of that, you're all doing great on defense, and Mia's making some excellent saves."

The rest of my team nodded and voiced agreement. My already hot face grew hotter. I made myself nod in acknowledgement of their praise.

"In three minutes, they're going to pull their goalie in hopes of the man advantage on offense. Stick to your man. When they empty the net, turn and shoot as soon as you get the ball. I don't care where you are. Shoot the ball."

The ref blew her whistle and we set up for a

defensive face-off. There was a bit of elbowing and shoving around the circle. The ref ignored it. The Scorpions gave off an energy of frustrated desperation. They wanted to score badly, but they had no plan, other than to keep on trying to out-skate us.

Like Coach said, the Scorpions abandoned all strategy and tried to take shots from everywhere. We made block after block, and I made a few more saves. The only reason we didn't get much of an offensive push was due to the Scorpions' superior speed, giving them the ability to beat us to rebounds. At the two-minute marker, they pulled their goalie and we were forced into a six on seven. Their coach yelled at them to slow down and make smart shots on the net. The Scorpions fell into the oh-so-familiar triangle formation. We forced them to burn sixty seconds on the clock before they finally got impatient and gave me an easy save. There was no one screening me. I had the whole goal box to myself.

Shoot the ball.

Screw it. Cranking my scoop arm back, I fired at the empty net. It arced over everyone, sailing past half court before making its first bounce, heading straight for their net. The stands erupted so loud that I was sure the ground would start shaking.

Players gave me the back of their jerseys as thirteen girls chased after the bouncing ball. A Scorpion player pulled ahead of everyone else as my shot made it halfway down their side of the court, on track to go in. The player bent lower, gaining momentum, gaining ground on the ball.

Fifteen feet from goal…ten feet from goal. It was definitely going to find the back of the net if the

Scorpions' number four didn't get there in time. But she was so close. Five feet from net. Number four dived and swiped her leading scoop as she slid on her belly.

Her swipe fell short. The ball bumped into the back of the net, followed by the player.

The stands erupted in cheers and next thing I knew six players were piled on top me, giggling and huffing for breath. I laughed with them. Among my huggers was Gwen. When our eyes met, all the joy left her face. She extracted herself from the group hug.

"This doesn't mean I like you."

Kelsi playfully elbowed Gwen. "Yes, it does. You just don't know it yet."

A smile fought to form on Gwen's face. She turned away.

The Scorpions went through the motions for the last minute of play, their goalie back in the net and us happily on offense. At the final horn, the announcer declared us the winners with a final score of 2-0 and we hurried off the court to make way for the next game.

Coach Tokket patted me on the shoulder in the locker room hallway. "Excellent goal." He popped a crooked smile. "You were the last player I expected to shoot on the net, but I'll take it. You could be the next Brodin Mar if you keep playing like that."

"Who?"

He waved. "A pro goaltender from back in my day. He holds the league record for most goals scored by a goaltender." He patted my shoulder again and gave me a nudge in the direction of the locker room.

I headed inside to clean off and change back into regular clothes. I wore a Hornets girl's tee of gold on purple, a pair of white skorts, and my sneakers. Gear bag over my shoulders and Vergo beside me, we headed out onto the main concourse.

Mr. Muradon stood outside the locker room, his brow drawn with deep lines. He removed his hands from the pockets of his long coat. "Mia, there you are. You've gotta hurry. It's Lyra. She's in trouble."

Vergo and I exchanged confused looks. I said, "Trouble how? What's happened?"

He waved for me to follow. "I'll explain along the way. Hurry!" Instead of running towards the main entrance, he ran deeper into the arena.

"Tradereth," Vergo said in a worried tone. "Go."

Hefting my bag higher on my shoulders, I hurried after him. I tried to catch up. His much larger stride forced me to focus on running. We plunged into a side hallway that spilled us out into a small lobby lined with tinted glass doors and widows. Mr. Muradon held the door open and pointed outside. "My car's over there."

I blew past him. His dark gray car was straight ahead. I recognized it from the day he pointed it out during the fire drill. I sprinted, footsteps close behind. The passenger door of the car opened as I crossed several parking spaces.

And then I rammed into an invisible wall.

Dazed, I landed on my bag, skates and goalie gear digging into my back.

The purple glow of a power circle flared to life, enveloping me. What on Aardra? I lurched to my feet. Vergo sat hunched on wobbly legs outside the circle, his collar in shreds by his white toes.

He shook out his head and took one look at the circle. "Mia, run!" Chains made of purple light shot out of the pavement, wrapping around his neck, each leg, and several times around his torso. Two more small chains shot upwards, securing his muzzle and covering his eyes. He fell still.

Mr. Muradon casually walked up to Vergo and accepted a metal cage from some robed figure. The figure had feminine hourglass curves and held a hand with painted nails towards Vergo, as if channeling a spell. Mr. Muradon stuffed Vergo into the cage and the robed lady drew a rune on the door.

A car door clicked open. A head of graying red hair appeared above the roof of the car.

No. Please no. Not him. This couldn't be. Mr. Muradon had helped me so much. He couldn't be with the Order of Tenebron, too. I liked him.

Mr. Redd rounded the car, wearing a black robe over his usual suit shirt, tie, and dress pants. His shiny shoes clacked on the pavement. "Put him in the car. He has to go wherever she goes. We won't be able to move her otherwise."

Mr. Muradon handed the cage off to the robed lady, who deposited it in the car.

"Miss Evers, I believe you have something of mine." He pointed a wand at my feet. The world went black and quiet.

Chapter 21

I woke up lying on dirt packed with rocks, my wrists tied behind my back. The earthy smell of desert and a burning campfire filled my nose. My body felt like it'd been hit by an entire bandyll team. This was so not the arena parking lot. Starlight and a full moon shone down on a cloudless night. What time was it? It'd been somewhere around midafternoon when—

Mighty Shinjan. I'd been kidnapped. And by someone I thought was a friend.

I groaned and tried to sit up. Something held me down.

Lines of purple light flared to life under and all around me. I stiffened. A light breeze kicked up and the circle hummed with power.

A familiar voice swore. Mr. Redd. "She's awake. Are we ready to start yet?"

A female voice that sounded vaguely familiar said,

"Almost. We have a few wards left. Please don't rush us. This is an archdemon after all."

"Right, right. Get them done right as quick as you can."

Gravity pressed down ten times stronger than normal as I rolled onto my belly. Bracing against my forehead, I got my knees under me and sat up on my heels. The world tilted this way and that as robed figures moved around with ease, drawing lines and runes in the ground with sticks. I tried to brush away the pebbles stuck to my forehead, only to be reminded that my wrists were bound. A very tall man tossed salt and an herbal concoction around the perimeter. While his hood obscured his head, that was unmistakably the towering figure of Mr. Muradon.

The light of Marohu glowed on the horizon off to the east. Where were we? Some dark corner of Toolena Mesa? The horizon was a bumpy, dark line of mountains in every direction. The southern range was dotted with lines of light from the mine. Work sites created clusters of light connected by dotted lines of light and more specs of light moved along the lines. Mine vehicles.

A pair of shoes crunched along the rocky ground. Mr. Redd stepped into the circle, hands in his pockets. He gave me a pitying look made sinister by the lines of shadows the power circle cast over his face. "Miss Evers, you have an annoying knack for getting yourself in trouble."

Vergo lay bound in chains of purple light in the cage. "Vergo," I called to him. He didn't so much as flick an ear.

"He can't come to your rescue this time." To

emphasize his point, Mr. Redd kicked the cage. It shivered and remained stuck to the ground, Vergo inert inside. "His presence has most certainly made it difficult to get to you."

"What do you want with me?" I tugged at the cloth binding my wrists.

"Nothing now." He let out a weary sigh. "I'm after only what's anchored to you. You would've made a great addition to the Order. So much talent, so much power, but no. Tradereth forced my hand. All your potential gone to waste. You've clearly been brainwashed by Lyra. I should've known better than to hire her. That was probably my wife's meddling. I knew ascending Lily to demonhood came with risks, but to turn on me like that? She'll be punished." He walked over and backhanded me, knocking me over. "I hope you felt that, Lily, you thankless traitor. I ascended you straight to archdemon and you turned on me the moment you gained a drop of power."

Tradereth bubbled up inside me, lifting me to my knees. Her energy settled in my throat and my mouth moved of its own accord. "The Demon King opened my eyes to my true potential." It was my voice with Tradereth's power. "You're weak and insignificant. I've found a better anchor."

Mr. Redd crinkled his nose. "Not for long. I have tasks for you, and you'll do them." He snapped his fingers. The circle pulsed with an extra burst of light. An unseen force pushed my mouth closed. Tradereth's presence returned to the back of my mind.

We must foil his plans. He cares not for either of us. We're mere pawns to him. You know I speak the truth.

321

That she did. As far as how to get out of this, I felt way over my head. All my tutoring and mentoring had focused on demons, power circles, and battling evil forces of a demonic kind and not of the human kind.

I hope you recognize this circle. It's the one he used when he killed and bound me to him. He's going to kill you to get to me.

Clearly, enough hours had passed between my kidnapping and this moment. What was he waiting for? "Why am I not dead already?"

Mr. Redd stood before an altar lined with candles and some incense. "That's the problem with uncooperative archdemons. If I kill you without making any preparations, then either she gets away or, more likely, she kills me and everyone present before retreating back to the demon realm." He sliced a palm with a blade and dribbled droplets of blood along the edge of the circle. Each drop sizzled and flared up with a flash of red light before getting devoured by the purple light. "Even with all the preparations, execution is a lengthy process. Everything must be done in the right way, the right order, and—" he glanced at the moon "—the right time." When done, the robed lady with painted nails bandaged his hand and drew a rune on the white cloth.

"We're on the last ward," she said. Again, I could've sworn I'd heard her voice from somewhere before.

My heart beat faster. I was running out of time. Maybe if I could stall long enough, someone would find me. It couldn't have taken long for Mom to figure out something was wrong when I didn't meet her at the entrance. She had to have called the police, Ms.

Weever, and Bylan. They had to be looking for me. "What is the Order of Tenebron trying to do?"

Mr. Redd did a double-take, his brows drawing together. "Unless you swear to join the Order, renounce everyone you care about, and join us, I'm afraid I can't tell you that."

"Payton said change is coming." *C'mon, keep talking.*

"Did he now?" A wicked smile formed. "Even in death, he fought against revealing too much. If only you had turned out to be as loyal as him. Anyway, I'm not going to stand here and monologue away my plans while you're alive and your friends are most certainly looking for you."

The robed figures, including the lady and Mr. Muradon, spaced themselves out evenly outside the circle's perimeter. Mr. Redd took the final spot. Each of them held a different object. One looked like a chicken foot, another a fistful of feathers, and the third—I shivered—a shrunken head. They began chanting. I clenched my fists. Not good. Not good at all.

Mia, they have wards up that block me from taking you to the demon realm. I can't buy us time. You need to make a decision, and quickly. Please strike a bargain. If we work together, we can get out of this.

"No bargain," I said under my breath. "I'd rather risk my friends finding me in time than give you what you want."

Damien's pawns most likely warded the location so it can't be probed. No one will find you until after they're done here.

"I don't believe you." Doubt trickled into the back of my mind. Mr. Redd's explanation about meticulous preparations might've included secrecy.

How do you think he's gotten away with so much over the years? He goes through great pains to not get caught. Strike a bargain with me and I'll get us out of this.

"Why do you need a bargain so bad? Can't you get out of this without my consent? You left Mr. Redd's body without his permission."

Tradereth sighed. *I don't think you realize how trapped we both are. He has wards and protections in place that use our anchor against us. I can't escape my binding to you any more than your stupid spirit cat can. Damien has been very thorough. He's clearly thought this out. That's probably why he left us alone for so long.*

"And why he had Mr. Muradon partially un-suppress me?"

Exactly. He probably didn't notice that you're no longer suppressed at all. I don't know how you managed that, but it works in our favor. Please bargain with me. There's a way out of this.

Despite my better judgement, I said, "How?"

With your consent, I can unleash my wrath on them. If our intentions are aligned, I can tap into your power and free us both. Mortal energy can more easily break bonds designed for immortal foes.

"Why don't you do that without a bargain?"

We don't have the time for me to explain to you the dynamics and energy demands of a demon invading the mortal plane, or for me to lecture you on willpower. Bargain with me and I'll save us both.

I shook my head before I realized I'd done it. "No. It isn't worth it."

Stupid girl, you're going to die if you don't let me help you.

"Then I die doing the right thing." My heart pounded away, not loud enough to drown out the chanting voices. I really didn't want to die, but I wanted even less to strike a bargain with a demon. It wasn't worth it. I knew it in my heart of hearts. She would—

Fine. Have it your way this once. Mia Evers, I offer you my aid freely. Do you accept?

"No bargain? No strings attached?"

I'm that desperate to never become his pawn again. Do you accept my free aid this once? I'll unleash my power as an archdemon fueled by your willing cooperation—just this one time, and then retreat back to the shadows. That's it.

The desperate terror in her voice and aura were genuine. On top of that, the chanting stopped. Hooded faces looked down at me. Uh, oh.

Please, Mia.

I hesitated, torn between worrying there was a catch and the instinctual need for self-preservation. Was her help really free? Could she save us or would she save herself?

No, she wouldn't be begging if she knew how to escape this ritual.

You must fight, Mia Evers.

I saw Bela's face and heard Mom's voice in that moment Bela had removed the final bit of suppression. Maybe this had been what she meant by fight.

"I freely accept your aid this one time."

Thank you. We'll show them the extent of our wrath.

Mr. Redd stepped into the circle, holding an open

book in one hand and a dagger in the other. My heart pounded so hard that my face hurt. He read from the pages, his voice harsh and guttural with demonic speech. I closed my eyes.

Tradereth's relief and elation filled me like air fills lungs. Her power gathered inside me, starting at the stomach. Her intensity grew and grew, pushing at my insides. She was so strong. How had I lasted against her for so long? Energy kept rushing inside. I clenched my teeth. More power rushed in, threatening to split me in half. It was too much. More forced its way in.

Fear not, Mia Evers. You can do this. Relax and let go.

Mr. Redd's speech stopped. For a moment, there was nothing but the body-splitting power growing inside me. "What is this?" Mr. Redd said, an edge to his voice.

Almost there. Tradereth willed me to my feet. My body obeyed like a clumsy puppet. I flopped into a seated position, and rose to my feet, knees touching, arms hanging limp, and head bowed, hair hanging down. The power throbbed inside me, pushing me a little straighter with every pulse. Instead of pain, there was excitement, a fiery thrill. My breath came in deep gulps.

I took one more deep breath.

Brace yourself. Your vengeance and mine are one.

Tradereth's power burst forth, flinging my arms out and throwing my head back. It coursed through me, head to toe, and then up, up, up like I rode on a lift moving as fast as a car. The upwards motion stopped. I opened my eyes. Instead of looking up at Mr. Redd, I looked down on the world from a hundred feet off the ground. I was inside Tradereth's body. The edges of the power circle nipped at her barely contained form head to toe, like its edge rose to envelop us. She stood on her hind legs, arms wrapped around her emaciated torso.

Yes, we are one. Behold our power.

We inhaled. "You dare try to take me again?" When she spoke, so did I. Both our voices came out as one. "I won't go. Begone, worthless mortal." We pushed to unwrap our arms. The circle sizzled and sparked, giving off smoke as it seared into our body. We took another deep breath and elbowed the circle with all our might. It shattered. Shards of light shot out in every direction and winked out. The robed figures flattened against the ground.

We dropped to all-fours, making the ground quake. We swiped outwards, sending the robed figures flying away from us and out of our immediate concern. They were no bigger than rats to us. We left Mr. Redd, though. He was going to need special treatment to make sure he never bothered me or Tradereth again. Yes, he was going to suffer before we squeezed the life out of him.

We slashed the ground over and over, destroying the wards, destroying the circles and all other protections one by one. With the last one gone, we tilted our head back and shrieked, releasing our exultation. The sound sent a chill through me, but at the same time gratification and relief coursed through me as well. The shriek sounded like a mix of hawk screech, elk call, and years of pent-up rage. With all of it out of our system, we could finally think clear enough to exact vengeance.

"Damien, you despicable creature," we yelled loud enough to make Mr. Redd clamp his hands over his ears. We snatched him up, taking a chunk of dirt and rocks with him, and squeezed enough to make it hurt, but not hard enough to break or tear anything. He cried out in pain. What a delightful sound, something that hadn't been heard enough from him. This was nothing compared to all the suffering he'd caused. "I loved you. I did everything to help you and make you happy, and you couldn't even bring yourself to say you loved me in the end. Was I really nothing more than a pawn to you?"

Mr. Redd grimaced, eyes closed, and let out a stifled cry. "I...loved you. I swear." Something about his declaration gave off a vibration, like a bug trying to fly off in a closed fist. Was that a—?

We shook his little body. "Liar. Don't lie to a demon. We can sense falsehood. You don't know what love is. You're incapable of it." We raised a clawed finger. His head was no bigger than one digit of our thumb. "If only I could raise you from the dead over and over to make you suffer as much as you should, but one life will have to do." We slashed his face with the tip of our claw, drawing out a line of red. He clenched his teeth, presenting his other cheek. We stabbed him with the tip of our claw, drawing more blood and making him cry out. "Yes, fuel us with your suffering, your rage. Let us feel what you have made others feel your entire life." We adjusted our grip, presenting a little arm, and pinched a finger between two claws. We jerked. Something popped. Mr. Redd let out a cry of pain. We studied his sweaty face, a mix of rage and pain. "Someone still doesn't feel sorry for all he did."

Twist. Pop. Scream.

Part of me knew I should feel sickened by all this.

My rage and pain blocked it out, making room for pleasure. A few broken fingers were totally justified.

Twist. Pop.

We screamed as something large and fiery rammed into us, forcing us to sidestep to regain balance. Beyond the campfire stood several little figures. Something white and gold lit up, growing and swirling, and then launched at us, hitting us square in the gut. We doubled over, searing pain leaving us gasping for breath. Among the figures stood one with a cascade of blonde curls I'd recognize anywhere. Ms. Weever held something large and wand-like in two hands. It ended in a crystal ball wrapped in wood fangs. The ball lit up in a swirl of white and gold.

We had enough time to shield our head with an arm before searing pain tore into us again. We doubled over and dropped Mr. Redd. He landed in a roll and popped to his feet, robes swishing around him. He held something long and clawed pointed at Ms. Weever while clamping his other hand to his side.

"You," Ms. Weever said with pure hate. Holding her wand thing aimed at Tradereth and me, she took another item out of one of her many pouches. Five other people poured out of a white limousine. Bylan, Zekary, Gerund, Nurse Kor and Ergon, all wielding weapons and looking quite pissed off.

Mr. Redd said, "How'd you find this place? We placed wards." His furious gaze bounced between us, Ms. Weever, and the team behind her.

Ms. Weever considered us and the principal a moment. With a flick of her arm, she shot another blast at Tradereth and me. A white brightness sailed right at our eyes, blinding us. We ducked and then screamed as

329

several branches tore off our head. We backed away, crushing bushes under our paws and clutching our head.

Mr. Redd sliced his arm with the clawed thing and sprayed blood all over the dirt. He chanted a quick spell. Shadowy tendrils shot out of the ground from where the blood fell and shot out at Ms. Weever. A fire blast filled the air. Water sprayed, combining with the fire, creating a massive steam cloud. Light flashed and we lost sight of them. The shadow tendrils recoiled and slashed again. Light lanced through the steam, severing some of the tendrils. It was like watching a black kraken attack sailors.

Mr. Redd drew a circle and scribbled some runes. Tradereth and I both knew we needed to stop him, but the searing pain was overwhelming. Every breath hurt. Every last square inch of our body hurt. Something black and sticky dribbled into our left eye. Demon blood. We wiped at it and took a step closer to the principal, and dripped more blood all over the ground.

Ms. Weever charged out of the steam cloud, one wand aimed at us and a second one with feathers and beads hanging off it pointed at Mr. Redd. Pipes played from within the cloud. A circle song. She yelled a spell we didn't know and stabbed the ground with the feathered stick. The music concluded. Blue and red light shot out from the stick, zigzagging along the ground to form runes, symbols and a circle. Ms. Weever stepped inside the circle and spoke in a guttural language that sounded similar to what Mr. Redd had used while holding a book and dagger.

"Lilimazshtu, I call thee forth."

Tradereth and I gasped. Ms. Weever was summoning a demon. We lurched forward, gritting our teeth against the pain.

Mr. Redd finished his chant, calling forth a demon inside a purple-glowing circle. Black tendrils shot out of both circles. Talons formed and gangly arms followed. The talons and arms clashed between Ms. Weever and Mr. Redd, coiling around each other. Some speared through the writhing mass, reaching for both humans. Little claws flashed against the edge of circles.

We lurched another step forward. "No! He's mine to kill." One more and we were within reach. We threw a paw down, pinning Mr. Redd to the ground. The demon arms and claws he controlled let out a screech sounding like a nail down glass. Ms. Weever's demon rose out of the ground and devoured them. Its hunched frame grew until its shoulders sat level with my tutor's blonde curls. Spikes shot out of its back. With a roar, it turned on our paw and clamped down with teeth and claws.

We growled, filling the air with a thunderous rumble, and stomped on that pathetic thing. "Begone, pest. This monster is mine." The demon transformed back into smoke and retreated to the demon realm. Served him right for biting.

Ms. Weever flailed her arms and got her feet back under her. She glared up at us.

"You, too," we said, Tradereth's voice coming out louder than mine. "This mortal's life belongs to me now."

"We need him alive," Ms. Weever said and took aim with her wand. The bulbous end glowed.

Not again, Tradereth said to me. *Mia, make her stop or she'll kill us both.*

Her terror filled me. This was no lie. We were

dripping demon blood everywhere, turning the dirt black and killing every shrub and cactus it drenched. Plants curled and shrank and turned to ash. We crouched, shrinking away and bringing our eyes to above her head.

"Ms. Weever, stop. Please. It's me, Mia." This time, my voice sounded predominant.

The wand thing lowered, and Ms. Weever's brows drew together.

Quick, say something that'll prove it's you.

Ms. Weever hesitated before raising the wand thing again.

I held out a clawed hand big enough to crush a car. "Wait. Please give me a chance to prove it to you."

Her eyes watered. "You struck a bargain with an archdemon."

"I didn't, I swear. Tradereth offered one-time help freely."

Hand over the tiny evil man as a gesture of faith. I can finish him later. Let him think he's safe. Let him think he's protected from my wrath. We gave him a slight squeeze, making him grunt.

With slow, deliberate movements, we set Mr. Redd's writhing form at her feet. "Mr. Redd was about to kill me so he could get Tradereth back."

Zekary, Gerund, Nurse Kor and Ergon edged closer.

Bylan stepped forward, holding a smoking silver ball attached to a heavy chain. He waved it like a pendulum. The smoke enveloped us, stinging us. We backpedaled on all-fours. Bylan said, "I sense Mia inside you, demon. What have you done?"

This time, Tradereth's voice overpowered mine. "I

saved her life, ungrateful mortal. If you strike me down, you'll kill her, too. Allow me to release my hold and she'll be all yours again."

Your turn. Say something to prove it's you.

I wracked my brain for something intelligent to say. It had to be from a moment when we were under a lot of protection, like a sage cloud. The day she pulled me from the demon realm after my failed attempt at banishing Allosyr came to mind. "Ms. Weever, remember the day you saved me from the demon realm? Our conversation was protected by a sage cloud. You told me about what happened to your baby boy." I lowered my gaze to the darkened ground. "That's what helped you pull through to help me save Deren."

Bylan's head snapped in Ms. Weever's direction. "Is this true?"

Eyes full of tears, she nodded.

Chain in hand, Bylan twirled it overhead several times before throwing the ball at our paws. It hit the ground and stuck there like a thorn in a beast's side. He shouted runic words. A power circle enveloped us, stinging our paws and causing pain from head to toe. We hissed.

Tradereth's voice overpowered mine again. "Do we have a moment's cooperation?"

Bylan held the chain in both hands linked to the smoking ball over thirty feet away. "Be quick about it."

We crouched, wrapping our shins in our arms. The power circle stung. We pushed the pain aside as best we could.

We should do this again sometime, minus the excruciating pain. Tradereth's power and presence withdrew into my stomach. A falling sensation filled me. Her control over my body kept our arms wrapped around our legs. Something gently deposited me on my knees. Blackness swirled around me, then pulled tight and forced my mouth open. The blackness pushed my knees into the ground as it rushed back inside me like one long inhale. My mouth snapped closed after the last bit dived inside. My body grew weak, tired. I needed sleep. Badly. My body tilted one way and the world tilted the other. Several pairs of feet ran towards me, and then everything went black.

Chapter 22

I woke to the aroma of mint and the sound of water bubbling away under me. Something steadily beeped beside me. I lay against something soft that shaped itself around the contours of my body. I opened my eyes.

A white ceiling spread overhead, sprinkled with round lights and calming colors painted around the lights. Buckeye Hospital? I turned my head, sending a line of pain down my side. Ow. Sure enough, a heart rate monitor beeped away. I lay on a gurney.

I tried to sit up. My body erupted with pain, and I cried out. Something small walked along the edge of the gurney, making a point to avoid stepping on my leg or torso. Vergo's furry face came into view, looking down at me.

"Little One?"

"It's me." I tentatively raised a hand. It stung, but I

was able to pet him, until I realized I couldn't feel his fur. I lifted my arm. It was wrapped in gauze from fingertip—I carefully turned my head—to shoulder. "What happened to me?" My whole body hurt.

"A lot. What's the last thing you remember?"

"Tradereth retreating back inside me so Ms. Weever wouldn't kill us both. And then a whole bunch of shoes running towards me."

"You didn't strike a bargain with her, did you? We didn't see any tattoos on you but—"

"No. She freely offered me help after pressing a bargain several times. She was that desperate to not go back to Mr. Redd."

"Wow. That *is* desperation. She obviously didn't do it out of the kindness of her nonexistent heart." He gently pawed my bandaged arm. "I was trapped in something Bylan had to free me from. I wasn't aware of anything that happened until after I spotted you lying on the ground, looking quite gruesome. Thankfully he and Amity were able to hold you together until an emergency unit took over."

I tried to move, but a sharp pain shot through me. I had bandages all over one arm, around my torso, and around one thigh. Tradereth had been blasted three times by whatever that golden white light was, but not me. Still, I'd felt the pain, too. "What happened to my body?"

"If you and Tradereth were working together, then the two of you took the same damage. No wonder Lyra feels so guilty."

"Is she here?"

"Yes. Let me get everyone. Might as well have them present so no one has to repeat anything." He hopped off the bed and paused, head bowed. His body twitched several times and then transformed into his human self on his hands and knees. He stood and smoothed down his tunic. "I'm getting good at this."

"Are you able to control it now?"

He turned, smoothing back his mane of long hair. "Somewhat. It appears there are rules as to when I can revert to human form. One, there must be a genuine need for it. Two, there's a time limit. And three, I seem to be able to transform only so often. I've experimented over the past few months while you slept, so as not to disturb or surprise anyone. I'll be right back." He strolled over to the doorway and stuck his head out into the hall, looking one way, then the other. "Ah, madame, would you be so kind as to call a few people over? She has woken."

Vergo helped me sit up and get me comfortable enough while wrapped nearly head to toe like a mummy. I had severe burns everywhere Ms. Weever had blasted Tradereth, along with muscle damage. No wonder I could barely move.

"You've been out cold for a few days. It'll take months for you to fully heal, maybe faster since you're so young and fit."

I choked on the water Vergo helped me sip. Apparently, I was weak from channeling an archdemon, too, on top of having a lot of tissue to heal. "But we have another game next week."

"You can forget the next few weeks of games. I'm sorry, Little One. I don't think Bylan and Amity can speed healing up much faster. The human body can heal only so fast before you do more harm than good."

"That's half the season," I said in a small voice.

There went my most favorite thing in the world to distract me from my problems.

Footsteps drew closer. Mom, Bela, Ms. Weever, and Bylan filed in. Everyone but Bela stopped and went wide-eyed. Bela broke into a jog.

"Kitty!" Standing only as tall as his waist, she wrapped Vergo's legs in a hug.

"Why hello there, Tiny One. How on Aardra do you recognize me?"

Mom said, "Who the—?"

"Vergo?" Bylan said, unsure. Inserting his hands in voluminous sleeves, he squeezed past Mom and Ms. Weever. "You certainly feel like him."

"Greetings, Bylan. I am Vergo. This form is temporary. The Light saw it fit to allow me to better aid Mia. I dare say I missed opposable thumbs."

Bylan studied Vergo in open wonder, placing a hand on his shoulder. He recoiled. "You're cold."

"I'm still dead."

"Right. It's…never mind."

Mom gave Vergo a wary look before wrapping me in a cautious hug. "You had me so worried when you didn't show up after the game. Bela got real fussy, and then she started crying and ran over to the locker room before I was able to catch her. I saw a couple of your teammates. I think it was Sussi who told me that you'd run off with your tutor. Something felt so off about the whole thing." She hugged tighter. I tensed as pain shot up and down my side, and it felt like my skin tried to stretch to cover too much space. Mom let go, eyes red with tears. "Next thing I knew, we were all crammed in Bylan's car, hunting for you. When I saw that…that *thing*, I couldn't leave the car, not with Bela with us."

"I stayed put, didn't I, Mommy?" Bela held two of Vergo's fingers in her little land. Vergo didn't seem to mind in the least.

Mom popped a wan smile. "Yes, you did, sweetie. Mommy's very proud of you."

"The bad thing is sleeping now. It's very tired."

Mom stiffened. "Let's not talk about that right now, okay? It makes Mommy very upset. Let's focus on your sister instead."

Face serious, Bela nodded.

Bylan gently placed a hand on my forehead. "How do you feel?" he said.

"When am I going to be able to play bandyll again?"

He chuckled. "Unfortunately, not for a while."

Ms. Weever shifted from foot to foot.

Bylan said, "Lyra, there's no way any of us could've known. All of us would've done the same thing in your place. She'll heal. She's young and strong."

"Ms. Weever, I'm not mad at you," I said as gently as possible. I agreed with Bylan, even though knowing I'd miss a lot of bandyll stung. I didn't know Darks and demons could do such a thing, much less that I'd share injuries like that.

"I'm not either," Mom said, putting a hand on Ms. Weever's shoulder. "Please forgive yourself."

My tutor shied out from under the hand. "Later. Let's discuss something else."

"How'd you find us?" I said.

"You can thank your sister for that," Bylan said. "A rare talent among all alignments is clairvoyance. She described the general area. Zekary and Ergon tried to pinpoint it with their Fire and Water senses, but the area had been warded against all types of probing. We were close enough the whole time to not only sense when all the wards fell, but also see when Tradereth surged above the terrain, making it very easy to close in."

"I can't handle this right now." Mom pressed a hand to her forehead and Bela followed her out of the room.

Ms. Weever glared as my mom exited. "I'm worried about her. She's not showing any signs of improving and she's not wearing any of the trinkets we gave her."

"We'll take care of that later." Bylan turned back to me. "The Light has greatly blessed your sister. Her alignment and the strength of it are no accident. Dangerous times are ahead. This is only the beginning."

"What happened to Mr. Redd?" I said.

Ms. Weever said, "He's been arrested and jailed in a location not associated with where Fabian slipped out of. Lyra and I suppressed his alignment. Gerund, Ergon and Zekary are taking turns guarding his cell, just in case. We're doing everything we can to avoid a repeat."

"We've also contacted the Grand Light Order," Bylan said. My heart sank. "Something this severe isn't worth hiding from them. Showing them there are Darks willing to fight the Order of Tenebron will work in your favor in the long term. They won't be thrilled at first, but you and Lyra have a chance to build trust as we help them take the enemy down. We can't afford another Necromancers War."

"No," Vergo said.

"So what happens next?" I said.

"There'll be a trial," Bylan said. "And with the

Grand Light Order involved, I can guarantee you that'll be a spectacle."

"Did you find any evidence surrounding Lily's death?"

"Not yet," Ms. Weever said, folding her arms. "I want to go back to where we found you. I wouldn't be surprised if that was the same place he sacrificed his wife. It worked for him once. Why not use it again?"

Bylan touched my arm, his gaze studious once again. "Mia, I can sense Tradereth's presence. She's still anchored to you, yes?"

"Yes." I lowered my gaze to the blankets covering my lap. I had a few vines inserted in my arm, delivering fluids and nutrients.

"Tell us what happened the other night. You didn't strike a bargain, did you?"

I told them everything I could remember, from how eager Mr. Redd was to get Tradereth back to how desperate she was to not go back, and how she reluctantly offered me one-time help. Both Bylan and Ms. Weever's eyes bulged at the revelation.

"Unheard of," Ms. Weever said under her breath.

"But not impossible?" Bylan said.

"Correct. It's just that demons never act without gaining something in return. Tradereth clearly wanted to avoid her murderous husband at all costs. She may prove useful in the future, especially when it pertains to Damien.

I'll show you where to find my bones, Tradereth whispered in a tired voice.

A tickle crawled down my spine. Ms. Weever stiffened. "Did she just—?"

I nodded and told them what she said.

Ms. Weever inhaled. "That'll help with the trial, if not guarantee a life sentence. He won't be able to make a pawn out of anyone ever again."

"That'll make us all happy," Vergo said. "I've had enough of that man."

Bylan said, "I'm amazed you didn't give in and strike a bargain with her. What gave you the strength to not give in?"

My chest rose and fell with a measured sigh. If I breathed too deeply, my side seared with a burning and stretching sensation. I shook my head. That also hurt. "I'm not sure. All I could think was how bad of an idea it was. I'd experienced what a partial bargain was like and Ms. Weever gave me a good idea of how bad deals with demons are. I couldn't bring myself to do it. Tradereth must've sensed my honest conviction, and that's why she finally gave in."

"Makes sense," Vergo said. "Demons are excellent lie detectors."

Bylan checked the machines and charms hooked up to me, read my charts and cast a healing spell over me that made my injuries tingle so badly that I had to fight the urge to itch them. "That's a burst of healing. It'll pass in a few minutes. Go ahead and get some rest, Mia. I'm going to go check on your mother." Hands hidden in his robe sleeves, he shuffled out of the room.

Silence followed, broken only by the gentle beep of my heart rate monitor and the small pool bubbling away beneath my gurney. Vergo and Ms. Weever stared each other down, standing tall and proud, looking so much like siblings about to fight.

"I'd appreciate it if you'd stop sneaking looks of death at me," Vergo said. "I'm your ancestor and you're my descendant. I'm no longer a demon, no longer the monster that took advantage of you in your darkest moment. You don't have to forgive or forget that, but you do need to learn to work with me. We're allies in all this. Mia clearly needs both our help, so stop trying to shut me out."

Ms. Weever's glare was so furious I could've sworn the temperature of the room dropped. Vergo returned her gaze, stern and resolute. Neither of them were going to back down.

I said, "Please get along. I like you both." They both turned. Vergo smiled triumphantly. Ms. Weever frowned and looked away.

"You're asking a lot of me."

"I'm not saying you have to like him. I'm asking you to work with him as needed. The Light sent him to me for a reason. We need him."

"No, we don't," she said under her breath.

"Damn it, Ms. Weever," I said, clenching my blankets. Both adults' eyes widened. Crap, I'd sworn out loud. I wasn't much of a swearer. A lot of my classmates were. It made them feel cool and adult. Mom and Dad had drilled into me to mind my tongue at all times, especially around adults. They hardly swore. Bad words leaked out only when they were upset, or when Dad listened to bandyll games. Apparently, my frustration with Ms. Weever's determination to hate Vergo was enough to remove my filter.

Well, I'd already gone this far.

"Now you're being—what's the word for acting stubborn even when you know you're wrong?"

"Obstinate," they said in unison. Their gazes met a moment before Ms. Weever lowered her gaze to the floor. She shook her head.

"I'm going to need time to adjust to something like this." She gestured to Vergo with a hand. "I remember him better as what he was and not what he is."

"That's fair," I said. And it was. I didn't entirely understand how she felt, what she'd been through, or what it was like to be tormented by a demon after losing a child.

She grimaced. "So you really have her best interest at heart?"

"The Light has left it up to me to decide whether or not to embrace my atonement. I must confess she's grown on me."

"Grown on you how?" She studied Vergo, her eyes narrowed.

"Her spirit, her determination, her incredible talent, and even her bandyll games. I get the best seat in the house every time."

My heart fluttered. This was the first time Vergo had mentioned liking me. It was always sarcasm and stoic suffering from him. Sure, he helped me a ton and even put up with Bela. I figured it was for the sake of his atonement and not out of genuine caring. Hearing that he actually liked and cared about me made my eyes sting. For some reason, I wanted to cry—not in front of anyone, of course.

I took one controlled breath after another, willing my emotions to level out. Vergo casually gripped the gurney's railing, letting his fingertips rest on the bandages on my arm. A cool calmness spread into me, alleviating the stinging in my eyes and the tightness in my chest relaxed. "Perhaps we should let our little hero rest. She's got a lot of healing to do."

"After I refresh my wards. We don't need a certain archdemon taking advantage of Mia's weakened state."

Not much to worry about at the moment, Tradereth said in a weak, tired voice. *Your sister was right. I must rest, too.*

Ms. Weever's icy gaze shot towards me. I said, "Doesn't she have to recover from the blasts, too? She said she's weak right now."

My former tutor tilted her head thoughtfully. "Makes sense. She must've been fully in our mortal plane." She stepped closer to me, clutching the gurney rail. "You can tell her there's more where that came from next time we get a chance to face off, so she has a choice—remove herself from you and stop meddling with our lives, or prepare to be forcibly removed and sent to the Light."

I said, "Why don't we send her now or within the next few days? She's too weak to fight back."

Both Vergo and Ms. Weever grimaced. Tradereth chuckled faintly. Ms. Weever said, "Not a good idea. You need to be strong enough to handle an exorcism."

I sank against my pillows. "It never is that easy, is it?"

"Welcome to how life is. Not all lessons are fun."

No, they weren't. I sat upright again and clutched my side from moving too fast. "Ms. Weever, I've been meaning to ask, but I kept forgetting. Did Mr. Muradon ever show any signs of being a bad person when the two of you went to school together?" My heart sank as I recalled the moment he helped cage Vergo.

Ms. Weever's face went blank with confusion. "Who?"

"Sig Muradon," Vergo said. "Taller than me, kind

of lanky, charming smile. He said he went to the same private Dark school with you."

Her brows drew together. "I never went to such a school and I've never heard of this person."

Vergo and I exchanged shocked looks. He said, "Oh, dear. He presented quite the compelling story."

"He does fit the description of one of several Order members that were also arrested." Ms. Weever gave me a pained expression. "Among them was one of the front office ladies—not Desi, but the other one."

"That's where I recognized her voice," I said and smacked my thigh. I regretted it as pain shot up my leg. Both Vergo and Ms. Weever reached out to me and stopped.

Vergo smirked. "May we one day bond over our love of this child here."

Ms. Weever glowered.

Chapter 23

I was back home a couple of days before the next bandyll game went on without me. I'd been sent home in an Air chair, with a bunch of bandages and burn salve, and supplements that quelled inflammation and promoted an optimal environment for muscle growth. My Air chair floated like a car, had comfy arm and footrests, and a tray I could pull out to put stuff on, like food and drink. The doctors and Bylan projected it would take me a good two months to recover, so, basically, I wasn't playing bandyll again until eighth grade. Life sucked. I told Vergo as much while I winced at Mattie trying her best in goal.

"When life sucks, suck it up," my personal spirit cat told me, eyes on the game. He wore a new charm collar courtesy of Bylan.

We sat in the front row tucked near the Hornets bench. I had a purple and gold blanket keeping my lap and legs warm, along with a cat sitting on my lap. The arena was kept relatively cool for the sake of the players. Mom and Bela sat behind me in regular seats, cheering my team on and also sporting our colors.

The seats on the other side of the arena erupted in cheers as the blue and orange Pumas snuck a goal through Mattie's five-hole. The horn blared and the announcer's sonorous voice filled the arena. Mattie fished the ball out of the net as my teammates skated around with slouched shoulders. Sussi rolled by, a pained expression on her face. Even Gwen had given me a look of horror when she first spotted me in my wheelchair at practice the other day. As much as I wanted to get out there, I'd regret the decision the moment I tried to stand. Widespread burns sucked. "That doesn't make me feel any better."

"It wasn't meant to," he said. "Life is full of pain and disappointment. You know this, or have you forgotten suddenly?"

I said nothing as the teams reset at center court. I knew he was right, but I wasn't going to say it to make him happy.

Vergo chuckled. "Your face is priceless."

Bite me, I thought, folding the one arm I could move without causing shooting pains. I probably looked ridiculous. I didn't care. I was going to feel sorry for myself until I felt ready to get over it.

I felt a little better by the end of the game when my team squeezed out a 4-3 victory. Our offense and defense were good. The Pumas had gotten a few lucky breaks that produced goals. I could've stopped all those shots, but oh well. I'd get back on the court as soon as I could. My team and Coach Tokket bumped fists with me before heading off into the locker room.

***

Due to my poor mobility, the school sent my schoolwork and song stones containing daily recordings home with Bela. It became a juggling act of song stones and notebooks. I kept up with the workload. Mom and Vergo took turns helping me, Vergo in human form every chance he got. Mom jumped half the time until she got used to seeing him like that. She even started talking to him more and invited him to eat dinner with us once.

"A thoughtful gesture," he said while inspecting my Algebra homework at the dining table, "but the dead do not eat."

"What about cultures who leave offerings for their deceased loved ones?"

Vergo shrugged, flashing us with a peek of his muscular chest through the "v" in his tunic. "It provides energy for a manifestation, that's all, but the food remains uneaten in the conventional sense."

Loved ones. That reminded me. I held onto the thought until I finished my homework. Vergo guided my Air chair back to my room even though I had charms that allowed me to control the direction and movement. He set me by my bed. I carefully slid myself onto the mattress and propped myself up against my pillows. Vergo stiffened and reverted back to cat form, shaking out his head.

His furry chest rose and fell with a sigh. "Goodbye, height and thumbs." He hopped onto my bed.

I smirked and finally sprang the question that'd impatiently sat in the back of my mind. "So you love me now, huh?"

Vergo's blue eyes bulged. He made a mix of snorts and coughs as he fought to get words out. He was probably trying to lie, but the Light wouldn't let him.

"I heard you at the hospital."

He looked away, chin held high. "I certainly do not hate you anymore. Anyway, don't you have some reading to do?"

I scooped him into a tight one-armed hug, enjoying his soft fur. He tensed, pushing at my grip for several heartbeats before sinking into my arm.

"Fine. You win. I have a feeling we're going to need each other as the future unfolds. Dire times are ahead." He curled up on my feet while I settled down with my latest Yuna book. The dryads had agreed to mobilize for war against the wizard, but only if she found more help. Wizards could shape their magic into armies of their own. It was going to take more than one warrior fairy and an army of dryads. They needed magically powerful beings on their side.

Of course, the dryad king wouldn't help unless Yuna was able to convince the frost giants to join them. Frost giants would most certainly help. The only problem was that fairies and frost giants *hated* each other. They were mortal enemies. Mom called me to dinner when the dryad king suggested a side mission to gain their favor instead of being met with the business end of an ice axe.

***

I was in the middle of a nightmare about a dust storm and spinning axes destroying my house when a polite knocking came from my bedroom closet. The thick dust cloud hardened and morphed into my bedroom walls and ceiling. The axes framed my room. I sat up in bed, not sure if I was awake or asleep. Vergo was absent, making me inclined to believe the latter.

My closet door slid open. I bolted to my feet and summoned my protection bubble with a hand gesture. Tradereth in her human form stepped out, head topped with draconic horns. Sharp ridges followed her brow ridge, curled over human ears and curved up and beyond her head. Short bangs covered her forehead, and more hair fell to her shoulders behind the horns. Instead of a professional skirt and blazer, she wore a black silk bathrobe with red trim and matching slippers. The soft material shimmered with every step as she crossed my bedroom and took a seat on my desk chair. Even though she wore casual attire, she looked elegant.

"Popping in quickly, my child. I don't know what your beloved tutor used on us, but it most certainly left its mark. I fare no better than you at the moment."

"What do you want this time? You know I'm going to turn down a bargain."

One corner of her mouth rose into a smile, revealing a small fang. "While that's not the purpose of this chat, it's still on my mind. One day, one year, Mia Evers, I'll wear you down."

"No, you won't. I almost died and you couldn't convince me."

"That's because the dynamics of the situation were not entirely under my terms. But anyway, I'll let you enjoy your conviction for now." She shifted in my desk chair, crossing one knee over the other and resting her hands on her knee. "I plan on sticking around, anchored or not."

"We're going to exorcise you one day and you know it."

She smiled. "I do. I already have plans in place. I've told you before. I have plans within plans, moves and countermoves to every move you and your allies take."

"You didn't have a countermove to Damien kidnapping me." It didn't feel right to call him Mr. Redd anymore. He didn't deserve such respect.

"Oh, really? Are you dead? Did he get what he wanted? Did I imagine combining our wills and freeing us from the trap? Hm?"

I said nothing.

"My dear child, when one plan doesn't work, you try another. If you hadn't consented to my free aid, I would've acted on my own and more than likely killed you in the process. Your consent to fight together saved your life. I want you alive, I'll have you know."

"Yeah, out of the kindness of your nonexistent heart," I said. The revelation sent a chill down my spine that hopefully she didn't notice. I believed it. When getting to me one way hadn't worked, Tradereth had forcibly broken her anchor with Damien and transferred herself to me. I didn't doubt for one instant that she would've sacrificed having me as an anchor to avoid going back to being anchored to her husband.

Smiling, she placed a long-nailed hand over said heart. "You wound me with your terrible manners. One day, you'll learn. Think of what we can accomplish together. Think of all that power you had in that moment. You know you liked it. You know it was thrilling. You want to feel that power again."

"No, I don't," I said so quickly that even I didn't believe myself.

Her smile widened, revealing both fangs. "Such a

terrible liar," she said.

My stomach flopped. That moment of power had been amazing. We were gigantic, imposing, destructive. Damien had been at the mercy of our wrath. All of them had. We'd knocked them down like Bela's blocks, and there'd been nothing they could do to stop us. We would've been unstoppable if I didn't care about leaving Ms. Weever alive. I'd love to feel that powerful while in goal, when getting picked on, when people hated me for being a Dark. I wouldn't have to take it in silence anymore. I could reshape the world around me and make it better.

Tradereth let out a pleasant chuckle that made me want to punch her. She stood and adjusted her bathrobe. "See? Told you."

"It's a temptation. I won't give in to it."

"Not even with a war coming?"

"I'm not going to be fighting in it. I'm just a kid."

"Oh, you think this is going to be the traditional battlefield war, something like the Necromancers War? There'll most certainly be moments like that, plenty of blood spilled. Those moments will be delicious." She ran the tip of her tongue along her lip. "War doesn't take place solely on one battlefield or another. You'll see in time. You'll participate in time. You all will, even your adorable little sister."

I balled my hands into fists, resisting the urge to lunge at her. "*You stay away from her*," I said in that other powerful voice. It sounded deep and resonant, big enough to be a giant's voice. My room shook. Tradereth's eyes widened. I hadn't used that powerful voice since sending Payton to the Light. It'd only happened when channeling my alignment. Why now, all of the sudden?

Tradereth popped an unnaturally wide grin. "So much power." She shivered with delight. "No wonder your soul shines so brightly in the demon realm. You may want to be careful about that. Just saying."

"I have my wards and protections," I said in a normal voice. Oh, thank goodness.

"Hm, you do, yes." She stood and smoothed down the front of her silky bathrobe. "Well, nice chatting with you. I'll leave you to recovering from your injuries. I have recovering of my own to do."

Words lodged in my throat, making it burn. For the first time ever, I wanted a demon to stick around and talk. I had questions. Many, many questions. While demons were full of lies, they were full of truths, too. I could sense when Tradereth told me the truth and wanted me to know it. The rest of the time was a mystery.

"Until we chat again, Mia Evers." She reentered my closet and I slipped into dreamless sleep.

***

I didn't bother telling anyone about the chat. What was the point? She was trying to manipulate me. That was it. As far as the whole thrilling power thing went, I'd turn it down next time she dangled it in front of me. That's all I had to do. Hopefully it'd be enough. For now, I wouldn't worry about it. She had to recover, too. She hadn't spoken to me telepathically during waking hours, ever since offering to lead us to her bones.

The week before spring break, Mom and I were sent a letter requesting our presence at the next board meeting. Ms. Weever called us, letting us know she and Bylan had gotten notices, too. As to why, none of us knew.

The five of us, plus Vergo, arrived around the same time. I was in the Air chair. My burns were taking forever to heal and my left side felt weak. It was annoying. Vergo sat in my lap. I navigated my chair to follow everyone inside the district office meeting room. Bylan and Ms. Weever cast protections over the room in case Tradereth had the strength to meddle, and in case we were among enemies.

Mom wore her necklaces and bracelets. After learning about the true nature of Mr. Muradon and one of the front office ladies, she more readily accepted acting like we all had our backs to the proverbial wall.

The center was packed with rows of empty chairs. We crowded the front. Everyone but me remained standing. Bela climbed onto the chair next to Mom so she was almost as tall as her. Mom wrapped a protective arm around her.

The five board members, including Mrs. Voliare, stood on the opposite side of a semicircular bench that looked like a wide judge's booth decorated with five speaking stones held up by fingers of vines. Positioned next to the speaking stones were metal wires encased in glass, charmed by Metalminds to light up with a touch. The board members wrapped up their conversation and dispersed into their respective seats. Each of them had a brass plaque with their name on it.

Mrs. Volaire, a plump, intimidating lady, waved for us to sit. Like her husband, she dressed well and held herself with an air of confidence. She had the same tawny hair and green eyes as Gwen. "Please sit. All of you. This shouldn't take long, but do make yourselves comfortable."

Mom plunked Bela one chair over and sat next to her. Bylan pinned his robes to the back of his legs and sat on the other side of the aisle. Ms. Weever remained standing.

Mrs. Volaire looked at my former tutor expectantly.

"Without causing any offense, I would like to remain standing. I hope you don't mind."

"Since you asked nicely…" Mrs. Volaire organized a pile of papers, giving them a few taps on the bench. She touched her light and it flared to life. "The regular board meeting doesn't start for another hour, so we shouldn't have any interruptions." She held up the top piece of paper. "Mia Evers, a lot has happened since the day you arrived at this school district. In light of three staff members getting arrested, it's been brought to our attention that you're not the true cause of all these… events. On behalf of the entire school board, I'd like to extend a formal apology."

"There's a surprise," Vergo said, an edge to his voice. "I wonder what's happened. People like her don't apologize. Ever."

I sat up straighter. My brain stretched to wrap itself around Mrs. Volaire's news. While her husband saw me as an asset to the club bandyll team, he hadn't so much as asked how I was doing or initiated other polite exchanges typical of compassionate people. Last year, Mrs. Volaire made it painfully obvious that she didn't like me with her attempt to expel me, until Bela unwittingly stopped that with Bylan's help. "Thank you," I said. What else could I say? I wouldn't make them stop being hateful if I acted hateful in return.

Ms. Weever studied Mrs. Volaire with a neutral expression. The slight lines in her brow clued me in to her buzzing thoughts. She must've shared Vergo's thoughts.

Mrs. Volaire nodded and set aside the first paper for the next. "I'd also like to extend our apology to Alexander Bylan and Lyra Weever. Both of you were wrongfully removed from your positions. We now see that this was all part of Damien's schemes. The rest of the district's staff is currently under intense scrutiny while we await his trial. We're hoping useful information will come to light over the next few weeks." She set aside the second sheet. "In the meantime…" She looked up, hands folded. "The Evers daughters are in need of proper tutors and mentors. Lyra, we would like to offer you your previous position back. We understand if—"

"I accept," Ms. Weever said. "There are children in need of protection, secrets that need unveiling. I'll do my part as tutor and protector."

Mrs. Volaire blinked. "You don't want any time to think about this?"

Ms. Weever placed a hand on my shoulder. "Not under the present circumstances, no."

Silence followed. Mrs. Volaire straightened her posture. "Then welcome back. If you're able to return immediately after spring break, please do."

Bela clapped. "Yay. Pretty lady's back."

A small smile appeared for a moment on Ms. Weever's face before she restored her air of cool detachment.

"Fancy that," Vergo said. "The insidious beast has some sense, after all."

My head spun. Ms. Weever was coming back? She was going to be my tutor again? I should've been clapping and cheering with Bela. All I could do was stare at Mrs. Volaire's sound stone. I had to be dreaming, like a real dream and not one of those stupid ones demons forced on me. Something good had happened. This couldn't be real.

"And Bylan," Mrs. Volaire said, her tone businesslike. "Damien informed us of your anathema status with the Order of Leo. A quick call to the basilica confirmed this as fact. What happened?"

Bylan rose, sticking his hands in his sleeves. "I have no regrets. If given the chance, I'd make the same decision that earned me my fate. You understand that the Light preaches love and acceptance, yes?"

"That it does. My family and I dutifully attend services every weekend."

"Then we can have a long conversation at a convenient time, if you wish. The short answer is that I discovered that the Order of Leo isn't living by its teachings. When they found out about me helping Mia and Lyra, two Darks, remove a demon from your campus, they were outraged. No matter how hard I tried to convince them that the cooperation was necessary, my superiors wouldn't listen. They cast me out." He held out a hand towards us. "If it weren't for these two ladies, you'd have faced countless more losses like Carlo, Payton, and Orton. Deren Sevine was almost another casualty, as was Bela."

"And my daughter," Mrs. Volaire said.

Bylan thought for a moment. "And your daughter," he said. He squared up with Mrs. Volaire again. "Terrible truths are going to come out of the impending trials. I'll let you hear them firsthand, should you attend."

"Oh, we plan on it." Mrs. Volaire analyzed a few pieces of paper, carefully reading each of them. "So what do we do with you? Bela clearly needs a proper mentor. The Order of Leo stopped answering our calls ages ago. I even called from my own home, only to be cut off when I mentioned Bela Evers' name. Totally uncharacteristic of what I'd expect out of a Light order. It's disappointing."

"I'm sorry my former Order treated you so."

She nodded. "I appreciate it, but clearly you share no blame. I'm not sure what's going on in the world. I have a feeling we need Light priests like you on our side. I'd like to offer not only your old position back, but also the vacant principal position. The school needs a person of your integrity filling such a critical role in a school. Would you like time to think about it?"

He broke into one of his grandfatherly smiles. "For a great many reasons, I accept."

Mrs. Volaire's shoulders visibly relaxed. "Thank you. Thank you both." She gathered the papers. "That concludes this bit of business. If you have any questions or would like further discussion on anything, we'd be happy to—"

A rumbling of footsteps sounded outside the heavy, closed doors. The entire school board looked up. I spun my Air chair around.

Two of the four doors burst open. Men clad in white and silver uniforms stepped inside and held the doors open for the stream of more men and women in matching uniforms march inside. Soldiers? They wore white combat boots with overlapping silver plates, white pants lined with several pockets and silver knee guards, silver utility belts, white jackets with triangular shoulder guards and gold buttons, white gloves, and a pair of hilts stuck above each of their shoulders.

An imposing man with a severe face marched into the meeting room, his arms moving in perfect unison with his stride. He wore a matching uniform made grander by the presence of an embroidered cape lined with silver, a white beret with a silver visor, and boot heels that clacked with every step. The doors closed behind him, revealing a flash of sword and axe on the soldiers' backs. What on Aardra were a bunch of armed people doing at a school?

The man had a name embroidered over his left breast pocket in all capitals. ZEIKAN.

Zeikan glanced over a shoulder as two soldiers moved in front of the doors and stood at attention, eyes ahead, gaze neutral, as if none of us existed. Zeikan headed down the aisle created by the rows of chairs. Ms. Weever grabbed my chair and moved us out of his way.

Bylan stood with his head bowed in deference, arms clamped at his sides. Zeikan considered the Light priest a moment before giving him a slight nod. "At ease, Bylan." His voice was deep and rumbly, and every bit as intimidating as his regal presence. While he spoke softly, his voice effortlessly filled up the room. Zeikan paused before Mrs. Volaire, who had gone pale.

She said, "I think I speak for us all when I say we'd appreciate an explanation."

"Certainly," Zeikan said. He clasped his wrists behind his back, revealing a flash of gold on the underside of his cape. "I'm Arnold Zeikan, Captain of the Grand Light Order, Marohu branch. We've received word of events surrounding Damien Redd and Mia

Evers, along with a request for aid. Rana Volaire, your school district is now under our control."

Acknowledgments

I have so much to be thankful for. So many people have cheered me on over the years. Every last one of you helped me see this through to publication. A big thanks to my mother, cousins Jessie, Jennie, and Jon, and my late grandmother for being my biggest fans of even the first chapters I dared called writing. You gave me the gumption to keep learning and growing.

Thank you to the WANA Tribe for all your support as well, for being my sounding board when I needed it, for all the help with the dreaded blurb, for helping me get unstuck on the rare occasion, and for just being there day after day, especially through the pandemic. We were not alone.

And of course, thank you to my husband who keeps me grounded and, for some reason, is willing to put up with my crazy. Well, I do put up with his stupid, so that makes us even.

About the Author

Angela Guajardo is an award-winning author, blogger, sports journalist, and editor whose heart lies with young adult fantasy. She currently lives in the Phoenix metro with her husband and fur babies. When not writing or editing, she nerds it out on various video games, walks her dog, or binges on various paranormal programs.

Join the Mailing List

Get informed on the next book release without worrying about any spam or filler. Keep an eye out for updates and chances to become a beta reader.

Sign up at AngelaGuajardo.com by scanning the QR code:

www.ingramcontent.com/pod-product-compliance
Lightning Source LLC
Chambersburg PA
CBHW070403260626
47161CB00001B/251